The Auctioneer

Debbie Tindle Parker

Our Front Porch Books

Published by Our Front Porch Books
Montezuma, Iowa 50171
www.ourfrontporchbooks.com

First Edition: February 2018

Cover design by Michael Reid.

ISBN-13: 978-1983871566
ISBN-10: 1983871567

Dedication

I would like to dedicate this book to my husband, J.O.
Thank you for always supporting my dreams.

Chapter 1

Trisha Jenkins couldn't believe her rotten luck.

And now she was going to be late. She hated being late.

She sat with a thump on the hard airport seat and glared at the woman behind the counter, sighing, still upset the plane malfunction had delayed her flight. Willing herself to calm down, Trisha slumped down in the chair and shut her eyes, thinking about the night before.

She'd stayed at her office until almost 1:00 a.m., working ahead so her absence wouldn't create a problem for her co-workers.

Then she'd taken a scary cab ride to her small apartment, sure the driver was some sort of zombie creature.

Thankful to be home in one piece, Trisha had spent the next thirty minutes packing her suitcase and had finally crawled between her covers a little after two. She'd been tempted to throw her alarm clock across the room when it rang at five.

She knew her bad mood was partially because she'd had less than three hours of sleep.

"And all of this to go to a work convention I don't need to go to."

"Ms. Jenkins?"

Trisha waved her hand at the woman she'd been glaring at.

"Good news. We got you on another flight. And it's a direct flight. Your plane's boarding now at Gate 3."

"I'll never make it," Trisha exploded, instantly feeling bad when the woman jumped.

"They're holding it for you, ma'am," the woman said through tightened lips.

"Oh, okay. I'm sorry. None of this is your fault. Thanks again for your help."

"No problem."

Trisha managed a small smile and took off at a trot.

Breathless when she arrived at Gate 3, she was thankful to see the plane was indeed still there.

"Ms. Jenkins?"

"Yes." Trisha handed over her paperwork.

Fifteen minutes later she sat in a plush seat feeling terribly guilty she'd snapped, especially since the woman had bumped her up to first class.

Once in the sky, the humming of the plane was too much to bear, and she fell fast asleep.

"Miss?"

"Hmmm."

"We'll be landing soon."

Trisha opened her eyes, embarrassed when she realized she'd fallen asleep on the plane.

"Already?"

"Yes. We'll be landing in Minneapolis very shortly. I thought you might like to be ready when we land. I understand you're in a hurry."

"Oh, well, yes. I'm late for a work convention."

"We made up some time in the air."

"That's great. Thank you," Trisha replied, once again embarrassed by her outburst in the airport.

While mentally scolding herself, Trisha sat up and ran her hand through her long, blond hair, hoping she hadn't messed it up too badly while sleeping.

She glimpsed out the window and noticed the tall buildings as the plane started its descent.

Before long, she stood at the baggage claim, holding her purse and her briefcase, watching as the bags whirled around.

Spotting her old, blue suitcase, thankful it had made the trip with her instead of getting lost in the shuffle, she fetched it and took off in search of a taxi.

Less than thirty minutes later, she was in her room, her clothes dumped on the bed, shaking her head.

"That's what I get for packing in the middle of the night."

She reluctantly dressed in the black skirt and silky blue button-down shirt, which were the only suitable dressy clothes she'd packed.

"Guess I'm going to have to go shopping tonight." Trisha shook her head. She had hoped she'd be able to crash as soon as the last meeting of the day wrapped up.

Glancing in the mirror, she decided she looked okay. She picked up her briefcase and reached inside for her tablet.

"Oh, shit. Don't tell me I forgot that too."

Soon, everything from her briefcase was mingled on the bed with everything from her suitcase.

"I don't have time for this," she declared as she stuck her card key in her skirt pocket, then turned her back on her mess and hurried into the hallway.

She rode the elevator down to the lobby and walked up to the front desk.

"How can I help you?"

"I'm here for the Communications and Marketing Convention, and I left my schedule at home. Can you tell me where I need to go?"

"One second." The woman clicked on her keyboard. "Looks like check-in is in the Prairie Sky Room on the third floor.

"Thanks," Trisha said before hurrying back to the elevator.

She got off on the third floor and studied the map on the wall. Spying the room, she took off as fast as she dared in her high heels. Her head tilted slightly to the right when she noticed the door to the room was shut.

Shrugging, Trisha pulled it open and froze, instantly realizing she was in the wrong place.

Charley Walker was nervous.

As he sat in the fancy room, surrounded by men in Western-cut suits and young women in short dresses, he felt like he was living a lie.

No one from back home knew where he was. He hadn't even told his daughter.

And he'd never stayed in a hotel that cost as much as this one did.

But he'd had no choice.

This was where he had to be.

"Kind of a crazy atmosphere, huh?"

Charley studied the man beside him, who was also wearing a fancy Western suit, and nodded, "A little."

"I'm Alex Coltrane."

"Charley Walker," he said, shaking Alex's outstretched hand.

"Ever been to one of these before?"

Charley shook his head. "I finished the classes in June."

"Oh, so you're a first-timer. I'm one of the directors. Don't worry, you'll learn a lot today, and tomorrow night will be fun."

Charley hoped that would be true.

"Show time," Alex said, glancing toward the front of the room.

Charley felt anxious when he noticed the man who'd taught his classes had approached the podium.

As he set down his glass of water, the door behind him opened and the most beautiful woman Charley had seen in a long time ran into the room.

He could tell she was confused as she peered at the room full of people, who were all looking back at her.

"Ma'am," his instructor said as he tipped his black cowboy hat.

"Uh, sorry. This can't be right."

"This is the Auctioneering Conference."

"Nope, this isn't right," the woman said, her cheeks turning a bright red. She waved to the crowd and offered an apology, then hurried back out the door.

But even as his instructor started the welcome speech, Charley couldn't get the beautiful, bewildered blonde out of his mind.

"Well, shit," Trisha mumbled, as she ran down the hallway to her room.

She tossed her keycard on the desk, then picked up her purse and dumped it out on her bed. She rifled through the tubes of lipstick, combs, receipts and papers until she found the folded-up schedule she'd printed off in her office the night before.

"Check-in will be held in Conference Room A on the second floor," she read, making a mental note. "A program will be available during check-in."

"Second floor, Conference Room A," she reminded herself as she hurried to the door and walked back into the hallway, realizing as the door clicked shut that she'd forgotten her room key.

"I should go back to bed," she moaned as she walked back to the elevator and hit the number two button.

When the elevator doors reopened on the second floor, she noticed several professional looking men and women were milling about and knew she'd missed the entire first session.

She called out a few friendly greetings as she zigged and zagged her way through the crowd to the check-in counter.

"Hi, I'm Trisha Jenkins."

She watched as the younger girl flipped through the files, then peeked back at Trisha before flipping through them again.

"Is there a problem?" Trisha asked when the girl glanced around.

"Um, well, I don't see you in the file."

"That would figure," Trisha muttered.

"Just a second."

Trisha watched as the young girl walked over to an older woman who was visiting with a group of ladies. The woman talked to the girl, then hurried over to Trisha, "Good afternoon."

"Hi. My name's Trisha Jenkins. I'm supposed to be registered. I work for The Milligan Group based in Los Angeles."

"Let me look through the file again," the older woman said as she started thumbing through the names of the others who were later than she was to check in. "Well, that's weird. Let me check the computer."

Trisha watched as the lady clicked on her keyboard. Then she got a puzzled look on her face and walked back over to Trisha, "I'm sorry. Your registration fee was never paid."

"Oh, crap."

"You can pay today."

"How much is it?"

"$450. That'll get you into every session and will include all the meals. We could charge the company credit card."

"I'm so sorry. I left my purse in the room. And my room key was in it too."

"Tell you what, why don't we check you in so you can get to the next session? You can bring the credit card first thing in the morning. Or I could call your company?"

"All great ideas," Trisha agreed. She grabbed the notepad and pen on the check-in table and scribbled down the company secretary's private number. "That should get you to the secretary. She should be able to get you the credit card information. I'll check in later and make sure things are okay."

"You can check with me in the morning, Trisha. Enjoy the rest of the day."

"Thanks," Trisha said as the young girl handed her a written nametag and lanyard, along with a bag full of freebies and a schedule book.

She opened the schedule and found the room number, then headed in that direction, unable to quit wondering why her fee hadn't been paid.

Charley's head was spinning as he walked down the hallway toward his hotel room.

After fumbling with the keycard, he pushed the door shut with his arm, walked to the plush recliner in the corner of the room, and sank down into the fluffy cushion.

He eyed the huge, king-sized bed and felt his cheeks flush when the beautiful blonde popped into his mind.

Shaking his head, he pulled his cell phone out of his breast pocket and turned it on.

"Pam called?"

He quickly dialed his code and listened to the message she'd left.

"Daddy, I know you won't tell me where you are, but I need to know you're okay. Plus, I really need to talk to you about something. And it's very important. First you went away for a whole week in June and wouldn't tell me where you were going, and now you're gone again. And if it's a woman, Daddy, I'm okay with it. Mom's been gone for a long time; it's okay if you want to move on. I want you to be happy. But please call me so I can quit worrying that you're lying in a ditch somewhere. I love you. Bye."

"Oh, Pammy, I'm sorry." Charley dialed her number, disappointed when he got her voicemail.

"Honey, it's Daddy. I'm sorry I haven't told you what's going on. I promise I will. I'm fine. I won't be able to call you tonight, but I'll try you again tomorrow. Love you."

He tossed his phone on the nightstand and pulled his folded schedule out of his aged suit jacket pocket.

"Let's see, I don't have to be anywhere for an hour."

He peered at the bed and yawned, then shook his head.

"I have to be ready for tonight. I have to get up in front of all these auctioneers and try to remember everything I learned."

Charley decided he should practice again. He scanned around the room and focused on the large TV resting on the mahogany stand at the foot of the bed.

"Who'll give me $500 for this thirty-six-inch color television set? I've $500; do I hear $550?"

A knock on his door startled him. He looked over and wondered if Pam had found him after all.

"No, that's impossible." He hurried to the door and opened it.

"Hey, Charley. How's it going?"

"Hey, Colonel Lewis."

"You can call me B.J., Charley. It's okay. I thought you might like to practice a little before tonight."

"I was practicing. But it'll be easier with some help."

"I know you'll do great," B.J. assured him, patting him on the back.

Trisha yawned as the last session of the afternoon ended. She stood up and stretched, then started for the door.

She stepped into the hallway and felt the collision at the same time she noticed another woman in front of her.

"Oh, damn," Trisha muttered, almost losing her balance in her heels.

The other woman's briefcase went airborne and crashed into the wall, bursting open with papers flying everywhere.

"Well, that figures."

"I'm sorry," Trisha said as they both hurried toward the mess and started gathering.

"Me too. I've had a rotten day," the dark-haired woman said as she tucked a strand of her long hair behind her ear and scanned Trisha. "Hey, you look familiar. Were you in my session this morning?"

"No. I was stuck at the airport this morning. I've had a rotten day, too."

"I'm Katherine Roe. I know I've seen you somewhere before."

"You didn't graduate from Hope Community School, did you?" Trisha asked, remembering a girl in her school a few years older than her named Katherine.

"Yeah, I did. Trisha?"

"Yep. It's Jenkins now."

"That's it! You were awesome in sports. Oh my gosh, I haven't seen you in, well, forever."

"It's been a long time. Your class was helper buddies with my sister's class. She really looked up to you."

Katherine frowned a bit. "It's really sad to see her how she is now."

A little taken aback by Katherine's comment, Trisha said, "I wouldn't know how she is. I haven't seen her in almost thirteen years."

"Really?" Katherine asked, raising her eyebrows.

"Yes." Trisha handed her the last pile of escaped papers. "The only member of my family I've heard from is my brother. And he just contacted me via email a few weeks ago."

"That's too bad, but I understand. It's been awhile since I talked to my folks. They moved out east to help my aunt with her bed and breakfast in Maine. They don't have any desire to come back to Iowa, and I don't have time to go out to Maine."

"So, you work in marketing too, huh?"

"Yes, I'm the Director of Communications and Public Relations at Just For You Insurance in Taylor. How about you?"

"I'm the Assistant Director of Creative Development & Communications at The Milligan Group in Los Angeles."

"Los Angeles? Wow, you really did move away."

"I got a scholarship to play basketball out there and never left."

"Well, I bet Los Angeles is a lot different than Hope."

"It is."

"Wait a second, Jenkins?" Kat snapped her fingers. "As in the Trisha Jenkins whose ad campaign won the top advertising award last year?"

"That was me."

"Oh my gosh, I loved that campaign. We were talking about it in my last session. We should catch up more. What are you doing for supper?"

Trisha smiled. It had been a long time since she'd heard someone call the last meal of the day supper. "I don't have any plans."

"Why don't you come with me? I'm meeting up at the lobby restaurant with a few women from my morning session."

"Sounds great," Trisha agreed. "I have to get my purse, and I'll meet you there. It might take me a bit, though, because I accidentally locked it and my key in the room."

Katherine smiled. "You are having a tough day."

Charley stood to the right of the podium and peered at the table where the two items he'd brought to auction off were sitting. He was up next, and he could feel his heart racing. The person before him was almost done selling her second item, and it wouldn't be long before all eyes were on him.

Even though he'd participated in mock auctions during his classes and had auctioned real items off for his ceremony after the class was over, this was the first time he would be auctioning items off in a room full of professional auctioneers.

He took a deep breath and let it out slowly. He knew B.J. had encouraged him to come to the convention to get more practice and gain exposure. B.J. had been impressed by his work ethic in the class and had been working hard to help him find a job.

Charley took another deep breath and wondered what his daughter would do when she found out he might have to give up his life as a farmer and become an auctioneer.

B.J. walked up to him. "Charley? It's your turn. Are you ready?"

"As I'll ever be."

Charley listened as B.J. announced his name, then he walked in front of the table and peered at the room of people who were looking back at him.

As if a switch had been turned on, Charley's training and practice kicked in and he started selling the Iowa photography book. Everything was on automatic as Charley raised the bid in five dollar increments. The price quickly shot up, and clapping erupted as the final bid reached ninety-five dollars.

"Wow, that's a record," B.J. announced as he took the microphone from Charley. "That's the most a new auctioneer at our Midwest Convention has ever brought for an item twenty dollars or less."

Charley grinned as the crowd clapped and hollered.

When B.J. held up the collector tractor Charley had selected from his own small collection, Charley didn't hesitate as he started calling out numbers again.

He noticed B.J. seemed pleased the tractor brought seventy-five dollars. Charley waved to the crowd as the next auctioneer walked up to him, shook his hand and took the microphone.

"Great job." B.J. slapped Charley on the back then shook his hand. "Now, go relax and enjoy the rest of your evening."

Charley grinned, then worked his way through the crowd. He shook hands as he went, finally feeling like an equal.

"Thank God you were with me," Katherine said as she and Trisha made their escape from the supper table. "I'm not in the mood to get drunk tonight. I'm much too tired."

"I don't drink much at all," Trisha said as they headed to the elevator.

"Hey, I know you mentioned you were going to have to go buy something to wear tomorrow. I think we're close to the same size, and I over-packed. You're more than welcome to borrow something of mine."

Trisha shook her head. "Oh, thanks. But I couldn't."

"Why not? You look as tired as I feel. You don't really want to get a cab and go shopping just for something to wear tomorrow at this stupid convention."

Trisha giggled. She knew she'd thought the same words hours earlier.

"Is it a deal?" Katherine asked as they reached the elevators.

"Yes, sounds great. Thanks."

They stepped in when the doors opened and Katherine hit the twelve button.

"Sometimes I wonder why I even come to these things. Seems like most people only come to drink and bullshit," Katherine said as the efficient elevator whizzed higher and higher.

"Yeah, me too. I wasn't planning on coming, but my boss insisted."

"Mine too," Katherine agreed as the doors opened and they stepped out, greeted instantly by two handsome men sporting cowboy hats.

"Hi, ma'am. Hope you found your convention," the taller one said as he smiled at Trisha.

"Oh, yeah. I did. Thanks." Trisha blushed as he tipped his hat before getting on the elevator.

As they started down the hallway, Katherine asked, "What was that about?"

Trisha quickly filled her in, still embarrassed by the entire scene.

"Well, seems like you made an impression on him. Here's my room."

Trisha followed her in, noticing how organized Katherine's room was compared to her own.

"Okay, what do you think about this?" Katherine asked as she opened the closet door and pulled out a short, black dress.

"You hung your clothes up?" Trisha blurted out before she could stop herself.

Katherine laughed. “It’s a habit. Well, do you think this would work?”

Trisha inspected the short, sleeveless dress, noticing the zipper in the front. “You don’t think it’s too sexy for the sessions, do you?”

Katherine shrugged, “I’ve worn it to work before. Why don’t you try it on? Then you can decide.”

Trisha agreed and took the dress into the bathroom.

She pulled it on and adjusted the zipper, then stepped out, “What do you think?”

“Oh, that’s cute. I think it looks perfect. What do you think?”

“It is cute,” Trisha agreed, as she looked at her reflection in the full-length mirror. “And it’ll work great for tomorrow. Thanks so much. I really didn’t want to go shopping tonight.”

“My pleasure.”

“Why don’t I run back to my room and change into some comfortable clothes, and then, if you’re not too tired, we could catch up for awhile.”

“That sounds good.”

Trisha retrieved her clothes out of the bathroom and waved. “I’ll be back in a bit.”

~

“You did great,” Alex congratulated Charley as he walked up to him.

“Thanks.” Charley replied.

“Hey, guys, have you met each other?” B.J. asked as he walked into the hotel suite where they were meeting, a bottle of beer in his hand.

“Briefly.” Alex shook B.J.’s hand. “Good to see you again.”

“You too. I want you to tell Charley about your career. You two are some of the top students I’ve taught,” B.J. praised. “I’ve been trying to help Charley find some work. I’ve gotta go and talk to Colonel Monroe about tomorrow’s championships. Good seeing you again, Alex. And great job tonight, Charley. Enjoy the party.”

Charley held onto his can of Pepsi and watched as B.J. disappeared into the crowd of mingling auctioneers.

“Let me grab a beer, and we can talk,” Alex said as he walked to the suite's refrigerator.

Charley followed him across the room. "So, tell me about your business."

"It's just me, now. After I graduated, I went to work for a group of auctioneers in Kansas. I worked for them for several years, but really wanted to start my own business. I was finally able to, and I'm so glad I did. It's great being your own boss."

"I know. I've been farming my entire life, so I'm used to working by myself and for myself."

"It was hard work getting the business up and running, but if you farm, you're used to hard work."

"So, how do you let people know about you? Advertising?"

"At first. And networking. Tell everyone what you're doing. Put your company name on your truck. Go and talk to the guys who get together and eat breakfast every morning. Get your name out there. Once you get a few successful auctions under your belt, you'll start getting more work than you can handle."

"How many employees do you have?"

"I mainly work alone." Alex took a swig of his beer. "But I do have a gal who does my bookwork. And she lines up people to help the day of the auction. But I don't have a set crew. I pay by the hour. Sometimes I'll get a group from the school, like the football players, to come and help me unload and set up."

Charley listened closely, taking in everything Alex offered.

"So, why auctioneering?"

Charley shrugged, not wanting to get into his financial mess with Alex. "Time for a change."

"I understand that," Alex said before taking another long swig.

Charley finished his pop. "Well, I think I'm gonna call it a night. See ya tomorrow."

"See you then." Alex waved his beer as Charley walked out of the room.

Charley dropped his pop can into the trash by the elevator, then got on and rode up to the twenty-second floor.

He started down the hallway and felt his heart skip a beat when he noticed the blonde from earlier was walking down the hallway toward him.

She smiled at him. "Hi."

"Hi. Did you find your convention?"

Trisha's light laugh made Charley grin as she said, "That was embarrassing, but yes, I managed to find where I was supposed to be. So, you're an auctioneer, huh?"

Charley felt mesmerized by her sparkling blue eyes as she stopped in front of him.

"I used to go to auctions when I was a little girl. I loved them. The way the auctioneer would talk always seemed like a different language to me."

"It takes practice, that's for sure. So, what convention are you here for?"

"Oh, nothing as exciting as yours." Trisha put her hand on his arm and smiled, "Marketing and communications."

Charley's arm felt on fire where her soft hand rested. "Well, I bet you're a very talented woman."

Trisha smiled as she gave his bicep a small squeeze. "Have a great evening."

"You too."

He unlocked his door, then looked back down the hallway. He waved when he noticed the woman had stopped and was smiling at him.

"Just breathe," Trisha reminded herself as she rode in the elevator, thinking about the man from the hallway.

She could still feel how strong his arm had been under her hand and couldn't help but wonder more about the stranger.

When the doors opened, Trisha made her way through the obviously drunk group that didn't wait for her to exit, and then she hurried down the hallway, knocking when she reached Katherine's door.

"Come on in," Katherine, who was now dressed in shorts and a T-shirt, said as she opened the door.

"Thanks." Trisha shut the door and followed Katherine, opting to sit down on the burgundy leather recliner in the corner of the room.

Katherine plopped down on the edge of the bed and handed her a bottle of water from the nightstand. "What's that look about?"

"What look?"

"You have a different look in your eyes. What are you thinking about?"

"Oh, well, I met this guy." Trisha blushed. "Sorry. I was still thinking about him."

"Another cowboy?" Katherine teased, thinking back to the guys waiting to get on the elevator.

Trisha shook her head. "I don't think he was a cowboy, but he was strong. I couldn't help myself; I had to touch his bicep. And, well, wow!"

Katherine giggled with Trisha. "This is such a nice way to end this hectic day."

"It is. So, if you weren't stuck here, what would you be doing back home?"

"I'm afraid I'd be at work. Not much different than being here."

"But aren't you married?" Trisha blurted, glancing at Katherine's ring. "Oh, I'm sorry. It's none of my business."

"No, it's okay." Katherine looked sadly at her own ring. "Yes, I'm married. My husband's name is Victor. We've been married for 11 years."

"Is there something wrong, Katherine?"

"Please, call me Kat. And yes, there's something wrong."

"Okay, Kat. If you need someone to talk to, I'm here. If not—"

"I don't know what's going on with him," Kat interrupted as she started absentmindedly playing with her wedding ring. "He took a leave of absence from his job back in December and went to Kansas to help his sister with their mother, who had a stroke. It's been the three of them for so long. Vic's dad was killed in a small plane crash when Vic was a little boy. Anyway, they didn't think his mother had long to live. But he's still there, and I think something's going on."

"Like what?"

Kat shrugged, "I'm not sure. He never calls me anymore. Hell, he doesn't even care that I'm here in Minneapolis. I think he's…well, I think he's up to something.'"

"I'm so sorry, Kat."

"Yeah, me too. But I don't want to talk about me anymore. Let's talk about you. Are you married?"

Trisha shook her head. "I'm divorced. Brad and I were married for a little over four years."

"I'm sorry."

"It's okay. We should've taken things slower when we met. Instead, we met in October, got engaged at Christmas and married on Valentine's Day. Then we had something major happen, and after that, our marriage fell apart. But we're still good friends and I'm all right with us just being friends."

"So, are you dating anyone?"

Trisha shook her head. "I've pretty much buried myself in work."

"And you haven't been back home since you left for college?"

"I was back, once, but it wasn't to see my family. And I didn't see them. I drove by the house but didn't stop. The last time I talked to my family was when I called my parents to let them know I was staying in California after college graduation. It wasn't a good conversation, and I've never called again."

"I'm so sorry, Trisha."

Trisha took a sip of her water. "You said something earlier about my sister. You most likely know about my father's drinking issues. Is that what's wrong with my sister? Does she drink too?"

Kat noticed the sad look on Trisha's face and slowly nodded, "I've run into her around town, and she's always either drunk or hung over."

"Have you run into my dad?" Trisha asked in a soft, almost meek, voice.

"Yes. I'm afraid he hasn't changed since you've been gone, Trisha. I'm so sorry."

"That's the reason I left Hope. I had to get away. And if my brother hadn't contacted me, I wouldn't be curious about them. But he found me and sent me an email saying he wants me to call him. I haven't, but I don't want to hurt him. We were always close growing up, and I hated leaving him in that house to deal with the family alone. But I had to get out. And to tell you the truth, I'm a little nervous to find out what he wants."

"It'll bother you until you do."

"Do you know anything about him?"

Kat leaned back and let out a low, slow breath while she was thinking. "Yeah, I guess I do. He works at the school. I think Chase said he works with the football program, but he might be a teacher too. I'm not sure."

Trisha had a light bulb moment. "Chase Locke. That's who you used to date in school." Trisha noticed the pained look on Kat's face and instantly felt terrible, "Oh, shit. What?"

Kat shook her head as she stood up and paced around the small room. "It's nothing. Really. Yes, we dated back then. I thought we were going to get married, too. But it didn't work out."

"I'm sorry. I really didn't mean to bring up bad memories."

"It's not that. It's just that…oh, hell…Chase and I almost kissed yesterday. I still feel guilty about it."

Trisha's eyebrows rose. "You almost kissed?"

Kat's brown eyes welled up. "It was wrong. It was so wrong, but he still loves me. I can feel his love when we're together. And it's so tempting…"

Trisha nodded as Kat's voice trailed off.

"I'm sorry, Trisha. But I think I need to get to sleep. I have an early morning session."

Trisha stood and started for the door. "Yeah, me too. Thanks for letting me borrow your dress. I'll see you in the morning."

Chapter 2

"Denied?"

"Yes," the older woman, whose nametag read Vivian, said. "And when I call, no one answers."

"I'm so sorry. I have no idea what's going on," Trisha apologized. "I'll pay for this with my personal credit card. They can reimburse me when I get back."

"Well, okay," Vivian agreed.

Trisha pulled her wallet out of her purse, then picked out her credit card with the most credit left on it. "Here you go."

She watched as Vivian typed on the computer, waited, and then smiled and handed her card back. "Okay, we're all set."

"Again, I'm sorry. Maybe our normal secretary is out or something."

"Enjoy your lunch, Trisha. I hear it's delicious."

Trisha managed a smile, but when she turned away, she frowned while wondering what was really going on with her company.

As she stepped out of the conference room, she pulled her phone out of her purse and dialed her boss' cell number.

"Voicemail?" Trisha questioned, angry, as she ended the call. "He always answers his cell, even on the weekend."

She scrolled through her contacts until she found the cell number for the company receptionist, Shelly.

"Hey, Trisha. What's going on?"

"Hey, Shel. I'm at this convention in Minneapolis."

"I wondered why I didn't see you yesterday."

"Yeah. Hey, is everything okay at the office?"

"Not really," Shelly voice suddenly hushed. "Strange things were going on yesterday."

"Like what?"

"Lots of closed-door meetings. And in the afternoon, none of the higher-ups were accepting calls and all appointments were cancelled. It was strange."

"Yeah, well, the company credit card apparently isn't working either, because I had to pay for this convention on my Visa."

"I could've told you it wouldn't work, Trish. I was told not to pay the bill."

"Shit," Trisha muttered.

"I know. With all the layoffs going around town, I'm not feeling real secure. When are you coming back?"

"Tomorrow. I'll see you on Monday."

"Okay, try to have some fun."

Trisha had just hung up when Kat walked past her, clearly preoccupied.

"Hey, Kat."

Kat stopped. "Hey."

"Are you okay?" Trisha asked, concerned when she realized how frazzled her friend looked.

"Oh, yeah. I was trying to process that last session. Where are you heading next?"

"Room twelve. The session on fresh marketing ideas. How about you?"

"That's where I'm headed too." They started walking together. "So, how's your day?"

"Pretty good, except something weird is going on with my company. I hope we're not in for layoffs."

"I hope so too, Trisha. But hey, if something does happen, look me up. Based on your award winning ad campaign, I'd be more than happy to have you on my team."

Just the thought of moving back to Iowa scared Trisha, but she also longed for the comfort of her hometown again. She managed a small smile. "I'll keep that in mind."

ꝏ

"Hey, guys, thanks for sticking around," B.J. said as he caught up to Charley and Alex in the hotel bar.

"No problem," Charley said.

Alex added, "There isn't anything else to do around here."

"I wanted to ask how you thought the convention went?" B.J. continued as he waved to the sole, clearly stressed waitress trying to tend the packed bar.

"One of the best," Alex answered.

"Good," B.J. said, as he relaxed his shoulders. "I was on the committee, and I was hoping we did okay. The fun auction tonight seemed like a good way to end things."

"It was helpful to watch you guys in action," Charley said.

"That girl's busy. Let me get the drinks." Alex stood and turned towards Charley. "Beer?"

"Pop, please."

"Beer's fine with me," B.J. said. After Alex walked away, B.J. continued, "Sorry Charley, I didn't think about you not drinking when I asked you two to wait in the bar."

"It's okay."

"Are you a recovering alcoholic?"

"No. My wife, Nancy, was killed in a car accident. I always thought someone who'd been drinking ran her off the road. I haven't touched the stuff since," Charley replied, his thoughts instantly on his wife.

"Oh, man. I'm sorry. I shouldn't have asked."

"No, it's fine. It was a long time ago."

"We can go somewhere else if you want to."

Right then, Charley noticed the blonde from the night before as she walked into the room surrounded by several other women. He felt his heart speed up when he noticed her formfitting black dress that showed off her sexy legs.

"Damn, this place got hotter," Alex mumbled as he joined them and handed out the drinks.

"It did," B.J. agreed, checking the women out.

Charley watched as the blonde looked in their direction and waved, and he felt himself waving back.

B.J swiveled to look at Charley. "Do you know her?"

"I talked to her last night in the hallway. She's the girl who walked into the conference room yesterday morning."

"Oh, yeah. I remember. She looks, I don't know, hotter, tonight."

"Do you know the brunette with her?" Alex asked.

Charley shook his head. "I don't really know her either. I just talked to her briefly."

"Well, that's a foot in the door. Come on, let's say hello."

B.J. slid up next to the tall table between a couple of the ladies. "Hi, I'm B.J. Why don't you ladies let us buy you a round?"

"I'm Suzy," the busty redhead next to him offered.

"These are my friends, Alex and Charley," B.J. continued.

"These are my friends Tara, Krista, Kat and um, I'm sorry. What was your name?"

"Trisha," she said, turning to Charley. "I'm Trisha."

Charley felt a warmness radiate through his body, all the way down to his toes, as she smiled at him.

"Charley," he repeated, smiling back.

Noticing the way they were looking at each other, Suzy said, "I think Charley and Trisha should dance."

Charley felt himself panicking. He hadn't danced with a woman in more than a decade.

"Would you like to?" Trisha asked, waking him from his thoughts.

Knowing he was doing a lot of things lately he didn't usually do, Charley managed to ask, "Trisha, would you like to dance?"

Trisha's heart raced as she took ahold of Charley's strong, calloused hand and led him in the direction of the crowded dance floor. She still couldn't believe Suzy had suggested they dance. She also couldn't believe how excited she was he had asked.

She turned to face him and felt her hip quiver as he placed his hand on it and took her hand into his.

Suddenly, Trisha forgot about everyone else in the room as they started swaying with the music, looking into each other's eyes.

"You're a good dancer."

"You are too," Trisha agreed, thankful to find her voice. "Thanks again for asking."

"I'm glad Suzy suggested it. I had hoped to see you again. You look beautiful, Trisha."

"I had hoped to see you again, too."

As their song ended and fast-paced rap music brought a crowd to the dance floor, Charley placed his hand on her back and they walked to the table, where the drinks flowed and the laughter was loud.

Trisha couldn't help herself as she glanced at Charley and noticed he was drinking a pop. Like she was. She noticed he looked at her again and smiled, feeling butterflies coming to life in her stomach.

"Would you like something more to drink? Could I get it for you?" Charley asked as he leaned close so she could hear him.

"I'm good," she said, her lips close to his ear.

She noticed Kat was leaning into Charley's friend, Alex and flirting. She wondered if Kat had seen the wedding ring he wore, and quickly scanned Charley's left hand, relieved when she discovered it was bare.

"Let's dance, Cowboy!" Suzy called, snatching B.J.'s hat before taking his hand and dragging him to the dance floor.

Trisha noticed the other two girls they had met at supper had disappeared while she and Charley had been dancing.

"Would you like to get out of here?" Charley asked.

Trisha looked back at Kat, who seemed to be completely caught up in whatever Alex was saying, and nodded, "Yeah, I'd like that."

She felt Charley's hand in hers again and felt the butterflies take flight as they walked out of the loud bar and into the quiet hallway.

Pleased when he kept her hand in his, they started toward the elevator.

"What would you like to do now?"

Anxious to spend more time with him, Trisha suggested, "We could watch a movie."

"That's what I thought too," Charley agreed, pushing the up button. "So, did you have a good conference?"

Suddenly remembering her work problems, Trisha managed a small smile. "Yes. Did you?"

"Yeah. It was my first time at one of these things, but it was good."

Several more partiers emerged from the elevator when the door opened, and they were alone as the doors shut and the elevator started climbing back up.

"So, how long have you been an auctioneer?"

"I'm just getting started. I took classes last June, and my instructor, B.J., suggested I come to this. He thought it would help if I networked some with other auctioneers so I can find a job."

The doors opened and they stepped out, still holding hands.

"Would you like to watch movies in my room or yours?" Trisha asked as they started down the hallway.

"How about yours? Mine's a mess."

"Well, so is mine," Trisha laughed. "But that's fine with me. Here we are."

Charley couldn't believe he was in a woman's hotel room. He watched while she picked up various items, shoving them into her suitcase. When he noticed a lacy, black bra in her hand, he felt a fire ignite deep inside that he hadn't felt in years.

"Let me make this up," Trisha said as she stuffed the last piece of clothing into the suitcase and zipped it shut, then tossed it onto the floor and flipped the bedspread over the bed.

Charley felt his mouth going dry as he looked at the bed, then back at her.

He couldn't stop his gaze as he peeked at the zipper that dove between her breasts, showing a modest amount of cleavage.

"We could sit on the couch and watch the movie."

"Sounds good." Charley agreed, willing himself not to lose his nerve.

He wasn't doing anything wrong. He was widowed and had been for several years. He wasn't cheating on his wife. He wasn't cheating on anyone.

Trisha grabbed the remote and started flipping as Charley walked over and sat down on the burgundy love seat that matched the recliner in his room.

Settling on a romantic movie, Trisha asked, "How about this?"

"Good choice."

He watched as she walked over and kicked off her black high heels, then she sat down beside him and tucked her feet, leaning in close.

It felt natural as he put his arm around her shoulders and pulled her closer.

As the first commercial came on, Charley turned toward Trisha and felt his heart racing as she leaned in and kissed him on the lips.

His body instantly responded as he took her into his arms, forgetting all about the movie as their tongues found each other.

When she pulled back slightly, he gazed in her eyes and noticed a hunger he'd never seen before.

He almost lost it when she took his hand and placed it on the zipper.

He slowly moved the zipper downward, revealing a lacy red bra that dipped low, and felt his pants tightening.

Trisha reached over and started unbuttoning his Western shirt, and he moaned as her soft hand started playing with his dark, thick chest hair.

"Oh, Charley," she said as she pushed his shirt off, then stood and pulled him to his feet.

Charley thought he was dreaming as she led him to the bed. Then she stopped and finished unzipping her dress. As if fell to the floor, she whispered, "Make love to me."

Chapter 3

The sliver of sun shining in through the heavy curtains was the first thing Charley saw as he started to wake.

He rolled onto his back and tried to remember where he was, and then he realized he could hear the shower water running.

"It wasn't a dream," he whispered as he sat up, quickly noticing the black dress on the floor next to his best pair of blue jeans. "It really happened."

A wave of panic followed by guilt swept through Charley as he thought about his wife and the fact he'd slept with another woman.

"But she's been gone for almost thirteen years," he reminded himself. "It's time to move on. But I don't even know Trisha's last name."

Not sure what to do, Charley found his underwear next to her black thong and pulled it on, his mind replaying their sweet lovemaking from the night before.

He sat on the edge of the bed, jeans in his hand, when Trisha emerged wearing only one of the soft, white, hotel bath towels.

"Running out on me?" she asked with a twinkle in her eyes.

"What? Oh, no." Charley dropped his pants as he stood. "Damn, you're so sexy."

He felt like someone else, someone much bolder, as he quickly crossed the room and yanked off the towel. Noticing water droplets on her collarbone, he leaned down and ran his tongue along them, enjoying her moan.

Before long, they were back in the bed, making love again.

As their bodies parted and they both lay on the sheets, Trisha said, "I want you to know…I don't…this is the first time that I've, um, hooked up like this. I'm not easy."

Charley looked over at her. "I didn't think you were."

"I don't want you thinking this is something I usually do. In fact, I haven't done…this…for awhile."

"I haven't either."

"You're a very special man, Charley," Trisha said as she sat up. "And there's nothing I'd rather do than make love to you all morning, but I have one last session this morning. And I can't miss it."

"And I need to get headed home," Charley agreed as they both got out of bed.

Charley watched her nakedness disappear as she dressed in red underwear and a black bra.

He instantly felt turned on again but continued pulling on his clothes from the night before.

Then he sat down on the couch and watched as she picked out a pair of shorts and a silk-looking tank top and pulled them on.

Trisha noticed he was watching and smiled.

"You're such a beautiful woman, Trisha. Dressed or naked. Just beautiful."

Trisha walked over and sat down beside him, then leaned over and rested her head against his chest, "I hate that we have to go our separate ways. I don't even know your last name."

"Walker. I'm Charley Walker. How about you?"

"Trisha Jenkins."

"Where are you from, Trisha?"

"California. You?"

"Iowa. California's a hell of a long ways away from Iowa."

Trisha instantly thought of her family. "I have some points saved up. Maybe I could come and visit you in Iowa. Or you could come on out to California. It's warm in California."

"I'd love to visit you sometime."

"Shoot, I'm going to be late," Trisha said, noticing the time on the alarm clock. "I'm sorry, but I have to finish getting ready."

He watched as she walked over to the desk and grabbed the complimentary notebook and pen.

Then she handed him a piece of paper with her name and a phone number.

"That's my personal cell number." She handed him the pen and notebook. "Can you give me yours?"

Charley wrote down his name and cell number, quickly realizing it was the first time in his entire life he'd ever done that.

He stood up and walked over to her, handing her the paper. "I hate leaving you."

Trisha smiled. "Me too. But I'm really glad we met."

"Me too." Charley hugged her. Then they kissed again before she opened the door and he stepped into the hallway.

After she shut the door, he pulled the paper out of his pocket and looked at her writing, already missing her.

Thirty minutes later, he rolled his suitcase past her door, fighting the urge to knock. He knew she most likely wasn't there, but couldn't help himself as he stopped and rapped his knuckles on the heavy, wooden door.

Time seemed to stand still as he waited, hoping her session had been canceled.

But her door didn't open, and he sighed as he continued down the hallway and into the elevator.

As he crossed the marble floor in the lobby, headed toward the front desk, he heard someone call his name.

He noticed Alex was sitting on one of the plush couches, waving him over.

"Hey," Charley said, then added. "You look terrible, what's wrong?"

Alex stood up. "Have you seen those girls from last night?"

"I…well…I left Trisha's room about a half hour ago. Why?"

"You left her room? You mean, you stayed with her all night?"

Charley ran his hand thorough his dark brown hair, "Um, yeah."

"Good for you," Alex said, patting him on the back. Then the worry fogged his eyes again as he asked, "Where's she now?"

"She had a session. Why?"

Alex took a deep breath. "Kat stayed with me last night. But she was gone when I woke up this morning. I've been sitting here hoping to see her checking out. I didn't get her last name, Charley. I don't know where she lives. I think she might be upset."

"Why? Did something happen?"

"I'm married, Charley." Alex waved his left hand. "And so is she. We didn't talk about it, but I saw her ring. We both got a little drunk last night, and things got hot and heavy really fast. I care for her. I want her to know my marriage is pretty much over. My wife and I are only staying together for our daughter. I want to tell Kat that and find out about her marriage. I wanna make sure she's okay."

"She's probably in the session with Trisha. And that lasts until noon."

"Shit. I have less than twenty minutes to get to the airport."

"I can give you a ride to the airport," Charley said, "but we need to hurry. Are you checked out?"

Alex nodded.

"Okay, let me get checked out, and we'll try to make your flight."

Trisha couldn't concentrate on the lecture, as her thoughts were still on Charley and their night together. She still couldn't believe she'd ended up making love with a man she hardly knew. She also couldn't believe how much she already missed him.

As the people around her started to stand, Trisha realized the session was finally over. She stood too and quickly noticed Kat, who looked miserable, was headed in her direction.

"Hey." Trisha said. "Are you okay?"

"No. I'm so ready to get out of here."

"Okay." Worried, she softly added, "Do you want to talk about it?"

Kat shook her head as a couple of tears escaped down her cheeks.

"Okay. That's okay."

"But, I did want to tell you how nice it's been talking with you. I'm glad you were here, Trisha," Kat said as she hugged her.

"It was great running into you too. I'll get your dress dry cleaned and mail it to you."

"Don't worry about it. And I hope everything works out with your job in California. But, if you ever find yourself needing a new job, give me a call. Okay?"

Trisha nodded, taking Kat's card when she offered it.

"Let me get you mine." Trisha pulled a business card out of her purse. "I'll email you my personal number."

Kat hugged her again. "I've already checked out, so I'm going to head home. Have a safe flight, Trisha."

Less than four hours later, Trisha walked down the hallway in her apartment building. She unlocked her door, walked in and jumped when she noticed her ex-husband lying on her couch.

"Hey."

"Oh, hey. Sorry, I musta fallen asleep."

"What are you doing here, Brad? I thought you were in London," Trisha said as she walked over and sat down on the chair across from him.

"I got in last night." Brad yawned as he sat up. "I've been hearing some things about your company, Trish. I wanted to tell you in person." Noticing the suitcase, he asked, "Did you go on a trip?"

"I had a convention in Minneapolis. And I ended up having to pay for it with my own personal credit card because the company one was declined. Shelly said the charge was rejected because she was told not to pay the credit card bill when it came in, and she also said weird things were going on at the office on Friday. What have you heard?"

"I've heard they're having money problems and there will be layoffs."

"Great," Trisha leaned back in the chair. "Just what I need."

"Well, you've been there several years, Trish. And you've worked your way up the ladder pretty quickly. I doubt you'll get laid off."

"I hope not. I'm barely making it the way it is," Trisha said, then stopped, putting up her hand. "No, Brad. I won't take any money from you."

"Too damn stubborn. I know your lease is up on this place at the end of the month. I also know you haven't renewed it. And you haven't paid this month's rent."

"They raised the rent." Trisha crossed her arms. "They've raised it every year, but now it's over $2,000 a month. I haven't paid it, because I can't afford it. I guess I'll have to find a new place to live. But, I'd better wait and see if I still have a job before I do."

"I really can't see you losing your job. But why don't you move in with me, Trish. That way you won't have to rush to find somewhere new to live."

"I don't think your girlfriend would be too thrilled to find out your ex is living with you."

"Scarlette knows we're close."

"I'll think about it, okay?"

Brad nodded and patted the couch beside him.

Trisha quickly moved and curled up against him, feeling safe in his embrace.

"What's his name?"

Trisha pulled back, her eyes wide. "What?"

"Oh, Trish. I know you. I can tell something's different about you. It has to be a guy. Tell me."

Trisha shook her head, not really surprised he could tell, as he knew her better than anyone else.

"I'm waiting."

"His name's Charley. I met him at the convention. He's really nice."

"Is he from here?"

Trisha softly said, "No…Iowa."

"Oh, shit."

"I know. I didn't think I'd ever want to go back there. But, there's something about him that has me rethinking that."

"Good." Brad pulled her tight. "I'm glad to hear you've found someone, Trish."

"Well, I hardly know him. But I do like him."

"Why don't I make us supper and we can watch TV?" Brad offered, then teased, "You look tired, like you hardly slept at all last night."

Trisha's cheeks turned red. She grinned as she stood and said, "Great idea. Wake me when it's ready."

The rumbling of the gravel road underneath his tires calmed Charley, and he was thankful he was almost home.

Trisha's smiling face popped into his mind, and he wondered where she was and if she was okay.

Then his thoughts went to his daughter, and he relaxed when he noticed her older blue car wasn't parked in its usual spot.

"Dodged that bullet for a little bit," Charley muttered as he parked. He smiled when he noticed his black and white border collie waited by his front door.

"Hey, Shooter!" Charley called as he opened the door and slid out of his aging pickup, thankful it had made the journey in one piece.

Shooter sprinted to Charley and started dancing around his feet, rubbing on his knees.

"I missed you too." Charley rubbed the excited dog between the ears before he walked around to the passenger's side and gathered his suitcase and bag of goodies from the convention.

"So, what's been going on around here?" Charley asked as Shooter darted around him and they started to the house. Noticing the feed pan by the door was empty, Charley unlocked the front door. "Did Pam forget to feed you again? Or are you just really hungry today. Either way, let me get you some more food, and I'll be right back."

He scanned his modest living room, thankful to be home as he dropped his suitcase and goodie bag on the sagging, old green couch.

His thoughts were instantly on the day Nancy had picked out the couch.

They'd been married for two weeks, and she'd taken the money they'd been given from her parents and had gone to the small furniture store in town. She'd picked out the green couch and matching green swivel chairs.

Charley thought about those chairs and knew they'd worn much faster than the couch and were now lining the local landfill on the edge of the county. But the worn couch was still in the same place in the living room where Nancy had placed it more than twenty five years earlier.

Guilt started coursing through Charley's veins as he scooped a generous helping of dog food out of the bin in the enclosed back porch off the kitchen.

His thoughts were bouncing between Nancy and Trisha as he carried the food back to the front porch were Shooter waited patiently by his pan.

"There you go," he said as he filled the dog's bowl and patted him again.

Shooter acted as if starved, as always, and started gobbling up the food, and Charley sat down on the wooden bench while he thought about Nancy.

He'd loved her since they were freshmen in school. He'd had a crush on her since third grade when she'd shared her peanut butter cookie with him during lunch.

Their love had been magical as they'd grown up together in school and life, and they had married shortly after graduation.

"I'm sorry, baby," Charley whispered as he thought about the way he'd spent his previous night.

It had been the first time in his life he'd been with a woman other than Nancy.

He leaned back and shut his eyes. Other women had tried to keep him company over the years. And he'd dated a few of those women, but had always ended the relationships when they had started to become serious.

"Why did I go back to her room?" he asked the quiet, Iowa countryside.

Shooter jumped up beside him on the wooden bench and laid his head down on Charley's leg.

Charley started rubbing him while looking at the growing cornfield across the road, his mind still on Trisha.

"Your cooking has gotten better," Trisha said as she nibbled on the chicken Parmesan dinner Brad had prepared for them.

"Scarlette. Her parents have several restaurants in Phoenix. She grew up working in them."

"Well, I need to thank her the next time I see her."

"So, tell me about your guy," Brad pried. "What's his name?"

"Charley Walker."

"And where's he from?"

"Iowa. I told you that already."

"Where in Iowa, silly?"

"Oh, hell, I have no idea. I had so many things running through my mind when he said Iowa that I didn't think to ask. I don't know if I could go back there, Brad. You know that. The relationship has to be over before it really gets started."

"I don't think it does." Brad handed her a piece of garlic bread. "Just because he's from Iowa doesn't mean this is doomed. Do you like him, or was it just sex?"

Clearly caught off guard, Trisha choked on her bread, her eyes welling up as she coughed.

"Are you okay?"

Trisha coughed a few more times as she cleared her throat. Then she took a drink before mumbling, "You ass. Just for the sex?"

Relieved she was okay, Brad explained, "It was a joke. Of course it was more than that. I was trying to get you to laugh, not choke."

Trisha rolled her eyes at him. "He's…I don't know. Intriguing."

"Well, that's a good place to start. But Trish, let me ask you something. What made you sleep with this man? You haven't been with anyone since me."

"You ruined me for others."

Brad smirked. "Thanks for that, babe. But I'm going for an honest answer here. Why have you been so cautious around men all this time to just sleep with one you hardly know?"

"I don't know, okay? I've been asking myself that same question all the way home. But it's…he's different. He's kind and cute and…sincere. He's not like the guys I've met around here. He's genuine."

"Sounds like a good Iowa guy."

"Maybe that's it. Maybe he seemed like home to me. I don't know. All I do know is I was very attracted to him. I haven't been that attracted to anyone since…well, you. And there was this sense of urgency. I knew the conferences would be over and we'd both be headed home. And I wanted to spend more time with him. I didn't want our time together to be over. I wanted him to spend the night with me. And now I miss him. I want to call him and tell him that."

"So, what's stopping you? You did get his number, didn't you?"

"Yes, but what if he thinks it was a mistake? What if he doesn't want to hear from me? What if he wants to forget about us?"

"Oh, God, Trish. He's not married, is he?"

"What? No," Trisha shook her head. "At least I don't think so. He didn't have on a ring."

"Doesn't necessarily mean…"

"He's not. Okay? I know he's not. He didn't seem the type to cheat."

"Well, then, call him," Brad suggested. "It's the best thing you could do."

After starting a load of laundry, Charley walked into the kitchen and noticed his favorite farming magazine sat on the edge of the kitchen table. When he picked it up, two envelopes fell to the floor.

"Oh, shit," Charley groaned as he picked them up and noticed one of them was from his bank. He dropped the magazine and other envelope back on the table, then carried the bank envelope into the living room and sat down on the couch.

"I've been dreading this all summer," he muttered as he stared at the envelope, his hands shaking.

Figuring he had to face it sometime, Charley tore open the envelope and pulled out the papers.

As he read the letter, his face turned a bright red.

"Damn that George Bailey," he growled as he thumbed through the financial papers attached to the letter. "Every single damn year I have to jump through hoops for that man. And this year he's finally going to get his damn wish. He's finally got me backed into a corner. He's going to be so damned happy. Damn him. Damn George Bailey!"

Charley flung the letter and envelope across the room, almost hitting Pam as she walked through the door.

"What's wrong? I could hear your yelling when I got out of the car," Pam said as she walked over and picked up the papers. "What are these?"

"Oh, nothing," Charley grumbled, crossing the floor and taking them from her. "Nothing you need to worry about."

"Damn it, Daddy. I can tell you're upset. Your cheeks look like tomatoes. Is that from the bank?"

"Yes, damn it. That damn George Bailey. Every single year he's been after me. Every single year I have to fill out all of this damned paper work to get my loan renewed. He never makes anyone else I know do that. Just me. It's because it's me. It's harassment, that's what it is. Damn him!"

"Why, Daddy? Why does he harass you?" Pam pried, shook up by her father's outburst.

Charley clenched his lips together as he fumbled with the papers, trying to fold them small enough to fit back into the envelope.

"Daddy, why?"

"You don't need to worry about any of this," Charley insisted, giving up as he tucked both the papers and envelope under his arm. "I thank the good Lord you came to your senses and quit seeing that Bailey boy. That family's nothing but trouble!"

Charley's ringing cell phone startled them both.

Charley peeked at the screen. When he noticed the 310 area code, his thoughts instantly turned to Trisha and the number he'd read on the piece of paper she'd handed him. "I have to take this."

"Okay"

Charley hurried through the kitchen and out the back door. "Hello?"

"Charley?"

"Yeah. Trisha?"

"Yeah. How are you? Did you get home okay?"

"I did." Charley felt his anger melting away with the sweet sound of her voice. "Did you?"

"Yes. It's kind of lonely, though. I can't stop thinking about you, Charley."

"You've been on my mind a lot too," Charley said, the words flowing freely off his tongue. "How was your flight?"

"Uneventful," Trisha leaned back on the couch and closed her eyes, picturing Charley from that morning in her bed. "I hate that I had to leave you this morning."

"It's okay, Trisha. I understand. You were there for work. But, I have to admit, I did stop by your room before checking out in case you were back early."

"Oh, damn. I wish I would've been there."

Charley smiled as he walked into the barn and sat down on the old lawn chair in the corner of what Pam called his primitive man cave, "I'm glad you called me, Trisha."

"Me too." Trisha agreed, thankful Brad had practically forced her to call. "I hope you aren't having second thoughts about last night."

"Not at all," Charley said, shaking off the memories of his wife. "You?"

"Never. I wish we would've gotten together Friday night so we would've had two nights together."

Hot desire coursed through Charley's veins at the thought of being with her again. "We'll have to make plans to see each other again. Trisha. And soon."

"I agree. Real soon."

"Don't come out," Pam ordered as soon as Tyler picked up the phone. "I'm almost there. We have to do this. We're running out of time."

"When I walked in the door, my daddy was cursing your dad. He was throwing papers across the room. Bank papers. My daddy says your dad's harassing him," Pam rambled, getting upset. "What are we going to do? My daddy doesn't want me with you, Tyler. He's never going to be happy we're getting married."

"He'll change his mind when he finds out about our baby. Think of our baby, Pam. Try to calm down. Okay? I won't come out tonight. We'll try it again another night. But honey, we're running out of time. We're getting married this weekend, and your dad doesn't even know we're back together. If we're not careful, he'll hear about this from someone else. Things get around in a town this small. You know that."

"My daddy doesn't hate anyone," Pam said as she plopped down on her bed. "He gets along with everyone he meets. What is it about your father that gets my daddy so upset?"

"I don't know." Tyler pulled off the gravel road into a field driveway and turned around, then started back toward town. "My dad ticks everyone off. It's his specialty."

"They're never going to be happy for us. Our baby's grandparents will never get along. What will that do to our baby?" Pam questioned as her voice cracked.

"Sweetie, you have to calm down. It'll all work out. I promise you it will. Besides, babies have a way of uniting people. Once our families find out there's going to be a little one, everyone will get along."

"You don't really believe that, do you?"

"I do. You'll see. Are you sure you don't want me to come out there?"

"I'm sure." Pam fought off a yawn. "I think I'm going to go to bed early. I'm beat. Let's try again tomorrow night."

"Okay. Did your dad tell you where he went this weekend?"

"I never got a chance to ask him. He was upset with your dad, then got a phone call and went outside. He's never taken a call away from me like that. It has to be a woman."

"So, your dad has a friend he's seeing without telling you. It's nothing different than what you are doing."

"He's not seeing the daughter of a man he hates," Pam mumbled, shaking her head.

"I love you. Everything will be okay. I'll see you tomorrow. Okay?"

"Okay. I love you too. Good night, Tyler."

Pam hung up her phone and walked into the living room. Realizing her father was still outside, she wrote a note and left it on the table, telling him she was going to bed. Then she continued to the bathroom and brushed her teeth. While glancing in the mirror, she noticed the glow on her cheeks that Tyler had mentioned seeing earlier in the evening.

"I have to tell him. And soon. But he's going to be so disappointed. Not just because of Tyler, but also because I got pregnant before getting married."

She absentmindedly rubbed her slim stomach, hoping her father didn't hold that against the little baby growing inside of her.

Trisha noticed the time on her television. "Oh my gosh, have we been talking for an hour? It's gotta be late there."

"A little before eleven," Charley said as he glanced at Shooter, who slept on his feet. "Time flies when we're together."

"It does. I don't really want to hang up."

"Me neither. But you have work tomorrow."

"And you probably have another auction to get ready for."

"Well, not really. I'm just getting started with that. But I do have some farm work to do. Mowing hay, actually."

"Oh, so you're a farmer, too. That would explain those strong muscles of yours," Trisha swooned, thinking about his arms.

Charley blushed.

"Charley?"

"Yeah, I'm still here. I'm a little surprised you like me, Trisha. It's been awhile since I've been in a relationship. I'm a little rusty at all this."

"Well, I think you're doing fine. Besides, it's been awhile for me too. We'll work out the kinks together."

"I'd like that. I'll be thinking about you all night, Trisha."

"Me too. Good night, Charley. Sweet dreams."

As their call ended, Charley suddenly felt more alone than he'd felt in years. He reached down and petted Shooter, then slowly moved his feet out from under the sleeping dog and started to the house, shutting off the makeshift barn light on his way.

As he walked along the moon-lit path, he noticed the lights were still on in the kitchen and wondered if Pam was waiting up for him. He knew she'd have several questions as to why he'd been on the phone for so long. He slowed down his pace, not sure how he was going to answer her questions.

"I don't want to lie to my daughter," he reasoned out loud in the darkness, "but I'm not ready to tell her about Trisha yet, either."

Deciding he'd try to change the subject, Charley braced himself as he stepped into the dated kitchen. He quickly noticed the pink piece of paper on the table and read it, instantly worried about his daughter.

"She's been tired a lot lately. I hope she's not sick," Charley said as he placed her note back on the table, then locked the back door and shut off the kitchen light.

He made his way through the familiar darkness to the front door and locked it, then continued down the dark hallway, glancing in the direction of his daughter's closed bedroom door before he walked into his own bedroom and shut his door.

After stripping down to his underwear, Charley climbed beneath the cool covers, Trisha on his mind as he fell into a deep sleep.

Chapter 4

"Oh, this is not good," Trisha moaned as she set her briefcase down beside her desk and inspected the note placed directly in the middle of her calendar. "I have to meet with Mr. Sadler at eight. He's not usually even in at eight."

She sat down with a thump and gazed out the window, once again admiring the view she had of the Los Angeles skyline. She'd worked hard from the complete bottom rung up to get to this office and worried it was all about to slip right though her fingers.

"Hi, Ms. Jenkins. Here's your coffee."

Trisha looked up at their intern, Marti, and took the insulated cup she offered. "Thanks Marti. But you don't have to bring me coffee. It's not part of your job, you know."

"I know. But you're always so nice to me. You make me feel like your equal. This coffee is my way of saying thanks."

"Well, it's no problem. If you're having issues with someone, let me know and I'll—"

"No, everything's fine," Marti interrupted. "How was your convention?"

Charley instantly popped into Trisha's mind. She couldn't help herself as a huge grin spread across her face. "It was good, Marti. I had a real nice time."

"I'd guess so. That's some smile. Well, I'd better get to work. Have a great day. I'll have those proofs you need on your desk as soon as they're delivered."

"Thanks Marti, and thanks again for the coffee."

As Marti walked out, Trisha noticed the clock on her computer screen. Realizing it was time to head to Mr. Sandler's office, she felt her stomach knot up.

As she made her way down the hall and around cubicles to Mr. Sadler's posh corner office, she called her hellos to others in her department. But as she got closer and closer, her mind was on her boss.

He'd always been a very pleasant man and great to work with. He'd been the one who'd noticed her potential way back when she'd been working as a part-time receptionist. And he'd also been the one who'd helped her all the way up to her office with a view.

"Hi, Trisha. Go on in," Mrs. Whit, Mr. Sadler's longtime secretary, offered when she noticed Trisha.

"Thanks," Trisha said, walking through the open doorway.

"Hi, Trisha. Please shut the door and have a seat."

Trisha closed the door, thinking it was another bad sign, then walked over to the overstuffed, straight leg, black chairs by his desk, sat down, and watched as he studied notes in front of him. She stared at the top of his bald head and knew all of her fears were right just by the way he acted.

"I've got some bad news, Trisha," Mr. Sadler started as he glanced at her. "The company's experiencing some financial troubles. We're going to have to cut corners. And it's been decided that we no longer need both a director and an assistant director in the Creative Development & Communications Department. The position is being merged into President of Creative Development & Communications, and that job has been given to me."

Trisha felt her face paling as she gripped on to the armchair.

"However, we don't want to lose you here at The Milligan Group. You are very talented, Trisha. I know how lucky we are to have you here. And I've been fighting for you. I was able to secure a position for you if you want it. But it does come with some major cuts."

"What kind of job and what kind of cuts?" Trisha asked, feeling her mouth going dry.

"We would like to offer you the position of entry-level communications assistant. It would be part time at first. And your salary would fall to $30,000 a year, and you would move to a cubicle on the fourth floor. But if you could hold on through this tough patch, you might be able to—"

"What? Work my way up?" Trisha interrupted, her cheeks turning red as her eyes burned. "That's what I did, Eric. We both know it. I finally made my way up, and you're ripping it away from me. Why send me to that conference if you knew this was happening? I had to pay for that damned thing on my own credit card. And unlike so many of you around here, I can't afford to do that."

"I'm sure you'll be reimbursed, Trisha. I'm so sorry. I tried for something better. I tried for something full time. But this is affecting several people, Trish, not just you. This is the best I could get. I'm sorry. I'm so sorry."

"Yeah, well, so am I. How long do I have to get out of my office?"

"End of the day."

"What, no escort off the premises?"

"I told them that wasn't necessary."

"I'm leaving this morning," Trisha informed him as she stood. "And thanks, but I think I'm going to have to refuse your job offer."

Eric jumped up and ran around the desk, blocking Trisha before she could leave. "I'm really sorry about this. Please, don't leave angry with me."

Trisha's anger subsided a little, and she felt a lump forming in her throat.

"You're like a daughter to me, Trish. I'm so proud of the work you've done here. I hate that this is affecting you. But it was between you or me. And I did the selfish thing—I chose me."

"You have a family to take care of. I'm a single. I knew if it ever came to this I would be the first on the list. It's what happens to single, unattached people. We're expendable."

"Not true, Trish. At least not in my department."

"You've always treated me as an equal, Eric. And I'm thankful for that. And I'm sorry I snapped at you. It's just that I worked really hard for this. I worked hard for the title and for the office. I feel like I've put my entire life on hold for this company, and to be let go, just like that, well, I think I put my trust in the wrong place."

Eric grabbed a sealed envelope off his desk. "I'm so sorry. You will be receiving a severance package. It's all out-lined in this letter. I hope it helps a little." Then he pulled out his wallet and handed her four fifty dollar bills.

"What's this?"

"I want to make sure you at least get some of your conference money back."

"You don't have to do that."

"It's the least I can do. And you don't have to leave until the end of the day, Trisha. Stay and say your goodbyes."

"I can't. I have to get out of here. I'm going to clean out my office and leave. I'm sorry, but I can't stay somewhere I'm not wanted."

Eric stepped out of her way as she hurried out of his office, ignoring Mrs. Whit as she called to her.

Trisha's eyes welled up as she grabbed a box out of her closet and started tossing her items into it.

Once she was sure she had everything, Trisha called a cab, then walked over to the window and took in her view one last time.

"Well, it was fun while it lasted."

Charley opened his eyes and noticed the bright sun shining in his window. Feeling as if he'd overslept, he picked up his watch.

"It's after ten? Shit!" He jumped up and opened his door. Realizing the house was still quiet, he eyed Pam's shut door. Then remembered she didn't have to be at the school until noon.

He continued across the hallway, and all through his shower and while dressing, Trisha was on the forefront of his thoughts. Their conversation had been replaying over and over in his mind. He still could hardly believe a woman as beautiful as Trisha had feelings for him.

Charley opened the door and quietly made his way to the kitchen, not wanting to wake Pam.

Worried about how tired his daughter had been lately, he decided to surprise her by fixing her favorite breakfast, French toast.

While beating the eggs and adding the vanilla and cinnamon, he thought back to the first time he'd made French toast. Pam had been six and had wanted her father to fix her breakfast. She'd been adamant about it, and Charley, being wrapped around her little finger, had wanted to give it a try.

Nancy had set the ingredients out and had slowly talked him through the process. And Pam had watched from the kitchen table, beaming the entire time.

"Are you making French toast?" Pam asked, interrupting his memories.

"I am. Doesn't it smell great?"

"It…uh…oh no."

Charley watched as Pam put her hand over her mouth and ran out of the room.

"Pam?" Charley called as he shut off the stove and followed her.

Noticing the closed bathroom door, he leaned it against and asked, "Are you okay?"

Sickness sounds were all that answered him, and his mind started swirling as he started wondering what was wrong with his daughter.

"Pam? Do you have the flu? What can I do to help?"

A few minutes later, the door slowly opened.

Charley stepped into the bathroom where Pam sat on the edge of the tub. Noticing she was as pale as a ghost, Charley said, "Baby, are you okay? Do you want me to call Dr. Mathes?"

"No. You don't need to."

"Well, you're obviously sick. And you've been so tired lately. I'd feel better if you went to the doctor."

"I've already been to the doctor, Daddy." Pam lowered her eyes to the old linoleum floor.

"Okay. Good. What'd he say?"

"Oh, Daddy. I didn't want to tell you this way." Pam peeked at him with tears streaming down her cheeks.

Charley's heart fell to his toes as panic set in. "Tell me what, Pam? Are you sick? Is there something wrong? Tell me."

Pam eyes were full of shame as he looked at him again. "I'm pregnant."

"Pregnant?" Charley leaned against the edge of the sink.

"Yes, I'm two months pregnant."

"Oh my gosh. I don't know…how did this…who's the father?" Charley rambled, as different emotions rushed through him.

"Tyler Bailey."

Charley's cheeks turned red. "I thought you quit seeing him."

"I did. We did. But we love each other, Daddy." Pam stood up and hurried over to him. "We ran into each other during Christmas break, and all of those feelings were still there. We couldn't shut them off. We've been secretly dating ever since. And we work together too, Daddy. He teaches high school math and is the assistant football coach."

"He's just like his father," Charley snarled as he hurried out of the room and down the hallway.

Pam ran after him. "Daddy, wait!"

She finally caught up to him outside the back door, grabbed his arm and turned him to face her. "Wait."

"I can't believe this. I was so proud of you in June for graduating from UNI with your teaching degree. You were following in your mom's footsteps."

"You and Mom got married before she started college. And I was born a year after she graduated. And, like mom, I landed my dream job teaching at Hope Community. Tyler and I obviously didn't plan this, but I'm happy, Daddy."

"This will change your life forever, Pam."

"I know. But I love him. We're getting married. This Saturday. I wanted to do it at the church like you and mom did, but it's booked, so we're getting married at that cute little chapel I showed you when you visited me at college. We've already hired a minister and photographer. And we have a cake. It's going to be a small wedding. I want you there."

"Sounds like you have everything taken care of already. What could you possibly need me for?" Charley questioned through gritted teeth.

"I want you to give me away," Pam said softly, still holding on to his arm. "And I want you to be happy for us."

"I need time to think," Charley muttered as her pulled away from her and stomped down the path toward the old machine shed.

Trisha struggled to carry her box, purse and briefcase down the sidewalk and up the ramp into her older apartment building.

"Keys, I need keys," she said as she set everything down but her purse and started fishing around for them.

She finally found the keys at the bottom, opened the entry door, and struggled to rebalance everything as she continued down the hallway, past the doors of her two neighbors, before she came to her own door.

She unlocked it, carried everything in and dropped it on the floor, then pushed the box out of the way with her shoe as she reset the deadbolt. She continued in through the small living room to the one bedroom, where she kicked off her black, high heeled shoes and changed into shorts and a T-shirt.

"I've got a lot of work to do," she mumbled as she left her discarded clothes on the bed and walked back into the living room.

Fumbling around in her purse again, she finally found her cell phone.

She carried it over to the couch and sat down, then scrolled through the numbers until she found Brad's picture and hit send.

"Hey, darling."

"You were right about my job. Can you come over?"

"Sure. I'll be there as soon as I can."

Figuring Brad hadn't eaten breakfast, and knowing she was starving, Trisha walked to the kitchen and opened a bottle of red wine, the only alcohol she occasionally allowed herself to drink. She carried the bottle and two glasses to the living room and set them on the coffee table, then she swung over and unlocked the door before hurrying back to the kitchen.

After grabbing the last of the shrimp out of the refrigerator, she started opening and shutting cupboard doors while gathering all the ingredients and pans she needed to make Brad's favorite meal.

Time flew as Trisha started mixing fresh, diced tomatoes and paste with basil, garlic powder, oregano and sugar in the large saucepan. As they started to simmer, she cooked the wheat spaghetti noodles, enjoying the smells as her mind got lost in the memories of eating that very meal with Brad on all of their special occasions.

"Something smells amazing," Brad called as he walked into the living room.

"It should. It's your favorite."

Brad walked over and poured them both a glass of red wine, then he carried the glasses into the kitchen and greeted her with a kiss on the cheek.

"Wine and shrimp at 10 in the morning? Huh?"

"I had some shrimp I needed to cook." Trisha took the glass he offered and set it on the counter. "Besides, I'm starving, and I figured you haven't had breakfast."

"You know me well. How long until that's done?"

"I'm ready to add the shrimp."

Brad handed her the bowl with the shrimp, and then he drained the noodles while Trisha started shredding the fresh Parmesan cheese.

Before long, everything was mixed together and on their plates and they were walking into the living room.

"This wine is wonderful." Brad took another sip as they sat down at the two-seat table in the corner of the living room.

"It's my last bottle of the case you brought back for me from Italy."

"Thanks for sharing it with me." Brad raised his glass. "To my beautiful ex-wife who's also my best friend."

Trisha raised her glass to him, then sipped on the wine, still fighting the emotions she felt every time she tried to drink anything with alcohol in it.

Memories of her father's breath laced with a heavy whiskey scent when he'd kiss her on the cheek or pat her on the back assaulted her, and she almost dropped her wine glass.

"Are the memories coming back again, Trish? We don't have to drink this. I got it for you because I knew you occasionally liked…"

"It's fine. You like it." Her mind jumped back to the present, and she set her glass down on the table. "You were right, Brad. I lost my job. Effective immediately."

"I'm so sorry. Didn't they offer you anything else?"

"Oh, yeah. Part-time, entry level work worth $30,000 a year."

"Damn, you can't live on that."

"That's why I turned it down." Trisha munched on her lunch. "And I have to get out of here immediately. Even with the severance package, I can't afford this month's rent, let alone the price hike. I gotta pack my stuff and find a new place to live."

"I could hire someone to help you pack. And I know somewhere you could live."

"I don't know. I'll think about it. I wanted to run something else by you."

"Okay, what?" Brad said between bites.

"While at the conference, I talked to Katherine Roe, who's the head of the communications department for an insurance company. I told her about my concerns and shared that I was worried I might lose my job, and she offered me a job with her company. I'm thinking about taking her up on her offer."

"That's great, Trish. Where's this company located? Malibu? Santa Barbara?"

"Iowa."

"Damn, Trish. You should have eased me into that instead of dropping it like a bomb. You're considering moving back to Iowa?"

Trisha shrugged. "Maybe. It's a job I can get."

"And this man's in Iowa."

Trisha nodded as she thought about Charley. "I took your advice and called him last night. We had a nice chat."

"Well, then maybe that's the right move for you to make now, Trisha."

As Trisha finished her meal, she said, "I hate moving so far away from you."

"But you'd be close to –

"I know," Trisha interrupted.

"I'm sorry that my actions back then caused our –

"We've moved past that."

"I know we have. I love you, Trisha. You know my job keeps me traveling all over the place. I'll be in Chicago and Minneapolis this fall.

That's not too far away from Iowa. We'll meet up. If you want to move back, then I'm all for it."

Charley wiped sweat off his forehead with his hand and scanned the hay field he'd finished mowing.

He killed the engine of the old, green tractor, and his ears continued to buzz from the loud sound.

"Wish this old thing had a cab," he complained as he stood up and stretched, then climbed down the three steps, the heat from the hot motor making him sweat even more.

He circled around the tractor, making sure everything was okay, then walked over to a patch of mowed hay. He squatted down and touched it, noticing it still felt damp, and then he stood back up and stretched again.

He turned to the south and noticed his friend, Darrell, whose farm abutted his, was out by his machine shed.

He took off in that direction on foot, arriving five minutes later.

"Did you get it all mowed?" Darrell asked, noticing him.

"Yep. I can't believe it's still damp."

"Well, I'm almost ready to go and rake it for ya. I got the gate open on my hayfield. Wanna drink before heading over?"

"Sounds great. It's sure hot today."

The two men started toward Darrell's two-story farmhouse.

"I need to stop in the first old chicken coop. I think I have a couple of old teeth there that I can use to replace the two missing from the rake."

Charley followed him into the old building and waited for his eyes to adjust to the darkness. His nose picked up the scent of mice, and he wondered what else lived in the old shed.

"I think they're over here," Darrell continued as he walked past the piles of sheet metal and stacked boards. "This place was organized once."

"Still looks like it to me. You've seen my old shed," Charley said as he started helping Darrell in his search.

"There they are," Darrell called, finally finding the piles of old teeth in the back corner. "Didn't realize I had so many. These came off that old rake I junked a few years back. Glad I kept them."

Charley helped Darrell carry them back to the rake, and then they started back down the worn path, past the barn, cattle lot, chicken sheds and back end of Darrell's cornfield.

"Crop's lookin' good," Darrell observed as they both studied the plants while they were walking. "Even with that wet spring, it looks like we'll have a good year."

"Yeah, but not good enough."

"What's goin' on, Charley?" Darrell inquired as they walked up the two steps onto the wraparound porch. "You seem miles away this afternoon."

"Not sure where to start." Charley followed Darrell into his spotless kitchen and sat down at the wooden kitchen table.

Darrell fetched two cans of pop out of the white refrigerator and a couple of chocolate bars, and sat down across from Charley. He took a bite of his candy and said, "The air feels pretty good in here; we've got time for a break."

Charley cracked open his can and took a long swig. "Pam's getting married."

"Married? I didn't even know she was dating anyone."

"Well, that makes two of us."

A puzzled look came over Darrell's face. "You didn't know either?"

Charley shook his head.

"I don't understand."

"She's marrying that damned Bailey kid," Charley muttered as he ripped the wrapper off his bar, anger coursing through his veins. "She's pregnant too. That damned family."

Darrell shook his head. "Oh, man. I'm sorry. He really is his father's son."

"I know. Old man Bailey got Betty Sue pregnant at 15. Guess I should be thankful Pam is 22."

"So, you're gonna be a grandpa, huh?"

"Looks like it. Me and ol' George Bailey are going to be connected forever. Ain't that swell."

"Man, I'm so sorry."

"That's only part of it. I also got a letter from the bank. I gotta fill out all that damned financial paperwork again. And we both know that ain't gonna turn out good. I know George ain't gonna do me any favors. Especially now."

"You've been dreading that since spring.".

"Yep. And now that I lost all my custom work, I don't have enough income to justify my bank loan. They're gonna try to take my land away from me, Darrell. I know that's what George Bailey has been trying to do all these years. And this year—well hell, he might get his wish."

"Do you have what you need to make your loan payment?"

"I should, as long as I sell all the crops right out of the field. And as long as the bank grants me an extension. It might mess up my taxes, but I gotta do it."

"Do you think George will let them grant you that extension if he knows he's close to getting your land?"

Charley shrugged, "Hell if I know."

Trisha sat on the couch, staring at her wine glass, which was still full.

Brad had left more than twenty minutes earlier for a job he had to get to, and she'd been sitting alone in her quiet living room thinking over her options.

On one hand, she wanted to let Brad take care of her. Although she knew they would never be romantically involved again, he really was her best friend. And she loved the security that came from letting him care for her both financially and emotionally.

But she also knew she'd prided herself on becoming more and more independent since their divorce four years earlier.

She'd gone from living in his large, spacious home with a maid to living in a cramped, one bedroom apartment. She'd also gone from having him pay all of her bills to making enough money to both pay her bills and put some away in savings.

"Then my rent went up," she said to herself, thinking about her credit card debt. She wistfully thought about the modest nest egg she'd been saving that had been drained to buy her another year in her apartment.

She peered at Kat's business card and wondered if she was really ready to go back to Iowa. And back home.

She knew she wasn't ready to see her parents. And she wasn't even sure she was ready to see her brother and sister.

She wondered if they had gotten married or had kids.

Just the thought of having nieces and nephews who didn't even know their Aunt Trisha made her heart ache for her own greatest loss.

She scanned the ultrasound photo placed lovingly in the heart frame on the end table and picked it up, her eyes welling as she rubbed her finger along the glass, then hugged the frame to her body.

"My little Sophie."

Her mind flashed back in time to the day they lost their little girl, and tears rolled down her cheeks.

A noise outside her door made her jump. She watched as an envelope was pushed underneath her closed door.

Sniffling as she stood up, she carefully set the picture frame on the coffee table, then walked over and picked up the envelope.

When she noticed her landlord's return address typed on the outside, she ripped it open, pretty sure what it was.

She skimmed through the second notice of her rising rent, then glanced over at her box full of items from her office. She closed her eyes, realizing what she needed to do next.

After dropping the letter down on the box, she walked back over to the couch and placed the picture frame back on the end table. Then she picked up her cell phone and Kat's business card and dialed the number.

"Hello. This is Kat."

"Kat, how are you? This is Trisha Jenkins."

"Hey, Trisha. How are you…oh, no…did you lose your job?"

"Yes. And I'm calling to see if you're still interested in having me on your team?"

"You mean you're ready to move back home?"

Trisha looked back at the box. "Yes, I'm ready to come home. And I'd love the chance to work for Just For You Insurance."

"Oh, this is great. Let me make a few calls and I'll get back to you shortly. Do you have a resume you could email me?"

"Sure, I'll do that right now."

"Great. Bye."

Trisha pulled out her lap top and emailed her resume and portfolio to the address on Kat's business card. Then she paced around the room, her thoughts bouncing from Charley to her family.

She jumped when her cell phone rang after only a few minutes.

"Great news, Trisha. I've been given the okay to hire you on a probationary basis. How soon will you be moving?"

"I'm going to start packing today," Trisha said, realizing she was actually excited about her upcoming change. "I'll probably put my things into storage here and get them later. But I'll have to find somewhere to live. That might take a little longer."

"How about with me?"

"With you?"

"Sure. I'd love the company. And you could take your time finding somewhere to live. You don't have to answer me now, but—"

"I think that sounds perfect," Trisha interrupted, liking how things were falling into place.

"Great. You see how the packing goes and let me know over the weekend when you think you'll be heading this way."

"Perfect. Thanks Kat."

Pam's car was already back by the house when Charley rolled in the driveway. He parked the tractor and mower by the back shed and felt his heart rate quicken when he noticed Pam was standing outside the shed with none other than Tyler Bailey, who was petting Shooter.

"Traitor," Charley grumbled, noticing how happy his dog was sitting at Tyler's loafer-covered feet.

"Hi Daddy," Pam said as Charley walked past them.

Fuming, Charley didn't respond and walked faster in the direction of the house.

"Mr. Walker, could we please talk with you about all of this? Pam's really upset about how you found out. We wanted to tell you together," Tyler called as he and Pam tried to catch up to Charley.

"Daddy, please stop!" Pam cried as Charley reached the back door of the house.

Hearing the pleading in her voice, Charley stopped, then turned to face them.

Pam almost knocked her father over as she hugged him. "Thank you for stopping. I'm sorry I dropped all of that on you this morning. I didn't want to keep it from you any longer. I'm sorry, you know. I'm sorry all this has been going on behind your back. But we both know you're keeping something from me too. That's something else I think it's time we talked about."

Charley glared at Tyler and his anger returned as he noticed how much he resembled his father, George Bailey.

"Daddy, please."

"I'll tell you what's going on with me, but not in front of him."

"But I'm going to marry Tyler. He's going to be my husband, and he is the father of my baby. And whether you like it or not, he's going to be your son-in-law."

Charley glared at Tyler and thought about the dreams he'd had for his son-in-law. Realizing Tyler Bailey was going to fill that role crushed all of those dreams. He took a deep breath and said, "You're an adult, Pam. I can't tell you whom you can or can't marry. And now I know I was wrong before for asking you to break things off with Tyler. I'll respect your choices. But you need to give me a little time to get used to all of this. I don't think that's asking too much."

"But we don't have a lot of time. We wanted to be married before I start showing. And before school starts. And I want you to be a part of the wedding. You're my father, and you're a very important part of my life. I don't want that to change."

"And I don't want that to change either. But you've got to give me time to process all of this. Remember, before this morning, I didn't even know you were dating anyone. Now you are engaged, pregnant and getting married this weekend. That's a lot for me to take in."

Pam let out a slow, long breath.

"I think we should give him that time, Pam," Tyler said. "I think I should give you both a little time to yourselves."

"You don't have to leave." Pam looked at Tyler, then back at her father.

"Thank you, Tyler. I think that would be a good idea," Charley agreed.

"Why don't I take your car back to town, honey? I'll pick you up in the morning for work."

Pam glanced back at her father, then back at Tyler and nodded.

Charley turned away as Tyler hugged and kissed his daughter, then he moved out of the way as Tyler started walking down the driveway towards her car.

Neither one of them spoke a word as Tyler started up her old car and pulled onto the gravel road.

"Let's go inside," Charley finally said, opening the door as the car disappeared in a cloud of dust.

Pam walked through the doorway, stopping in the kitchen to fill her favorite *Wizard of Oz* coffee mug with water.

Charley watched the familiar action and sadness weighed him down as he realized once again she'd be moving out of his house. Except this time, unlike the time she moved to college, she wouldn't ever be moving back.

"What?" Pam asked, noticing the look on his face.

"I can't believe you're leaving me. I mean, I knew someday you'd get married and move out. But you just got back from college. And we were getting into a comfortable routine. And now, well, now it's all over. Again."

"I'm not moving far."

"Where will you live after you get married?" Charley asked, trying not to focus on how weird that sentence sounded to him.

"The Bailey mansion. At least at first."

"No, Pam. Please, tell me you aren't moving into that place. Please, anywhere else but there. Live here. We could all live here."

"Daddy, there's not enough room here. Tyler says there's more than enough room for all of us in the mansion. Besides, they have maids and a cook. Isn't that exciting?"

"No." Charley shook his head. "Nowhere near George Bailey is exciting."

"Why don't you like Mr. Bailey? You always find a way to get along with everyone else."

"I will never be able to get along with that man."

"Well, I'd like you to try. I want my baby growing up surrounded by family."

Charley felt his heart breaking as he gazed at his baby girl.

"I'm sorry, Daddy. I know this is the last thing you expected from me. But I want you to know I'm happy. Both with Tyler and with the idea of having his baby. I tried not to love him, but I couldn't. It's like what you had with Mom. We love each other."

Charley studied their family portrait on the wall, which was taken a month before Nancy was killed. They all looked so happy. Nancy, who after several miscarriages had finally been able to get pregnant again, was carrying their baby boy. And she simply glowed in the picture.

Charley wondered how Nancy would handle the situation. He knew she wouldn't want Pam to marry George Bailey's son any more than he did.

"Daddy?"

"Just thinking about Mom."

"Yeah, I think about Mom a lot too." Pam glanced up at the photo. "Especially now. There are so many questions I have about being pregnant. And I don't have anyone to ask. None of my friends are mothers yet. I've been looking most things up online."

"I'm sorry your mother's not here."

"Me too. But I'm so glad I have my daddy."

Charley hugged his daughter tightly. He vowed to try harder to be happy about her news for her sake and for the sake of his unborn grandchild.

"Where's our son?" Forty-nine year old George Bailey asked his wife as he breezed into the living room where she was reading the *Hope Gazette*.

"I have no idea. He's disappeared. Again. I asked Helen, but she didn't know. I swear, George, what do we pay that woman for? She's supposed to know things like that."

"Dear, she's the head cook. It's not her job to keep track of our children."

"Well, fine," Betty Sue huffed as she pulled the paper up between them.

George walked over and plopped down on the leather couch beside his wife, pushing the paper away. "I love it when you're mad at me, Sue."

"That must be why you tick me off all the time."

George laughed and leaned over, kissing his angry wife on the cheek.

Betty Sue pushed him away but smiled a little.

"So, you really have no idea where he is?"

Betty Sue gave up reading her paper and folded it. "No. He's been very secretive lately."

"Hey."

George and Betty Sue looked up as their son, Tyler, walked into the room.

"Son, we were just talking about you," George informed him. "We were hoping you would've joined us for supper."

"Oh, sorry." Tyler ran his fingers through his blond hair as he scanned his parents.

Betty Sue took note of his agitated state. "Is something wrong?"

"Wrong? No. But there's something I need to tell you. Both of you. And I'm not sure how to do it."

"Tell us, son," George prodded, although his heart was almost beating out of his chest with concern. Tyler was a very grounded child. He'd never caused them any trouble, and because of that, he had been treated like an adult long before he was one.

"Okay. Here it goes. I'm engaged. And I'm going to be a dad."

"What?" Betty Sue asked, shocked, as her mind was instantly back in time when she was 15 and found out she was pregnant with George's baby.

"I'm sorry. This isn't what we wanted to happen. But I love her. And she loves me. And we're very excited we're having a baby."

"Is this someone you just met?" George pried, his mind racing with the possibility of who his soon-to-be daughter-in-law might be.

"No," Tyler shook his head. "We've been dating for several months."

"And you never told us about her? Never invited her to the house? Why, Tyler? What's wrong with this girl?"

"Nothing's wrong with her. It's…well…it's Pam Walker."

"Not Charley Walker's daughter," George said, the terrible pieces falling into place.

"Yes. Pam is Charley's daughter. That's why we've been keeping our relationship a secret. We knew neither you nor Pam's father wanted us dating, but we love each other."

"I thought you quit seeing that girl," Betty Sue said.

"I did. But we're meant to be, Mom. We ran into each other during her Christmas break. Neither one of us wanted to hurt you two or Mr. Walker, so we kept things quiet. But we're in love and pregnant and we're getting married. Saturday."

"What Saturday? Not this Saturday."

"Yes, Mom, this Saturday. I want you both to be there."

"Son, you're acting irrationally." George stood up and started pacing around the couch. "Just because you got this girl pregnant doesn't mean you have to marry her. Hell, you might not even be the father."

"What's that supposed to mean?" Tyler demanded, rushing to his father and grabbing his arm.

"I mean, she's a Walker. Are you sure she's even telling you the truth? Maybe she's trying to get her hands on our money!"

"She's not like that." Tyler's cheeks turned red. "You'd better be careful. You're talking about the woman I love."

"George, Tyler, stop this." Betty Sue ordered as she ran in between them, thinking about their past arguments that had turned into fist fights. "Let's all calm down. I'll get Helen to fetch us some tea."

"I don't want tea, Mother." Tyler rumbled, stepping back from his father. "I wanted you both to know. I'm not asking for your permission.

And I'm not asking for any money or favors, either. I want you at my wedding because you're my parents. But I'm not going to beg. I'll be getting married Saturday to the woman I love, the woman who's pregnant with my baby, whether you're there or not."

Betty Sue grabbed George and held him tightly as Tyler stormed out of the room.

"What are we going to do?" George pulled away from Betty's grip. "We know this is wrong."

"Calm down. Fighting with our son, making him defend that girl, isn't going to help matters. You know that, George."

George eyed the doorway and looked back at Betty Sue, then started pacing around the couch again.

Betty Sue walked over and shut the French doors that led out of the posh room, and then she walked back to the couch and sat down.

"Sue. We can't let this happen."

"Sounds to me that it's already happened. We have to be smart about how we react, or we'll be the bad guys in all of this."

"What do you mean?" George asked as he walked over to her.

"Look at the facts, George. There's a baby on the way. Our grandchild and…"

"It might not be his."

"I imagine it is. We don't want Charley Walker getting the upper hand in this situation. We need to be supportive and kind. We need to welcome that hussy into our family."

"Why?"

"Because I don't want to lose our son or our grandchild. And that's exactly what will happen if we push this issue. We need to act like we're happy about this. We need to be at the wedding, and we need to support them with all of this. It's what we have to do."

"Sue, you've lost your mind." George hurried over to the bar and poured himself some whiskey. He slammed it back, then poured another and started pacing again.

"I have not. That man's been a thorn in our side for years. I refuse to let him win this time. If we turn our back on our child and grandchild,

Charley will win. Our son will side against us with that…that…*man.* I don't want that to happen. I want the upper hand. We need to tell Tyler that he and Pam can live here. With us. And with the baby."

"No Walker offspring is going to set foot in my house!" George bellowed, temporarily startling Betty Sue.

She took a deep breath, then calmly replied, "Yes, she is. And the sooner, the better."

ග

"Looks like you started packing," Brad said as he walked into Trisha's apartment a little after midnight and noticed the piles of clothes scattered around the room.

"I have." Trisha peered into the living room from the bedroom. "Did you get the boxes?"

"Yeah, they're in my car." Brad glanced at her. "Oh wow, you must be serious. You're ponytailed up."

Trisha grinned. "Things are going great. I'm almost all done in the closet."

"So, what do these piles mean?"

"Well, that pile is to donate, that pile is trash, and that pile is to be stored," Trisha pointed as she talked. "The pile to pack is on the bedroom floor."

"Help me with the boxes, and I'll give you a hand."

"Oh, you don't need to do that. I'm sure you're tired." Trisha grabbed her apartment key and stuck it in the hip pocket of her shorts.

"Nope, not tired at all. I'm yours until I have to fly out."

"Great, I can put you to work," Trisha teased as he opened the outside apartment door and propped it open with a brick from inside.

"You should have seen the look they gave me at the grocery store when I stopped and asked if they had boxes. I'm sure they thought I'd been given the old heave-ho from my wife."

"If they only knew," Trisha said as they made one trip with boxes and then went back for more.

After a few more trips, Brad locked his car while Trisha moved the brick and let him in.

"You might want to give me your keys while I'm thinking of it." Trisha unlocked her apartment door again and they walked inside. "I think it costs like fifty dollars if I don't return both sets."

"I hate to give them up," Brad teased as he took the keys off his key ring and handed them to her. "Does this mean you're moving to Iowa?"

"Yes. I called Kat, and they have a job for me. She even said I could live with her until I find a place."

"That's great, Trish. It's gonna be weird around here without you, though."

"I'm gonna miss you too. But you said earlier you'd be by to visit me. And I don't know why, Brad, but it feels right."

"Have you told Charley you're moving to Iowa?"

Trisha shook her head. "I didn't call him tonight. I was hoping he'd call me, but he must be busy."

"I'm sure he is. What does he do?" Brad asked as he started following her lead by folding the first pile of clothes.

Glancing at him, Trisha said, "He's a farmer."

"Never known a farmer."

"Well, there're lots of them in Iowa." Trisha started carefully packing the clothes he had folded. "I'm sure it keeps him busy, too. Plus he's just starting off his career as an auctioneer."

"Sounds like a very motivated man." Brad handed her another blouse. "You're giving away some nice clothes."

"I have too much stuff." Trisha got up and started searching for tape. "Someone else might as well get some use out of the things I hardly wear anymore."

Trisha noticed Brad was yawning. "You look tired, Brad. Why don't you spend the night instead of driving all the way back to your house?"

"Sounds good to me. I can sleep on the couch."

"That's crazy. I'm going to keep working until I have all these piles packed up. You take the bed. I'll take the couch."

"That's not very gentlemanly." Brad shook his head then yawned again.

"Go." Trisha gently pushed him in the direction of her bedroom. "There's nothing piled on the bed. Get a good night's sleep."

Brad turned and gathered her in a bear hug, then he kissed her on the forehead before disappearing into her bedroom.

Trisha continued folding, packing and taping until she had more than fifteen boxes neatly stacked along the wall by the front door, all carefully marked as to where they were going. She also had three trash bags full of clothes that shouldn't or couldn't be donated.

Giving into her own yawn, Trisha walked to the bathroom, brushed her teeth and changed into her nightgown, and then she walked to the couch and curled up with her Iowa blanket and pillow, quickly falling asleep.

Charley sat at the kitchen table, rolling his coffee cup around in his hand while staring at the letter from the bank.

He scanned the time on the microwave and shook his head, noticing it was well after 4:00 a.m.

"I need to go to sleep, but how the hell am I supposed to sleep? My daughter's pregnant and getting married to the son of the man who is responsible for me getting that damned bank letter. How can this possibly be okay? How can any good ever come from any of this?"

Charley glanced through the questions on the form and decided that since he couldn't sleep, he might as well get to work.

He got up and walked to the small office desk in the living room corner, then opened the bottom drawer and sorted through the manila files until he found the one marked "Bank Land Information." Then he pulled it out and carried it back to the table.

After refilling his coffee cup, he sat down and started figuring.

By five thirty, he'd filled out all the information that never changed – like the number of acres. He'd also found all his receipts from his crop expenses from the spring and hand-entered them, along with the information from his last year's tax return.

He skimmed the section regarding his current projected income and knew that was the section that was going to get him.

He rubbed his stinging eyes and decided he was finally ready to try to sleep.

After dumping his cold coffee in the kitchen sink, he checked the living room and back doors, then shut off the lights before walking in the darkness to his bedroom.

Leaving his door open a crack, he stripped down to his underwear and climbed in the bed, his mind instantly on Trisha Jenkins.

"I wonder why she didn't call me tonight?"

His insecurities teased that she might have decided he wasn't right for her after all, which made him feel worse than he thought was even possible.

Then he drifted into a fitful sleep.

Chapter 5

"You have until Friday," Brad said as he walked into Trisha's apartment the next morning. "He said he's sad to see you leave."

"You spoke to my landlord without talking to me first?" Trisha asked, as she pulled her robe tighter.

"You weren't up yet, so I thought I'd handle it." Brad breezed past her and walked into the kitchen, pouring himself a cup of coffee.

Trisha stood in the middle of the living room, watching as he carried his cup and sat down on the couch.

Noticing the look on her face, he asked, "What?"

"It wasn't your responsibility to talk to him. It was mine. Why do you keep doing things like that?"

Brad shrugged. "It was something that needed done, so I took care of it. I also rented a storage unit for you."

Trisha threw her arms up in frustration. "This is one of the reasons our marriage ended, Brad."

"Don't you need a storage unit?"

"Yes, but I can find one. I can handle it."

"You needed your sleep. It's handled. Now, what needs done next? Are those boxes going into storage?"

Deciding to let it go, as she had done so many times before, Trisha nodded.

"You don't have to leave for Iowa on Friday, Trish. You could stay at my house for a few days," Brad suggested, as he wrote STORAGE on the box.

Trisha shook her head. "Scarlette comes home Saturday. You two need some alone time. Besides, if I leave on Friday, I could get things rolling at work on Monday. Kat sent me an email and said I'd need to fill out some paperwork, take a drug test and meet with some people before I officially start. And I want to get started as soon as possible. That severance package money is going to come in handy, but I've got a lot of bills and I don't want to get behind."

"Why don't you let me pay your bills for a few months, Trisha? Consider it a going away present."

"Brad, I—"

"Please, Trish. I insist," Brad interrupted as he hurried to her side. "I'm really going to miss you. I think it's starting to sink in that you're really, truly, leaving me."

"Brad, we've been divorced for years."

"We both know we'll always love each other. Just not in that way. You're so important to me. Please, let me pay your bills for the month of August and your storage bill for one year. And I also insist on paying for your plane ticket. Okay?"

Trisha noticed the determination in his green eyes and knew it was useless to try to fight him. "Yeah, okay."

"Great. What are you going to do about a car?"

"What do you mean?"

"When you get back to Iowa. You're gonna need a car to drive, aren't you?"

"Oh, shoot. I hadn't thought about that. I don't have enough money to get a car. Not even a junker."

"Let me get you a car, too."

"No." Trisha crossed her arms in front of her. "Absolutely not. You're already doing too much."

"Come on, Trish. Don't get like that. We both know I'm able to do that without it being a hardship on me. I'd feel better if you had something safe to drive around in. Please. I'd be worried to death if you bought a junker."

"I'll be fine. Maybe I could car pool with Kat until I get enough money saved up for a car."

"We both know you aren't going to do that. You already feel bad enough you're crashing at her place. I know you, Trisha Marie. You're going to go and get some crappy car."

"Sometimes you know me too well," Trisha grumbled as she started angrily folding towels and shoving them into one of the boxes.

"Okay, fine. I won't buy you a car. I'll loan you the money to get a good car. How's that?"

Trisha turned and faced him, her head tilted slightly to the right.

"Good, you're thinking about it."

"How in the world do you know that?"

"I was married to you, woman. I know all your cute, little mannerisms. You tilt you're head to the right when you're thinking about something."

Figuring she wouldn't be able to stop him anyway, she shrugged. "Okay. Fine. Can I borrow enough money to get a safe, but inexpensive, car?"

"Yes."

"Thank you. Now, get back to work."

Brad started wrapping her knickknacks in newspaper. "So, have you told Charley yet?"

"No. I'm not sure what kind of schedule he has during the day. I'll call him tonight."

"I bet he'll be thrilled, Trisha."

"But I'm not moving because of him. I'm moving because of this job. And I want to make sure I do a good job for this company. Kat might've gotten me in the door, but I'll have to prove myself."

"I'm not worried, Trish. You'll do great."

ꙮ

Charley made his way through his hayfield with the old rusty baler on the back of Darrell's modern green tractor.

The air conditioning felt good, but Charley's mind wasn't on the field. It was going between Trisha and the wedding.

"I can't believe she hasn't called me," Charley moaned. "Maybe I should call her. I don't want to bother her, though. I should've asked her when was a good time to call her. I thought she'd call me when she had a chance. I hope she's not having second thoughts. I hope she hasn't decided a long distance relationship isn't worth it."

Just the thought of not talking to Trisha again made his heart hurt, and that made him think about his daughter and the fact that Thursday night would be the last night she'd stay under his roof as his little girl.

"Damn that Tyler Bailey. Damn that whole Bailey family!" Charley balled his right hand into a fist, wanting to hit something.

But he didn't want to break anything in Darrell's fancy tractor, so he released his fist and shook his head.

Before long, he had all the bales made on his hayfield.

He pulled out of the narrow field driveway and onto the quiet, gravel road, then traveled down the road a few feet and pulled into Darrell's field.

While making Darrell's hay into large, round bales, he started thinking about his financial papers. He knew he had most of the forms filled out already and also knew he'd left the hardest for last.

As he started down the next windrow of hay, his cell phone started ringing.

He pulled it out of his pocket, hoping to see Trisha's number.

His shoulders dropped when he noticed it was B.J.'s.

"Hey, Charley. Did I catch you at a good time?"

"Yeah, this is fine. I'm doin' a little baling."

"Well, I got some good news. You created a lot of good buzz at the conference, and I had someone inquire about you. They'd like to hire you to work for their auctioneering company."

"Really?" Hoping that would put an end to all of his financial problems, he asked, "Who?"

"Well, that could be the problem. It's for a big company out of Omaha."

"Omaha? That'd be a long commute."

"You'd have to move there."

"I'll have to think about it, B.J. I don't really want to give up my farm."

"I understand. I'll email you the details, and you can think about it for a few days. I told him you'd get back to him by Monday. Does that sound like enough time?"

"Yeah. I'll know by then," Charley agreed, thinking about the weekend wedding he was dreading. "Thanks, B.J."

"Sure thing. Have a great day."

Charley put his phone back in his pocket, more confused than ever. He knew he should take the job because he needed the money. But he didn't want to move. He never wanted to move away from his farm.

"But if I did move, Pam could stay at the farmhouse with the baby. Then she wouldn't have to move into that awful place. And the baby could grow up where my baby grew up."

Charley felt conflicted. His father had moved off the family farm when Charley and Nancy had gotten married, but his father had done that so Charley could continue farming the ground that had been in their family for over 100 years.

"Tyler Bailey isn't a farmer," Charley muttered, shaking his head, once again reminded that all the hopes and dreams he'd had for his son-in-law were dead.

"Thank God I don't have to decide this now," Charley declared, deciding it was time to focus on the field in front of him.

Trisha felt good giving back as the Community Shelter and Outreach volunteers from down the block carried out her boxes of donated clothes, kitchen items and books.

"Your donations will have a huge, positive impact in our community," the head volunteer said as she hugged Trisha. "Good luck with your move and new job."

"It was my pleasure."

"You've helped more than you'll ever know. I think we have everything."

Trisha walked around, reading the instructions on the boxes. "That looks like everything."

"Thanks for assisting us with the trailer, Mr. Jenkins," the woman said as Brad walked into the apartment, sweat dripping down his forehead. "I hope you and your wife enjoy your new home."

Brad smiled as he watched as the lady shut the door, then turned to

Trisha. "She seemed happy."

"Very. You didn't correct her and tell her we're divorced."

"It didn't seem important." Brad started setting up more boxes. Then he turned to her. "I'm sorry, Trisha."

"Sorry? For what?"

"This morning. I'm sorry I did it again. I should've let you handle things on your own."

"It's a stressful time for both of us. It's okay, Brad."

"Thank you. I guess we'd better keep going, Trisha. I want to help you as much as I can before I have to leave for the airport. The moving crew will be here before noon on Thursday."

"I have all day tomorrow. Besides, we're doing great."

"And I've been thinking."

"That's a shocker," Trisha teased as she joined him in preparing the boxes.

Brad grinned. "I want you to take me to the airport. Then you can keep my car and use it to run your errands tomorrow."

"Oh, I can't do that."

"Yes, you can. Besides, you'd be doing me a favor. I hate leaving my car in the parking lot. It always gets scratched."

Trisha thought it over for a little bit and knew it would save her quite a bit of money if she didn't have to pay for a cab to take her all the places she needed to go. "Okay, I'll do it."

"Great. Thanks."

"What time do you need to be at the airport?"

"Five."

"It's after three. And you said you wanted to shower and change before you go."

"Oh, shoot. Didn't realize it was that late."

Charley walked in the back door and froze when he noticed Pam, who was standing in front of the stove cooking their supper, wearing the apron her mother had always worn while preparing their meals.

Noticing him, Pam said, "Hi Daddy."

"Something smells great," Charley said, wishing for the millionth time that day, that his little girl wasn't pregnant or getting married that weekend.

"I wanted to fix you your favorite supper. I know how hard all of this is on you."

"How are you feeling?" Charley kicked off his work boots and walked in his socked feet across the kitchen floor to the sink to wash his hands.

"Great. I haven't been sick all day. And I got my room almost all ready at school."

"Those second graders are lucky to have you as their teacher this year."

Pam flashed him one of her beautiful smiles, and he fought back the tears that were threatening him again.

"The spaghetti's almost ready. And I made garlic bread, too. Will you set the table?"

"Sure." Charley retrieved two plates from the cupboard.

After setting them on the table, he grabbed the silverware, then filled two glasses with milk and set them by the plates.

"Can you help me get this to the table?"

Charley carried the pan of noodles, hamburger and sauce to the table while Pam carried the plate with the garlic bread.

After saying grace, they both hungrily dug into the delicious meal.

"What'd you do today, Daddy?"

"I baled hay. I'll have a lot to sell to Darrell for his cattle this winter."

"Do you ever think about getting cattle again?"

"Oh, sometimes. Why?"

"Well, I think it would be nice for my child to see their grandpa farming," Pam said as she helped herself to another piece of garlic bread. "Growing up on the farm was fun and rewarding, and I want my little girl or boy to experience that with you."

"I want that too," Charley agreed, making up his mind then and there to stay put on his farm and not take the job in Omaha. He knew it would mean the world to his daughter, so Charley asked, "How are the wedding plans?"

"Oh, great. I called today to make sure everything was going to be ready for Saturday. And everything's on schedule. We have the chapel reserved for the both the ceremony and the rehearsal on Friday night. Our friend Paul is going to officiate. I also checked with the bakery, and the cake will be delivered Saturday morning to the community center. And the photographer will meet us Saturday morning for photos at 11:00 a.m."

"When does the wedding start?"

"1:00 p.m."

"What do I need to do to help you, Pam?"

Overwhelmed with gratitude, Pam smiled across the table at her father.

Charley couldn't help but flash through the years they had sat at the same table talking about the day and their future plans.

"I'm so glad you asked me that, Daddy. I want you to give me away at the wedding. And I want your blessing."

"I won't lie to you, Pam. All of this really caught me off guard. But I've had some time to think about it. I know I raised you right. I raised you to be independent and honest. I also raised you to be bold and confident. I love you. And I will love your baby. And because of those two things, I'll both give you my blessing and give you away."

"Oh, Daddy." Pam jumped up and ran around the table, taking his hands and pulling him to his feet. "I love you so much!"

Charley hugged his little girl, knowing he was doing what she needed him to do.

As they sat down and continued eating, Charley asked, "What do I need to wear, Pam? Do I need to rent a tux?"

"Oh, no. This isn't going to be formal. I'm wearing a white summer dress, and Ty's wearing a suit. My attendants are also wearing summer dresses, and Ty's attendants are wearing black pants and dressy shirts. I don't know what Tyler's mom and dad are wearing, but you could wear a pair of black pants, a dressy shirt and a suit jacket."

"After we get done eating, let's look in my closet and pick something out," Charley suggested, not wanting to think about Tyler's parents.

"Sounds great, Daddy."

The apartment seemed too quiet when Trisha got back from dropping Brad off at the airport.

"I've got to keep working on this," she muttered, ignoring how tired her eyes were feeling.

She walked into the bedroom and opened her dresser drawers, pouring the contents out onto her made bed. Then she started sorting out piles of bras, underwear and socks.

"I don't need all of these," she said to herself as she started going through the piles, picking out what she wanted to take with her to Iowa as well as tossing the socks with holes in the toes and the underwear with stretched out elastic into a pile on the floor. Then she started going through the bras left on the bed, feeling her heart rate speed up when she noticed the red bra she'd been wearing under the dress she'd borrowed from Kat.

Her mind was quickly back to her time with Charley, and she could almost feel his rough, callused fingers against her soft skin as he had traced along the edges of the bra before gingerly releasing the clip between her breasts.

"I've gotta call him. I can't keep waiting for him to call me," Trisha moaned, longing for his touch again.

She hurried into the living room, still carrying the bra, and found her purse tossed onto her couch.

She rummaged around in the unorganized bag until she found her cell phone, and then she scrolled through the numbers until she found the one marked Charley Walker.

Her heart was beating louder with each ring as she clung on to the red bra, fearful he was going to tell her he'd made a mistake and wasn't interested in her any longer.

When his voicemail cracked to life, Trisha cleared her throat, listening to his message, then said, "Hi. It's me, Trisha Jenkins. I'm calling to let you know things have been pretty crazy around here. I lost my job on Monday and am having to move out of my apartment. Luckily, I met up with an old friend at the conference. Thanks to her, I have a new job. I want to tell you all about it, so call me when you get a chance. Thanks,

Charley. Bye."

Worried he really might be avoiding her, Trisha carried the red bra to her bedroom and threw it into her suitcase along with the other items she was taking with her. Then she gathered all the items she was throwing away and tossed them into a trash bag.

"Okay, I'm done with the clothes. Now, I need to go through the books in this room."

She squinted at the two wooden, floor-to-ceiling bookcases in the corners of her room and let out a low sigh.

Knowing she'd always want to surround herself with her favorites, she grabbed some boxes to start packing them to go with her. Then she walked back to the bedroom and started carefully placing the books into the boxes, hoping Charley would call her back.

"This looks perfect, Daddy," Pam said as she laid his good black jeans on his double bed with a blue, Western dress shirt. "Where's your suit jacket?"

"It ripped."

"Since graduation?" Pam asked, thinking back to May.

"Yep. It was almost twenty years old, Pam. It hardly fit. My, um, muscles have gotten bigger."

"Yes, Daddy. Your muscles are what got bigger."

Charley laughed as she patted his stomach. "Well, maybe my gut's gotten a little bigger, too. But I'm not too much bigger than I was back in the day."

Pam smiled. "My handsome Daddy. All my friends had crushes on you in high school."

"I know." Guessing where she was heading, he changed the subject by asking, "So, I probably need to get a new suit jacket before Saturday, huh?"

"Yes. I have to go to Des Moines tomorrow to pick up some things for the ceremony. Why don't you come with me, and I'll help you find something? It doesn't have to be expensive, Daddy. We'll find something in your budget."

"It's supposed to rain tomorrow," Charley agreed, thinking over the long list of things he needed to be doing on the farm. "But are you sure we should go to Des Moines? The state fair's going on. It'll be nuts up there."

"I'm sure. That's where I need to get my stuff. We'll have to leave early, though. I have to be back to the school for a meeting in the afternoon."

"Then we'd both better get to bed," Charley suggested, noticing it was already after nine. "What time should we leave?"

"Eight?" Pam asked, yawning.

"Sounds good. Thanks for supper and for helping me find something to wear."

Pam smiled and hugged him, then took off for her bedroom, her phone in her hand and Tyler on the line before she shut the door.

Not wanting to think about Tyler Bailey again, Charley walked into the kitchen and started doing the dishes they had stacked in the sink.

Trisha glanced at her cell phone, noticing it was already after midnight. "I can't believe he didn't call back."

Worried he was having second thoughts about their relationship, and wondering if she'd made a huge mistake agreeing to move back to Iowa, Trisha's mind raced as she stretched out her lower back.

"I forgot how much work packing is," she continued as she scanned her now-empty bookshelves. "Okay, I've got the bookshelves done, the dresser's empty, and the closet's empty. That leaves the nightstands."

Trisha studied the nightstand on the right side of the bed and picked up the lamp and tissue box.

"There, that was easy. Now for the left side. My side."

She carried the lamp into the living room and set it on the couch, and then she fetched a couple of boxes and walked back in, stretching again before sitting down on the floor.

As she started pulling out books and packing them, she noticed something was wedged in the back corner of the nightstand's bottom shelf.

She pulled all the books out and laid them on the floor, and then she reached back and picked up the small photo album.

"Oh my gosh. I did have it."

She stood up and flipped open the book, hearing the sound of something dropping to the wooden floor below.

Trisha looked down and felt her heart racing as she noticed the gold necklace lying at her feet. Memories of the forbidden man who had given her that necklace when she was 22 assaulted her mind as she bent over and picked it up.

"I didn't need to find this. Not tonight. Not ever," Trisha growled, willing herself to toss the forgotten piece of jewelry into the trash.

She wrapped her fist around the gold metal and carried it to the trashcan in the bathroom, but as she stood with her hand poised over the small, white container, memories of that time almost knocked the breath out of her.

"Damn it, why am I so weak?" Trisha cried out as she abruptly turned around and carried the necklace back into the bedroom. Then she carefully tucked it in her small jewelry tin and placed it into her purse.

"Okay, enough of that," Trisha willed herself, hoping she could suppress the memories, as she'd done so many times before.

Her eyes peeked at the album, and she resisted the urge to open it, knowing the photos would lead her mind back to the man who had led her to make the biggest mistake of her life.

"I need to get rid of this, once and for all," Trisha declared as she carried the photo album into the living room and set it on the couch beside the lamp. "And tomorrow, I'll do just that."

Suspecting if she went to bed now the memories would take over, Trisha ignored the grainy feeling in her eyes and quickly threw herself back into her work, packing the rest of the books in the bedroom.

"Everything's done in here except for the bedding," Trisha told herself as she stood up and studied the room, suddenly realizing how bare it looked.

"No time to change your mind, Trisha Marie. You're moving to Iowa. And you're running out of time to get out of here."

Chapter 6

"Daddy, what are you doing?" Pam asked as she stood in the living room, watching as her usually calm father stomped around, throwing couch cushions and papers into the middle of the room.

"Oh, hey. I didn't see you there." Charley ran his fingers through his dark hair as he looked sheepishly at the mess he'd made.

"What's going on? You've made a terrible mess," Pam scolded as she picked up the papers and stacked them on the coffee table.

"I lost my cell phone," Charley said, thinking again as he started helping her how much she acted like her mother. "I can't find that damned thing anywhere."

Pam grinned. "You've lost the cell phone you didn't even want, and you're upset about it?"

"Yep."

"What's the big deal? I have mine. You can find it when we get back from Des Moines."

"But I need to find it before we go in case…uh, yeah, you're right. What am I worried about?" Charley quickly changed gears, not wanting to tell Pam he was worried he'd miss a call from Trisha if he didn't have his phone.

The truth of the matter was he couldn't believe she hadn't called him yet. And it bothered him more than he wanted to admit to himself.

"Who are you expecting a call from Daddy?" Pam put her hands her hips. "This has something to do with these disappearing acts you've been doing. You've met a woman, haven't you?"

Charley took a deep breath before nodding.

"Oh, Daddy. That's great! Tell me all about her."

Figuring he'd have to tell her something, Charley was ready to confess everything. But Pam's ringing phone interrupted him.

"Oh, shoot, it's the photographer. I have to take this. We need to leave as soon as I get off the phone."

"I'll be in the truck." Charley picked up his ball cap and took off out the front door.

After petting Shooter, Charley got into his truck and looked around, wondering if he'd dropped his phone there.

"When did I have it last?" Charley asked himself aloud as he stuck his hands down seat cushions while thinking back. It worried him when he realized he couldn't remember the last time he'd even had his phone.

"She probably has called. And she probably thinks I don't want to talk to her. Oh, shit. I have to find that damned thing. And soon."

Trisha's ringing phone woke her up. She reached over to the nightstand, grabbed it and mumbled, "Charley?"

"Uh. Is this Trisha?"

"Oh, yeah. This is Trisha Jenkins."

"Trisha. This is Betty from the maintenance office at The Milligan Group. You forgot to turn your keys in when you left on Friday."

"Oh. Sorry. I'll bring them in today."

"Great. Please leave them at the front desk."

"Sure. Bye."

Trisha pushed the covers off and sat up.

Thinking of all she had to accomplish before Brad returned, she hurried into the bathroom and took a shower. Then she fixed her hair and put on her makeup, something she hadn't been doing all week.

After dressing in a nice pair of shorts and a blue top, Trisha located her work keys and threw them in her purse. Then she checked her cell phone again, making sure she hadn't missed any calls from Charley.

"Nothing," she moaned, tossing her phone into her purse.

Trisha picked up the photo album and Brad's car keys, and hurried out of her apartment.

Her mind was focused on her driving as she weaved in and out of the busy, morning traffic. Noticing the familiar buildings and houses flashing by her window, Trisha slowed down, enjoying the drive.

Before long, her large office building came into view. She thought of all the times she'd been on that road and her hands started shaking as her eyes started burning.

It seemed weird to park in the guest parking spot by the front door.

Trisha took a moment to gain her composure, then opened the door and got out. Her legs felt like lead as she walked down the sidewalk and into the lobby, the hot summer sun beating against her skin.

"Oh, Trisha. I've missed you," Shelly said.

"I forgot to hand in these." Trisha held up her keys. "Betty from maintenance called me this morning. She said to leave them with you."

"Thanks. And I have this for you."

Trisha took the envelope Shelly handed her. "What's this?"

"It's your severance package check. I have a whole stack of them to either hand out or mail. I think over 50 people were let go, Trisha."

"Wow, that's a lot."

"Trisha!"

Both Shelly and Trisha turned toward the elevator and noticed Marti running to them, "Are you back?"

"Just turning in my keys."

"I can't believe you're gone. You were they only one who knew what was going on around here. It's unbearable now. I can't stay here. I've already requested to transfer my internship."

"I'm sorry, Marti. I'd be happy to give you a reference. You did a great job for me."

"Would you? Oh, that'd be great!"

Trisha nodded and fished around in her purse for her business card. She crossed through her old work contact number and replaced it with her personal cell phone number.

"Use this number if you need to get ahold of me. I'll do what I can."

Marti almost knocked her over with a hug. "Did you get another job?"

Shelly leaned forward, clearly waiting to hear her answer.

"Yes, but not around here. I'm moving to Iowa. Flying out Friday. I'll be working for an insurance company."

"Iowa? Damn it." Shelly shook her head, her slicked-back blond ponytail swishing around. "I'm gonna miss you."

"Me too," Trisha agreed.

Shelly hurried around the desk, her platform heels clicking on the marble tile, and gave Trisha a bear hug. "Come back and visit us, okay?"

Before Trisha could answer, Shelly's phone started ringing, and she waved at Trisha while pushing the button on her headset and saying hello.

"Thanks again, Trisha. And good luck in Iowa," Marti said.

"Thanks." Trisha hurried out, jumping into Brad's car and taking off, ready to leave her old job in the rear view mirror.

"Well, that didn't take too long," Pam commented as she and Charley flew down Interstate 80 back to Hope.

"No, it wasn't too painful either," Charley teased.

"And you got a nice suit jacket. I'm glad it didn't cost too much."

Disappointed Pam considered $350 as "not too much," Charley bit his tongue while wondering if Tyler was to blame for that, too.

Pam's cell phone rang, and Charley was curious when Pam said Darrell's name. He waited until she was done talking, then asked, "What was Darrell calling about?"

"He found your phone. It was in his tractor cab's seat."

Charley snapped his fingers. "Oh, yeah. I remember having it there. Good. I can quit worrying about that."

"So, Daddy. You never did tell me about this woman you've been seeing," Pam said, turning her full attention toward him.

Knowing it was time, Charley cleared his throat. "I've met someone, Pam. But just this last weekend. My trip back in June and my trip this weekend weren't about her."

"I'm confused."

"I have two different things to tell you about," Charley clarified, thinking about the bank letter. "I want to wait until after the wedding to tell you why I was gone back in June. It's nothing major and can wait. But

I did meet someone this weekend, and she's the person I'm expecting a call from. But she's not from here. She doesn't even live in Iowa. We're just friends."

"Well, shoot. I was going to tell you to invite her to the wedding."

"Really?"

Pam nodded. "I know you and Tyler's family don't get along, and I'm afraid you aren't going to have anyone to talk to at the wedding and during the reception. The only people invited are you, Tyler's family, and our friends from college and school."

"Well, I know some of the people from school."

"That's true. But I didn't invite any family. There wasn't time. Besides, Tyler's only inviting his immediate family, too."

Charley's thoughts quickly turned to George Bailey, and he felt his fist tightening again.

"Daddy, please tell me why you don't get along with Tyler's parents."

"Oh, honey. I don't want to get into that."

"You don't have to tell me everything, just tell me something," Pam begged. "Help me understand this, because I'm so confused. I've never known you to have a problem with anyone before. It's very upsetting that you hate Tyler's family so much."

"I don't hate his family. I just don't get along with his parents. This goes way back to high school, Pam."

"So, you went to school with Tyler's parents?"

"Yes. George was a few years ahead of your mother and me. Betty Sue was a year ahead of us."

"Okay. So what happened?"

Charley thought back and shook his head, wishing once again Nancy were there to guide him. "I don't want to talk about that. All you need to know is that I love you. And I respect your decision to marry Tyler. He may not be the person I pictured you with, but I accept him and I'm excited to be a grandpa. Even though I think I'm way too young."

Pam giggled as tears started streaming down her cheeks. "Oh, Daddy. You made me cry."

ꟹ

"Damn traffic," Trisha moaned, her knuckles turning red as she gripped the steering wheel. "Now I remember why I don't drive, especially during the lunch hour."

She carefully followed the flow of traffic, alternating between slower than she wanted to and faster than she was comfortable going.

What should have been a twenty-minute drive took more than an hour, and Trisha let out a sigh of relief as she pulled onto the quiet side street smack dab in the middle of the college campus.

Memories flooded Trisha's mind as she drove past her freshman dormitory and the buildings where she used to go to class and study.

Her excitement continued to build as she moved her way closer to the athletic training area and the gymnasium where she practiced and played basketball.

After parking, Trisha gathered her purse and the small photo album and got out of Brad's car.

She walked up to the heavy, wooden doors, and her memories came flooding back as she remembered going to practice and games in that very building. Then the memories of the summer after she graduated—the summer when she'd helped the coach with the incoming players—assaulted her with a vengeance, and she took a deep breath, willing those memories to go away as she opened the door on the right and walked inside.

The scent of the freshly oiled gym floor mingled with the smell of the leather balls. She glanced in the direction of the closed doors that led to the gym and was instantly back to the night when her team won the game that gave them the first place standing in their league.

"What a great win," she said as she walked down the hallway, noticing her own smiling face in the photo on the wall with the years she was a Tiger listed along with her numerous awards.

"Trisha. Get out! What are you doing here?"

"Hey, Shawna, you're the lady I'm looking for." Trisha high-fived her favorite teammate, who was now the assistant coach of the basketball team. "I've got something for you."

"Great, what?"

"This." Trisha handed her the album.

"Oh my gosh, is this *the* album?"

"Yep. I guess I did have it. And I think it's time someone else enjoyed it."

"My team's going to love looking through these photos. Are you in a hurry? We could talk about some plays I've been working on."

Trisha sighed, suspecting Shawna wasn't going to like her news.

Quickly picking up on her mood, Shawna asked, "What is it?"

"I'm moving home."

"What? To Iowa?" Shawna crossed her arms. "No way."

"It's true. I got a job back there."

"What about your job here?"

"Laid off, effective last Friday. And my lease was up too."

"You loved that job. I'm sure you could get a job here. They're looking for another assistant."

"It's time to go back home."

"You don't owe your family anything, Trisha. They turned their backs on you. Remember?"

Hurt feelings and anger coursed through Trisha's veins as she thought about her troubled relationship with those whom she was supposed to be the closest.

"Hey, sorry. I'm sorry. That was out of line," Shawna tapped Trisha's arm, which brought her back to the present. "It's okay; I understand. If you get back there and decide it's a mistake, call me. I'll help you get back here."

Trisha hugged her. "Thanks."

"Do you have to leave right away? I'm getting ready to go to the cafeteria for lunch. I could bring my playbook, and you could help me with some things I've been having trouble with. What do you say?"

"Make it the café instead, and you've got a deal."

Anxious to get his phone, Charley dropped Pam off at home, then hurried down the road to Darrell's house. He was disappointed when he noticed Darrell's truck was gone and his wife's car was sitting by the garage.

Not wanting to wait a minute more for his phone, Charley pulled up beside Tess' car. As he walked down the sidewalk to the front porch, he thought about the mysterious woman who had somehow convinced his life-long bachelor friend to marry after only a few months.

"Hi, Charley." Tess opened the door and walked onto the front porch barefooted. "Darrell said you'd be stopping by for this."

"Thanks." Charley anxiously took his phone from her outstretched hand. "Where's Darrell?"

"Town. He's planning on doing some work with the cattle tonight. I'd help, but I have my book club meeting. Don't suppose you're free?"

"I can help," Charley said, not surprised Tess had found a way out of farm work. "Thanks for the phone. Tell him to call when he's ready."

"I will, thanks."

Charley walked back to his truck and studied his phone, mumbling some cuss words when he realized the battery was long gone.

"Great, just great." Charley mumbled as he started the truck and coasted back to his house.

He waited on the road as Pam flew down the driveway, waving at him before she turned onto the gravel road and headed off to her meeting at the school.

Charley pulled up by the house and hurried inside, plugging his phone into the charger on his desk in the living room.

"Guess it's time for lunch," he declared as he walked into the kitchen and fixed himself a bowl of cereal.

He sat down at the kitchen table and started browsing through the *Hope Gazette* while enjoying his light lunch. He snorted when he noticed a photo of Darrell's wife on the front page.

"Not a fan of that woman," Charley grumbled, shaking his head, still suspicious of her.

Darrell had been a bachelor his entire life. When his mother died, he'd inherited a substantial amount of money, his mother's house and all of her farmland. And several women had attempted to woo him in order to get their hands on his fortune.

And Darrell saw through every one of them.

But then Tess, a complete stranger, had waltzed into town less than a year after Darrell's mom had passed away. And Darrell had been instantly smitten with her.

Charley had tried to warn him to get her checked out to make sure she wasn't after his money.

But for the first time in his life, Darrell had fallen in love.

And after less than three weeks of knowing her, he'd asked her to marry him.

"And she's a good cook," Charley declared out loud as he eyed his soggy cereal. "But she's no farmer's wife, and she doesn't mind not working, either."

"But it's none of my business," he reminded himself as he finished his cereal and carried his bowl to the sink.

Then he walked back into the living room and checked his phone, thrilled when he noticed it had charged long enough to come to life.

Noticing he'd missed a call and had a message, Charley punched in his security code. His eyebrows raised as Trisha's message informed him about her lost job and her impending move.

"Well, she can't get much farther away than California," he reasoned as he saved her message and sat down at the desk, the phone still plugged in and charging.

He scrolled through his contacts and pushed the button when it came to her name, feeling butterflies coming to life as he thought about hearing her sweet voice on the other end.

"Damn it," he muttered, getting her voicemail. "Hey, it's me. Charley Walker. Wow, you've been having quite a week. I'm sorry I didn't call you back last night. I accidentally left my phone in the neighbor's tractor. I'll try you again later, or you can call me. I miss talking to you. I can't wait to hear all about your new job. Okay, I'll talk to you later. Bye."

Knowing he needed to get to work on his tractor, Charley left the phone charging and headed out the back door.

∞

"I can't believe you talked me into this," Trisha scolded as she stood in the gym after helping Shawna with the afternoon basketball practice.

"I didn't try that hard, Trisha. You wanted to help," Shawna teased her. "Besides, you get to keep the Tiger's Pride Camp shirt and practice shorts."

Trisha peered down at her outfit and laughed, then caught the ball as Shawna passed it to her.

Unable to help herself, Trisha took off in the direction of the basket. She made a lay-up, then grabbed her rebound and dribbled past the three-point line, sinking the ball again.

"You've still got it," Shawna praised as she ran over and stepped in front of Trisha. "But let's see how you handle a little pressure."

"You're on."

For the next fifteen minutes, they played a brutal match, both falling to the court a time a two, neither one of them letting that stop them from playing with passion.

Every time Trisha would make a basket, Shawna would make her pay with tougher defense than the time before.

Both of them were so caught up in their game they didn't notice a small crowd had gathered in the corner of the gym, watching them.

After Trisha sunk another three-point shot, someone started clapping, which brought their game to a halt.

"Hey, it's Coach Halley." Shawna pointed to the crowd. "Oh, this is great. Like old times."

Trisha glanced over at their old coach and felt her heart racing as he hurried to them.

"Oh my gosh, Trisha. I can't believe it's you! I haven't seen you in—"

"A long time," Trisha interrupted as she handed the basketball to Shawna. "Hey, it's been fun. But I gotta get out of here. I'm supposed to pick Brad up at the airport in less than an hour. And traffic will be a nightmare."

"Are you sure you don't have time for a cup of coffee?" Coach Halley asked as he grabbed her elbow.

Trisha glared at him and pulled her elbow away. Then she turned to Shawna. "I need in your office to get my things."

"It was really good to see you again, Trisha," Coach Halley called as Trisha bolted for the door, not stopping until she was standing outside of Shawna's office door.

"What the hell was that?" Shawna asked as she finally caught up to her. "What's with you and Coach?"

"I can't get into that now," Trisha declared, her cheeks bright red. "I just can't. I'm sorry. And we were having so much fun, too. I thought he quit helping with summer practices."

"He did. But sometimes he comes back for a couple of days," Shawna explained as she unlocked her office door and they walked inside. "Something happened between the two of you, didn't it?"

Trisha looked up from where she was gathering her purse and clothes, and she shook her head. "Nothing important. We aren't close anymore. It happens. Enjoy the album."

"I will." Shawna hugged her. "Be careful and call me when you get settled in. Okay?"

Trisha nodded and hurried out of the office, her entire body tensing when she noticed Coach Halley waited by the door.

"Trisha, please, we need to talk."

Trisha rushed past him. "I have nothing else to say to you."

"Give me a few minutes, please," Coach Halley begged as he chased her through the deserted hallway.

"I'm not interested in talking with you," Trisha declared as she reached the exit and took off at a jog toward Brad's car.

She peered back as she pushed the button on the key ring to unlock the door and tried to calm down when she realized he wasn't following her any longer.

Then she tossed her things into the passenger's seat and took off faster than she should.

Trisha was several blocks away before she finally calmed down, her hands finally still.

"Damn him. I shouldn't have gone back there. I promised myself I'd never go back there!"

Upset, Trisha forced herself to concentrate on her driving in the busy afternoon traffic.

She was almost forty-five minutes late as she pulled into the airport parking lot and located a spot.

Her cell phone started ringing as she parked the car.

Trisha pulled it out of her purse and sighed when she noticed she'd a missed call from Charley.

"Hello?"

"Hey, where are you? My plane got in early."

"I'm sorry. I'm here now. In Lot B."

"Stay put. I'll be right there."

Trisha ended the call, then listened to Charley's message. A smile instantly popped onto her face as she listened to his voice.

Then she pushed the call button and waited as it rang and rang, disappointed when she got his voice message again.

"Wow, we're playing phone tag. I'll try calling you again later tonight. It was great to hear back from you Charley. I miss talking to you, too."

Fifteen minutes later, Brad emerged from the shuttle bus. Trisha got out of the car and handed him the keys, "Here, you drive."

"Nice outfit," Brad teased.

Trisha laughed when she realized she was still wearing her gym clothes and Shawna's extra gym shoes.

"Don't tell me you had time to go to the gym?"

"I went to see Shawna, and she conned me into helping with summer training. But I'm almost all packed. You'll be proud of all the work I've done."

Brad was quiet as they merged with the crazy, rush hour traffic, and Trisha's mind was swirling with memories, both good and bad, as they headed back to her apartment.

"Thanks a lot for coming to help me," Darrell said as he and Charley walked down the worn dirt path toward his barn, cows mooing at them from the lot. "Tess really didn't want to miss out on this meeting. She said they read one of her favorite books."

"No problem." Charley bit his tongue so he wouldn't tell his friend what he really thought about Tess' excuse. "So, what are we doing?"

"Building fence." Darrell squinted his eyes. "Tess didn't tell you?"

Charley shook his head, "She said you needed help with the cattle."

"Oh. Well, they've been testing the northeast corner of the pasture and managed to break out. I was out chasin' 'em all morning. That's why they're stuck in the lot now. So, what'd you do today?"

Charley filled him on his trip to Des Moines while they gathered the items needed to repair the fence.

Soon, they were both riding on four-wheelers to the corner of Darrell's property, each holding on to a bucket of fence-repairing supplies.

"See where they've been pushing?" Darrell asked as they stopped the four-wheelers and climbed off. "They want Old Lady White's corn."

"Well, better hers than mine," Charley chuckled.

Being experienced at fence repair, both men got to work, quickly finishing their task.

"That went good," Darrell declared as they stood back and admired their work. "Should hold 'em too."

"Good. Sounds like they're ready to run again," Charley noted, still able to hear their bellowing.

"Sounds to me like they're scolding us for fixing their escape route," Darrell joked. "Why don't we park these four-wheelers in the machine shed?"

"Okay." Charley enjoyed himself on one of Darrell's newest purchases as they flew through the pasture and open gate and down the path to the machine shed.

"You go ahead and open their gate. I'll shut the field gate," Charley said as they started toward the lot.

After shutting the gate, Charley walked back and watched as the herd of thirty raced to the pasture. He smiled as the mamas started munching and their several-month-old babies started frolicking.

"You got some nice-looking cattle," Charley said as Darrell climbed over the fence.

"Miss yours, don't ya?"

"It's pretty quiet with no livestock."

Darrell patted him on the back. "Why don't we go on up to the house? Tess fixed us something in the slow cooker for supper. She said it'd be ready about dark."

Charley admired the setting sun as he followed his friend toward his house. As soon as they walked in, Charley could smell the delicious scent of Tess' cooking.

"She really is a good cook," Darrell praised as he kicked off his boots and headed for the kitchen sink. "And our house is always spotless."

Charley nodded and glanced around the clean kitchen that never had a pile of anything, unlike his house.

While Charley washed his hands, Darrell scooped up two bowlfuls of the beef and vegetable stew and carried them to the table.

"Milk?"

"Yeah, thanks." Charley walked over, sock-footed, and sat down at the table.

Both men were quiet as they dug into their meals, making quick work of the stew.

"More?" Darrell asked as he hopped up and walked back to the counter.

Although tempted, Charley shook his head and held up his hand. "I gotta fit into that stupid suit jacket."

"Your parents want me to come over to the mansion?" Pam asked Tyler as they stood in the school parking lot beside her car.

"Yes. Dad called me before our meeting. He said they wanted you to feel welcome and asked me to invite you over for dessert. Do you wanna go?"

"Well, I think I should," Pam started, fighting off a yawn.

"Honey, if you're too tired, that's okay."

"No. I think it's a good idea. It's just that last time we were dating, they wouldn't let me anywhere near that house."

"I know. And I'm sorry about that. I should've insisted."

Pam shook her head. "We both agreed not to push the issue last time. Besides, it's nice they've invited me now. It makes me hopeful that everything will go smoothly at the wedding."

"Maybe, but it's hard telling with my parents. You know, if you don't want to get married this weekend, we don't have to."

"I want to be married before this baby comes, Tyler. School will be starting soon. And, I love you. Nothing will change that. Yes, I'm tired, but let's go and have dessert with your parents. I think it's nice they asked."

"Okay. You can either ride with me or follow me."

"I'll follow you. But I can't stay too long. Tomorrow's going to be a busy day."

"I understand." Tyler leaned in for a kiss. "Park beside me, and we'll go in together."

Pam got into her car. She felt her heart racing as she started following Tyler down the quiet Hope streets.

As the Bailey mansion came into view, Pam thought about all the times she and her friends had driven by, wondering what it was like inside the fancy estate.

"Now, I'm going to know," Pam said. "And it terrifies me to walk in the house of the people my father hates."

She pulled her car up beside Tyler's and shut off the motor as Tyler opened her door.

"Ready?"

"Let's go."

Tyler held tightly on to her hand as they walked up the cement sidewalk lined with fancy, black park lights.

She expected a butler to open the front door, but Tyler reached down and pushed the door handle, opening it.

"After you, my dear."

Pam walked in and found herself in a fancy, marble foyer.

"This is the way to the kitchen. We'll let Helen know we're here, and then we will go and find Mom and Dad."

Pam looked around as she walked with Tyler down the carpeted hallway lined with artwork.

Before long, they stepped into a large, spotless kitchen filled with stainless steel appliances.

Pam noticed the older woman with a rounded belly and gray bun and smiled, feeling as if she were looking at the grandmother she lost way too soon.

"Hi, Tyler. You must be Pam. I'm Helen," the woman said as she hugged Pam. "It's so great to meet the girl who stole Tyler's heart. Do you like chocolate?"

"Oh, yes. I'm craving chocolate."

"Great. I'll bring dessert to the study in a few minutes. That's where your parents are, Tyler."

Tyler smiled at Helen, and then they walked out through another door.

"This is the dining room," Tyler said as they walked past a long, wooden table.

"Do you eat in this room?"

"As much as we can."

Pam tightened her grip as they walked through a room with bookshelves that lined one side and couches and chairs scattered throughout. She noticed the windows along the wall and asked, "Is that a pool?"

Tyler nodded and started in that direction.

He opened the glass french doors, and they both stepped out.

"Oh my," Pam said, instantly smelling the chlorine as they walked up to the edge of the pool. "This is huge."

"It's heated, too." Tyler pointed to the other side of the pool. "And that's the pool house."

"That's the pool house?" Pam's eyes grew wide. "It's bigger than my house."

Tyler smiled as he pulled her close and hugged her. "Ready for my parents?"

"Yes," Pam said, hoping she sounded more confident than she was.

Tyler led her back into the living room and then into the hallway.

Pam noticed the family photos on the wall as they continued deeper into the mansion. When Tyler stopped at a partially closed door, Pam felt her hands starting to shake.

Tyler turned and smiled at her, then pushed open the door.

"Oh, good. You're here," Betty Sue said as she jumped up and hurried to them. "Come in. Oh, Pam. It's so good to have you here."

"Thank you, Mrs. Bailey."

"Now, now. I'm going to be your mother-in-law in a few short days. Call me Mom or Betty Sue."

Pam smiled as Betty Sue gathered her into a hug.

"Such a petite little thing," Betty Sue continued as she studied her, amazed how much she resembled her mother.

"Hi, Dad," Tyler said.

Pam turned toward the man walking to them and noticed his ashen skin. She made a mental note to ask Tyler if his father was sick, as George shook her hand.

"Welcome to our home."

Pam felt a little uncomfortable when George's hand lingered in hers and noticed he seemed to be inspecting her.

When she was finally able to pull her hand away, she said, "Thank you. It's a lovely home."

"Dessert's here," Tyler announced, noticing Helen was carrying in a tray with four plates of chocolate cake.

"Come on, Pam. Let's sit on this couch. Son, please bring Pam and me our treat."

Tyler fetched the two plates and carried them over to the women, then returned with a cup of coffee for his mother and a cup of tea for Pam.

George sat down at his desk, and Tyler took the matching burgundy leather chair beside the couch.

"Oh, this is delicious," Pam said, her taste buds melting from the pure chocolate flavor as she started to relax.

"So, Tyler tells us you're a teacher?"

"Yes. This will be my first year teaching second grade at Hope Community School. I'm very excited about it."

"I also understand you're carrying our grandchild."

Pam almost choked on her cake, and Tyler shot his mother a warning stare.

Before anyone else could speak, Helen appeared in the doorway.

"Sir, there's a call for you on line one. It's the sheriff's office."

"Oh, hell. Now what?" George growled as he picked up the phone on his desk.

"You got a lot done while I was gone," Brad praised again as they sat at the table, munching on the fast food hamburger and fries they had picked up on the way to her apartment. "But did you get any sleep?"

"Not much. But I'm glad I stayed up. The kitchen's packed and so is the bathroom, except for the stuff I need in the morning. The only thing left in the bedroom is the bedding. And the only thing left in here is the bedding on the couch. We can take those boxes over there down to the shipping store in the morning and get that stuff on its way to Iowa. Then the movers can come and we can get all that stuff into storage."

"You've been working hard. Now, tell me why you're upset. Is it Charley?"

"Charley? No, not Charley." Trisha shook her head. "We've been playing phone tag for the last two days."

"Then what is it? You're clearly upset about something."

"Coach Halley," Trisha mumbled, suddenly back in the gym.

"Oh, shit. Where was he?"

"At the college."

"Why'd ya go back there, Trish? I thought you weren't—"

"I know - ever going back," Trisha interrupted. "I found a photo album Shawna's been wanting. It's got team photos and pictures from our days on the road. I thought I'd given it back to her a long time ago. I found it while I was packing. I was just going to drop it off, but she wanted my help with some plays she's working on. We went out for lunch, and then she talked me into helping with the afternoon session. And it was fun. But then, *he* showed up. He wanted to talk to me. He acted like…like…"

"Oh, come here." Brad jumped up and hurried over to her, pulling her to her feet and taking her in his arms. "I'm so sorry you ran into him again."

Sobbing, she melted into Brad's arms as he held her tight.

"I can't believe I ran into him," Trisha whispered as she started to gain her composure and pulled away. "All these years and I managed to avoid him. Until today."

"Put it behind you, honey. I think a good night's sleep would do us both good."

"But it's only eight," Trisha said as she glanced at the clock on the microwave that stayed with the apartment.

"Doesn't matter; I'm beat. And you are too."

"Okay, but please stay again, Brad. You're too exhausted to drive home. You can have the bed, and I'll take the couch."

"I'll stay, but you take the bed. It's your last night to sleep in your bed in your apartment. I'll be fine on the couch. I'm gonna call Scarlette and see how things are going, then I'm going to sleep."

"Okay. Good night, Brad. I'm so glad you're here."

They hugged again, and then Trisha took off for her bedroom.

As soon as she heard Brad laughing on his cell phone, she pulled out hers and called Charley.

"Darn it, voicemail again." Trisha mumbled. "Hey, Charley. It's me, Trisha. I was hoping to talk to you tonight, but I'm going to bed early. This packing is wearing me out. Hope you had a good day. And I hope we're able to talk tomorrow. Good night."

She set her phone down on the empty nightstand, then gathered her pajamas off her bed and walked into the bathroom, smiling as she listened to Brad's laughter.

After changing, washing her face and brushing her teeth, Trisha walked back to her bed and lay down, staring up at the ceiling.

Part of her was sad as she glanced around the dark room, knowing it was her last night in the apartment she'd called home for the last four years.

But she also knew she hadn't spent much time in the apartment, because she'd given herself completely to her job.

"And we see how well that turned out," she muttered to herself as she turned onto her right side.

"I'm not making that mistake again," she whispered as she thought about her new job and Charley. "I need someone in my life again. And I hope that's you."

ꕥ

Charley and Darrell had just finished eating the angel food cake Tess had made when she breezed into the kitchen.

"Hey, guys. How was supper?"

"Delicious. Thanks for cooking," Charley said, waving his fork at her.

"I'm glad you liked it." Tess helped herself to a piece of cake and sat down beside Darrell at the table. "Did you get the cows all fixed up?"

"Yes. How was the book club?"

"Oh, good. Well, until this drunk lady showed up. Do either one of you know a woman named Jessica Donohue?"

Darrell shook his head and looked at Charley, "I don't, do you?"

"Seems familiar, but I can't figure out why."

"Well, she made a scene tonight. Her daughter, Danni, was at the library. Danni had been checking out some books and was waiting for her mom to pick her up. Her mom hadn't shown up when the library closed, so Casey, the head librarian, brought her to the book club. She said she was only 11, but oh my gosh, that kid is smart. She listened to our discussion and asked questions about the book. Thank goodness it was a mystery this week instead of a romance. Anyway, we were picking a book for next month, when Danni's mother showed up. This woman was dressed like a hooker and was drunk. She smelled drunk, looked drunk and definitely acted drunk. She started yelling at that little girl, telling her she should be home because they have court tomorrow. I guess this Jessica woman's husband wants custody of Danni. But Danni isn't his kid. And he's already been granted custody of their other kids. Char said they had two boys. Anyway, she yelled at the girl and dragged her out of the library.

Someone called the cops, and we ended our meeting early. Char said her dad would bail her out. Everyone else seemed to know who that was, so I didn't ask. Thought you two might know."

"I bet that was George's daughter," Charley said, snapping his fingers. "Tyler's sister."

Darrell nodded. "Yeah, it was the Donohue that threw me off. He's in construction."

"Who? Her dad?"

"No, her ex-husband. I think his name's Clay. Her dad's George Bailey; he owns several banks."

"Bailey?" Tess asked, her cheeks suddenly turning pale.

"Yeah, do you know him?"

"No." Tess shook her head as she stood up. "I'd better get to work on those dishes."

Darrell glanced over at Charley, who was looking back with a confused expression on his face.

"I'd better get on home," Charley said as he stood, wondering why Tess had reacted the way she had when he'd said George's name. "Pam should be home from her meeting. It's our next to last night in the old house."

"Are you moving?" Tess asked, as she turned away from the sink where she was running dishwater and peered at Charley.

"I'm not. Pam's getting married on Saturday."

"Married? I didn't even know your daughter was dating anyone."

"Neither did Charley," Darrell explained.

"She's marrying Tyler Bailey. The brother of the drunk woman you met tonight."

"Oh, no," Tess said, shaking her head.

"He seems like a good kid. And I know my daughter wouldn't be with someone who drinks. Not after her mother's accident was most likely caused by a drunk driver," Charley declared as he started for the door. "Thanks for supper. It was great."

Darrell followed him to the door and waited while Charley put on his work boots. "Thanks again for your help."

"No problem. I'll talk to you tomorrow."

Charley started for his truck, pulling his cell phone out of his shirt pocket as he climbed in the cab, not wanting to wait a minute more before he called Trisha.

"Missed call? It never rang. Or beeped. Or nothing," Charley growled, annoyed with his phone as he put in his code and listened to Trisha's message. "Damn it. Another day without talking. This is gettin' serious."

Disappointed, Charley made his way back to his house, missing her more than he had all the other nights combined.

Noticing his house was dark and Pam's car wasn't in the driveway, Charley continued driving and made the five-minute trek into Hope.

He coasted by the school and found the parking lot empty. "Where'd she go?"

Worried Pam might be getting herself mixed up in Tyler's sister's drama, he changed directions and headed to the mansion on the west side of Hope.

His heart almost broke in two when he spied his daughter's old, blue Pontiac parked next to Tyler's fancy Mercedes outside the front door of the two-story, white mansion.

"Damn the Bailey's," Charley snarled, as he turned around and headed home.

"Are you sure I should stay?" Pam whispered to Tyler as they sat in the living room, waiting for George and Betty Sue to return from the sheriff's office.

"That's what they said to do. We'll wait a little longer. If they don't come, then you can go home."

"Why would your parents be called down there?" Pam asked, thinking over the one-sided conversation she'd heard when George had taken the call from the police.

"Probably has something to do with my sister, Jessica." The tips of Tyler's ears turned red. "She's a mess, Pam."

"What's wrong with her?"

"Well, she's…I think I hear them."

Tyler and Pam both jumped up and were headed toward the door when a woman wearing a short black skirt and tight red tube top stomped through the doorway.

Pam noticed her mascara-streaked eyes and tussled, short blond hair and was shocked with how old Tyler's younger sister looked.

"Damn it, Jessica!" George bellowed as he stormed into the room, followed closely by a crying Betty Sue who held the hand of a clearly frightened young girl.

"Who the hell are you?" Jessica demanded as she glared at Pam. "Who's this?"

"Your brother's fiancée," Betty Sue said.

"Why the hell didn't anyone tell me you were gettin' hitched?" Jessica demanded, putting her hands on her hips as her glare moved to her brother.

"Don't you dare change the subject. I had to come down to the county jail to get you. This has got to stop, little girl. You've been nothing but trouble since you turned ten!"

"George, let's not have this conversation in front of Danni." Betty Sue waved Pam over. "Will you please take Danni and go out to the pool house?"

Pam turned to Tyler, who nodded.

"Okay, Danni, my name's Pam, and I'm going to marry your Uncle Tyler. Would you like to go out to the pool house and talk about the wedding with me?"

Danni glanced at Betty Sue, who gently nudged Danni in Pam's direction.

Danni slowly walked over to Pam, and they walked out of the house, hearing the yelling break out in the main house before they even got around the pool.

"So, Danni, do you go to Hope Community?"

"Yeah." Danni trudged over and sat down on the plaid couch in the middle of the small living room in the pool house.

Pam walked over and sat down beside her. "Let's see, are you going to be in fifth grade?"

Danni raised her eyebrows as she nodded.

"What's your favorite subject?"

Danni shrugged.

"Well, I always liked history. And recess," Pam said, trying to get Danni to relax. "And sports. I played softball and basketball. Do you play any sports?"

"Basketball and softball. I want to be the pitcher."

"That's an important part of the team. I was the first basemen."

"That's real important too," Danni agreed. "There's pop in the refrigerator. Want one?"

"Sure, thanks," Pam said, thankful Danni was warming up to her.

Chapter 7

Trisha felt refreshed as she walked down the sidewalk in her neighborhood and glanced at the familiar houses, apartment buildings and stores.

"I'm going to miss some things," she whispered to herself as she entered her apartment building and walked down the hallway to her closed door.

"Hey," she called, noticing Brad was sitting on the couch, awake. "I got breakfast and coffee."

"I wondered where you had gone." Brad took the coffee from her. "You must have been up early. It's only eight."

"I was." Trisha sat down beside him and handed him the Styrofoam container.

"Is this one of Terry's omelets?" Brad asked, smelling the onions through the box.

"Yes. And I got one, too. Had to have one before leaving."

They both were quiet as they enjoyed their breakfast.

"I have a surprise for you," Brad said as they finished their food and he carried their cartons to the trashcan in the kitchen.

"Oh, what?"

"Nothing much. I bought you a car."

Trisha's eyebrows raised, "What?"

"While you were gone. I called a few places in Des Moines and found a great deal. They're going to deliver it to the airport for you. Isn't that great?"

"Damn it, Brad, I was going to pick out my own car. We had a deal," Trisha muttered as she got up and started folding his bedding.

"I know we did," Brad started as he took the blanket away from her.

He grasped her hands and held them tightly in his. “I’m going to miss you and worry about you, Trish. This way, I know you’ll always have wheels. You’ll have a way around. I did this for me, not for you. Please, don’t be mad. I was lying here on your couch, tossing and turning most of the night. You’re leaving, Trish. You’re really leaving.”

Trisha noticed the sadness in his green eyes. “I know. I’m sorry.”

“I’m happy for you. But, I’m sad for me. I’m so used to you being here when I need someone to talk to or hang out with. You really are my best friend, Trisha. I don’t want to make you feel bad about moving and starting a new adventure. It really hit me last night; you’re really leaving California.”

“You can come and visit me anytime you want to, Brad. Our friendship will never change.”

Brad gathered her in a big bear hug.

A knock on the door startled them both. Brad stepped away and made his way over to answer it.

“Hey. We’re here to move you.”

“You’re early.” Brad glanced at his phone. “I set up the appointment for ten.”

“We had some cancellations. We can come back later.”

“No, this is fine.” Trisha hurried to the door. “Everything’s ready to go except for the bed. It still needs torn down.”

“We’ll do that.” The mover blatantly checked out Trisha. “Why don’t you show me to your bedroom?”

Noticing, Brad said, “I will. Honey, why don’t you fold up our sheets?”

Trisha grinned at his over-protectiveness as she followed Brad and the movers.

Charley was still fuming as he drove down the quiet, gravel road toward Hope. He’d waited up until after midnight to talk to Pam, but she hadn’t returned home.

“And when I got up this morning, she was already gone,” he said, thankful she had at least come home and slept in her own bed.

“Not that it really matters. Tonight’s our last night in our house.

Tomorrow we'll be in the hotel in Cedar Falls and Saturday night she'll be…well, she will be a married woman."

Tired of being upset, Charley flipped on his radio and listened to the midday market report. He pumped his fist in the air when he heard the price of corn had risen higher than the analysts had expected.

"That's good news," Charley said as he pulled up to the small parts store and shut off his truck.

As he was getting ready to open his door, his cell phone started ringing.

He pulled it out of his shirt pocket and felt his heart start to race when he noticed it was Trisha.

"Hello?"

"Oh, thank goodness. I got the real you this time."

"Yeah, we've had a hard week connecting," Charley agreed. "So, how's the moving going?"

"Great. We got one load to the storage shed and have one more to go. And I just ran some boxes to the post office to have them shipped out. I'm on my way back to the storage unit, as the movers should almost be there with the last load. Then I have to go back to the apartment and get my things, hand in my keys and get out."

"So, where are you moving to? Hopefully it'll be closer than California."

"Well, Charley, I'm moving to Iowa."

Charley was sure he'd heard her wrong. "What?"

Trisha's laughter made him grin.

"You heard me right. I'm moving to Iowa. I got a job in the communications department at an insurance company. I'm flying out tomorrow. I was hoping that maybe we could see each other this weekend."

Charley's thoughts were instantly back on his daughter. "I don't think that's possible."

"Oh, um, okay."

"It's not that I don't want to see you," Charley quickly clarified. "It's, well, I have a daughter, Trisha. And she's getting married this weekend."

"Oh, wow. I didn't know you had kids."

"Only one. My daughter, Pam. But she did say I could bring you."

"You told her about me?"

"Yes. She saw me going crazy the other day when I lost my phone. She kinda guessed it. Anyway, I'm not real thrilled with the family she's marrying into. They're going to have a small wedding in Cedar Falls. I don't know what part of Iowa you're moving to, but I'd love to have you as my guest if it works out."

"I'll be close to Cedar Falls," Trisha reasoned. "I'd love to come."

Charley felt his toes curl. "That'd be awesome, Trisha. I can't wait to see you again. And I'm thrilled you're moving to Iowa."

"What time's the wedding?"

"Saturday at one o'clock. It'll be at a little chapel west of Cedar Falls. The reception will be right after the wedding, down the road from the chapel. I'll text you the information. Do you want me to pick you up somewhere?"

"I'll drive up, Charley. You'll have your hands full."

"So, what town are you moving to?"

"Oh, shoot. I'm getting another call. I'm sorry, Charley. It's probably Brad about the movers. I'll try to call later; otherwise, I'll see you on Saturday."

"Great, bye." Noticing he was talking to the dial tone, Charley hung up.

"Guess I've got a date for the wedding," he said to himself, beaming as he started into the store. Then it hit him as he said out loud, "Who's Brad?"

"Hi, honey. How's your day going?" Tyler asked as he walked into Pam's second grade room.

"I'm exhausted." Pam glanced up at him from where she sat on the floor, organizing a pile of books.

"Yeah. Again, I'm sorry about last night." Tyler helped her to her feet when she offered him her hand.

"How's your sister this morning?"

Tyler shrugged. "She never came back after running out during our talk. She's pretty upset."

"What about her court appearance? Danni said they had to go today."

"Dad stepped in. His lawyers handled it," Tyler answered as they walked over and sat down at her desk. "There's something I need to talk to you about."

"Okay."

"I know you didn't get to hear a lot of what was talked about last night. And my mother wanted me to thank you again for taking Danni out to the pool house. My niece is exposed to too much the way it is."

"I didn't mind. Danni's a smart girl."

Tyler smiled. "She really is. She reminds me of …well, never mind. Anyway, Jessica made a deal with Mom and Dad. She and Danni are going to move into the pool house so Mom and Dad can help with Danni. The lawyer's going to present that to the judge in the hope Clay won't take Danni away from Jessica."

"But maybe Danni should go with Clay. Maybe she should be with her brothers, Tyler. She misses them."

"I think she should. But that's not what my dad wants to happen. He wants to help Jessica again. He always wants to help Jessica. And he almost always gets his way. But that's not what I wanted to tell you."

"Okay." Pam took ahold of his hand when he offered it. "What do you want to talk about?"

"My dad's giving us Jessica's house."

"What?"

"The house where Jessica and Clay lived was a gift to them from my father. But he kept his name on the deed. Part of deal Jessica made with Dad last night was that you and I get the house. They're moving Jessica's stuff out today. We can move in when we get back from our honeymoon. If you want to."

"A house?"

"Yes. It's a really nice house. They are going to clean it and paint it before we move in. Mom said she'd pick out the colors. I said that was fine. But if you want to do it then—"

Pam threw her arms around Tyler and squealed, "We're going to have our own house. My daddy will be thrilled to hear we aren't living in the mansion."

"I'm kinda thrilled about it myself. Do you want to go and see it?"

"Yes, I do. But I have so much work to do, Tyler. I thought I was about done, but I forgot about the decorations."

"I have a couple of free hours. Let me help you."

"Ok." Pam smiled, then pointed at the cardboard letters and numbers on her desk. "Are you good with scissors? Because those all need cut out."

"I'm on it." Tyler kissed her before grabbing the scissors off her desk and getting to work.

The humming of the old, clunky refrigerator bellowed throughout the empty, small apartment.

Trisha studied the noisy beast that had been a constant annoyance when she first moved in and sighed, realizing she'd gotten used to the noise sometime over the years.

But now that it was almost time to move out and the apartment was almost empty, the noise echoed around the quiet room.

While Trisha slowly sauntered around the empty rooms, making sure she'd packed everything, it saddened her that the humming sounded like home. A home she really was leaving.

As she stood in the middle of the living room, where the couch had resided the entire time she'd lived there, she started thinking about the changes that had happened to her over the years.

This had been the place she'd retreated to after the divorce and after leaving Brad's spacious home.

It had felt so cramped those first few months.

Part of her wondered if that was the real reason she'd spent most of her waking hours at her job.

She thought back to the first and only party she'd hosted. It had been a March madness game-watching party with a handful of her former teammates, including Shawna. She could almost taste the fattening sausage cheese dip they'd devoured while swearing each other to secrecy that they would indulge in such an unhealthy snack. They had also watched as their brackets had gone up in smoke when most of the higher ranked teams had fallen during the first round.

Her last company in the apartment had been her neighbors, the Millers, before they'd moved out. They had always enjoyed challenging each other in heated matches of trivia games with the tenants in the apartment building and had pestered Trisha until she'd finally agreed to have them over.

Brad had joined them, and the Millers had gotten upset when Brad and Trisha had skunked them at their own game.

Trisha grinned, thinking how much fun she and Brad had enjoyed in the apartment. She knew it was strange to people that they got along so well even though they were divorced.

"I turned your keys in. Are you ready?" Brad asked as he stuck his head through the open doorway and grabbed the handle on her suitcase and the strap on the matching bag.

"Yes. I'll be right out."

"Take your time, Trish. I'll be in the car."

"Goodbye old place," Trisha whispered as she glanced around once last time. Then she picked up her purse and slung it over her shoulder, trying to maintain her composure as she walked across the threshold and pulled the door shut one last time.

Charley wiped the sweat off his forehead with his red and white handkerchief as he sat on the tractor. He studied the line of bales he'd made by Darrell's barn and counted.

"Great, 24 bales." He made a mental note before he started the tractor up and drove down the lane toward the house.

"Can you get the ones off my field too?" Darrell hollered as Charley pulled up beside him. "I gotta run to town and get parts."

Charley nodded and waved, then took off down the road to the field. Sweat continued to roll down his back, and he wiped his forehead again, wishing it wasn't so hot.

While he started making trips back and forth from Darrell's field to Darrell's barn, Charley started thinking about Trisha again. He was both thrilled and a little scared she was going to the wedding with him.

"Everyone will know," Charley muttered, thinking how people would react when they found out he was seeing someone. A younger someone. He thought about the name Brad again and grumbled, "A younger someone I don't know much about."

After thirty minutes, Charley had all the bales moved. He stopped his tractor in the middle of Darrell's driveway and headed to the machine shed, where Darrell worked on his combine.

"How's it going?" Charley asked as he walked in.

"Great. Thanks for helping with the hay while I worked on this. You look hot. Want something to drink?"

"Wouldn't turn it down."

"I'm ready for a break myself. Let's go to the house," Darrell said as they started in that direction. "Tess' in town getting groceries, but I think we have some Pepsi left. Sound good?"

"Heavenly," Charley agreed. "There's a good breeze out here. I'd better not go in the house. I'll leave a trail of dirt."

"Okay. I'll be right back."

Charley sat down on one of the two fancy Adirondack chairs and took off his sweat-soaked Pioneer Seed ball cap, resting it on his knee. The breeze felt good, and he once again admired Darrell's manicured lawn.

"Here you be," Darrell said as he handed him a can and sat down in the chair beside him. "It does feel good out here. The combine should be ready by harvest time. We'll get an early start so we can get all of our crops out in a decent amount of time."

"Thanks again for helping me out with the combine situation. My old one was going to cost too much to repair this year."

Both men seemed lost in their thoughts as they drank their pop.

"Darrell, I got something to tell ya."

"Okay, shoot."

"I met a woman."

"That's great," Darrell said, surprising Charley. "Who is she? Where'd ya meet?"

"Last weekend, when I was gone. Can we keep this between us?"

"Sure, Charley. Won't tell a soul. Not even Tess."

Charley took another drink. "Last June, when I was gone, I went to auctioneer school out in western Iowa. I knew I was going to be short on money and thought it was something I'd enjoy doing."

"Sounds good to me. Why you keepin' it a secret?"

"Well, two reasons. I didn't want George Bailey finding out about it, because I hoped he'd have a heart this time and not demand my financial records. And I haven't told Pam. I don't want her to worry about me."

"And you met this girl out there?"

"No." Charley took another swig. "My instructor thought it'd be good for me to go to the annual convention they had in Minneapolis. That's where I went last weekend. And that's where I met her. She was there for another convention. We hit it off, Darrell. We hit it off really well."

"Okay. Isn't that a good thing?"

"Oh, yeah. It's great. I was kinda bummed because she lives in California. But she's moving to Iowa. She'll be here this weekend, and Pam even said I could invite her to the wedding, so I did."

"So, it's not a secret."

"Trisha's not a secret, no. But the auctioneer thing is. For now."

"Kind of coincidental she's moving to Iowa right after meeting you."

"I know. But I'm glad. Last weekend, she was worried something weird was going on with her company. She was worried she might lose her job. I'm thrilled she's moving to Iowa."

"Where in Iowa?"

Charley shrugged. "We'd just gotten to that when she had to go. She's moving her stuff into storage today."

"Well, if she makes you happy, then I'm thrilled for ya. Having a woman in my life has made me a lot happier, Charley. It's time for you to be happy again, too."

"I've been happy raising Pam."

"I know. But this is something you're doing for you. I know it wasn't easy for you. I know how much you've missed Nancy all these years. But she'd want you to be happy, Charley. She really would."

Charley took another drink, hoping Darrell was right.

*

"Home sweet home," Brad said as he unlocked his front door and they walked inside.

Trisha took the time to admire the beautiful house that used to be her home too. "Does Kennedy still work here?"

"No. I don't have anyone on staff right now. Scarlette loves to cook when she's home, and she doesn't like having anyone around. I did hire a cleaning service, but they only come when I call them. I'm starving; how about you?"

"A little." Trisha followed him into the large living room. She glanced up at the second floor, which was visible from the living room, and memories rushed through her mind of their time together living and loving in the house.

"If you wanna rest, you can. I have dinner covered tonight."

"I'm going to look around. It's been awhile since I've been here."

Brad smiled, offering her a little peck on the forehead before he took off in the direction of the kitchen.

Trisha walked over to the curved stairs that led up and took her time climbing them as she thought about all the times she'd been up those very stairs.

She started down the hallway and turned into what had been their bedroom.

It saddened her a little when she noticed everything had changed.

The fuchsia flowered bedspread she'd lovingly picked out had been replaced with a plain white one. All the scenic photographs she'd special ordered and hung on their walls were replaced with paintings of fruit and trees.

Trisha peeked into what had been their master bath and thought it was odd that her shampoo and favorite hairbrush no longer sat in their places.

She glanced over at the wall where they had set up the baby crib and blinked back the instant tears.

Trisha took a deep breath and hurried out of the room as a feeling of sadness started to wash around her. She thought about all the times Brad had tried to get her to come back to the house to visit and was glad she'd always come up with an excuse not to. The pain of losing Sophie still cut like a blade.

Trying to shake the sadness, Trisha continued down the hallway. Glancing into the numerous guest bedrooms, she stopped in her tracks when she realized that Brad and Scarlette had turned the room she'd used for her library into their master bedroom.

Blue silk sheets lined the bed, and various photos from Scarlette's modeling shoots decorated the walls.

Trisha's face flushed when she noticed the photo at the end of the bed showed Scarlette almost nude. She quickly turned and hurried out of the room, feeling like an intruder.

She took the back stairs down to the main level and followed the hall around until she was at the back of the house. Then she stepped out into the garden and followed the path until her favorite place in the entire estate, the pool, came into view.

Trisha sat down on one of the lounge chairs and shut her eyes, feeling the warm sunshine against her bare legs and arms.

She thought about Charley and wondered what he was doing as she fell into a deep sleep.

"Hi Daddy," Pam said as Charley walked through the back door.

Charley kissed her on the cheek. "I didn't figure you'd be home this early. I've been sweating all day. I'm going to take a shower."

"Supper will be ready when you're done. I fixed your favorite—minute steak and baked potatoes."

"It smells wonderful. Thanks honey. I'll be right back."

He hurried to the bathroom and quickly showered, then threw on a clean pair of jeans and a blue, Carhart T-shirt. He walked back into the kitchen as Pam was setting their food on the table.

"Great timing, Daddy," Pam said as she poured milk in his favorite glass.

"Thanks for fixing us supper."

Pam bowed her head as Charley said grace. Then they both started eating.

"So, you were out late last night."

"I know. It was kind of crazy. Tyler's parents wanted me to stop by for dessert after our meeting at the school. We had just started eating this absolutely delicious chocolate cake when the cops called."

"The cops?"

"Yep. Turns out, Tyler's sister, Jessica, had been going around town causing a scene. She was so drunk, Daddy. And she had her daughter, Danni, with her. Danni's such a good kid. I spent time with her in their pool house while the rest of the family had it out in the main house. Turns out, Jessica and her husband are getting a divorce, and he wants custody of all three kids. He and Jessica have two boys. No one knows who Danni's father is. But anyway, George pulled some strings, and Jessica and Danni are moving into the pool house. And Tyler and I are moving into Jessica's house. Isn't that great Daddy? I won't have to live in the mansion."

"That's great," Charley agreed, relieved he'd be able to visit her without stepping foot in the Bailey mansion. "I heard about Jessica's escapades from Tess, who had her book club at the library last night. I wondered if that had something to do with you being out so late last night."

"I'm sorry. I was really hoping we could spend these last few nights together, Daddy. I'm going to miss you. And living in our house. But at least I'm not going too far away."

"That's true. Hey, I have some good news."

"What's that?"

"Remember I told you I met someone and you said she could come to the wedding with me?'

Pam nodded.

"Well, she's coming."

"Really? I thought you said she was in California."

"She is. But she lost her job out there and got another one. Here, in Iowa. She's moving here this weekend, so I invited her to the wedding. That's still okay, isn't it?"

Pam offered him a smile, although Charley didn't think she looked too happy.

"If you don't want her to come, I can tell her not to."

"No, that's okay. I want you to have someone with you. I was just caught off guard. That's all. I think it's great. I want to meet her. But it's kind of weird she's suddenly moving to Iowa. Is it because of you?"

Charley felt a little excitement in his stomach with that thought, but shook his head. "No. She had a job lead for an insurance company here in Iowa. I don't even know what town she'll be living in. We didn't get that far in our conversation before she had to go. She's been packing all week and has been really busy. How about you? Do you need help packing?"

"No, but thanks. Tyler and I are going on a short honeymoon to Minneapolis. It's not fancy, but it's the best we can do. We were lucky to get any time off with school starting next Thursday. I'll probably pack up my stuff next weekend and live out of a suitcase until then."

Both of them seemed lost in their own thoughts as they finished their supper and cleaned off the table.

"Daddy, can we watch our movie tonight? You know, like we always used to do when it was snowing outside?"

Charley smiled. "That's a great idea."

Trisha and Brad sat on the lounge chairs by the pool.

"This lemonade's really good. How's your wine?"

"Good. It's been a long time since I sat under the lights out here, enjoying the night. The last time was probably back when you were here."

"We had some good times, Brad." Trisha admired the full moon. "It might take a bit to get up here, but it's so peaceful."

Brad thought back to when he bought the house long before he met Trisha. His friend had told him about it, and Brad knew it was exactly what he'd been looking for. Something close enough to get to all the places he need to get to, but far enough away he could forget he was living in the middle of a rat race.

"I've always loved this place, but it wasn't until you moved in, Trish, that this place became a home. Our home."

"We had a good run, Brad. You truly are the best friend I've ever had."

"Well, you let me know if Charley is ever a jerk to you, because I'll let him have it."

Trisha's blue eyes met his green ones and she smiled.

"I'm going to miss you so much, Trish. It's almost unreal you're leaving tomorrow. And not just on a trip. You're moving. For good."

"You're out of the state more than six months every year, Brad. And now that you got that new client and are going to be exclusively directing all their print ad campaigns you'll be traveling even more. I'm not that far away. Once I get a place of my own, you can come and visit me."

Brad reached his hand across, and Trisha latched on to it.

"I'm glad you decided to stay here tonight, Trisha. It seems right. We were so in love once. And if Sophie wouldn't have—"

"Don't!" Trisha interrupted as she pulled away and sat up. "Please, don't. Don't go there. Not tonight."

Brad nodded and drank the rest of his wine.

Trisha stood. "Let's do something fun."

"Like what?"

"Our tournament," Trisha said, snapping her fingers. "There's no way I'm leaving with you ahead of me. Where's your gaming system?"

"In the basement." Brad followed her into the house. "Sure you wanna go there? I'm going to beat your score even worse than before."

Trisha grinned, loving the challenge. "You're on."

Chapter 8

"I guess it's time," Brad said as they walked slowly down the crowded corridor at the airport.

Trisha nodded and fought hard to maintain her composure. When she noticed Brad's tears, she lost her fight and let her tears fall, too.

"I can't believe how hard this is." Brad hugged Trisha tightly. "I'm so glad you came to California, Trish. And I'm so glad we met. You gave my life purpose. The time we were married was the best time of my life. I wish we would've worked out. But I'm thankful we're still friends. Best friends."

Trisha buried her face in his chest, trying hard to control her sobs.

Slowly, Brad pulled away and kissed her on the forehead.

"A new adventure," Trisha said, managing a small smile for him as she brushed the tears off her cheeks. "I'm starting a new adventure. And just because I'm not going to be here anymore doesn't mean you won't be in it."

Brad hugged her again. Then he kissed her on the forehead and let her go. "Have a safe flight, Trish. Call me when you get to Iowa. And tell her hi, from me. Okay?"

Trisha nodded and quickly turned away, not wanting to cry anymore.

She waited in line at the metal detector and didn't look back in Brad's direction as she was cleared to continue to her gate.

As she sat down near the desk, looking out the window at the airplanes, her mind was suddenly back thirteen years earlier.

She remembered arriving at this very airport, a scared, small-town girl.

Everything in California seemed so big back then—the crowds, the airport, the traffic.

Her first day in California had been confusing as a van from the college had picked her up and delivered her and her two suitcases to the gym entrance. Trisha had struggled to carry the only items she'd brought with her from home into the gym.

Inside, she'd found more than twenty other girls who had looked as confused as she had.

"Then Coach Halley appeared," Trisha muttered, remembering how exciting it had been to finally meet the man who had wooed her into coming and playing for his college.

Trisha sighed as memories of those years ticked though her mind.

Her memories were interrupted as her cell phone started ringing.

"Shoot, I thought I shut that off." Trisha quickly pulled it out of her purse. "Hello?"

"Trisha, it's Kat. Sorry I didn't get back to you yesterday. How are things going?"

"Great. I'm waiting to board the plane. I did ship a few things to your house, but they aren't supposed to get there until next week some time."

"Do you need someone to pick you up?"

"No, I have it covered." Trisha thought about Brad's gift. "I'll probably get to your house around eight."

"Well, I should be home by then. But if I'm not, there's a key under the flower pot by the back door."

"I'm really excited about my new job."

"We're happy you'll be joining us. I can't wait for you to meet Rick. You'll like him; he's a great guy to work for."

"Sounds perfect. See you soon."

Trisha hung up and shut off her phone, then watched the flurry of activity begin as they called for passengers and started boarding her flight.

Charley was checking the oil in his truck when he heard Pam's car pulling into the driveway.

"Hey Daddy."

"Wow, you're back already?"

"Yes. It's almost one. Tyler will be here to get me in less than half an hour. I have so much to do. Have you packed?"

"No." Charley shut the hood of the truck. "But I don't have as much to pack as you do. Want some help?"

Pam giggled as she examined his oil-covered shirt and hands, "I got it, but thanks, Daddy."

Charley offered her a grin as he followed her into the house.

As she took off for the bathroom, he walked into the kitchen and washed off at the sink. Then, he continued into his bedroom and changed his shirt.

After that, he walked into the hallway and watched as his little girl ran from the bathroom to her bedroom, gathering the items she needed during her last few hours as his single, little girl.

"Daddy, Tyler's supposed to be here any minute. Can you ask him to come on back when he gets here?"

Charley bit his tongue but obliged and walked to the front porch, where Shooter waited for him by the bench.

Just as he sat down, Tyler's fancy car came crawling down the gravel road and pulled into his driveway.

"Hello, Mr. Walker," Tyler said as he got out and started to the house. "How are you doing today?"

"Fine. You?"

"I'm happy. No, thrilled! I can't wait to marry your daughter, sir."

"Well, I always thought the boy who married my daughter would have the decency to ask me for her hand."

Tyler's cheeks turned a deep shade of red. "Sorry."

Charley took a deep breath and begrudgingly gave him Pam's message.

Not wanting to think about Tyler Bailey being in his daughter's bedroom, Charley pulled out his cell phone and dialed Trisha's number, disappointed when it immediately went to voicemail.

"Probably already in the air," he reminded himself. He ended the call and stuck his phone back into his pocket as Pam and Tyler both came out, carrying bags.

Charley waited out of the way as they went into the house again and came back out, Tyler carrying more bags, and Pam carrying a dress.

"We're ready to go." Pam walked up to her daddy on the front porch.

"I love you."

"I love you too," Charley said, his voice cracking. "I'll be leaving in less than an hour."

Pam wiped her wet cheeks. "I'm always going to be your little girl. No matter what. And this will always be my home."

Those words made Charley lose his battle, and he brushed away his own.

Pam smiled before turning and hurrying to Tyler's car.

Tyler opened the door for her and then shut it after making sure she was seated. He waved at Charley as he walked around and got in.

Charley tried to ignore the silence as they drove away, but his heart felt as if it were breaking in two.

"Damn this wedding. Damn that family!" Charley cried out, tired of the silence as he jumped to his feet and hurried into the house.

He took a quick shower, trying not to notice all the empty spaces around the tub where Pam's shampoos and conditioners had been stored.

After drying off, Charley dropped his towel into the hamper and walked into his room, pulling on his underwear before he started to pack.

When he noticed his best pair of jeans in the closet, his thoughts were instantly back to the moment when he was sitting on Trisha's bed looking at his pants lying beside her black thong.

"Can't believe I'm gonna see you tomorrow," he commented out loud, feeling a little better.

After packing the rest of his things, he dressed in the jeans and a nice Western shirt Pam had picked out for the rehearsal. Then he carried his duffel bag into the living room and set it down on the couch.

After feeding and watering Shooter, he carried his bag outside and locked the door. Then he climbed into his truck and took off on the almost two-hour drive.

❧

It felt weird to Trisha to be driving again as she left the parking lot.

"Brad shouldn't have gotten me a brand new car."

She was still trying to get used to all of its special features as she made her way to the interstate.

Traffic on I-80 was crowded and she found herself gripping the wheel as she maneuvered her way through the lanes congested by multiple construction projects.

"Wow," she whispered, noticing all the new buildings on either side of the interstate. "This is all new. Altoona has really grown."

As she noticed the Adventureland exit, her thoughts were suddenly back to the many summer days she'd spent there during her sophomore year in high school. Several of her softball teammates had taken turns driving, and they had splurged for season passes to the amusement park that also had a water park.

Trisha smiled, thinking about all the fun they had that summer.

Before long, the traffic started to thin out and Trisha started to calm down, relaxing her fists and stretching out her fingers.

The landscape, which was dotted with farmhouses tucked among rolling fields of corn and soybeans, looked beautiful to her, and she suddenly realized how much she'd missed her home state.

"And Charley's a farmer," Trisha reminded herself, unable to stop from smiling.

She'd been friends with numerous schoolmates who lived on farms, but she'd never paid much attention to what a farmer actually did.

"Maybe Charley will show me," she said, suddenly very interested in how the food she'd been consuming got from the Iowa fields to her plate.

Lost in the beautiful countryside, Trisha almost missed her exit.

As she pulled off and started down the quiet, two-lane road, she noticed the massive Just For You Insurance complex on the north edge of Taylor.

"I wonder if Kat's still at work," Trisha said as she pulled into the driveway and stopped by the front door, parking in the visitor spot.

She scrolled through the contacts on her phone until she came to Kat and pushed the button.

"This is Kat."

"Kat, this is Trisha."

"Oh, hi. Are you in Iowa yet?"

"Yes. I'm sitting in the parking lot of Just For You. You wouldn't happen to still be here, would you?"

"Of course I am." Kat chuckled. "Would you like a tour?"

"I'd love that. I'm anxious to get to work."

"Great. Where are you parked?"

"The visitor spot out front."

"I'll be right down and let you in the door."

Trisha hung up and tossed her phone back into her purse. Then she studied her reflection in the mirror on the visor above the steering wheel and fluffed her hair.

Deciding she looked good enough, Trisha got out, slung her purse over her shoulder, and started for the front door.

"Hi," Kat called as she held the door open and waved her in. "This is great. You can meet the president and owner of the company, Mr. Richard Marlin."

"Oh, crap. I'm not dressed to meet him," Trisha said, shaking her head, as she noticed her wrinkled shorts and T-shirt. "I have airplane clothes on."

Kat laughed. "Rick's been running on the track in the basement gym. He's got gym clothes on. It'll be okay."

Trisha smiled at Kat's enthusiasm and nodded, hoping to make a good impression on her new boss.

"We'll start here. This is the receptionist area. You probably won't be down here too often. More than likely, you won't deal with any of the walk-in traffic. And you'll park in the back parking lot, so you won't be entering through this doorway either. Let's see, why don't we go this way, and I'll show you some of the other offices."

Trisha tried to memorize everything Kat was telling her as they started making their way through the maze inside of Just For You Insurance. The farther they went, the more her internal compass was off track. She felt completely turned around as they started going down in the elevator.

"So, how was your flight?"

"Fine. How's your day been?"

"Very busy. But I like my days busy. I'm still catching up from being gone last weekend. Okay, here's the basement level. This is where the gym is, and this is where Mr. Marlin will be."

Trisha felt a little nervous as she followed Kat around an impressive gym that included a small track, half basketball court and lap pool.

"He must be in the weight rooms," Kat said as they walked on the side of the basketball court, through a set of doors and into another hallway.

Kat opened a door. "Here he is."

"Oh, hey, Kat."

Trisha surveyed the older man with dark black hair that was starting to turn gray. He was wearing a muscle shirt and gym shorts, had a killer smile, and was sweating like crazy.

"Mr. Marlin, I'd like you to meet the woman I was telling you about. This is Trisha Jenkins. Trisha, this is Mr. Richard Marlin."

"Please, call me Rick," he insisted as he offered his hand to her.

Trisha shook it. "Trisha."

"She stopped by on her way to my house. I thought I'd give her a tour."

"This is a huge place."

Rick grinned. "Business has been very good to us over the years. We've finished expanding to the west, where we added several offices. And we updated down here about three years ago. Our next project is to remodel our cafeteria. We want to have a healthier eating area for our employees."

"Well, I think it's amazing what you're doing for your employees," Trisha said, thinking how much better it was than The Milligan Group. "Thank you for giving me a chance."

Rick wiped sweat off of his forehead with a white towel. "Kat told me about your award-winning ad campaign. I trust her completely."

Trisha watched as Rick and Kat smiled at each other and wondered if they had been more than just boss and employee at some point.

"Well, let's go to your office," Kat said as she turned back to Trisha.

"Nice to meet you, Trisha." Rick called as they started for the door. "I'll see you tomorrow, Kat."

Kat smiled and waved and they continued down the hallway.

ꟼ

"Have you seen him?" George whispered to Betty Sue as they sat in the overstuffed chairs in the lobby of the chapel.

"No. But I'm sure he's scampering around here somewhere. Remember, we have to be nice."

"Hell, Sue. I can't be nice to that…that…"

"You have to be. I don't want any scenes during our son's rehearsal or wedding. Remember, we want the upper hand in all of this."

George let out a long, low, frustrated sigh and messed with his tie. "Why did I have to wear this thing? I thought the rehearsal was supposed to be casual."

"We are the Baileys, dear. This is our casual wear."

"Hi, Grandpa." Danni bounded into the chapel wearing the flowery spring dress Betty Sue had bought for her. She was closely followed by Tyler.

"Hi, Mom and Dad. Our flower girl is ready for this rehearsal to start."

"I'm a junior flower girl," Danni reminded Tyler. "I'm too old to be a flower girl."

"You look lovely, Danni," Betty Sue praised, smiling at her.

"Why don't you go on down that hallway to the second door on the right? Pam's in there getting ready, and she has your flower basket," Tyler said to Danni. As soon as she was out of the room, he turned to his parents. "Thanks for bringing her."

"We can't rely on Jessica to even show up," Betty Sue said through tightened lips.

"She'll be here. She wouldn't miss her own brother's wedding," George vowed, not yet ready to give up on his baby girl.

"You need to admit that girl has a problem!"

"Mom, not now. Okay?"

Betty Sue noticed the look on Tyler's face and quickly hurried to him, hugging him. "I'm sorry, honey. You're right. Not now. And your father's probably right; she probably will be here shortly."

"Hello."

Everyone turned and looked at Charley, who had entered the chapel.

"Hello, Mr. Walker. I'm so glad you could come. Let me take you to Pam." Tyler shook Charley's hand and then led him past his parents and down the hallway.

"Smug son of a—"

"We're in a church," Betty Sue interrupted, then whispered. "But you're right, he is."

"You must be Tyler's parents."

George and Betty Sue turned and noticed the pastor as he walked into the room. "I'm Pastor Paul Ninnen. It's so good to meet you both."

"I'm Betty Sue, and this is George."

"You have raised a wonderful man. We attended school together. Tyler was always focused on his schooling. We got along great."

"You went to UNI? To be a pastor?" George questioned.

"I started at UNI. I was going to be a lawyer. But my younger sister was diagnosed with cancer when she was in the 8th grade. I returned home to help care for her. She made a full recovery, and that was when I decided I wanted to serve the Lord. Tyler and I have kept in touch over the years. I was thrilled to find out he was with Pam. They're so perfect together."

"Yes, they are," Betty Sue quickly said before George could admit his true feelings.

"Paul."

George and Betty Sue turned and watched as Pam hurried to Paul and hugged him.

"I want you to meet my father, Charley. Daddy, this is Paul Ninnen."

"Nice to meet you, Paul."

"You too, Charley. I was telling Mr. and Mrs. Bailey how right your daughter and Tyler are for each other. They're both very special people."

Charley noticed that both George and Betty Sue were glaring at him, but managed to say, "They seem happy together."

"There are Bill and Brit," Tyler said, spying the couple who had walked in.

"Oh, great. The McEntires are here."

"I'm here too," a petite, dark-haired woman said as she hurried in behind the McEntires.

"This is my best friend, Jessie. She's my matron of honor."

"Hey, guys, hope we're not late."

"And this is Mitch Hines and Marley Williams. They're the other couple standing up with us."

"Nice to meet you all," Pastor Ninnen said. "It looks like we're all here. We might as well begin."

Trisha carried her briefcase into the office building and down the hallway to her new office, deciding she might as well drop off the things she would need for work while she was there.

After showing her around the rest of the building, Kat had returned to her office to finish up some work. And Trisha had decided there was no time like the present to start making her new space feel like home.

She stood by her desk, amazed she was starting off with an office bigger than the one she'd left in California. She walked over to the row of windows facing south and smiled as she noticed the stalks of corn waving in the warm, August evening breeze.

"This is so much better than the skyline of LA."

She glanced at the solid wooden desk complete with a new Mac computer, wireless keyboard and wireless printer and set her briefcase down on the floor under the desk. Then she opened her purse and pulled out one of her photos of her sweet Sophie, which she placed in the top drawer, not ready to answer questions that were sure to come if anyone saw it sitting on her desk.

She sat down in her leather chair behind her desk and sighed, noticing how comfortable it was.

Then she looked across at the twin leather chairs and down the long wooden conference table that matched her desk, thinking about the weekly communications meetings Kat said they would hold in her office.

Not having anything else to unpack, Trisha leaned back in the chair and shut her eyes, thankful to have a new job and thankful to be back home in Iowa.

"Okay, I'm ready to go. How about we get something to eat before we head out to the farm? I don't know about you, but I don't feel like cooking tonight."

"I don't either," Trisha agreed as she grabbed her purse and stood up.

"Great, there's a—oh, wait a second," Kat said, answering her phone on the second ring.

Trisha listened as Kat's mood changed from relaxed and happy to upset and angry.

"Ugh." Kat shook her head as she hung up the phone.

"What's wrong?"

Kat started pacing. "Some of the job ads we sent to the local paper got lost and need to be replaced. They are short-staffed and don't have anyone who can recreate them. The deadline to make this next week's paper is in two hours. I don't have any experience with their program. I don't know what the hell I'm going to do."

"Let me do it. I make ads all the time. You tell me what you want it to look like and say, and I can create it."

"Really?"

"Yes."

"Let's go to my office."

ꕥ

Charley felt like an outsider as they sat in a back room at a restaurant down the road from the chapel, eating the rehearsal supper.

Pam and Tyler were laughing and joking with the Pastor, the McEntires, Jessie, Mitch and Marley. Danni was enjoying the attention she was getting from Tyler's group of friends and was laughing and joking around with all of them.

And George and Betty Sue were sitting at the opposite end of the table, staring at him as if they were plotting something.

"Daddy, did you enjoy supper?" Pam asked as she broke from the group and walked over to him.

"I did, honey. It was delicious. Do you mind if I go on back to the hotel now?"

"No, that's fine. Let me walk you out."

Charley offered his goodbyes before he and Pam walked out of the restaurant to his truck.

"Thanks for coming, Daddy. I know it wasn't easy for you to be in the same place with Mr. and Mrs. Bailey."

"Don't worry about me. This is a very special time for you, honey. I wouldn't want to be anywhere else."

Pam hugged her father tightly.

"When will your friend get here?"

"I'm not sure. I'm going to call her when I get back to the hotel. I sure wish your mom could be here, Pam."

"Me too, Daddy. Me too."

Charley kissed his daughter on the forehead, then climbed into his pickup and watched to make sure she got back into the restaurant.

Then he started his truck and drove five miles back to the small hotel where he was staying.

After checking in, he carried his duffel bag up the stairs to the second floor and walked into his room, his mind instantly on Trisha Jenkins when he noticed the two queen beds.

He sat down in the chair beside the bed and pulled his phone out of his pocket, then dialed her number.

"Hello?"

"Trisha, it's Charley. Are you in Iowa?"

"Yes. I arrived a few hours ago. I decided to stop at my new job to get a tour, and they need me to help them with an ad. We have to make the deadline. I'd love to talk to you, but I need to work on this."

"Oh, okay. I was wondering if you're still planning on coming to the wedding tomorrow?"

"Yes, I am. I can't wait to see you. I got your text, and I'm pretty sure I can find the chapel."

"Great. I can't wait to see you either, Trisha. I'll let you get back to work."

"Thanks, Charley. Sorry about this. I'm really excited to see you tomorrow. I'm a little nervous to meet your daughter, though."

"She's gonna love you, Trisha."

"Hope so. Bye, Charley. I'll see you tomorrow."

Charley hung up the phone, leaned back in his chair and shut his eyes, able to see Trisha clearly in his mind.

"What a beautiful farm," Trisha said as she and Kat stood in Kat's yard. "Is this where you grew up?"

Kat nodded. "I didn't want to leave. My folks were counting down the days until I graduated with the idea we'd all move out east and I'd go to college there. But I love it here and I wanted to stay."

"I can see why."

"Can I help you carry anything?"

Trisha shook her head. "I don't have that much."

Kat walked ahead and unlocked the door, then waited as Trisha carried her two suitcases into the enclosed porch.

Trisha kicked her tennis shoes off on the welcome mat next to Kat's dress shoes, then followed her friend into the kitchen.

"I updated it a few years ago," Kat said as Trisha admired the stainless steel appliances. "Victor enjoys cooking, so he wanted the very best."

Trisha joked, "Heck, I might even be inspired to cook."

Kat smiled and continued into her living room with Trisha following.

"This is a pretty small house. Here's the hallway. To the left is my bedroom, and to the right is the bedroom you can use. We will only have one bathroom."

"That's fine. Thanks again for letting me stay here. I'll try to find someplace as soon as possible."

"No rush. It's been pretty lonely around here with Victor gone."

Trisha noticed the sad look on Kat's face and wanted to ask questions but held back as they both walked into the spare bedroom.

"I only have a single bed in here. I hope that's okay."

"It's fine, Kat. Perfect."

"I got you some space in the closet, and that entire dresser is cleaned out," Kat continued. "And off the back porch is the laundry room."

"It's all perfect. Thanks again for letting me stay here, Kat."

"My pleasure. Why don't you go ahead and get unpacked? I'm going to put on my pajamas and get a glass of wine. Would you like anything?"

"Some hot tea would be great."

"Okay. Holler if you need more hangers."

Trisha opened her large suitcase and pulled out the strapless blue dress she'd chosen to wear to Charley's daughter's wedding. She knew it hugged her curves and that she looked good in it. She smiled as she thought about seeing his reaction to her wearing it.

"One more day, Charley."

Deciding to leave her bathroom items together in her other suitcase, she quickly hung up the rest of her dress pants and shirts and placed her shoes in the closet. Then she organized her underwear, bras, socks, shorts, T-shirts and pajamas in the dresser.

"Home sweet home," Trisha said as she zipped up her now-empty suitcase and pushed it under her bed.

Then she walked into the living room and sat down beside Kat, who was sipping on a glass of red wine.

"Your tea's very hot," Kat warned. "Would you like some water or pop while you wait for it to cool down?"

Trisha shook her head. "I'm good. Thanks for buying supper. That restaurant was really good."

"It was the least I could do after you helped me with those ads. You were truly a lifesaver tonight, Trisha. Rick's going to be thrilled."

Trisha smiled, but she couldn't help but wonder about Kat's relationship with their boss. Not wanting to pry, she instead asked, "So, how's your week been?"

"Okay." Kat took another sip. "It's been a little rough. It's always hard coming back from those conventions. The work continues to pile up while you're gone. Is your family thrilled you're moving back? Or haven't you told them?"

Trisha shook her head. "I haven't told them. I haven't talked to my brother yet either. It was such a crazy week."

"I bet it was. I'm really sorry about your job, Trisha. But we are thrilled you're joining our company. I'll be going in to the office tomorrow. I usually go in on Saturday morning unless I have something else going on. It's a good time to get things done without the phone ringing. I hate to leave you home alone, though. You're welcome to come with me."

"Actually, I have a wedding to attend tomorrow."

"Wow, really? A relative?"

"Not exactly. The wedding's in Cedar Falls. Do you remember those guys we talked to last Saturday night in the bar?"

Kat's face paled a little as she nodded.

"Well, I kinda hooked up with that guy, Charley. Turns out he's from Iowa. His daughter's getting married this weekend, and he invited me to the wedding. I guess it's pretty low-key."

"Wow. You two must have really hit it off."

"We did. I'm a little nervous about meeting his daughter for the first time at her wedding. Plus, we hardly know each other. But, I really want to see him. And she told him to invite me. So, we'll see what happens."

Kat quickly drank the rest of her wine, then filled up her glass and gulped down another.

"Is something wrong?"

Kat's eyes welled up as she blurted, "I slept with Alex. Charley's friend. We're both married, Trisha. I was such an idiot."

Trisha was speechless as Kat got up and started pacing around the living room.

"It's been bothering me all week. I knew I shouldn't have done it. I knew it was wrong. But we were drinking. And he was hitting on me. And it's been too long, Trisha. I know something's going on with Victor. I'm afraid he's cheating on me. And then Chase and I almost kissed before I left for the convention. And things have been so…I don't know…heated when we're together. But I don't want to hurt Chase. He's still in love with me, and I don't want to take advantage of that. I didn't expect to meet anyone. But Alex was so handsome and charming. And he was a stranger, and there were no strings attached. But I can't get him out of my mind. I don't even know his last name. We didn't talk about being married. I don't know if he has kids. I feel so ashamed."

"It's okay, Kat. You're not responsible for his actions."

"But I am responsible for my own." Kat plopped back down on the couch beside Trisha. "I'm sorry to lay all of this on you. It's been eating away at me all week, and I haven't had anyone to talk to about it. I wasn't going to burden you with it either, but when you mentioned Charley, I lost it."

"It's okay, Kat. I'm not judging you. I'm the last person in the world who would judge you."

"Thanks," Kat said as she filled her glass again.

"Victor should be more open with you about what's going on. Do you want me to ask Charley how you can contact Alex?"

"No." Kat shook her head. "He was so kind to me, but I can't ever see him again."

"Where the hell are you, Jessica?" George yelled his message into his cell phone as he sat alone in the hotel room. "You were supposed to be at your brother's rehearsal tonight. I stood up for you. You'd better get your little butt here tomorrow in time for family photos, or I'm kicking you out of the pool house!"

George threw his phone onto one of the queen-sized beds, and then he stomped over to his suitcase and pulled out the silver flask filled with whiskey. It burned as it went down his throat, but the shaking in his hands subsided. He took another drink, then tightened the lid and hid it under his swimming trunks.

"Grandpa, we're going swimming," Danni said as she and Betty Sue hurried into the room. "Come with us."

"Grandpa doesn't feel like swimming, but I'll come down and watch you," George promised, smiling at Sue as she picked up her swimming suit from the bed.

As Danni walked into the bathroom to change, George suggested softly, "Why don't you get dressed out here, honey? I'd love to see the show."

"Smells like you've already been with your real true love," Betty Sue snipped before carrying her suit into the bathroom and slamming the door.

"Sorry, Sue," George muttered under his breath.

He sat down in the chair and waited until they had left for the pool before finding his keys and taking off. Fifteen minutes later, he returned with three bottles of whiskey. He hid one in the bathroom behind the trashcan and one in the nightstand drawer.

The last one he opened and tipped back, feeling his throat burning as the liquid worked its way down.

After consuming more than half the bottle, George poured the rest in his flask, then he took off out of the room, stumbling a little as he started down the hallway.

"It's you, you son of a bitch!" George cried when he ran into Charley by the ice machine.

"Get out of my way, George," Charley ordered, able to smell the stench of alcohol more than a few feet away from him.

"Make me," George dared as he took another step closer and blocked Charley into the small area where the ice machine and snack machine were housed.

"George, this ain't high school, and I ain't gonna fight with you. You don't have your posse to back you up, either. Move out of my way."

"Make me," George repeated.

"Dad?"

George spun around at the sound of Tyler's voice and staggered to the right, coming to a rest against the wall.

"Excuse me," Charley muttered as he hurried past both of them.

"Are you drunk?" Tyler asked, the tips of his ears turning red.

"I just had a little. Damn that Charley Walker. He was tryin'…tryin' to hit me!"

"I heard it all, Dad," Tyler growled. "If you can't quit drinking for one night, then I don't want you at my wedding at all!"

"Tyler?" Pam asked as she emerged out of the stairwell. "What's going on?"

"Nothing, honey. Let's get you to your room."

George leaned against the wall and watched as they walked by.

He was going to go on to the pool to see Danni swimming, but his stomach started churning. He hurried as fast as he could make his way down the hall, then ran in and shut the bathroom door, making it to the toilet as he started vomiting.

The red blood in the toilet scared him, just as it had the first time he'd seen it.

"Doc says there's nothing to do now," George reminded himself, feeling tears coming to his eyes. "Sue needs to know. But how can I tell her I'm dying?"

Deciding he'd had enough for one day, George flushed the toilet. Then he stumbled back to the bed and was asleep the moment he lay down.

"Are you sure you're okay, Daddy?" Pam asked as she sat down on the edge of the bed in their hotel room.

"I'm fine. It was just George being George," Charley insisted, not wanting to ruin his daughter's special weekend. "Where are your bags?"

"I got ready for the rehearsal in Tyler's room. He's bringing them down. Then I won't see him again until pictures tomorrow. I wish we could wait until the ceremony to see each other, but this is how the photographer wanted to do it."

"I thought the rehearsal went well. Is Jessie staying overnight too?" Charley asked, thinking about Pam's best friend since grade school.

"Yes. Her sister has an apartment. She's going to school here. Jessie's going to stay there tonight."

There was a knock on the door, and Pam opened it, letting Tyler in. He handed her the dress, then carried her two suitcases over and set them down by the window.

"Thanks, honey." Pam hugged him. "We'll be married by this time tomorrow."

Tyler smiled and kissed her on the forehead. "I can't wait. I'll see you tomorrow, darling."

Pam kissed him on the lips and hugged him again, then walked him to the door, kissing him again before shutting it and turning back to her father. "Did you talk to your friend?"

"Briefly. She's planning on coming to the wedding, but I didn't get to ask her when she thought she'd get here. She stopped by her new job, and they already put her to work."

Fighting off a yawn, Pam said, "She must be good at what she does."

"Why don't we call it a night, honey? We both have a big day tomorrow."

"Sounds good to me, Daddy."

ꟹ

"Hi, Mom. Looks like you two are having fun," Tyler said as he walked up to his mother, who sat at the edge of the pool dangling her feet in the water.

"Watch this, Uncle Tyler," Danni called before climbing out of the water and jumping back in, spraying both of them.

"Hey, I don't have my suit on," Tyler teased, laughing as he pulled his wet shirt away from his skin.

Danni giggled. "Have you seen Grandpa? I want to show him too."

Tyler thought about his father and shook his head, "I don't think he's coming down, Peanut. He looked, um, tired when I saw him."

"He'll come down. He said he would," Danni said before she took off swimming across the empty pool.

Betty Sue stood up. "Tired?"

"Drunk, okay?" Tyler whispered, following his mother as she walked to a table and started drying her feet with the white hotel towel. "He had Pam's dad cornered by the ice machine. He was trying to get Charley to hit him."

"Damn it. Can you keep an eye on Danni for a little bit? I want to talk to your father."

"Yeah, sure. Good luck."

ꟹ

Betty Sue pulled her cover-up over her dark blue, two-piece suit and hurried down the hallway and up the stairs, wishing again the old hotel had an elevator.

She stomped down the hallway to their room and let herself in, preparing to yell at George.

When she found him in the bed, passed out, she shook her head, the anger reaching a boiling point.

"Damn you, George Bailey. Your granddaughter was counting on you."

When he didn't stir, Betty Sue hurried over to her purse and pulled out the silver pill tin. She grabbed the small, white pill Dr. Hartman had prescribed to help with her nerves, then decided if one was good, two would be better. She swallowed them down dry, then tossed her tin back in her purse, fetched her clothes and headed to the bathroom.

She hung her damp suit up on the back of the door, then started dressing in the best lounging suit she'd been able to find on such short notice.

When she dropped her hairbrush on the floor, she bent down to pick it up and quickly noticed the stashed whiskey bottle.

"Just like home, damn you," Betty Sue complained as she picked it up and poured the contents down the sink.

She carried the empty bottle in by the bed and slammed it down on the nightstand, huffing when George didn't even flinch.

"Damn drunken stupor." Curious, she started opening the drawers around the room. She quickly found the second bottle and dumped it out as well.

"I don't want your granddaughter to find you like this. Like always, I have to be the strong one. I have to cover for you."

Betty Sue stomped to the desk in the corner and picked up the phone. She secured another room for Danni and herself and was gathering some of Danni's things when the room started spinning.

"Oh, shit," Betty Sue muttered as she sat down the edge of the bed and put her hand against her head. "I shouldn't have taken that extra pill. My head."

After a few moments, the dizziness subsided, but she felt weighted down and tired.

When there was a knock on the door, Betty Sue slowly made her way over and opened it.

"Here are the keys to your extra room," the hotel receptionist offered. "I got you down the hall in room 234."

"Could you be a doll and carry some things for me?" Betty Sue asked as she turned and walked back into the room, gathering up the clothes she'd collected. She handed them to the girl before she could complain, then started down the hallway to the new room and unlocked the door.

"Set them down over on that bed. Thanks," Betty Sue said as she pulled a twenty dollar bill out of her pocket and handed it to her.

"No problem, ma'am. Please call if you need anything else."

"There's one thing. My granddaughter and son are down at the pool. Could you tell them what room I'm in and tell Tyler to bring Danni up? It's time for her to go to bed."

"Sure. Good night ma'am."

Betty Sue shut the door, managing a smile, then slowly made her way to the chair, where she sat down and tried to control her breathing, hoping the spinning in her head that had started up again would go away before Danni got back.

Chapter 9

Charley was anxious as he paced around the hotel lobby. Although it was only 9:00 a.m., he felt like he'd been up for hours.

After falling asleep shortly after 10:00 p.m., he'd awoken just before midnight, his heart pounding from a nightmare he had in which Nancy had told him to make Pam leave with him and to not let her marry George Bailey's son.

Charley had managed to fall back into a fitful sleep, but had been tired when the alarm clock on Pam's phone had started ringing a little after seven.

Pam had jumped out of bed, excited and smiling, and Charley hadn't been able to ruin her happiness by telling her about his dream.

While he'd been in the shower, Pam's friend Jessie and the best man's wife, Brit, had arrived and started helping Pam prepare for her special day.

Charley had quickly dressed and escaped the room. Although he was happy his daughter had been giggling and glowing, he needed some time alone to think about his dream.

"I can't ruin her special day because of a dream," Charley said to himself as he started for the door, deciding pacing outside might keep him from running into any of the Bailey family members.

Once outside, he paced up and down the sidewalk, thinking about Nancy and the dream.

"Was she trying to tell me something? Should I act on this? Or did I just have that dream because of George's actions last night?"

Charley took a deep breath and let it out slowly, accepting the fact that he couldn't do anything to stop the wedding. No matter how he felt and no matter what he did, Pam was going to have Tyler Bailey's baby.

"I have to let them get married," Charley declared as he stopped pacing and plopped down on the bench near the side door of the hotel. Depressed by his decision, he leaned forward and buried his face in his hands.

"Good morning, Mr. Walker."

Charley glanced up and noticed that Tyler's best man, Bill, was standing in front of him.

"Good morning, Sheriff McEntire. Please, call me Charley. I didn't realize until last night Tyler was friends with you."

Bill shook his hand, then sat down beside him. "Tyler and I were in the same class in high school. We've been friends for years. It's a beautiful day for a wedding."

"It is a beautiful day," Charley agreed, finally noticing the bright blue sky and light, warm breeze.

"I know all of this has been a surprise for you, Charley. And I don't blame you for being a little upset at Tyler. But I want you to know Tyler's a good man. And he loves Pam very much."

Charley studied Bill's face, wanting to voice his doubts, but instead turned away.

"Tyler doesn't drink, and he isn't anything like his father," Bill continued. "In fact, he's embarrassed by his father and has been since junior high. He loves his family but isn't blind to their problems. He loves your daughter more than anything in this world and will do anything to make her happy. And you should have seen his face when he told me Pam was pregnant. He'll take good care of both Pam and their baby."

Charley remained silent, so Bill continued. "I can tell you're struggling with all of this, and I don't blame you. Tyler wishes things would have gone differently. And I think they both should've clued you in on what was going on sooner. But their love is real and it's strong. If I didn't believe in this marriage, I wouldn't be standing up with them."

Charley reached his hand over and shook Bill's hand, "Thanks. It's nice to hear such good things about my future son-in-law from a man of the law."

Trisha woke with a start and sat up, glancing around completely confused.

"Where the hell am…oh, Kat's. I'm in Iowa."

She swung around and slipped on her fuzzy house shoes, then padded down the hallway and peaked into Kat's room.

"Her bed's made. Is she gone already?"

Trisha continued through the living room and into the kitchen and noticed the note lying on the table next to a fluffy blue bath towel and a washrag.

"Good morning, Trisha. Sorry I had to leave so early, but I was having trouble sleeping. Help yourself to whatever you need. Have fun at the wedding. Call if you have any questions. Kat."

Trisha glanced at the clock on the microwave and stretched, then picked up the towels and headed for the bathroom.

Thirty minutes later, she was curling her long, blond hair into spiral curls.

"This is turning out great. Thank goodness," Trisha said as she glanced into the mirror and noticed her hair was doing exactly what she wanted it to do. She grabbed her hair spray and used it to keep everything in place. Then she brushed her teeth and put on her makeup.

"I'm going to be seeing you so soon, Charley."

She glanced into the mirror again and retouched her mascara and lipstick, and then she walked into the bedroom and carefully slipped into her blue dress.

Noticing the full-length mirror on the wall, Trisha walked over and looked herself up and down, a smile slowly spreading across her face.

"This is going to drive him wild." Trisha grinned as she noticed how the dress seemed to hug her womanly curves. "But it's still appropriate for this wedding."

After slipping her feet into her black pumps, she grabbed her purse and cell phone.

"Shoot, is it eleven already? I have to get going. It will take me almost two hours to get to Cedar Falls, and then I still have to find this chapel. I can't be late."

Trisha hurried through the house, only stopping long enough to lock the back door.

As she slowly walked to her car, careful not to turn her ankle on the gravel driveway, Trisha noticed a fancy blue pickup as it pulled in and drove past her, the man in the driver's seat looking curiously at her.

Trisha waved before she climbed into her car. She figured it was Chase Locke, remembering that Kat had said he'd be popping in and out.

Then she started the car and took off, counting down the minutes until she could see Charley.

ෛ

"You look like shit," Betty Sue whispered angrily in her husband's ear as they sat in the chapel, watching the photographer take photos of Tyler and Pam. "That's what you get for drinking so much."

George pointed a shaking finger at her. "I guess that's why you dumped it all out."

"Your son doesn't want you drunk at his wedding. I don't think that's too much to ask."

"You didn't have to take our granddaughter and go to another room. Don't you think that was a little crazy?"

"I'm not crazy," Betty Sue insisted, her voice growing loud enough Pam's friend, Jessie, turned around.

"Keep your voice down, Sue."

"Danni was counting on you last night," Betty Sue informed him in a hushed voice. "She wanted to show you some tricks in the pool. It broke her heart you didn't come down and watch. She gets her heart broken enough from her mother; she needs to be able to depend on us, George. I thought you agreed with me on that."

"I do." George leaned closer and put his arm around her bare shoulders. "I'm sorry. I didn't mean to let either one of you down."

Betty felt her heart softening as she gazed into his intense blue eyes, and she slowly nodded. "I'm sorry too."

"I can't believe Jessica didn't show up last night."

As if on cue, Jessica picked that moment to sashay into the church, dressed in a black leather mini-dress that left little to the imagination. She clung to the arm of a man dressed in jeans and a black T-shirt, who was puffing on a cigarette.

"Jessica?" George questioned, latching on her arm and leading her into the lobby before anyone else noticed her. "What the hell are you wearing, and who the hell is this?"

"This is my boyfriend, Dad. His name's Glen. And he thinks I look hot in this dress."

"You weren't supposed to bring anyone to the wedding, Jessica," Betty Sue reprimanded as she charged toward them, looking the stranger up and down as she snatched the cigarette out of his mouth. "And that's not proper attire to wear in a church."

"Chill, Mom. I'm here. That's what you wanted. I want Glen in the family photo."

"Absolutely not. There's no way."

Jessica grinned as she leaned into Glen and wrapped her arm around his waist. "But he's my lover, Mom."

"Oh, you are such a disappointment!" Betty Sue cried out, forgetting where she was.

Jessica laughed. "Yep, I know."

"What's going on out here?" Tyler stepped into the lobby and shut the heavy wooden doors to the sanctuary behind him. "We can hear you."

"I brought my boyfriend, Ty. Mom's not happy about it." Jessica hugged him. "I'm so happy for you big brother."

"No drama today. Please." Tyler reminded them.

"Ty, I want a photo with Glen. Is that okay?"

Tyler studied the greasy-haired man who was latched on to his sister, and he wanted to say so many things to him. But instead, he took a deep breath. "Go ahead and have a picture or two together, but remember we're in a church. I would appreciate it if he's not in the family photos though, okay Jess?"

Jessica hugged him. "Sure. Thanks Ty."

"It's our turn. Please, let's get through this. Okay?"

After everyone nodded, Tyler opened the doors and they started down the aisle.

ல

"Well, shoot." Trisha pulled into the gas station in a small town, completely lost. "I thought I knew my way to Cedar Falls. I must have taken a wrong turn."

She pulled her phone out of her purse and checked the time, moaning when she noticed it was almost one.

"There's no way I'm going to make it to the wedding. Oh, shoot. I'm so sorry, Charley."

Knowing sitting in the parking lot and feeling sorry for herself wasn't going to do her one bit of good, Trisha pulled up the map app on her phone. She started working her way through the map until she realized what she'd done.

"I should've turned left. Darn it, they changed that," Trisha mumbled, thinking back. "I've driven more than twenty miles the wrong way."

Trisha dropped her phone back into her purse, then merged onto the busy two-lane highway and pushed down on the pedal, gaining speed until she was just pushing the limit.

ல

"Daddy, where's your friend?"

Charley scanned the church parking lot through the window and shrugged. "She must have been delayed. It's okay, though, honey. I'm anxious to see her again, but this is your time. And I don't want any distractions."

Pam smiled as she looked in the mirror one last time, her dark eyes meeting his gaze in the glass. "I look like mom's wedding picture."

"Yes, you do." Charley walked up behind her. "You're beautiful, Pam. I'm very proud to be your daddy."

Pam turned and hugged him.

"Okay you guys, it's time," Jessie announced as she walked up to them, followed closely by Danni and Marley. "Ready to get married, Pammy?"

"I'm ready."

Charley followed the girls into the church lobby at the end of the aisle and listened as the music changed.

"Okay, Danni, your turn." Jessie smiled at her. "Are you ready?"

Danni nodded and grinned at Pam, then took off down the aisle, dropping red rose petals as she went along.

"I love you," Jessie said as she smiled at Pam, then turned to watch Marley following Danni down the aisle.

"I love you too," Pam agreed, smiling at her best friend before she started her walk down the aisle.

"Don't forget to breathe, honey. And remember that I'll love you forever," Charley said as he lined up beside Pam and she lovingly wrapped her hand around his arm.

As the music once again changed, Charley started walking his daughter down the short aisle. He purposely ignored Tyler's family, who were sitting on the right side, and instead smiled at some of Tyler and Pam's co-workers.

Once they reached the end of the aisle, Charley stood in between Pam and Tyler, like Pastor Ninnen had instructed him to do.

Charley flashed back to his own wedding as he stood before the pastor, thinking how beautiful Nancy had looked in her long, white gown.

He noticed the happiness in his daughter's big brown eyes and smiled, suddenly feeling as if everything was going to be all right for her and Tyler.

Hearing his cue, Charley kissed Pam on the cheek, then placed her hand in Tyler's hand before walking over and sitting by himself in the front pew.

"Finally," Trisha sighed as she reached the outskirts of Cedar Falls. She carefully read the signs and before long, had turned left and was heading out of the west side of town.

"There's the chapel," Trisha noted as she drove by a beautiful small church on the side of the road. "The community center should be down the road."

Noticing a small white building with a few cars parked around it, Trisha flipped on her signal and turned to the right, and then she slowly coasted through the lot and parked in the farthest spot.

Her phone started ringing as soon as she shut off her car.

"Hello?"

"Hey, Trisha. Is everything okay?"

"I got lost. I'm so sorry. But I'm here now. At the community center. I'm in the parking lot."

"I'll come out and meet you. I've missed you so much."

"Okay, I'm in a blue Impala, and I'm parked at the west end of the lot."

Trisha hung up her phone and put it in her purse, tucking it under the passenger's seat. Then she peeked into the rearview mirror, touching up her hair before she pulled the keys out of the ignition and got out of the car.

She felt the breath sucked out of her when she saw Charley, who was dressed in a fancy suit jacket and black jeans, hurrying toward her.

"Wow." Charley slowly looked her up and down. "You look amazing."

"Funny, I was thinking the same thing about you." Trisha rushed to him and hugged him tightly. "Oh, I have missed you so much."

Charley couldn't help himself as he leaned in and pressed his lips against her ruby red ones.

Trisha felt the butterflies stirring to life as she kissed him back and pulled him tight, feeling his excitement through his formfitting jeans.

"I want to take you back to the hotel right now," Charley whispered in her ear, making her shiver with anticipation.

"Soon, I promise you. We'll do that soon," Trisha said as she reluctantly took a step back and wiped the red lipstick off his lips. "But your daughter wouldn't be too happy if you left her reception."

"No, that's true. But it's already pretty much over. They aren't having a dance or anything. Just cake. Most of the guests have already left. Are you ready to go in and meet her?"

Trisha nodded, feeling nervous. "Can you keep my keys in your pocket?"

The gleam sparkled in Charley's eyes as he looked her up and down again and whispered, "I see you don't have a pocket."

Trisha smiled, then took ahold of his hand as they started for the door.

"Is your dad's friend here?" Tyler asked as he and Pam waved goodbye to their last guest.

"That's what he said when he went outside. I'm anxious to meet her."

"Why don't we go out by the door? That way, your dad won't have to introduce her to us in front of my parents."

"Good idea."

They walked hand and hand toward the door and met up with Charley and Trisha as they entered.

Trisha and Tyler took one look at each other and both turned pale.

"What is it?" Pam asked, instantly noticing when Tyler's body grew tense.

"Oh my gosh. Trisha?"

"Tyler?" Trisha felt the blood draining from her cheeks. She looked at Pam, then at Charley. "Is that your daughter?"

"Yes." Charley turned to Tyler. "What the hell's going on here?"

"Trisha's my sister. But…but I haven't seen her in almost thirteen years."

"Your sister's dating my daddy?" Pam asked, shocked.

Trisha felt Charley's hand pulling out of hers, and turned to him. "I had no idea my brother was marrying your daughter. I haven't talked to anyone in my family since I graduated from college."

"What's going on out here…oh my gosh, Trisha?" Betty Sue said as she barged into their conversation. "You came for your brother's wedding? Oh, this is so wonderful. Oh, my beautiful daughter."

Trisha studied her mother and realized they looked more like sisters than mother and daughter.

"You didn't tell me your sister was coming," Betty Sue scolded as she rushed to Trisha and gathered her in her arms. "Oh, I've missed you so much Trisha."

"I didn't know she was," Tyler said. "She's Charley's guest."

"Charley's guest?" Betty Sue asked, staring him down as she kept her arm around her daughter. "What kind of game are you playing now, Walker?"

"I had no idea Trisha was your daughter," Charley said, his mind spinning.

"Trisha?"

Trisha's head whipped around at the booming sound of her father's voice. Her jaw dropped slightly when she noticed how pale his skin was and how his once-vibrant blue eyes were sunk slightly into his skull.

She longed to ask if he was sick, but the anger and hurt from how her parents had treated her when she left for college started bubbling through her, and she quickly pulled away from her mom's grip and hurried back to Charley's side. "I'm here for Charley. I'm sorry, Tyler, I was going to call you back."

"Well, no need now, really. I was going to invite you to my wedding. But you missed it."

"Daddy? What's going on?" Pam asked, feeling lightheaded as she took a step toward her father.

"Baby, are you okay?" Charley asked, noticing how pale she'd gotten.

"Pammy?" Tyler called, also noticing. "You need to sit down, honey."

"Take me back to the hotel." Pam latched on to Tyler's arm, and he helped her out of the building.

"What the hell is she doing here?" Jessica boomed, startling them all as she marched up to Trisha and got only inches away from her face. "You're not welcome here."

"Jessica, stop it," Betty Sue demanded, looking at George. "Stop her."

"Jessica?" Trisha asked, putting her hand to her heart as she examined her little sister. "Oh my gosh, what happened to you?"

"I grew up." Jessica put her hands on her hips and took another step closer. "Dad disowned you. Get the hell out of our lives. We don't need you!"

"Oh my gosh," Betty Sue cried as Jessica punched Trisha directly in the nose and blood started running down the front of Trisha's beautiful, blue dress.

Jessica looked at the blood, then ran out of the building, followed closely by her boyfriend.

"Trish." Charley rushed to her side and gingerly placed his white handkerchief against her nose. "Come with me."

"Get your hands off my daughter!" George yelled as he ran to Charley and grabbed his arm.

"Let go of me, George," Charley warned, glaring at him. "She needs help."

"She's my daughter; I'll take care of her." George tightened his grip on Charley's arm.

"You made it perfectly clear I wasn't your daughter anymore when I refused to come back from California," Trisha reminded him as she fought through the pain and blood. "You have no claim to me now."

"Grandpa?"

All eyes turned to Danni, who stood beside George, pulling on his fancy suit jacket. "Come on, Grandpa. Let's go."

"Grandpa?" Trisha questioned as she looked at Danni and felt the guilt of missing the little girl's entire life weighing down on her.

"Come on." Charley pulled his arm free from George and put it around Trisha. "Let's find some ice."

"Sue?" George questioned as he turned toward her.

"Let's go back to the hotel, Danni. I bet Grandpa will swim with you this afternoon."

"Sue?" George repeated, glaring at Charley as he and Trisha walked down the hallway.

"Let's go swimming with our granddaughter," Sue ordered, as she started toward the door.

"I'm so sorry, Charley. I didn't know," Trisha declared as they sat in the kitchen of the community center.

Even though Charley had quickly gotten her some ice, Trisha's nose throbbed, and her head felt as if it were going to explode.

"I don't know how this could happen." Charley shook his head. "How could we not know?"

"Well, I haven't talked to anyone in family since I graduated from college. My parents didn't want me to stay in California, and I didn't want to come back to Iowa. Up until that point, they'd been financially supporting me, but as soon as they found that out, they took the money away. I know they thought I'd come crawling home, but I found a way to survive."

"They left you to fend for yourself?"

Trisha nodded.

"But they have plenty of money."

"And they use it to control everyone around them."

Charley quickly thought about his bank loan papers. "Yeah, I know all about that."

"What do you mean?"

"My farm loan is through your father's bank. He's made me fill out financial papers every year to prove I can afford to pay back the loan. He doesn't make my friend Darrell do that. But he doesn't like me, so every year, I have to fill out those damned papers. Except this year, he's going to be thrilled when he gets them back."

"Why's that?"

Charley took a deep breath. "Because he'll probably be able to take away my ground. I lost the rest of my custom farm work this year. Old farmers are dying and leaving their land to their kids and grandkids. They're so far removed from the land that they just want the money. They sell the ground to one of the large farmers who can afford to pay top dollar for the ground, and us little farmers are knocked off one by one. I'm afraid this might be my year to be picked off."

"That's why you're becoming an auctioneer."

"I needed a career to fall back on."

"I'm sorry my father's treating you that way. And I'm sorry for this mess. I really had no idea that—"

"I know you didn't," Charley interrupted, believing her. "It's okay, Trisha. I know you didn't plan this."

Trisha felt tears coming to her eyes as she nodded, relieved.

"Do you think we should go to the emergency room? She might have broken it," Charley said, glancing at her nose.

"I don't have any insurance. I know it was foolish, but I was hoping to stay healthy until my new insurance kicks in."

"Your sister should pay for it."

"I just want to get out of here," Trisha said as she stood.

"Why don't we find somewhere to stay tonight, Trisha? I know where everyone else is staying, so we can avoid them." Charley took ahold of her hand. "I'm sorry your sister hurt you. Hell, I'm sorry all of them hurt you."

"Whose child is Danni?" Trisha asked as they started for her car.

"Jessica's."

"I had no idea I was an aunt."

"Pam and Tyler are going to have a baby too. That's the reason for this rushed wedding."

"You're gonna be a grandpa?"

"Yes. I just found out this week. About the wedding and the baby. Truth is, they started dating last summer, and I told Pam she couldn't date your brother because I didn't want her to be hurt by your family."

"I don't blame you for that. Do you need to go and check on your daughter? I don't mind if you want to."

"Well, I would like to tell her goodbye. They were planning on leaving for Minneapolis. I don't know if they have left yet or not. But I don't want to run into your folks."

"Call her."

Charley pulled his cell phone out of his pocket. He was handing her car keys to her when his phone started ringing.

"Daddy?"

"Pam. Are you okay, honey?"

"Yeah, I'm fine. Tyler and I are almost ready to leave. I'd like to see you before I go."

"Why don't I meet you in the hotel parking lot?" Charley said. "I don't want to run into Tyler's family."

"Okay. We'll wait in the car."

Charley hung up his phone and turned back to Trisha.

"Go ahead."

"I would like to stay with you tonight." Charley reached for her hand. "Nothing's changed for me, Trisha. I still care about you."

"I still care about you too," Trisha agreed, thankful to hear those words. "Why don't I find us a place to stay?"

"Baby, you're covered in blood."

"I'll clean up and change before I leave," Trisha said. "I drove by a nice hotel down this road back toward Cedar Falls."

"I remember it."

"I'll get us a room. Call me when you get back."

"I won't be long. Call my cell if you need anything."

Trisha watched as he walked to his truck and climbed in, then waved as he pulled out of the driveway.

"What a mess," she moaned as she reached into her car and picked up her suitcase, then walked back into the community center.

The center's staff was busy cleaning up the reception area and Trisha felt badly when she noticed an older lady was down on her hands and knees cleaning up the floor where Trisha's nose had bled the most.

Embarrassed, Trisha ducked into the one-stall bathroom and locked the door.

She looked down at her once-beautiful dress and sighed as she slipped out of it and let it drop to the floor.

"Won't be able to wear that again."

As she slipped out of the thigh-high black panty hose, she thought about how excited she'd been just a few hours earlier when she'd thought about Charley taking those off her.

"I can't believe his daughter married my brother. I can't believe I saw my family. What a big, freaking mess."

Doubting their evening would be full of romance, Trisha settled for a pair of jean shorts and a dark blue T-shirt.

She thought about throwing the stained dress away, but instead tossed it over her arm and carried her suitcase back through the center and out to the car, not wanting to talk to anyone.

"I can't believe my sister's back in Iowa," Jessica grumbled before taking a long swig on the whiskey bottle in her hand. "That bitch."

"I can't believe you didn't tell me you had a sister," Glen said.

"Why, do you want her?" Jessica demanded as she turned and glared at him.

"She's hot, but you're all the woman I can handle, Jessica. You really nailed her one."

Jessica laughed as she took another drink. "That felt so good. I've been wanting to do that for years."

"Why? What happened between the two of you?"

"She left. As soon as she graduated from high school, she was gone. And she left me and Ty home alone with two pissed-off parents. Our lives were hell after she left. But she didn't care. She didn't come to my wedding, and she never called to ask how I was. Hell, she didn't even know about my kids."

"Did she come back for your brother's wedding?"

Jessica shrugged. "Hell if I know. Doubt she's staying though. And that's a good thing. But just in case she was thinking about it, I wanted her to know she's not welcome here anymore."

"Oh, I think she got that message."

Jessica slid across the front seat of the Cadillac she'd borrowed from her dad's collection and placed her hand on Glen's knee. Then offered him a drink, laughing when he swerved, causing an oncoming car to honk.

"Pull over up here," Jessica demanded as she reached over and unfastened his pants.

"Jess, stop."

Jessica laughed and took another drink as he pulled off on a gravel road and drove until they reached a field driveway.

"I want you so bad," Jessica informed him as she pushed the tight top of her dress down and climbed on his lap. "Let's do it in Dad's car."

❧

"I can't believe we're swimming while our daughter is with that man," George said only loud enough for Betty Sue to hear as Danni splashed around the pool.

"I have to think about all of this. We have to play this the right way."

"Oh, like we played the Tyler-Pam situation. She married our son, Sue."

"They're having a baby, George. It was too late to stop the marriage but…oh no."

"What?"

"What if Trisha gets pregnant with Charley's baby?"

"I'll kill him." George vowed, slapping the water with his fist.

"What Grandpa?" Danni asked as she swam back to them.

George offered his granddaughter a smile. "Just making waves, honey. Grandpa's getting tired. Is it okay if I watch you from that chair over there?"

"That's fine, Grandpa. Thanks for coming in with me this time. I'm so glad we get to stay another night."

George got out and dried off, then sat down on the chair and watched his wife as she swam back and forth.

He noticed some other men were checking her out, and he puffed with pride. His wife was still one of the most beautiful women he'd ever seen.

She was 46, but had aged so beautifully she looked as if she were still in her 30s. It always turned him on when men checked out his wife. He knew he'd been her one and only lover, and that made him stir with delight.

He thought back to high school and once again cursed himself for not noticing her beauty when she'd started hanging around him. Of course, she'd been a sophomore when he had been a senior. But he knew the real reason he'd never noticed her was because he'd only had eyes for one girl in high school. And she'd been Betty Sue's one-time best friend. And it had made him angrier than he'd ever been before when that girl had turned down every advance he'd ever made to her.

Charley pulled into the parking lot at the hotel and coasted up beside Tyler's fancy car. He killed the engine and got out, then walked around to Pam's side and opened the door.

"I'm glad you came." Pam got out and hugged him. "I'm going to miss you, Daddy. And I'm so sorry about Trisha."

"Well, that definitely was a surprise."

"Do you really believe she didn't know?"

"I do, honey. But we can talk more about all of this when you get home. You'd better get going so you can get to Minneapolis before it gets too late. Have a great time. And call me if you need anything, okay?"

"I will. I love you, Daddy."

"I love you too, Pammy. Have fun."

Pam hugged him again, then climbed back into the car.

Charley waved as they drove out of the parking lot, then he climbed back in his pickup and hurried to the hotel where Trisha waited.

Noticing her car in the lot, he parked beside it, fetched his duffel bag and started in, dialing her on his phone on the way.

"Room 134," Trisha said after the second ring.

"I'll be right in."

He followed the signs and smiled when she opened the door for him.

"How's your nose?" Charley asked, noticing she was still icing it.

"Hurts like hell. But I took some Tylenol. It should be better soon."

"Looks like you might have a pair of black eyes."

"Great look for my first official day at my new job, huh?"

"Oh, shoot. I forgot about that." Charley set his duffel down on the table in the corner of the room. He smiled when he noticed the giant, king-sized bed.

Trisha followed his gaze and smiled back, "This wasn't how I had planned our day would go, but I'm glad we're staying together tonight. I've missed you."

"I've missed you too." Charley carefully took her in his arms and hugged her. "I don't want to hurt your nose."

"I'll let you know." Trisha gingerly kissed him. Then she set her bag of ice on the table and took his hand, leading him to the edge of the bed.

Charley smiled as she took off his suit jacket and carried it over to the closet, carefully hanging it up.

"As much as I want you right now, Trisha, I think we need to talk about this. Don't you?"

"Yes, I suppose we do," Trisha reluctantly agreed as she picked up the ice pack, then sat down on the edge of the bed.

Charley pulled the chair from the table over by the bed and sat down facing Trisha. "How'd this happen?"

"How'd what happen?"

"This mess? How could we not know your brother was marrying my daughter?"

"It's my fault, really. I don't talk to my family anymore. You know how they are. I wanted to get away from my dad's drinking and all the whispers behind our family's back. When I was offered a chance to play college basketball in California, I took it. My parents weren't happy."

"But you went anyway?"

"Yes. It was a great opportunity. I had a complete scholarship. And I foolishly thought they'd come around. I thought they'd come out to see me play or see where I went to school. But they never did, Charley. Not once. With my schedule, I couldn't come back home for Christmas. I invited the entire family to come to Hawaii at Christmastime during my freshman year. We were playing in a big tournament, and I really believed they'd come. But they didn't. Over time, I started feeling as if California really was my home. My teammates and their families and my coach started including me in their holiday celebrations. And, over time, it started hurting less that my family suddenly didn't need me in their lives. Sure, I talked to Tyler several times during that first year. My folks thought I'd come home for summer break, and I'm sure they thought they'd talk me in to staying home. But I didn't make that mistake, Charley. I stayed in California. I took summer classes and worked with summer basketball camps."

"I'm so sorry they treated you that way."

Trisha shrugged. "It hurt me a lot. But I was surrounded by new friends who felt like family. The final nail in the coffin was when I decided not to come back home after graduation. They'd made me promise I would when I first went out to California. And at the time I'd made that promise, I'd planned to do just that. But in those four years away from home, I'd made a new life for myself. I couldn't bear to come back and be under their roof again. So I didn't. And I haven't heard from anyone in my family since that day, except for an out-of-the-blue email I received from Tyler the Wednesday before I met you."

"What did it say?"

"That he missed me and he wanted to talk to me about something important. He gave me his phone number, and I tried to make myself dial it several times. But I was worried that if I talked to him, my parents would find out where I was and they'd start trying to control me again. My mind was going crazy with possibilities about what he might want. I never dreamed he was going to tell me he was getting married. I wish he'd just said that in the email."

"How come you never asked me where I lived in Iowa? Weren't you curious?"

"Very. But I was afraid you'd tell me you lived near Hope. If that were the case, I'd have to walk away from you for fear that if I ever came to see you I might run into my family. I care for you so much, Charley. I know it's crazy to say that, especially since we obviously don't know each other very well. But I just do."

"Is your new job near Hope?"

"Yes. In Taylor at Just for You Insurance. I'm staying with Kat Roe in the country north of Hope."

"Wow, you're staying in Hope?"

"Yes. I know. It was a gamble. I figured it wouldn't take long for my parents to find out I was back. But two things happened, Charley. I needed a job and Kat offered me one. And I met you. Although I didn't know you were going to be that close to me, I figured Iowa wasn't that big and I'd be able to see you again. I never dreamed you lived in Hope. I'd never heard of your family when I lived here."

"I don't suppose you did. Pam's my only daughter. My wife was killed in a car accident thirteen years ago in the fall."

"She must have been killed shortly after I left in August."

"It was September."

"I'm so sorry for your loss, Charley." Trisha got up and set the ice bag down on the table. Then she hurried to Charley and wrapped her arms around him.

ை

"So, what do you think about your sister with my daddy?" Pam asked as she and Tyler drove north down the highway toward Minnesota.

"I'm not sure what to think. I don't really know my sister anymore, Pam. I haven't talked to her since she graduated from college, and I haven't seen her since she left for California. Really, she's nothing more than a stranger to me."

"That's really sad, Tyler. Were you close before she left for school?"

"Yes. Extremely close. She was my best friend. We're only a year apart, so we had a lot of the same friends. Trisha made school fun. And she was really smart. Danni's always reminded me of Trisha. I really missed her when she left. She called me often that first year she was gone. And I admit, once I went off to school, I didn't reach out to her either. And life got busy after college. I hadn't really tried talking to her until a couple of weeks ago. I found her email address and wrote her. I didn't know until today she even got the email."

"So, this isn't something your parents set up?"

Tyler shook his head. "I'm sorry, Pam, but my folks don't like your dad. Even though they turned their back on Trisha, they wouldn't want her anywhere near your father."

"Would Trisha use my daddy to hurt your folks?"

Tyler thought about what she said for a few moments. "The old Trisha I knew would never do anything like that. But I don't know this Trisha. I can't answer that, Pam."

Silence overtook the car as they continued down the road, passing semi trucks and other cars.

Finally, Tyler said, "Pam, we're on our honeymoon. We only get one. I know it's hard to do, but let's put whatever this is between our families on hold for now. And let's just enjoy us this weekend. Okay?"

"I'm so glad you said that, because that's exactly what I was thinking."

꩜

Betty Sue checked on Danni one more time to make sure she was sleeping, then she glanced back at George, who was also asleep in the other queen bed.

She grabbed her phone and slipped into the hallway, not stopping until she was sitting on the bench outside of the hotel.

She scrolled through the numbers on her phone, then pushed the one she never thought she would.

"Hello?"

"Charley? This is Betty Sue Bailey. Are you with my daughter?"

Charley looked at Trisha, who slept peacefully beside him, propped up on the pillows. "I don't know if that's any of your business, Sue."

"Damn it, Charley. That's my daughter. Please tell me, is she okay?"

"Yeah, she's okay," Charley said, studying the bruising forming between Trisha's eyes and noticing how much her nose and face were swelling.

"Oh, thank God. I can't believe Jessica did that to her. Can I talk to her? Is she with you now?"

"She's asleep, Sue. I don't want to wake her," Charley said, not wanting to say much, but understanding a parent's need to know her child was okay. "I'll tell her you called."

"Are you sleeping with my daughter?" Betty Sue demanded, her voice rising with anger.

"That, Sue, really *is* none of your business. Goodbye."

"Oh, that man," Betty Sue grumbled, tempted to throw her phone across the parking lot when she realized he'd hung up on her. "Damn Charley Walker."

꩜

When Trisha opened her eyes again, the hotel room was dark.

She smiled, realizing Charley was curled up tightly beside her.

Thankful the throbbing in her nose had finally subsided, Trisha made her way out of the bed, then walked into the bathroom and softly shut the door. She then flipped on the light and cringed when she noticed the dark bruising around both of her eyes.

"This is not a good look for my new job. Why'd she do that? Why is Jessica so mad at me? Why doesn't she blame Mom and Dad?"

Saddened her little sister had so much anger for her, Trisha used the facilities, then used the light from the bathroom to find her suitcase. She rummaged through it until she found her nightgown, then grabbed her cell phone and walked back to the bathroom.

After changing into the gown, she texted Kat that she was staying in Cedar Falls and that she'd be back sometime on Sunday. Then she shut off the light and made her way back to the bed.

Charley sighed but didn't wake as she snuggled up against him and carefully laid her head on his arm.

She thought back to the moment when she saw her father and wondered why he looked so terrible. Was he sick? Was he dying?

Trisha eyes burned as it hit her just how far removed she was from the family she'd once loved with her entire heart. She had a niece who didn't even know her. And if Jessica had any influence over Danni, Trisha doubted she would want to know anything about her Aunt Trisha.

Her heart ached as she thought about her little Sophie.

She tightened her grip on Charley's arm and fell into a fitful sleep.

Chapter 10

"Good morning, beautiful."

Worried she was dreaming again, Trisha opened her eyes and turned to her right, smiling when she realized Charley was looking back at her. "Good morning."

"How'd ya sleep?"

"Okay. Sorry I fell asleep on you."

"It's okay." Charley turned onto his side and examined her nose. "How does it feel?"

She touched her nose tentatively. "Better. It's not throbbing any more. It's still tender to the touch, but it doesn't feel as swollen."

"It doesn't look as swollen, but you do have a couple of shiners. I'm sorry you walked blindly into that situation. And I'm sorry she did that to you."

Trisha reached over and touched his cheek with her hand. "It's not your fault."

"I know. But I'm still sorry. I led you right back to the family you've been trying to stay away from."

"You didn't know, and neither did I. But I figured I'd see them sooner or later."

Charley's eyes scanned the lacy nightgown. "You changed clothes."

"I woke up about midnight and put on something a little more comfortable."

She felt Charley's hand as it made its way down her side and under the short gown, then watched as he smiled when he realized the gown was the only thing she was wearing.

A fire heated up inside of her as his hands continued their journey up her belly and his fingertips traced the tips of her breasts under the lace.

"I've been dreaming of having you in my bed again all week." Charley's fingers worked their way down again. "And I've been dreaming about making love to you. Do you feel okay for that? Do you want to?"

Trisha didn't answer, but instead climbed on top of him and pulled the gown over her head, smiling down at Charley.

"Are we going to be late?" Danni asked for the tenth time as they raced down the highway toward home.

"We'll be fine dear," Betty Sue promised. "Your friend Kiley isn't expecting you until eleven. It's not even ten yet."

"I can't believe I get to have a sleep over with Kiley! Oh, thank you Grandma and Grandpa."

Betty Sue smiled, knowing Danni had wanted to stay with her friend all summer. She also knew Jessica had continually promised Danni could, but had never followed through on that promise.

Betty Sue was lost in troubling thoughts of their youngest child as George hurried into Hope.

"We're home," Danni called.

"Well, almost," George said.

Fifteen minutes later, they were all standing in the pool house. Betty Sue folded clothes as Danni handed them to her, and George watched them.

"Hi."

All three of them turned and looked at Jessica, who stood in the doorway of Danni's bedroom.

"I can still go, can't I?" Danni asked, the panic clearly written all over her face.

"Of course you can," Betty Sue promised. "I'm going to keep helping you get ready. George, why don't you and Jessica go outside and have a chat?"

George grabbed his youngest by her arm and led her out the door, stopping by the pool.

"Stop it," Jessica growled, pulling away.

"You caused quite a scene, little girl," George said, staring at his baby who was wearing dark shades, jean shorts and a man's T-shirt that was several sizes too big.

"I didn't do anything you didn't want to do. Trisha's no longer a part of this family. She shouldn't have been at Ty's wedding."

"You don't hit people because you're angry with them. You might've broken her nose."

"Good, I hope I did. Come on, Dad. She left us. We haven't even see her for years, and nobody's mentioned her name since she didn't come back after graduation. She's dead to us. Why am I the only one who did something about her crashing the wedding?"

"She's still your sister, and she's still welcome in this family," George informed her. "We've been waiting for her to come to her senses and come back home. And now, she has. Your little stunt better not drive her away, Jessica, or I'll hold you personally responsible for that."

"Are you kidding me? You're just throwing the door open and inviting her inside? She's a stranger, Dad. You don't know her anymore. And neither do I. She's never met any of my kids. Time didn't stop while she was gone. And why should we change everything in our lives just because she's decided to come back?"

"I know it hurt you when she left, Jess. It hurt all of us. But we're a family. I still love your sister as much as I did the day she left. Loving your children doesn't stop because they leave. And I expect you to welcome her back, too."

"No way." Jessica crossed her arms.

"Yes, you will. Your mother and I've bailed you out more times than I can even remember. Now Trisha's getting a second chance with this family. You'll be kind to her. End of discussion."

"Where the hell do you think you're going?" Jessica demanded, angry at her father but turning that anger toward her daughter, who picked that very moment to come out of the pool house carrying a suitcase.

Terrified, Danni ran behind her grandfather, clinging tightly to the suitcase handle.

"Your daughter's going away for a few days," George said.

"The hell she is. She's my daughter, and I never gave her permission to go anywhere."

"Jessica, stop this. You're scaring her," Betty Sue scolded as she latched on to Danni and held her tightly.

"You forget, little girl, you wouldn't even have her with you if it wasn't for your mother and me. Clay wants that little girl, and if you keep acting the way you've been acting, I'm going to call the judge and tell him she needs to be with Clay and her brothers."

"I hate all of you," Jessica yelled as she took off running and disappeared in the main house.

"I'm so sorry about that, Danni." George turned to face his scared granddaughter.

"I want to live with Dad," Danni admitted softly. "He's kind to me."

Betty Sue noticed the look on George's face and said, "You don't have to worry about that right now, honey. Today's a fun day. You're going to spend some time with Kiley's family at her grandfather's ranch. Promise me you'll have fun."

"Oh, I will Grandma."

"Great. Why don't I drive you over?"

"Can Jim do it, Grandpa?" Danni asked, referring to the man who worked for them. "I want to ride over in the black Cadillac."

"Of course he can. Let's go find him."

Charley set a tray of donuts and coffee down on the table. "Breakfast is served."

"Thanks for getting it for me." Trisha kissed him on the check. "I just didn't want to face the breakfast crowd looking like this."

"I think you look beautiful," Charley said, smiling, while his thoughts were back on the shower they had shared moments earlier.

"What time is it?"

"Almost 11. We'll need to check out shortly."

Trisha finished her donut, then she took a sip of coffee before she started gathering her items and putting them into her suitcase.

She noticed Charley was sitting in the chair by the table, munching on a chocolate donut and watching her, and smiled.

"Such a beautiful woman. I'm so lucky to have you in my life, Trisha."

"Even though I'm a Bailey?" Trisha asked while her back was to him, worried about his response.

Charley got up and walked over to her, gently placing his hands on her shoulders, "I like you for who you are, Trisha. You're a beautiful, kind, thoughtful woman. That's all that matters to me."

Trisha turned and leaned in for a kiss, pulling away when she hit her nose on his cheek. "Oh, ouch."

"I do need to tell you something though," Charley said as she zipped her suitcase and picked out another donut off the tray.

"Okay, what?" Trisha asked, glancing at the clock on the nightstand, noticing they had 10 minutes left in the room.

"Your mother called yesterday while you were sleeping."

"Called you?"

"Yes. I don't know how she got my cell phone number. I wasn't going to tell her anything at first. But she is your mother, Trisha. And she was worried about you. She wanted to make sure you were okay. I told her you were fine and that you were sleeping, but..."

"But what?"

"She asked me if we were sleeping together. I told her it was none of her business. Then I hung up."

"She has no right to ask that. I'm so sorry you're in the middle of this."

"It's okay. I just wanted you to know. I'm sure she's going to try to contact you again, Trisha. Do you want me to give her your number if she calls me back?"

"No. She hasn't tried in all these years to get my number. Or to talk to me at all. I've been through a lot since I left home and survived all of it without my mother holding my hand. Please, ignore her call if she tries to get ahold of you again. Okay?"

"If that's what you want. Let me get your bag for you."

Trisha nodded and opened the door, and they rode the elevator down, stopping briefly at the front desk to make sure everything was okay before they continued to their vehicles.

Charley placed her suitcase in her car, then turned to face her, taking her in his arms. "I don't want to leave you."

"I don't want to leave you either."

"Are you busy today?"

Trisha shook her head.

"Come to my farm," Charley suggested. "Let me show you where I live."

Trisha smiled. "That sounds like a great idea."

"Do you remember how to get back to Hope?"

"Yes, I just took a wrong turn on the way up."

"Okay, you follow me back, but if we get separated, I'll wait for you on the town square. Then you can follow me to the farm."

Trisha kissed him when he leaned in, feeling the butterflies once again springing to life.

They hugged. Then Trisha got into her car and waited while Charley put his duffel bag in his truck and started it up.

As they drove through Cedar Falls and started the journey home, Trisha's mind was back in the hotel and on their lovemaking.

"I'm falling in love," she said out loud. Then clarified, "I'm falling in love with a man I hardly know."

"It's such a nice day," Betty Sue said as she and George sat by the pool, enjoying their lunch.

"What are we going to do about Trisha?" George asked, as he picked at the salad and sandwich Helen had made for them.

"I'm not sure."

"Well, we have to get her away from that bastard."

"I know we do, but we have to be careful how we do it. We don't want her running away from us again. Or getting closer to him."

"I don't want to wait to get her away from him. Heaven only knows how long they've been together. What if she does get pregnant, Sue? It's one thing having Pam carrying a Bailey child. But if my sweet Trisha gets pregnant with a Walker child, I'll…I'll…hell, I'll kill him, Sue."

"Now, calm down. I want to find her and drag her home by her hair and never let her leave again. But we can't do that. We've learned Trisha doesn't respond to threats. She knew she'd lose all of her financial freedom if she didn't come home from California, and she chose that life over money. If we made her choose right now, I'm sure she'd choose Charley over us."

"I don't believe for one minute he didn't know she was our daughter. He knew I knocked you up in school. He knew that's why we got married. What if he's with her to get back at us?"

"I've thought about that, but I don't think that's what is going on. No matter how much we hate him, we both know Charley isn't capable of purposely using our own daughter against us."

"Then what, Sue? He really cares for her?"

"She's beautiful, George. And Charley's a lonely man. I'm not surprised he's attracted to her. What does amaze me is she's attracted to him."

George took a deep breath and pushed his salad away. "Now I've completely lost my appetite."

"Now, honey, don't get down. I think there's a way to get her away from him and get her to come to us."

"Oh, yeah? What?" George asked as he leaned in closer to Betty Sue.

"We make her think he is indeed using her to get to us. And we tell her something awful he's done to us to get her sympathy. To bring her over to our side."

"But he's never done anything to us; not really," George reminded her.

"I'm not above lying to protect our daughter, George. And I know you're not either."

George nodded.

"Good, now I just have to figure all this out, and then we'll put our plan into motion."

"You were always good at keeping the kids in line," George praised, hungry again as he started eating his turkey sandwich. "No matter what it took, you always got them to do what we wanted them to do."

"I'm their mother; that's my job. But I failed with Trisha. She got away from me once, and there's no way in hell she's getting away from me again."

"Let me in, damn it." Jessica hollered as she pounded on Glen's apartment door.

"Babe, damn. You're loud," Glen informed her as he latched on to her arm and pulled her inside the apartment. "Shut the hell up. You're makin' a scene."

"I hate her!" Jessica shouted as she marched into his kitchen and picked up the almost empty bottle of whiskey she'd left on his counter. She tipped the bottle up and tapped on the bottom, sucking out the last few drops.

"Hate, who? Your old lady?"

"Well, yeah. But I'm talking about my sister."

"How's her nose?"

Jessica laughed at his comment. "Hopefully broken."

"So, what's got you so uptight, Jess? I thought you were goin' home to sleep it off."

"My parents were in my house, packing up my daughter to go on some trip. They didn't even ask me if she could go."

"So, she went somewhere with your sister?"

"Shut up." Jessica swatted his arm.

"Okay, babe. I'm confused. You're mad at your sister because your daughter went somewhere?"

"I'm mad at my sister because she's my dad's favorite. I'm mad at my parents because they're trying to take my daughter away from me."

"Let them. Get out from under the responsibility, baby. Come live with me."

"Be serious. Danni's mine. She'll always be mine."

"I don't get you, Jess. Your ex-old man wants that brat, and she's not even his. And your parents want her too. Why are you fightin' it? Let someone else have her and move in with me. It's simple."

"You don't get it cuz you don't have kids."

"We could get to work on that." Glen grabbed her and kissed her hard on the lips.

As they parted, Jessica said, "I'm serious."

"So am I." Glen promised, rubbing his hands against her.

Fifteen minutes later, they were curled up together in his cramped double bed in the corner of his apartment.

"I wish my sister would just go away," Jessica mumbled as she rubbed Glen's arm.

"I could make that happen."

"How?"

"I got some people who owe me some favors."

"What do you mean? Kill her?"

"Whatever you want it to mean, Jess."

"I gotta think about it," Jessica said, possibilities rolling around in her head.

"It's so beautiful out here," Trisha said as she and Charley walked down the driveway, hand in hand, toward the old barn.

"Thanks. I wish you could have seen it when I had cattle. I'm afraid now the barn is just full of stuff."

Able to sense Charley's sadness, Trisha patted his arm. "Tell me what it was like when the cattle were here."

Charley got a gleam in his eyes as they stepped into the barn.

"This is where the mamas would have their babies," he started, pointing at small areas sectioned off with rusted metal gates. "We could have up to six calving at a time."

"How many cattle did you have?"

"The most we ever had was thirty-five head. The last few years I kept it at around fifteen. We'd sell off the babies when they got old enough. It was always hard on Pam. She would get attached to them even though she knew they were going to be sold. Of course, she'd show some of them at the county fair, so they'd stay around until the competition was over. She'd work with them from sunup to sundown in the summertime."

"Did you have horses, too?" Trisha asked, noticing an old, brittle bridle hanging from a rusty nail on one of the wooden beams.

"Yes. When I was growing up, we had about ten horses. I learned to ride when I was four. Nancy and I had two horses, but she was so scared Pam would get hurt on them that we sold the horses and got two ponies. I don't know if Pam sensed her mother's fear, but she never cared much for those ponies, so we sold them, too, and got a sheep. Pam liked her sheep, but she loved those cows, so we focused on those."

Trisha smiled. "Sounds like you're a great father. Is Pam an only child?"

Sadness seemed to weight down Charley's shoulders. "Yes. We wanted a whole house full, but Nancy kept suffering from miscarriages. She did manage to get pregnant again. With a boy. She was more than six months pregnant when she died."

"Oh, Charley, I'm so sorry," Trisha said as thoughts about her own loss assaulted her.

Charley felt his cheeks dampening and quickly turned his back to her while he wiped them off. "That was a real sad time around here."

"I'm sorry you had to go through that."

Charley faced her. "Why don't we go over to the machine shed? I'll show you my old tractors."

Enjoying his hand in hers, Trisha walked with him out of the barn and down the lane back to the old metal shed. Charley opened a walk-in door, and Trisha smiled when she noticed his man cave area, complete with several lawn chairs and a small dorm refrigerator.

"Well, at least now I know where to look for you."

Charley chuckled as he opened the refrigerator and pulled out two ice-cold cans of Pepsi.

Trisha sat down on one of the chairs, and Charley pulled the other one closer. "I couldn't stand to be that far away from you."

After taking a sip, Charley said, "Can I ask you a question?"

"Sure."

"Why did you tell me your last name was Jenkins?"

"Because that's my married name. I was married for four years to Brad Jenkins."

"Brad? Is that the same Brad who helped you move?"

"It is. I didn't realize I told you about him."

"Well, you didn't. You just said Brad was calling and you had to go. I got to admit, it's been driving me a little crazy wondering who Brad is."

Trisha smiled. "You have nothing to worry about. We're still best friends, but there's nothing romantic between us anymore."

"Why'd you divorce?"

Sophie instantly popped up in Trisha's mind, but she shrugged. "We grew apart. He works as a director for an ad agency and is gone a lot. It's hard to grow as a couple when you're never together."

"How long have you been divorced?"

"Four years ago, last February."

Charley leaned back and took another sip, his mind running crazy with questions he had about her ex-husband. But he didn't want their time together to be spent focusing on him, so he asked, "Would you like to see the tractors now?"

"Yes," Trisha agreed as she stood up and took his hand when he offered it.

They walked deeper into the old shed, and Trisha noticed the older looking tractors crammed into the small shed.

"This is my newest one." Charley patted the huge tires on one of them. "I bought it used in 1998, the year Pam started kindergarten."

"And this is your newest one?"

"Yes. They're real expensive, Trish. A new one costs at least $170,000."

"Wow, I had no idea they cost that much."

"Yeah, they do. My neighbor, Darrell, has a newer one. We help each other out, and sometimes I get to drive it. It's much nicer than this one, but this one does get the job done."

"That's good," Trisha agreed, feeling completely out of her element.

"How would you like to see my house, Trisha?"

She smiled. "Let's go."

❧

"Have you talked to Trisha yet?" George asked as Betty Sue walked into his study and sat down across from him.

Betty Sue shook her head, and her long, blond hair waved around her face, "No. It keeps going to voicemail. I can't believe you haven't found Trisha's cell phone number for me yet. I hate having to call that man's cell phone."

"I'm sure he's been lying to her about us, Sue. We've got to do something. I know where he lives. Let's go out there and—"

"No!" Betty Sue interrupted, startling him. "If we did that, she'd never talk to us again."

"That's the problem. I haven't talked to my daughter in nine years and haven't seen her in thirteen. I miss her. I've missed her so much."

Betty Sue hurried around the desk to George as he started crying and put her arms around him. "I know this is hard. But I'm working on it. Okay?"

George scanned his wife's beautiful blue eyes and nodded, feeling a little bit better.

"Have you checked around to see if anyone knows where she is? Did she come back to Hope or did she go back to California?" Betty Sue asked.

"I thought you didn't want me spying on our daughter."

"We both know I was wrong when I made that decision after she graduated from college. I really believed she'd come back home. But now, I want you to find her. This will be easier if I know where she is."

"I'll get to work on that," George said, relieved Sue was finally coming around to his way of tracking their daughter.

"Let me know the minute you find something out. I'm going to get on the phone and start calling my friends to see if they've heard anything about her."

❧

"There's not really much to it," Charley said as they walked in the back door of his small farmhouse.

"What a nice kitchen." Trisha instantly felt at home as she noticed the older table and four swivel chairs to her right. She smiled when she realized his refrigerator both looked and sounded like the noisy one from her apartment in California. Cabinets with a countertop lined the wall beside the back door, and along the other wall was the stove and sink with a few more cabinets and a small countertop.

"And through here is the living room."

Trisha followed him into the small living room and smiled when she noticed the family portrait on the wall. "Pam looks like her mother."

"I've always thought that too."

Trisha followed him into the room and glanced at the couch and older recliner chairs. To her right was a desk scattered with papers and an older-looking computer. Next to the desk was an old, cabinet-style television set.

"Would you like the rest of the tour?"

Trisha nodded and felt the butterflies coming back to life as they started down a short hallway. Charley grinned at her as he passed the first door on the right and continued all the way to the end of the hall.

"This is Pam's bedroom. And back down the hallway on the right is the bathroom. And this is my bedroom." Charley grinned as he stepped inside the room they had passed.

He glanced at the bed and then back at her.

"Your bedroom," Trisha repeated. A hunger that been dormant before she met him suddenly raged to life again.

"And my bed."

"It's a nice bed," Trisha agreed, eyeing the double bed. "Looks cozy."

"It is," Charley agreed. "Would you like to see how cozy?"

Trisha smiled as she quickly crossed the room and fell into his open arms.

Darrell and Tess were driving down the gravel road toward home when Tess noticed Charley was sitting on his front porch with a woman.

"Who's with Charley?"

Darrell slowed down and, while they both were straining their necks to see, said, "He mentioned he was seeing someone."

"Let's stop and meet her."

They pulled in the driveway and parked. Then they both jumped out and hurried to the house.

Tess suddenly felt her heart sink to her feet when she recognized the woman was Trisha Bailey.

She wanted to turn around and run back to the truck, but instead latched on to Darrell's arm.

"Hey," Darrell said, noticing she was wearing Charley's shirt. "What's going on?"

"Hey, guys. I'd like you to meet my girlfriend. Trisha Jenkins."

"Nice to meet you." Darrell noticed Trisha and Tess were both looking intently at each other. "I'm Darrell Whiteshell, and this is my wife, Tess."

"Theresa?" Trisha asked, finally recognizing her.

"Yes, it's me, Trisha," Tess said, deciding there was no point in delaying the inevitable. She turned to Darrell. "We've actually met before, but I used my full name, Theresa."

"Your full name's Theresa?" Darrell asked.

"You know each other?" Charley asked at the same time, glancing at Trisha.

"We met in college out in California, didn't we Theresa? Then I helped her get a job." Trisha turned to Tess. "Why are you in Hope? Did you come here looking for me?"

Charley noticed how angry Trisha sounded. He glanced back at Tess, wondering if his suspicions about her had been right all along.

"Can we talk in private, please Trisha? I want to explain a few things to you."

"Why can't you explain them to all of us?" Charley pried, glancing at Darrell and then back at Tess.

"Please, Trisha?"

Trisha took a deep breath, "Charley, can we talk in your living room?"

Trusting Trisha, Charley nodded.

Trisha walked into the living room, followed closely by Tess.

As soon as the door was shut, Trisha insisted, "What the hell are you doing in Hope? Did you come here to twist the knife some more?"

"We used to be friends, Trish."

"Yeah, well, maybe once. But you made sure we weren't anymore."

"You're not some innocent bystander, Trisha. You needed to take responsibility for what you'd done."

"You had no right to tell her," Trisha demanded.

"Why? Because you were going to tell her? I don't think either one of you were ever going to tell her."

"Sounded like you'd known about the affair from almost the beginning. Why did you wait until you needed to save you own butt?"

"Because we were friends. And because I was waiting for you to come to your senses. He was your coach, Trisha. And he was married. I knew it was wrong, and deep down, you did too."

Trisha felt the memories of her worst mistake swirling around in her head and sat with a thump on Charley's couch.

"I'm sorry, Trish. I didn't want it to ruin our friendship. But I was desperate. I didn't want to go to jail. And I did confess what I'd done when you were getting blamed for it. I didn't have to do that, but I couldn't stand by and watch you get blamed for my mistake."

"And I appreciated that. I was going to help you get out of that mess. But you turned on me. You told Mrs. Halley I was sleeping with her husband."

"She told me she wouldn't press charges against me. I was so grateful I wasn't going to jail, Trisha. I felt like I needed to repay her kindness."

"By telling her that her husband was cheating on her?"

"She needed to know the truth. I would want to know if my husband was cheating on me."

Shame washed over Trisha in waves as she thought about the three months after graduation when she lived in her coach's house. His wife was gone weeks at a time for work, and he and Trisha were together both at work at the college, where she was helping with the new class of basketball recruits, and then at home. It started to feel as if they were playing house.

He started sharing his marital problems with her, and she started letting herself admit how attracted to him she'd always been. Their affair was quick and full of passion. And she'd convinced herself she wasn't doing anything wrong. Until Tess, who had been working as the live-in maid, ratted her out.

"I'm sorry, Trisha," Tess apologized again, waking her from her thoughts.

"Why are you really in Hope?"

"Because I wanted a new start. You always talked about how peaceful and quiet Hope was and how beautiful Iowa was. I got a little money and decided to move here."

"Were you looking for me?"

"No. And I wasn't trying to get anything out of your family either. I never told them I knew you. I never told anyone I knew you. I promise. If your parents or anyone in your family found out anything about your life after college, I was not the one who told them."

Trisha examined her face and slowly nodded, believing her. "How'd you end up with Charley's friend?"

"I was working at the grocery store, and he came in to get groceries. We hit it off right away. I love him, Trisha. I mean, really love him. He's good to me, and we live on a beautiful, peaceful farm. Iowa's just as wonderful as you always described it. I'm happy here, Trisha. And I'm sincere. I love Darrell."

"Well, I'm glad you're happy."

"Charley doesn't trust me. He thinks I'm after Darrell's money. But I'm not. You have to convince him of that, Trisha. Charley's Darrell's best friend, and I don't want Charley causing any problems for us."

"Does Darrell know what you did?"

"No. He didn't even know I lived in California. I haven't told him about my brother, either. Please, don't, Trisha."

"Is your brother still troubled?"

"As far as I know. I never told him I was leaving. And I haven't tried to contact him."

"I'm not going to tell Darrell anything," Trisha said, making up her mind. "But I'm going to tell Charley. And I'm telling him all of it, including what happened with Coach Halley. But I think you should tell Darrell yourself what happened, Tess. I can't promise Charley won't tell him, and it'd be better if he heard it from you."

Tess stood up and started pacing around Charley's living room.

"No secrets, Tess." Trisha stood up and walked over to Tess, stopping her pacing. "I've learned the hard way that's the best way to live life."

Not ready to focus on her own issues, Tess asked, "What happened to your face, Trisha?"

"My sister punched me."

"Jessica?"

"Yes. Charley invited me to be his guest at his daughter's wedding. I didn't realize his daughter was marrying Tyler, my brother."

"Oh my gosh. You were there? That means you ran into your parents too."

"I did. It wasn't a happy reunion. That's why I'm trying to tell Charley everything about my past. I want to get it all out on the table. I hadn't planned on telling him about Coach Halley yet, because it's still painful for me. But I need to."

"Okay, Trisha. I'll tell Darrell. And I'll do it tonight."

"I'm sorry about all that happened back in California."

"Me too."

"Trisha seems nice," Darrell said as he and Charley stood on the porch, catching a word here or there when the ladies' voices grew loud.

"Thanks. You know her parents."

"I do?"

"She's a Bailey."

"Oh, shit. Not George Bailey's daughter."

"Yep. I didn't know until she showed up at the reception. She and Tyler recognized each other, and all hell broke loose."

"Is that where she got the shiners?"

"Her sister punched her in the face."

"So her name's Jenkins now?"

"Yeah. That's why I had no idea she was a Bailey. And we never talked about who Pam was marrying, so she didn't know it was her brother."

"Sometimes this ol' world's too small."

The squeaking of Charley's front door opening ended their conversation as Tess hurried out. "Let's go, Darrell. There's something we need to talk about."

"Oh, well, okay." Darrell waved at Trisha and Charley. "Nice meeting you, Trisha. I'll call you tomorrow, Charley, and we'll figure out where to take the tractor to get it fixed."

"Okay, bye," Charley called, waving as they walked back to their truck.

"I haven't been able to find out anything," Betty Sue admitted as she walked into George's study and sat down on the dark leather couch. "No one's heard anything about our daughter. At least not our oldest daughter. The only thing on people's minds is what's going on with our youngest daughter. They want to know why we are helping her keep Danni away from Clay. I don't know about you, George, but I'm starting to think we need to let Danni live with Clay."

"But he'll take her to Nebraska and we'll never see her," George reminded his wife. "He's already planning on taking our grandsons."

"Maybe that's exactly what needs to happen, George. The boys need their dad in their life if they are ever going to grow up to be responsible men. And poor Danni is scared of Jessica. That's no way for a little girl to live. And what if she follows in her mother's footsteps and gets pregnant while she's still in school? We need to do what's right for Danni, not what's right for us, George."

"I gave Jessica an ultimatum."

"You did? What'd you say?"

"I told her to be nice to her sister or we aren't going to help her fight for custody of Danni anymore."

"Oh, George, what a great idea," Betty Sue gushed, forgetting all about her mission to help Danni when it came to getting Trisha back home.

"She wasn't very happy about it. But I'm serious this time, Sue. If Jessica can't get along with Trisha, then I'm done trying to help her out. You know, I've felt like her drinking problems were all my fault because, let's face it Sue, I'm the one she learned that behavior from. But I'll do anything to get Trisha back home where she belongs. She's been living on her own for too long. Jessica's had everything handed to her, and she's never appreciated a single damned thing. It was time to put our foot down, and that's exactly what I did."

"Well, I'm proud of you. Have you heard anything? Did you find a private investigator who will look into Trisha's past for us?"

"Not yet. I've got some calls in. I'll probably hear from them in the morning, Sue. It is Sunday evening."

"I guess it is," Betty Sue concluded. "All of this is making me so tired. I'm going to bed. Want to come?"

George jumped to his feet and followed her out of the room.

"I knew she was no good," Charley said, amazed by everything Trisha had told him.

"I know you don't care much for Theresa, um, Tess. But what about me, Charley? What about what I've done?"

Charley shrugged. "You were just a kid, Trisha. Your coach was the married one. He should've been more responsible. He knew about the situation your parents put you in and knew you didn't have anyone else to turn to. He took advantage of that. You're not to blame for anything that happened between the two of you."

Surprised Charley felt the same way Brad always had, Trisha shook her head. "I'm not innocent, Charley. Far from it."

"It sounds to me like you've been holding on to this guilt for far too long. Let it go. He cheated on his wife, and all the trouble they had because of that is his fault, not yours. I don't think any less of you because of what happened. It's your past, Trisha. We all have a past."

"It's not that simple," Trisha said, the guilt coursing through her veins as if it had all just happened.

"It can be."

"I can't forgive myself for cheating with him."

"Well, I can." Charley hurried to her side and hugged her tightly. "I forgive you for everything that happened with your coach. It doesn't affect how I feel about you in any way. And I'm going to help you forgive yourself."

Trisha gazed into his brown eyes and offered him a small smile when he smiled at her.

"That's better," Charley said before kissing her.

"Thank you," Trisha said as their embrace ended. "It's hard for me to talk about Coach Halley."

"I understand why. But I do have one question."

"Okay, what?"

"What did Tess do that she was worried she'd go to jail for?"

"She stole Mrs. Halley's jewelry. She pawned the jewelry and used the money she got for it to pay her bills."

"I see," Charley said, his mind racing. "So, she probably is after Darrell for his money."

Trisha shrugged. "I don't know Darrell, and I don't know Theresa anymore, but she swears she loves him."

"Darrell became very wealthy when his mother passed away, Trisha. Before that, he had a hard time catching the eye of women and seemed content being a bachelor. But once he had money, women came looking for him. He sent them all on their way, except for Tess. I don't want him to get hurt, Trisha."

"I can't say Theresa won't hurt him," Trisha said. "But I told her she needed to tell him the truth about what happened in California. If she doesn't follow through, then I'd be concerned she's using him for money. But if she does tell him, then I'd be inclined to think she really cares for him."

"Or she's backed into a corner and will only come clean because she has to."

"But at least you know the truth. Her brother's the hardened criminal though, Charley. I'd be more worried about him finding out his new brother-in-law has money."

"What's her brother's name?"

"Um, let me see," Trisha said as she took a deep breath and thought back. "I only met him once, and he was very creepy. I wouldn't want to be alone with someone like that. Oh, I know. It was Carl. Carl Hooper."

"Carl Hooper," Charley repeated. "Okay. Thanks."

"I hate to do this, but I really need to get back to Kat's house. I need to get a good night's sleep before my first day at my new job."

"Okay. Let me walk you to your car."

They held hands as they walked to Trisha's car, then Charley took her into his arms and kissed her on the lips while holding her body tightly to his.

"Thanks for loving me today," Charley said, his mind back on their late-afternoon lovemaking session.

"Oh, Charley, it was all my pleasure."

Kat was sitting at the kitchen table working from home on her laptop when Trisha walked in.

"Oh my gosh, what happened to you?" Kat asked, instantly noticing the bruising on Trisha's face. "Did that man do that to you?"

"Charley? Oh, no. Charley's a good man," Trisha said, shaking her head as she sat down beside Kat at the table. "My sister did this to me."

"Wait, I'm confused. I thought you've been with Charley all weekend."

"I have been. Oh, Kat, you're never going to believe all of this. Charley's daughter married my brother, Tyler."

"You're dating Charley Walker?"

"Yes. You know Charley?"

"He gets his insurance through us. I've been out to his place a few times for work-related things. I didn't know your Charley lived here in Hope."

"Well, I didn't either. I just knew he lived in Iowa. I got to the reception and came face-to-face with the happy bride and groom. And Ty and I instantly recognized each other. After that, everything's kind of a blur, as my parents got in on it and Charley thought I'd lied to him. Then Jessica sucker-punched me and I started bleeding everywhere."

Kat put her hand to her mouth. "Oh my gosh, this is all so terrible. I take it Charley and you patched things up though."

Trisha nodded and smiled, thinking about their time together.

"Well, that's good. But we have a little problem, Trisha."

"What's that?"

"You're not going to be able to go in to the office tomorrow. Sharon, the head of HR, is going to be gone for a few days. Her mother fell and she has to care for her. Sharon's very particular about new hires." Kat sighed. "I wish I would've had her do the paperwork on Friday."

"Oh, shoot. I really need this job," Trisha said, her heart racing.

"You still have the job, Trisha. As soon as Sharon's able to come in, we'll get the ball rolling."

"Ok," Trisha said as Kat's cell phone rang.

"It's Rick," Kat announced before she turned and paced into the living room.

Trisha fixed herself a ham sandwich as bits of Kat's conversation with Rick filtered into the kitchen from the living room. She'd just sat down at the table to eat her sandwich when Kat joined her.

"Rick wanted me to tell you that we're going to pay you for helping with that ad on Friday, and your official start date will be last Friday. That way, your insurance will start faster. Again, I'm really sorry, Trisha."

"It's okay, Kat. Things happen."

"So, except for your family drama, how was your weekend?"

Trisha grinned. "Wonderful. It's so nice being with Charley again. But I was wondering, if you knew Charley, how come you didn't recognize him at the convention?"

"Because I hadn't met him in person, just on paper. He had some crop damage a few years ago, and I went out to his farm with the adjuster to take some photos for a story we were doing to promote our crop insurance protection. I was at his farm, but he couldn't be there. I've met Pam before, though. I've seen her at the grocery store several times. I guess Charley and I never hung out in the same places."

Trisha yawned.

"I think I'm about ready to call it a night. How about you?"

"I think that's a great idea."

Trisha was drifting off to sleep when her cell phone started ringing. She quickly grabbed it off the small nightstand by her bed, hoping it wouldn't wake Kat.

"Trisha, it's me. Brad."

"Brad. What's wrong?" Trisha asked, instantly able to tell something was.

"It's Scarlette. She left me."

"Scarlette left you?"

"Yeah. She got home yesterday and kept picking fights with me. When I asked her what was wrong, she said…well, she said she was mad at me. And said I was being disrespectful to her. I tried talking to her, but she kept getting angry. I slept in the guest room last night, and this morning, when I went in to check on her, she was packing her things. I tried to talk to her, but all she kept saying was that we're over and she can't even stand to look at me. She just got her last bag and left."

"Oh, Brad. I'm so sorry."

"And you're hundreds of miles away, Trish."

"I'm so sorry, Brad. What did she mean you were disrespectful?"

"I told her you'd stayed here Thursday night, and she wasn't happy about it. I think she thought something happened between us."

"But it didn't. I could talk to her."

"No, don't bother. I told her nothing happened. But she wants to be mad at me. I think it's really over Trisha. And I'm sorry if I made you feel guilty for leaving. I didn't mean to. I'm glad you're moving on with your life. I have to leave in a few hours and fly over to Paris anyway. But I just was so shocked she left me. We've been together for more than a year, Trisha. I never saw this coming."

"Are you're sure she isn't seeing someone else?"

"I have no idea. She was acting really different, Trish. I almost wonder if she's on drugs again."

"What do you mean, again?"

When Brad didn't answer, Trisha insisted, "Brad, what do you mean? Again? Was she taking something before?"

"Yeah."

"Oh, Brad. Why didn't you tell me?"

"She promised me she'd quit. I thought she had. She insisted at the time she only took the pills because one of the other models gave them to her. But I can't help but wonder now if that was a lie too."

"What can I do to help?"

"You're doing it. Just being able to talk all this through with you has helped me. Thank you for always having time for me, Trish."

"I love you, Brad. You know that."

"I love you too, Trish. Oh, shoot, it's like midnight out there, isn't it? I'm sorry. Don't you start your new job tomorrow?"

"Well, I was supposed to, but I can't because the HR lady had a family emergency. And it's probably a good thing, too, because I have two black eyes."

"If Charley hurt you, I'll…"

"It wasn't Charley," Trisha interrupted. "It was my sister, Jessica."

Brad listened as Trisha explained what had gone on over the weekend. "Sounds like we've both had wild weekends. And I can't believe you ran into Theresa, either."

"I know. That was a shock," Trisha agreed through a yawn.

"Hey, go to sleep, Trish. I'll call you tomorrow. Thanks for listening to me."

"Anytime, Brad. Goodnight."

Chapter 11

"You didn't have to fix me breakfast," Kat said as she rushed into the kitchen, following her nose. "But it smells wonderful."

"It's the least I could do." Trisha scooped the vegetable omelet onto a plate and set it down on the table. "Hope you like it."

"I'm sure I will. I'll call you on your cell phone if I hear anything from Sharon," Kat informed her as she started eating.

"Is there anything I can do around here to help—"

"Don't worry about it," Kat interrupted as she finished the omelet and stood up. "Thanks for breakfast, Trisha. It was great. I'll see you tonight."

"Okay, have a great day."

Trisha stayed out of the way as Kat gathered her laptop and slipped on her black heels that were still on the welcome mat by the back door. Then Kat turned and waved before rushing out of the house.

Trisha started running water in the sink and was adding the dish soap as Kat zoomed down the driveway.

The house seemed too quiet as Trisha washed the skillet and other dishes she'd used that morning. She dried them and washed off the counter and stove before letting the water out of the sink.

"What else can I do around here to help out?" Trisha asked herself out loud.

She searched around the house until she found the vacuum cleaner in the closet by the back porch, then she spent the next 15 minutes cleaning all the carpet in Kat's farmhouse.

Deciding that was a good start, Trisha continued to the bathroom and took her shower. After dressing in a pair of jean shorts and a red tank top, she found the cleaners she needed in the same closet where the vacuum resided and cleaned Kat's shower and bathroom sink. Then she scrubbed the bathroom floor.

She was carrying the cleaners back to the closet when she noticed Chase Locke had pulled into the driveway.

Deciding it was a good time to say hello, Trisha walked out the back door and continued down Kat's driveway until she reached where Chase had parked by the barn.

She walked inside and watched as he fed Kat's two brown quarter horses. Then she said, "Hi."

"Oh, hey, Trisha. Kat said you were staying here for a while. It's great seeing you again."

"You too," Trisha agreed, shaking his hand when he offered it. "Kat's horses are gorgeous."

"They are. Kat said you moved here from California. Must be a big change comin' back to the slow life."

"It is. But I love it here. I missed home."

"I wouldn't want to be anywhere else. Hope I'm not prying or anything, but what happened to you, Trisha? Who gave you those black eyes?"

"My sister, Jessica."

Chase shook his head. "Sorry your sister did that to ya'. She's got some problems."

"I've heard," Trisha agreed. "But we don't talk."

"Well, she's drunk. A lot. It's just not right, either. I'm glad Clay took the boys when they split up. I hope he gets the girl, too. Those kids need to be together."

"She has boys, too?"

"Yes, two. I think they're both under ten. My boy helped with their T-ball teams a few years ago."

"You have a boy? With Kat?"

Chase shook his head. "No. Kat and I broke up, and I did something stupid. Nine months later I became a father. Don't get me wrong, I love my son, but that mistake cost me Kat."

"I'm so sorry, Chase. I wondered what had happened between the two of you."

"It was my fault. I'm just glad we're friends again."

❧

"I love you," Tess said, kissing Darrell before he headed out the front door.

She was humming as she walked into their bedroom and made the bed while thinking about their talk the night before.

Somewhat true to her word, she'd told him about being in California and how she and Trisha had met while they both had been taking classes at the small, private college. And how Trisha had helped her get the maid job for Coach Halley and his wife. She also told him Trisha was the reason she came to Hope.

"He doesn't need to know about the jewelry," she said out loud as she finished making the bed and moved on to cleaning the bathroom. "And he doesn't need to know anything about my brother. That part of my life is dead to me."

After cleaning the bathroom, she vacuumed the upstairs hallway and bedrooms, and then she went downstairs and started cleaning the kitchen.

A knock on her door at nine startled her, and she thought about ignoring it until she remembered the neighbor girls to the east were supposed to bring over some sweet corn. She fetched her purse and hurried to the door, dropping it immediately when she noticed the greasy-haired man standing on her front porch.

"Hey, Sis. Surprise!"

"Carl?" she questioned, as the color all drained from her face. "Oh my God."

"What, no hug?" Carl grunted, his jaw tight as he glared at her.

"What are you…how did you…"

"Find you?" Carl said as her voice trailed off. "Wasn't easy. You wanna have this conversation on the front porch?"

Tess shook her head and pulled him in, glancing nervously around before shutting and locking the door.

"I don't much like being left, Tess."

"I'm sorry, but I had to get out of there."

"You had to get out of there?" Carl said, his voice rising. "What about me, Tess? You left me. And after what I did to help you."

Tess peered up at him. "I'm sorry. I really am. But what was I supposed to do?"

"I don't know; visit me? I bailed you out. And what did you do to repay me? You just took off. Do you have any idea how lonely a jail cell is?"

Tess shook her head. "No, thanks to you, I've never had to find that out."

"You owe me, little sister. And I'm here to collect."

"I don't have much money…" Tess started, completely caught off guard when Carl slapped her across the face.

"Don't you dare lie to me," he yelled as he grabbed her arm and spun her around to face him again. "I've been in town a few days, Sis. I know all about your rich farmer husband."

"Leave him out of this. Please." Tess held her free hand to her throbbing face while her mind flashed back to all the times he'd hit her in the past.

"You owe me," Carl repeated. "And you have money. It's time to pay."

"How much do you want?"

"I think ten grand will work." Carl grinned, "For a start."

Figuring he'd never leave her alone, Tess started racking her brain, trying to come up with a way out. Trisha's face popped into her mind, and she squinted at Carl. He'd told her he wanted Trisha the first time he'd seen her in Coach Halley's house. Deciding sacrificing Trisha was the only way to save the life she was building, Tess offered, "I know something you want more than money."

Carl released her arm. "What?"

"Trisha Bailey."

Carl raised his eyebrows. "What about her?"

"She's here. Back in town. I saw her last night."

"So." Carl crossed his arms.

"So, we both know you've always wanted her. How about you get her. And leave?"

"Like she's gonna go with me," Carl huffed.

Tess shrugged, "I'm sure you can figure out a way to get her out of town. And I'll even give you the $10,000 if you promise to leave and never come back."

Tess could tell Carl was thinking over what she said, and she latched her hands together to keep them from shaking as the guilt started getting to her for what she was offering.

"How would I get close to her? It's not like I can call her up."

"No. But I can."

"I gotta think about this."

"Fine. Let me know what you decide. But either way, I can only get $10,000."

"I'll be back when I make up my mind. And if this is some sort of trick—"

"It's not," Tess interrupted, then added, "I'm not that stupid."

Trisha was folding a load of clothes when her cell phone started ringing. Not recognizing the Los Angeles area number, she hesitated for a moment before answering.

"Trisha?"

"Yes. Who's calling, please?"

"Scarlette."

"Scarlette? This isn't your regular number. Where are—"

"How dare you sleep with my man?" Scarlette accused, interrupting her. "I should kill you!"

"I didn't sleep with him. I stayed at your house that night because I had to leave my apartment."

"We both know you two were together all week. And you were sleeping with him all week. Why can't you let him go?"

"I swear to you, Scarlette, there's nothing romantic going on between me and Brad. We're friends. That's it."

"Bullshit."

"Calm down, please Scarlette. I don't understand where this is coming from. We've known each other for almost a year. I think you and Brad are great together."

"Shut up, you're trying to confuse me."

"No, I'm not trying to confuse you. I'm trying to tell you the truth. I have a new boyfriend. I don't love Brad like that anymore."

"But you still love him."

"Well, yes, but—"

"I knew it. You bitch."

"Scarlette, I—"

"You're gonna regret this," Scarlette interrupted. "I'm going to make you pay for hurting me."

"Scarlette?" Trisha questioned, her hands shaking as she held on to the phone. Realizing Scarlette had hung up, Trisha gripped her phone tightly and paced around Kat's living room. When it started ringing again, Trisha jumped, dropping her phone onto the ground.

"Oh, shoot." Trisha picked it up and checked the number. Noticing it was Kat, she took a deep breath then said hello.

"Hey, it looks like Sharon might be gone all week. Her mother's not doing well."

"Oh, okay." Trisha murmured, her mind still back on her call.

"Are you all right?"

"Well, I don't know."

"What's wrong?"

"I don't want to bother you while you're at work."

"It's fine, Trisha. I'm taking a little break. What's up?"

Trisha quickly filled Kat in on Brad's call the night before and Scarlette's threats.

"Wow, Trisha. That's scary stuff. I could come home on my lunch hour if…"

"No, I'm fine. Scarlette's in California. I'm not even sure if she knows I'm in Iowa. She's always been a little bit of a drama queen. I've just never known her to act like this before. I thought things were great between us."

"Well, drugs can really mess with people. If I were you, I'd let Brad know about her call."

"I'll call him tomorrow. He's flying to Paris today. I'll be fine, Kat. Really. I just got off the phone with her, and I'm still a little shocked by all of this."

"Well, maybe it's a good thing you can't work this week. Maybe you need a little time to adjust to all the changes."

"Yeah, maybe you're right."

"What's Charley doing today?"

A smile came to Trisha's lips. "I don't know. Maybe I'll call him and find out."

"Sounds like a great idea. I know it's bad timing, but I have a meeting tonight with the business leaders in Taylor. I'll be home really late."

"I'll probably go over to Charley's tonight, Kat. I might stay all night."

"Have fun."

Betty Sue was reading a book by the pool when her cell phone started ringing. Noticing it was her best friend, Donna, calling she quickly answered.

"You never told me Trisha was home," Donna accused.

"Oh, well, she wanted to come to her brother's wedding," Betty Sue said, her mind racing. Finally, someone knew something about Trisha. "How'd you find out?"

"Grace Locke," Donna continued. "Her grandson, Chase, told her."

"Trisha's been keeping a pretty low profile. How'd Chase know?"

"Well, he works for Kat Roe. He's seen Trisha at the house. Why is she staying with Kat instead of you?"

Excited to finally know where Trisha was staying, she tried to keep her voice even. "You know how independent she is."

"I figured it was because Kat gave her a job so she felt the need to give Kat some company. You know, Kat's husband never has come back from Kansas."

"I don't really know Kat."

"Sure you do. She was Kat McBelle. She's the daughter of Percy and Vivian McBelle. They moved out east after she graduated, and Kat stayed here to run the farm. Her parents made her buy it from them. She works over at Just For You Insurance. I think she's the head of some department over there. Didn't Trisha tell you all of this?"

"No. We've hardly had time to catch up," Betty Sue said, hoping Donna couldn't see through her.

"Well, I was surprised to hear Trisha's working. I didn't figure George was very happy about that."

"No, he's not. But again, Trisha's very independent."

"Okay. I must go, Sue. I've got a golf lesson this afternoon. Will you be at the tea tomorrow afternoon?"

"I wouldn't miss it. Good bye, Donna."

Betty Sue jumped to her feet and took off at a trot, catching George as he sipped on the bottle he thought no one knew he kept hidden in his top desk drawer.

"Oh, Sue," George said as he dropped the bottle below the desk and struggled to screw on the cap.

"I know where Trisha is," Betty Sue announced, too excited to yell at him about the liquor. "She's staying with someone named Kat Roe, and she's working at—"

"Just For You Insurance," George interrupted.

Betty Sue put her hands on her hips. "How'd you know that? Did you find that out and not tell me?"

"No." George shook his head. "I know Kat. Sometimes she comes to the Tuesday Business Lunches. This is good news, Sue. Trisha's moved back home. She's close, honey."

"Yeah, but not quite close enough. I want her living in this house. I want to find out what she's been doing for the last thirteen years. I've missed too much time with her, George."

"Didn't you tell me that we had to take this slowly?"

"Yeah, you're right. I did. The good news is she's still in town. That gives us more time to figure out a way to get her home."

"But it also means she's still around Charley."

"And he might be the reason she moved back. But at least she's not staying with him."

"Not yet."

"Oh, don't even suggest that." Betty Sue shivered. "I've got to think."

"Danni called," George said before she could walk out of the study.

"Oh, really? How's she?"

"Great. She's having a wonderful time with her friend."

"I'm glad. How about her mother? Have you heard from Jessica?"

George shook his head. "Not since I told her she had to get along with Trisha."

"Do you think she's with that loser she brought to the wedding?"

"I imagine she is. I'm going to try to call her this afternoon."

"I wonder how Tyler's doing."

"I'm sure he's fine. Their house is all ready for them."

"What'd you do with Jessica's things?"

"Threw the junk away and put the rest into storage. She's never even asked about it."

"Did they find a lot of bottles when they were cleaning?"

George nodded, knowing they had found more than he had hidden around the mansion.

"Well, that girl has a problem. Maybe a bigger one than we can fix," Betty Sue admitted, feeling helpless when it came to her youngest. She noticed the wince on George's face but continued, "That's why I'm going to concentrate on helping Trisha. I haven't done enough for her over the years, and now that she's back, that's all going to change."

"Hey, Trisha. I just noticed you called."

"Where are you?" Trisha asked, hearing yelling in the background.

"A livestock auction in McGlover. Darrell and I came over. He's buying some cattle."

"Oh, okay."

"How's work going?"

"I didn't go," Trisha said, filling him in.

"Darn, you could've come with us. I won't be home for awhile."

"That's okay. Call me when you get home, and I'll come out."

"Sounds great. I miss you Trish."

"Me too."

Not sure what to do next, Trisha started playing with Kat's adorable black and white border collie. She had just tossed what appeared to be the dog's favorite toy and was watching her run for it when she noticed a fancy, black Cadillac slowing down in front of Kat's house.

"What the heck?" Trisha questioned as the dog brought the toy and dropped it at her feet. "Oh, shoot. Mom."

"Trisha," Betty Sue called as she climbed out of the car and took off across the grass to her daughter. "Thank goodness I found you."

"What are you doing here, Mom?" Trisha asked, watching as Dixie fetched her toy and ran to Betty Sue, dropping it at her feet.

"Oh, get back, dog," Betty Sue scolded as she waved her arms around.

"She's not going to hurt you," Trisha said, feeling sorry as Dixie whimpered and ran toward the garage, disappearing from view.

"Oh, Trisha. Look at your nose." Betty Sue walked closer to Trisha. "I'm so sorry your sister did that to you."

Trisha crossed her arms. "What do you want, Mom?"

"What do I want? I'm your mother. I haven't seen you for thirteen years. I want to spend some time with you. I want to be a part of your life."

"Now?" Trisha asked, years of anger bottled up inside of her.

"Why, yes. Now. Didn't Charley tell you I called? Damn that man. He was supposed to tell you."

"He did. I chose not to call you back."

"Why on earth would you do that?"

"Because, you made it perfectly clear when I was twenty-two years old that if I didn't want to play by your rules, then I was no longer welcome in your family. That was your choice, not mine."

"Trisha, stop speaking such nonsense. We had a disagreement."

"What we had wasn't a disagreement." Trisha shook her head. "No, what we had was another one of your attempts to control me."

Betty Sue flung her hand to her heart. "What? I've never tried to—"

"Save it, Mother. I've had plenty of time to think over the years. All the while I was growing up, you were always trying to control me. You controlled who my friends were and then who my boyfriends were. If you decided someone wasn't good enough for me, you found a way to get them out of my life. I'm sorry, but I'm not looking for a mother anymore. I've grown up."

"You're never too old to have your mother in your life."

"Do you have any idea how much it hurt that no one from my family ever attended any of my college ballgames? Or that not one of you came to see me graduate from college?"

"Well, your father—"

"Isn't that handy? Blame it on him when he isn't here to blame it on you."

"Trisha, I—"

"Don't even get me started on what you two did to me after college. Do you have any idea how hard it was to survive in California when all of your financial support is stripped away from you the day you graduate from college? When most kids were getting financial gifts from their parents, mine were taking them away from me."

"I didn't want to do that. That truly was all your father's doing. He thought you'd come home if you didn't have any money to live on."

"Well, he was wrong, wasn't he? I found a way to survive," Trisha said, her memories quickly back on her mistake with Coach Halley.

"What'd you have to do, honey?"

Trisha looked at the concern on her mother's face and tried to maintain her composure as her feelings of shame and her desire to have a mother's love swirled around in her heart and mind.

"Trisha, what'd you have to do to survive?" Betty Sue demanded.

"Wouldn't you like to know? But you don't deserve the truth. I don't owe you anything anymore."

"Trisha, come home with me. Let me make it all up to you," Betty Sue begged as she took a step closer to Trisha and held out her hand.

"No." Trisha shook her head. "I don't need my mommy any more. You weren't anywhere around when I did need you and I learned how to fend for myself."

"Fine. Stay here. But promise me you won't get close to Charley

Walker. Please, Trisha, he's not the man you think he is."

"Leave," Trisha yelled, startling her mother. Trisha pointed to the car and added, "Get the hell out of here and never come back."

"But Trisha, I—"

"Leave," Trisha hollered again before turning and running to the house, slamming the door and locking it behind her. She ran into the living room and watched as her mother stood staring at the house. After a minute, Betty Sue turned and walked to her car, and Trisha watched as her mother backed down the driveway and turned onto the gravel road. Then, Trisha fell down on Kat's couch and sobbed.

Jessica woke with a start and sat up, quickly realizing what a mistake that was as the room started to spin.

"Hey, baby. Where ya' goin'?" Glen asked, reaching for her.

"Beats me." Jessica plopped back down and curled up beside the man she'd been seeing for almost six months.

"You stayed all day with me," Glen observed as he noticed the sun was going down outside of his dirty apartment window. "You ain't done that before."

"I had no reason to go home."

"Thinking about your sister?"

Jessica pulled away from him. "Yeah, why? You wanna go and do her too?"

"Wow, hey, no. You're all the woman I can handle, Jess. I don't even know your sister."

"How could you? She's been gone forever."

"Ran away from home, huh?"

Jessica snorted. "Hardly. Ran away to college, then forgot to come home. Forgot all about us back here in Hope-less-ville."

"Well, if you'da left, you'da never met me."

"That's true." Jessica curled back up against him.

They had just begun making out when Jessica's cell phone started to ring.

"Wait a sec." Jessica checked the number on the screen. "Ah, hell, it's my dad."

"Want me to answer?" Glen teased.

"Shut up and be quiet," Jessica demanded as she jumped out of his bed and answered her phone.

"Jess, where are you?"

"You care?"

"You know I care about you. I'm worried about you, Jess. Come home so we can talk about all of this."

"You've got Trisha now; you don't need me."

"Jessica, I love both of you and your brother, too. We have a chance to have the family all back together again. I want you to be here when your sister comes home to stay."

"Is she coming home to stay?"

"Well, eventually she will. We've just got a few things we'll have to work out first. I'm worried about you, Jessica. Where are you?"

"With my boyfriend. Until Danni comes back, I'm staying here."

"No, you need to come home. Now," George demanded, thinking about the thug Jessica had brought to the wedding.

"No. You guys didn't even ask me if my daughter could go on a trip. You don't need me around until she gets back. When will that be?"

"Damn it, Jessica. Your mother and I have given you so much over the years, why can't you ever—"

"What? Be more like Trisha?" Jessica interrupted. "Well, actually, I am. I ran away from home."

"Listen, little girl. You get your butt back here within the next hour if you want your mother and me to continue helping you keep Danni. Otherwise, I'm going to do what everyone thinks I should do. I'm going to call Judge Martin and tell him to let Clay have full custody of Danni. I'm serious, young lady. Either get your butt back to my house or be prepared to be out on your own. Permanently."

"Oh, shit," Jessica growled after her father hung up.

"What is it, babe?"

"I hate her," Jessica yelled as she jumped up and started running around the room, picking things up and throwing them as she went. "Hate her!"

"Who?" Glen sat up. "I thought that was your old man."

"He threatened me. He said if I don't come home now, he's going to give my little girl to Clay."

"Is that all?" Glen asked, lying back down. "I thought somethin' was wrong."

"Something is wrong. She's my daughter, not his. Damn Trisha for coming back home. She's messin' everything up."

"Ready to get rid of her?" Glen propped himself up on his elbow.

"I don't know. Maybe." Jessica felt dizzy again as she sat down on the bed with a thud. "But for now, I'd better get home."

"Let her go, Jess. Stay with me and let that brat move in with your ex. Permanently. Stay here, please."

"You don't get it, Glen. She's my daughter."

"Fine, go," Glen conceded as he climbed out of the bed and walked into the kitchen. Standing naked a few feet away from Jessica, he opened the bottle of whiskey and took a long swig.

"You're not playin' fair," Jessica moaned, wanting both the alcohol and him.

He held the bottle out to her. "I'll share."

Unable to stop herself, Jessica hurried over and took the bottle from him, then she started guzzling it.

Glen took her in his arms and started kissing her neck as she drained down the rest of the bottle, then he picked her up and carried her back to his bed.

❧

Trisha sat in the cemetery's driveway, staring at the gravestone of their little girl, her entire body shaking with fear and shame.

Her mind was back to the day they buried her. No one had known she was in Hope that day. And she assumed no one had ever found out after she'd left. It had just been her and Brad with a minister they had flown in with them from California. A generous bonus had sealed the lips of the people from the funeral home.

The burial service had been short, but Trisha still felt as if she'd buried part of herself on that gray, dreary day.

Trisha's mind flashed further back to the day Brad had informed her they were burying their daughter in the very place she didn't think she ever wanted to return to again. Trisha had been livid when she found out Brad had made all of the arrangements without even consulting her.

Like many other times in their relationship, Trisha had held her anger and opinions inside of her. But as soon as they had returned to California after the burial, she'd exploded, letting him know exactly how she felt about her baby girl being more than 1500 miles away from her in the middle of what she had considered enemy territory.

She bristled as she remembered pounding on Brad's chest, while angry words that she'd bottled up time and time again, flowed as freely as the tears that had streamed down her face.

Trisha took a deep sigh, still able to feel deep in her heart the pain of losing both her baby and her marriage in what seemed like one moment in time.

Willing herself back to the present, Trisha took a deep breath, then reached over and grabbed the pink teddy bear she carried with her everywhere she went. It had been the first stuffed animal they'd purchased when they had found out they were having a baby girl.

Trisha climbed out of the car and carried the bear over to the stone.

"Hello, my sweet baby, it's mommy." Trisha rubbed her fingers along the lettering that spelled Sophie Sue Jenkins as a lump formed in her throat. "I'm sorry I haven't been here for a long time. But I'm here now. And I'm going to be back to visit you a lot now. Mommy moved closer, baby."

Trisha's ringing cell phone startled her, and she dropped the bear onto the ground.

"Oh, shoot," Trisha said as she picked it up. Noticing it was Charley calling, she cleared her throat before saying hello.

"Hey, Trisha. Sorry I've been gone so long. Have you had supper?"

"No, I haven't," Trisha answered, leaving out that she hadn't had lunch either.

"Well, why don't you meet me at The Tasty Cone in Hope? Do you remember where that's at?"

"Sure. It's still open?"

"Oh, it's changed owners a time or two. They've done a little remodeling, but yeah, it's still open. And as delicious as ever. If you don't want people seeing your bruising, you can stay in the car. I can order it for us, and then we can take it back to my house."

"No, that's fine. I don't mind," Trisha said, tired of hiding. "I'm a few blocks away from there. I'll be there shortly."

"I'll see you there, honey. I've missed you today."

Trisha smiled. "I've missed you too."

She placed her phone into her pocket, then kissed her fingers and touched the cool stone.

"I love you little girl, and I'll be back real soon."

After getting in her car, Trisha drove toward The Tasty Cone and happiness washed over her when she noticed Charley was waiting in front, talking with a couple she didn't know.

Finding a parking place in the busy lot wasn't easy, and Trisha finally pulled around the back of the shack and parked where the employees parked.

She took a deep breath, fetched her purse and got out of the car. "Here goes nothing."

A few people stared at her, clearly noticing the bruising. But she continued on, not stopping until she was at Charley's side.

"Hi Trisha. Ready to eat?"

"I am."

"See you later, Charley," the man said while the lady studied Trisha before they turned and walked back to an old Chevy pickup truck.

"Can I help you?" a teenager asked as she poked her head through the open window.

"Yeah. I want a double cheeseburger with tomatoes, lettuce and mustard and fries. Trisha, what do you want?"

"Oh, a…" Trisha started, looking up at the menu above the window.

She couldn't believe the prices were so high. "How about a hamburger with lettuce and pickles."

"It will be few minutes," the teenager said as she shut the window and disappeared.

"How was your day?" Charley asked as he took her hand in his.

Trisha shrugged. "Did Darrell find some cattle?"

"Yes. He bought fifteen head. They're delivering them tomorrow."

"Why don't you let me pay for this and you go and find us a place to sit?" Trisha suggested, looking around at the families who were eating.

"Sure. Thanks."

"Here you go." The girl handed her the bag of food through the window. "That will be $13.50."

Trisha paid her the money and waited for the change, then picked up a handful of napkins and headed for Charley, who was waiting for her on a bench.

"All the tables were taken. Is this okay?"

"Yeah, sure."

"You didn't tell me about your day," Charley reminded her as he started eating his double cheeseburger.

Trisha quickly went over the events of the last few hours, including her conversation with Scarlette and her argument with her mother.

"Sounds like you've had quite a day," Charley said, stunned with everything she was telling him. "How well do you know this Scarlette person? Do you think she'd hurt you?"

"No. I don't think so. I'm sure she's still all the way out in California."

"What did Brad say about this?"

"I haven't told him yet. He's flying to Paris today, and with the time change, I didn't think I'd call until tomorrow."

"Well, I think you need to tell him so he knows how she's acting. And as far as your mother goes, how in the world did she find you?"

"My parents have their ways." Trisha took a bite of her hamburger. "I figured they'd find me, but I didn't figure they'd find me so quickly."

"Have you seen your sister?"

Trisha shook her head, "Not yet."

Charley reached over and took ahold of her hand. "Well, I'm glad we're together now."

Trisha smiled, feeling the butterflies coming to life again.

"What the hell is going on here?"

Trisha shook her head when she noticed her father's friend, Robert Townsend, was standing in front of them, glaring at Charley.

"Trisha? My God, it is you. Does your Dad know you're here?"

"No. Why would he?"

"He wouldn't approve." Robert crossed him arms. "What are you doing, Walker? Making a move on George's daughter to get back at him?"

"Just walk away, Townsend," Charley demanded as he crumpled his napkin in his fist while he stood up.

"Stop this," Trisha ordered as she jumped up and stepped between them, her half-eaten sandwich falling to the green grass below.

"Your dad wouldn't want you anywhere near this bastard," Robert said, looking at Trisha. "Go home, Trisha."

"First of all, I decide whom I associate with," Trisha started, getting angry and embarrassed all over again as some of the families still eating turned their way. "And second of all, Charley's been nothing but nice to me. My brother married his daughter."

"I know all about that doomed marriage," Robert snarled as he took a step back but started wagging his index finger at Trisha. "And you, young lady, don't know what you're getting in to. Your dad wouldn't like this. Not one bit."

"Why?" Trisha asked, her hands on her hips as she took a step toward Robert. "Come on Robert, why wouldn't my dad like me talking to Charley? What's the big deal?"

"You'll need to talk to your father about that. I'll be sure to let him know so he can put an end to...to whatever the hell is going on here."

Trisha kept her ground, standing between Charley and Robert as Robert glared again before stomping away and climbing into a black town car, one Trisha suspected was a gift from her father.

"I'm sorry about that Trisha. And I'm sorry about your supper. Let me see if the girls can get make you another sandwich," Charley said as Trisha walked over and sat back down on the bench.

"It's okay. I lost my appetite anyway."

Charley sat down beside her. "I'm so sorry."

"I don't blame you. I've never been a fan of Robert Townsend. He uses my father. That man hasn't worked an honest day in his life. I don't know if people know this or not, but my dad bought Robert's house and car, and got him a cushy job at one of the banks we own. That man is worthless."

"He's retired now."

"I'm not surprised." Trisha shook her head. "Sometimes I forget I'm not 18 anymore. Being here again has really taken me back in time."

Silence fell over them, and Charley munched on his french fries before offering them to Trisha.

"That tastes so good," Trisha said as she nibbled on a fry. "It's been a long time since I ate fried food."

"Can't get fine dining like The Tasty Cone out in California, huh?"

Trisha giggled. "Nope, you have to travel all the way to Hope, Iowa to find that."

"There's that beautiful smile," Charley said, glad to see it again.

Betty Sue was still upset as she pulled up to the garage, almost clipping the large lion statue she had insisted they place there.

"Move that damned thing. It's in the way," Betty Sue yelled as soon as Jim came out the door of the garages.

"Yes, ma'am."

Betty Sue hurried into the garage and took off down the hallway that led to the main house. She stopped before opening the door and started moving things around in her purse until she found her small silver tin, and then she opened it up and pulled out two white pills.

She threw them into her mouth and tossed back her head, swallowing them. Then she continued into the kitchen.

"Helen.

"Yes, ma'am," Helen called as she walked into the room.

Betty Sue put her hands on her hips and ordered sharply, "I need a glass of water."

Helen pulled one of the spotless crystal glasses out of the cupboard and filled it with distilled water, then handed it to Betty Sue.

She took a long drink, then handed it back.

"I expect a pitcher of water in my room in twenty minutes. I want it cold, too, not like last night's water was. You'd better get it right."

"Yes, ma'am."

Betty Sue stormed out of the kitchen and through the dining room, then stomped down the hallway and slammed George's study door open.

"Sue?"

"Our daughter," Betty Sue started as she hurried to his couch and plopped down.

"What's Jessica done now?" George pried, thinking about their earlier conversation.

"Not Jessica, Trisha."

"I thought we were going to give Trisha some time," George said, then crossed his arms as he walked over to the couch. "Did you go see her? Without me?"

Betty Sue nodded. "I'm sorry. I had to. It's been so long since I've seen our precious daughter. Once I knew where she was, I had to go. I didn't expect to see her standing outside the Roe girl's house. But there she was, playing fetch with some mutt. I stopped, George. I stopped to talk to her. But she's angry at us, George. She's so very angry."

"I wish you would've taken me with you," George said as he sat down beside her on the couch. "How was her nose?"

"Oh, she's bruised terribly," Betty Sue said, putting her hand to her own nose and shaking her head. "Jessica hurt her badly."

"Well, I'm done with Jessica. I've already called the judge. We're meeting in the morning."

"What happened?"

"She's with that man, Sue. I told her she had to be home within the hour or I was going to tell the judge to grant Clay full custody of Danni. That was almost three hours ago. I've been out to the pool house more times than I remember; she's not there. She never came home. She's doesn't really care about her own daughter, and because of that, I can no longer care for Jessica."

"You're doing the right thing, George. I know it's hard, but you're doing the right thing. We need to concentrate on Trisha now. We need to give her our full attention."

George's private cell phone started ringing, and he quickly got up and hurried to his desk, secretly hoping it was Jessica calling to tell him she was on her way home. When he noticed it was Robert, and knowing Sue didn't want him talking to his friend, he turned to Sue and lied, "This is one of the private eyes I called this morning."

"Take it."

George stepped into the hallway and shut the door, "Hello?"

"Your daughter's back in town."

"Trisha?"

"Yeah. I need to see you, George. You're not going to believe what I found out about her."

"I'll meet you in twenty minutes at the Downtown Bar & Grill," George said, then hung up and hurried back into the study, finding Betty Sue sound asleep on his couch.

"She's taking those damned pills again, isn't she?" He walked over to the closet and pulled out a blanket and a pillow. Then he carefully placed the pillow under her head and lovingly covered her with the blanket.

"I'll be back, my dear."

"The stars are so beautiful out here," Trisha said as she and Charley stood in his front yard, looking up.

"Yeah, they are. But none of them are as beautiful as you, Trisha." Charley walked up behind her and put his arms around her waist, pulling her tightly against him. "I thought about you all day, Trisha."

"I thought about you too," Trisha said, butterflies darting around in her stomach again.

She turned to face him, and they both leaned in for a kiss.

"Let's go inside." Charley took her hand and they walked up to the front door.

Trisha waited while he unlocked it. Then they walked into the dark living room and started kissing again.

"Make love to me, Charley," Trisha said between kisses. "Now, please, make love to me."

Charley pushed the door with his foot, and then he picked her up and carried her to his bedroom, laying her gently on his bed.

George pulled his car up in front of Downtown Bar & Grill and stopped, taking a deep breath as his mind went crazy, wondering what Robert could possibly know about his daughter.

He walked through the door and blinked a couple of times, trying to get his eyes to adjust to the darkness while his nose quickly caught the scent of his favorite drink—whiskey.

"George, over here."

George noticed Robert was sitting at a table near the back of the establishment, which was bustling with the late night drinking crowd.

"These are the only seats they had left," Robert explained as George sat down.

George shrugged. "It's okay. What do you know about Trisha?"

"I ordered for you," Robert explained as a cute blonde waitress wearing too much makeup and too small of a shirt stopped at their table and juggled the mug of beer and shot glass of whiskey.

"He gets the whiskey," Robert said, pointing to George while his eyes were fixated on the stretched-out letters spelling State Champs on her shirt.

George could feel his patience wearing thin as Robert tried his best to flirt with her.

"Damn, she's hot," Robert said as she walked away.

"She's a kid."

"Has to be at least twenty-one to be working here. That's legal."

"Okay, whatever. What about Trisha?"

"I saw her a little bit ago."

"Where?"

"The Tasty Cone, but it's not where, George, it's who she was with."

"Damn it, Robert. Tell me."

"Charley Walker. Your daughter was with that SOB at The Tasty Cone. And they seemed real cozy to me."

"Shit."

"I know. I went to get me a cone, and there they were, sitting on a bench. Real close too. I'm telling you, George. He's making a move on your daughter. He's trying to get back at you, man."

"I'll kill him." George's face turned a bright shade of red.

"Hey, George, since I shared this information with you, do you think you could give me a little more money? I know Sue's against it, but I really need some to get by. It's the last time I'll ask, I swear."

George sat back in his chair, studying his friend while thinking about everything he'd already done for him. He'd gotten him a job when they were young and then a generous retirement package when he had made too many mistakes. Over the years, he'd also gotten him numerous cars and had even paid off his house when he'd been close to being foreclosed on. And that didn't even count all the times he'd given him money for various purchases.

But Betty Sue had been adamant the last time he'd given Robert a $10,000 check. She said that was the very last time they were giving him anything.

George shook his head. "I'm sorry, Robert. I can't."

"Well, I see what kinda friend you are," Robert huffed as he jumped up and hurried out of the bar.

"I'm glad you're staying the night," Charley said as he and Trisha lay curled up together in his bed.

"I really missed you today." Trisha snuggled in tightly against him. "I think I'll stay with you tomorrow too, if that's okay. Kat said she'd call my cell if she needs me."

"I think that'd be great. I'm so happy you're in my life, Trisha."

"There's no where else I'd rather be."

൏

After several drinks, George started for home.

His heart hurt as he wondered how involved his daughter was with Charley Walker. And he was angry they'd be flaunting it in public.

His mind quickly went back to Tyler's wedding. He remembered how excited he had been when he'd realized Trisha was back in Iowa. And how that happiness had turned to dread and then anger that she had been there with Charley.

The honking of a horn brought him back to reality quickly, and he slammed on his brakes, narrowly missing a truck that was coming toward him.

"Idiot," George yelled, even though he knew he was to blame, as he was driving down the wrong side of the county highway.

George gripped the wheel tightly in an effort to fight off sleep, and forced himself to focus on his driving.

Finally arriving at his house, he parked in the garage and quickly fell into a drunken slumber.

Chapter 12

"I think we're gonna make it," Tyler said as he slowly drove down the gravel road to Pam's house. "Do you want me to wait for you, or do you want to drive yourself?"

"I'll drive myself. I don't have to be at the school until nine. Your meeting starts at eight thirty. You go on, and we'll meet at lunch."

"I'm going to miss you, Mrs. Bailey," Tyler said as he pulled into the driveway of Charley's house and turned toward her.

Pam leaned over for a kiss, then smiled. "I'm going to miss you too. I can't believe they moved those meetings to today. And in the morning even. They knew we weren't supposed to be back until tomorrow."

"Oh, well. We can continue celebrating our honeymoon tonight at our own house."

"I like the sound of that. See you at lunch."

She stood outside, waving, as he backed up and slowly took off down the road, and then she petted Shooter before hurrying up the stairs to the front door.

"It's not even shut all the way," Pam said, noticing the door wasn't latched.

Worried something had happened to her father, she started down the hallway and stepped into his room, stopping cold in her tracks when she found her father and new sister-in-law wrapped up in each other's arms.

"What the hell?" Pam gasped, turning around quickly.

"Pam?" Charley called as he slid to the edge of the bed.

"I didn't know…what are you…oh dear," Pam mumbled as she ran down the hall and slammed her bedroom door.

"Oh, Charley," Trisha whispered, embarrassed beyond words.

"Pam," Charley called as he jumped up and pulled on his jeans before running out of the room, shutting the door behind him.

Trisha quickly got up and dressed, then she sat down on the edge of bed and shut her eyes. "What a mess."

ꙮ

Pounding with his fists, Charley insisted, "Pam, open this door."

"Go away. I don't want to talk to you right now," Pam hollered as she stomped around her room, angrily looking for the dress clothes she needed for her meeting.

"Pam, we need to talk. Now."

Pam quickly changed into her pants and blouse, then threw her door open. Face-to-face with her father, she ordered, "Get out of my way, Daddy."

"Pam, I'm sorry. I didn't think you were coming back today. I didn't mean to upset you."

"Why are you still with her?" Pam demanded as she glared down the hallway at the closed bedroom door. "She lied to you."

"No, she never lied to me, Pam. It was just a big misunderstanding."

Pam snorted and put her hands on her hips. "Yeah. And I was born yesterday. Clearly, she's up to something. Why else would she not tell you she's a Bailey?"

"Her last name's Jenkins. It's her married name, Pam."

"She's married?" Pam asked, her eyebrows rising.

"She was. She's divorced now. I never told her whom you were marrying, because we never had a chance to talk about it. She's a good person, Pam. I care very deeply for her."

"How do you know she's not trying to get you in trouble, Daddy? She's a Bailey, and you have made it perfectly clear that you don't trust the Baileys."

"I trust Trisha."

"So you can decide to trust Trisha, but you're mad at me for trusting Tyler?"

Charley ran his fingers through his dark hair, pausing to think, then said, "I'm sorry I was so hard on Tyler. I shouldn't have judged him."

"It's not just because she's a Bailey," Pam mumbled, her eyes burning. "She's not that much older than me, Daddy. I think she's too young for you."

"I know she's younger, but I'm happy with her. I've waited a long time to find someone like her."

"You barely know her."

"I'm not going to stop seeing her, Pam. And you need to respect that."

"I have to get to work," Pam growled as she pushed past him and stomped down the hallway.

"Pam, please?" Charley called as he followed her outside, only stopping when they both reached her car. "Think about the baby, Pam. Don't drive when you're this upset."

"I have to get to a meeting. That's why we're back early."

"I wish you would've told me you were coming."

"I didn't realize I needed to make an appointment to see my daddy."

"You don't, honey. And I'm sorry you walked in on what you did, but this is my house. And I can have a woman over in my house."

"Yes, I guess you can. Just be careful not to get her knocked up, Daddy. You said it yourself, it's the Bailey way," Pam sarcastically warned before jumping into her car and backing out of the driveway.

"I'm so sorry, Charley," Trisha said as Charley walked back into his house.

"It's not your fault." Charley walked over and plopped down on the couch. "She's very protective of me. Like I am of her."

"Well, I don't want to cause a problem between your daughter and you."

"You're not." Charley patted the couch beside him. "Come and sit down."

Trisha walked over and sat down, then curled up beside him. After a bit, she asked, "Why did Pam say you don't trust my family? Are there more than just the bank issues? And what did Robert mean last night when he accused you of making a move on me to get back at my father?"

There was a long silence, then Charley said, "Your parents and I don't get along, Trisha. Our troubles started in school and never really stopped."

"I need to know more, Charley."

"I want to tell you the whole story," Charley agreed, "but most of this you need to hear from your parents, not me."

"But I don't want to talk to my parents," Trisha reminded him as she sat up and looked him the eyes. "Why won't you tell me?"

Charley got up and started pacing, clearly thinking. Then he said, "Your parents and Nancy and I had a long, complicated history. As much as I want to tell you my side of things, I really think you should give them a chance and hear their side first. Hell, Trish, I've never even told my daughter about any of this."

"But you didn't want her to date Tyler because of whatever this is."

"No, I didn't. That's true."

"I need to go and see my parents, then, because I want all of this out in the open. I want to know what happened so it doesn't come between us in the future. We're getting everything out in the open, right Charley?"

"Except for this, my life's an open book, Trisha. But please, if they start trying to badmouth me, don't believe them. I don't know if you will be able to get them to tell you the truth, but I think the truth should come from them."

"I already trust you more than I'll ever trust them again," Trisha said as she stood up. "I'm going to take a shower, and then I'm going to have a chat with my parents."

෴

"It's done." George walked out by the pool where Betty Sue was swimming.

"That was fast." Betty Sue swam over to the edge and climbed out, covering up in a white terry cloth robe before sitting down at the patio table. "How'd Danni take it?"

"She was all for it." George thought back to his early morning conversation with his granddaughter. "She's thrilled. The judge talked to Clay's lawyer, and they're going to get everything in order today. Danni won't be coming back here. Clay's going to pick her up from the ranch. I told them we'd mail her things to Clay's mother's house. Most of it's still packed from their move here."

"I hate not seeing her before she goes, but I think that's the safest thing to do. We don't want Jessica finding any of this out before Danni's gone," Betty Sue agreed.

They both looked up as the assistant maid walked out to the pool.

"Ma'am, Sir, you have a guest. She said her name's Trisha, and she's waiting in the foyer."

"Oh. My baby," Betty Sue said as she got up and ran into the house, worried she was dreaming again when she noticed Trisha was standing by the front door.

"I need to ask you some questions." Trisha stepped back when her mother tried to hug her.

"Sure, Trisha," George said as he put his hands on Betty Sue's shoulders. "Let's sit by the pool."

❧

Trisha tried to fight off the memories as they came flooding back while she followed her parents down the hallway and into the main living room. She noticed little had changed.

The antique couch and matching straight back chairs still stood in the middle of the room. The piano her mother had tried to force her to learn how to play was still in the far corner. Bookcases with the same knickknacks and books lined the wall near the door. The only things different were the paint and carpet colors.

"It's so nice having you here," Betty Sue said as she opened the French doors and they all walked outside by the pool.

The smell of the chlorine tickled Trisha's nose, and she was instantly back in time to the pool party she'd held for her softball teammates after they had won their first league championship title.

She'd been thrilled when her parents had agreed to let her have the pool party without them being in attendance. It was the only time she'd invited more than one or two close friends over to her house. She'd been sure at the time that her parents had only agreed to the party with the hope that it would change her mind about leaving for California.

"Please, honey, have a seat," Betty Sue said, waking her from her thoughts.

She noticed both of her parents were already sitting down at the patio table and sat down in the empty chair.

"How does it feel to be back home?" George asked.

"It's different."

"Well, I'm just so glad you're here," Betty Sue said, still finding it hard to believe Trisha was indeed in their home again. "We've missed you so much, honey."

"I missed this place for a long, long time."

"You are always welcome here, Trisha. This is your home."

Trisha studied her father and felt tears burning her eyes as she once again noticed how pale and sickly he appeared. Unable to stop herself, she blurted, "Are you sick, Dad?"

Terrified she'd been able to see what no one else had noticed, George rambled, "What? Um, no, I'm fine dear."

"George?" Betty Sue pried as she turned and inspected him. "You are looking a little pale."

"I'm fine, honey. I just need more sun." Trying to get the attention off him, he said, "We'd love to have you move back, Trisha."

Trisha shook her head. "That's not why I'm here."

"Can you stay for lunch?" Betty Sue asked. "I can have Helen fix your favorite. You still like meatloaf, right?"

"I do." Trisha was caught off guard that her mother knew her favorite food. All the time she was growing up, Helen had been the one who remembered her favorite foods and knew her favorite shampoos and perfumes. "Helen still works here?"

"Yes, she does, honey. She'd love to see you," George said.

"But before she does," Betty Sue interrupted, once again jealous of the close relationship her daughter had with their head cook, of all people, "why don't you ask us the question you said you had?"

Trisha took a deep breath. "Why don't you two get along with Charley

Walker?"

"Damn him!" George bellowed, jumping up and startling both women. He pointed his finger at Trisha. "I can't believe you're…involved…with that man. What's wrong with you?"

"Nothing's wrong with me."

Betty Sue noticed the tips of Trisha's ears were turning red, just like Tyler's did when he was angry. Knowing that was usually right before Tyler rushed out of the room or came to blows with his father, Betty Sue ordered, "George, sit down."

George sat down, but crossed his arms and glared at Sue.

"I'm not going to quit seeing him. I asked him what the deal was between the three of you, and he said I should talk to you. So, I'm here."

Betty Sue's mind raced. She couldn't believe Charley would suggest that Trisha actually talk to them about their past, but knew she couldn't tell her the truth. She had to think of something quickly that would keep Trisha from defending Charley but would make her question everything she knew about him.

"Mom?" Trisha asked, noticing her mother seemed miles away.

"This goes back to high school," Betty Sue started, glaring at George when he shot her a panicked look. "Did Charley tell you we were all in high school together?"

"What happened?" Trisha demanded, ignoring her mother's question.

"I don't like to even think about it," Betty Sue insisted as she managed to squeeze out some tears. "I can't believe he'd send you over here to ask me about this. He really is a terrible, horrible man."

Trisha jumped at her mother's outburst. "What happened?"

"It's too upsetting for me to even talk about it," Betty Sue mumbled through the waterworks she had managed to conjure up. "All you need to know, Trisha, is that man cannot and should not be trusted. And I hope you'll stay away from him before it's too late. I thought he was a nice person, too. That was the worst mistake I've ever made. Please, don't make me talk about this anymore."

George got up and walked over to Betty Sue's chair and pulled her to her feet, taking her in his arms and holding her tightly, even managing to offer up a few tears of his own.

"I think I need to go," Trisha mumbled as she stood and took off for the front door, never once turning around.

"So, what do you think she thinks happened?" George asked after Trisha had disappeared into the house.

"Doesn't really matter," Betty Sue answered as she wiped the fake tears off her cheeks. "I think we just planted the first seed of doubt in her mind. Let's hope it grows."

❧

The bells on the old courthouse were chiming as Charley walked out of the bank, his mood about as low as it could get.

"Well, that didn't go very well," he moaned as he walked slowly to his truck and climbed in.

He slumped down in the seat and shut his eyes, trying as hard as he could to keep from crying.

Real men didn't cry. He remembered his father telling him that when he was a little boy and his dog had been hit by a truck on their country road.

He had tried to live by the lessons he'd learned from his dad and could only remember crying three times in his life from then until he'd become a father.

Suddenly, thoughts of that awful night when he'd found a sheriff's deputy standing on his front porch made him shudder.

He and Pam had been fixing a tater tot casserole to surprise Nancy, who was working late at the school. Pam, who'd just started 4th grade, had been super excited to fix her mom supper, talking about nothing else that night after arriving home on the school bus.

The casserole had been ready for almost thirty minutes, and he had just started worrying about his wife when the sheriff's car had pulled into his driveway.

Pam hadn't noticed it, and he'd sent her to her room to start her homework before he'd gone to the door, arriving just before they knocked.

Suddenly, he was back in the moment when the sheriff had told him

Nancy had lost control on the first curve out of town on their gravel road. He had said that her car had flipped several times and that she had been killed instantly. They hadn't been sure if there had been any other cars involved.

He'd gone through so many emotions so quickly that night.

What had stopped him from going completely out of his mind had been his little girl, who had run out on the porch.

The sheriff had left shortly after that, and Charley had told Pam what had happened. Then, they had sat on the couch, Pam curled up in his arms, and they both had cried and cried and cried.

Pam had actually fallen asleep crying, and Charley had taken her to her room and tucked her into her bed.

Then he had gone back to the couch and sat all night, staring at their family picture on the wall.

He hadn't cried again after that except for happy tears when his little girl had done something that had made him proud.

Suddenly, Trisha's smiling face popped up in his mind.

Feelings of excitement and happiness started mixing with sadness and guilt. And Charley felt more confused than he had been in a long time.

"I'm gonna have to deal with my financial mess," Charley reminded himself, talking out loud, before he started his truck and headed out of town.

"Trisha? What are you doing here?" Tyler said as he rushed into his empty classroom at the school.

"I hope it's okay I came here. I wanted to talk to you."

"Yeah, it's fine. Actually, I'm really glad you came to see me, Trisha."

"Really?"

"Oh, Trisha. I'm so sorry about everything." Tyler grabbed his big sister in a tight bear hug. "I'm sorry we grew apart, I'm sorry Jessica hit you, and I'm sorry our parents turned their backs on you."

Trisha buried her face into his chest, thankful for the support and love of her brother.

"Are you staying for awhile, Trisha? Because I'd really like to spend some time with you."

"I'm moving here, Tyler. I got a job at Just For You Insurance."

"Really? Oh, that's great. You'll be here to spend time with your niece or nephew then."

Trisha smiled, noticing the proud papa grin on her little brother's face. "Charley told me about the baby."

"So, how'd you two hook up?"

Trisha took a deep breath, knowing Charley hadn't told anyone about his time in Minneapolis. Finally, she said, "I met him last weekend, and we hit it off. He's a great guy."

"Did you move here because of him?"

Trisha shook her head. "I didn't even realize Charley lived here. I just knew he lived in Iowa."

"Did you move here to be close to home?"

"I moved here because I had a job offer. But I want our close relationship back, Tyler. We were best friends growing up, and I want that friendship back."

"Me too. So, how'd you know where to find me?"

"Kat Roe, my boss, mentioned you worked at the school. I knew you and Pam had meetings today, so I asked at the office where I could find you. They told me to wait for you in your room."

"So, you've seen Pam?"

Thinking back to their morning, she nodded, "You haven't?"

"Not since I dropped her off at Charley's. We were supposed to have lunch together, but her meeting's running late."

"Well, she caught us at a bad time, Tyler. She walked in on something I'm sure she's wishing she could forget. And I feel awful about it."

"Oh, shoot." Tyler leaned on his desk.

"Yeah. It was terrible. That wasn't a good way for me to start trying to win her over."

"No, but she's a good person, Trish. She'll think about it and come to realize you're good for her father. I'm sure she will."

"I hope so. I also had a chat with Mom and Dad this morning."

"Wow, way to jump into the fire."

"Do you know why they don't get along with Charley?"

Tyler shook his head as he noticed the time on the clock. "Neither Pam nor I do. I'm sorry, Trisha, but I have to get to my next meeting. Can I call you? Maybe we could all go out to eat soon?"

"I'd love that." Trisha pulled out her cell phone. "Put your number in there, and I'll give you a call."

"When the hell did that happen?" Jessica demanded as she talked to her lawyer's secretary on the telephone.

"My father can rot in hell." Jessica ended the call and threw her phone into the passenger's side of her car. "I can't believe he did that. I can't believe he followed through on his threat. No one takes my daughter away from me. No one."

Deciding she needed something to make the day go away, Jessica drove to Stu's, the nearest bar, and parked, fetched her purse and hurried inside.

Blinded by the darkness, she made her way to her favorite bar stool and sat down, pounding her fist on the counter. "Give me whiskey."

After slamming down the first shot, Jessica nursed the second one while she thought about her daughter and the fact she was most likely already on her way to live with the only father she'd ever known.

"Damn my family," Jessica growled as she slammed down what was left of the second shot of whiskey and pounded on the counter until the bartender set the bottle down in front of her.

Carl sat in the corner booth of the small dive bar, watching the woman at the bar getting toasted, and couldn't believe his eyes. She looked a lot like Trisha Bailey, but rougher than he remembered.

"Could that be her?" he said as he watched her finish an entire bottle of whiskey.

Deciding there was only one way to find out, he walked over and sat down beside her. When she glanced his direction, he whispered, "Trisha?"

"What?" Jessica asked, glaring at him.

"Are you Trisha Bailey?"

"Get the hell out of my face," Jessica demanded, flinging her hand in his direction and almost falling off her bar stool.

"So, you're not Trisha?"

"No, I'm not that bitch." Jessica shook her head. "I'm her sister. Why, you wanna screw her, too?"

"No," Carl lied, shaking his head as he stood up. "I haven't seen her for years. Thought you were her. Sorry."

"Wait," Jessica said as she tried to get up to follow him and instead fell to the sticky floor as her head started spinning.

"Are you okay?" Carl asked as he hurried over and helped her to her feet.

"No," Jessica's eyes welled up. "Why does everyone love my damned sister so much?"

"I don't love her," Carl lied again, his body coming to life as he felt her soft skin against his and smelled the flowery smell of her shampoo. It had been too long since he'd been in the arms of a woman, and this woman was as close to Trisha Bailey as he'd ever gotten. "Need a ride somewhere, sweetheart?"

"I'm not done drinking yet."

"Oh, yeah you are, Jess. Take her home." The owner of the bar ushered them toward the door, handing Carl her purse. "She hasn't paid yet."

"I got this," Carl said as he placed his last $50 on the counter, then helped her outside. "Your car or mine, sweetheart?"

"Mine." Jessica pointed at her purse. "Keys are there."

"Which one is it?"

"The Cadillac," Jessica sputtered, frustrated. "Help me."

Carl helped her to the passenger's side and fumbled with her purse until he found the keys. Then he opened the door and helped her in, dropping the purse beside her as he shut the door.

"Sweet, a Caddy."

He hurried around and climbed in behind the wheel, feeling like a king as he started it up and let it purr.

"Take me home."

"Where's home?"

"Or your place." Jessica shut her eyes and leaned her head against the closed window.

"As you wish," Carl said, noticing Jessica was already passed out.

He drove across town to the small rent-by-the-week motel he'd been staying at and shut off the car, then poked her. "We're here, Princess."

"I like that," Jessica said, waking. "Take me inside, peasant."

Carl rolled his eyes as he got out and walked to her door. Then he opened it and helped her to her feet. Noticing she was almost passed out again, he picked her up and carried her to his door, then leaned her against him as he unlocked the door and they walked inside.

Jessica started pulling off her clothes. "I want you, Glen."

"I want you too," Carl agreed, ignoring the fact she'd called him Glen. He watched anxiously as she struggled to strip down to her birthday suit, then took her to his bed.

Trisha's mind replayed her conversation with her parents over and over again in her mind as she drove down the road and pulled into Kat's driveway.

Noticing Kat's car was home, she hurried into the house.

Kat walked into the kitchen carrying a suitcase. "Hey," she said. "I was just getting ready to call you."

"Are you going somewhere?"

"Yes. Vic's mother passed away this morning. I'm leaving for Kansas."

Trisha hugged her. "Oh, I'm so sorry for your loss."

"Thanks. Of course, I feel terrible I cheated on him. And I need to confess what I did. But now isn't the time. He's going to need me to be strong for him. His mother and I were never close, but Vic was very close to her."

"There'll be plenty of time to work through your issues," Trisha reassured her. "Do you need a ride to the airport?"

Kat shook her head. "Rick's taking me. He has to fly to California for meetings anyway, so that worked out well."

"I hate staying here while you're gone. I'm sure I can find…"

"You don't need to leave, unless you have somewhere else you want to stay. I don't mind you staying here while I'm gone, Trisha. I trust you."

"Thank you. Do you want me to do your chores for you?"

Kat shook her head. "I've left Chase a list of things that need done. He usually takes care of the cows, horses, and cats and dog for me while I'm out of town. Of course, we aren't speaking right now, so he doesn't know I'm leaving. But I left a note for him in the tractor. He should be here shortly to start mowing the hay."

"How come you two aren't speaking?"

Kat sighed and shrugged her shoulders. "Just a misunderstanding. We have them a lot anymore. So things are going well for you and Charley?"

Her mother's warning came back to her, and Trisha nodded while asking, "Do you know anything about Charley's parents?"

"No. I don't really know Charley," Kat reminded her. "But I know someone who would know his family. Chase's grandmother, Grace. She's lived in the house down the road her entire life. You should go and talk to her if you have any questions. She's really nice and would love to see you."

"Oh, I don't know—"

"She's a sweetheart, Trisha," Kat interrupted. "I know she wouldn't mind if you stopped in. Oh, and I hate to tell you this, but since I'll be the one training you, you'll have to wait to start working until at least next Monday. I'm sorry, Trisha."

"Don't worry about it, I'll be fine. Oh, I think Rick's here."

Kat looked out the window. "That's him. I'll call and let you know how things are going. Call me if you need anything."

Trisha nodded and waved as Kat hurried out the back door.

"Hey."

Darrell stopped working on the fence he was patching. "Hi, Charley.

How'd your meeting go at the bank?"

"Terrible." Charley walked over and leaned across the fence. "They want their money, Darrell. And they refuse to wait until after the crops are out. Damn that George Bailey. He's doing this out of spite. That's what it is—spite!"

"And because you're dating his daughter."

Charley glanced over at Darrell. "Yeah, there's that too."

"Let me help you." Darrell stood up and walked over to Charley. "How much do you owe?"

"I can't take your money, Darrell. It wouldn't be right."

"We'd work something out, Charley. It's a way to keep your farm. I don't want some other neighbor. We've been friends for way too long for me to just sit back and watch that bastard take your ground right out from under ya. How much?"

"Darrell, I—"

"How much?" Darrell interrupted.

"$75,000. But I can't ask to borrow that much, Darrell. It's not right."

"What's not right is George Bailey winning after all of these years." Darrell's cheeks turned red. "If I loaned you that much, you'd be able to be done with George? For good?"

"Yes. That'd pay off the loan for the eighty acres and my operating loan."

"And how much do you think you'll get on crops?" Darrell continued as he started figuring prices in his head.

Charley pulled the now-wrinkled yellow paper out of his pocket. "I have thirty-two acres of corn and thirty-two acres of soybeans."

"How much crop share land?"

"Forty-eight acres of corn and forty acres of beans."

"So, after harvest, you should be able to pay me back some and still have money to live on," Darrell calculated.

"But it all depends on whether it rains or not," Charley reminded him. "If this drought continues, my bushels will be way down. And I won't be able to pay you back hardly any at all."

"Well, I'm not that worried about it, Charley. Let's get the bank paid off first. Come on in the house, and we'll get all this figured up on paper."

"Hi, Charley," Tess called as they walked into the house. "Are you boys hungry? I just fixed a batch of chocolate brownies."

"That's what smells so good," Charley complimented as his stomach growled loudly.

Obviously hearing it, Tess grinned and teased, "Charley's stomach wants some. How about you, honey?"

"Yeah, that'd be great. Thanks, honey. Charley and I'll be in the den."

"Oh. Is everything okay?"

"Yes. We just have some business to go over."

Trisha wasn't sure she was doing the right thing as she pulled into Chase's grandparents' driveway and parked in front of their white, two-story farmhouse. She noticed the curtains moving in one of the windows and took a deep breath. "I've been spotted, so there's no backing out now."

She was halfway to the house on the old, cracked sidewalk when the front door opened and a gray-haired, rounded woman with flour on her cheeks smiled and said, "You must be Trisha Bailey."

"Um, yes, I'm Trisha."

"Chase told us you were living with Kat. That's so nice. I was hoping you'd stop by to say hello. Come on in."

Trisha smiled as she was whisked in the door. Smells of cinnamon and apple tickled her nose, and she couldn't help but wonder what her life would have been like if she hadn't lost her grandparents when she was only five.

"I hope you like apple pie, because I just pulled one out of the oven five minutes ago. I'm Grace, by the way."

"Nice to meet you, Grace. And yes, I love apple pie."

Grace smiled. "Most folks do. Come on into the kitchen and have a seat. Would you like ice cream?"

"Oh, no. I'd better stop at the pie."

"All you health conscious youngsters," Grace said, clicking her tongue as she cut a generous slice of pie and placed it on the table in front of Trisha. Then she cut a piece for herself and sat down across from Trisha. "So, Trisha, what can I do for you?"

"Well, I wanted to stop by and say hi. Kat mentioned I should."

"Oh, Katherine. I love her to pieces." Grace slipped another forkful of pie into her mouth. "I was so hoping she and Chase would work things out. They belong together, you know. But now that she's married, I have to keep my mouth shut."

Trisha offered a sympathetic smile. "I thought they'd get married some day, too. I was surprised when I ran into Kat and found out she'd married someone else."

"Well, my grandson messed up. And he regrets his mistakes every single day. He doesn't regret having his son. He's a great dad. It's just that he and Katherine were meant to be together."

Silence fell over them as they both enjoyed their pie while lost in their own thoughts. Finally, Trisha said, "I wondered if I could ask you a question?"

"Sure, dear."

"I wondered if you knew why my father doesn't get along with Charley Walker?"

Grace winked. "I heard you two were getting friendly."

"Really? You heard that? From whom?"

"It's a small town, dear."

"Do you know why they don't get along?" Trisha asked again, trying not to show how much it bothered her that people were obviously talking about her relationship with Charley.

"I do know a lot about Charley. I was close friends with his mother, Joyce. We went to school together. And my husband, Douglas, was good friends with Charley's father, Ray. We stood up with them at their wedding."

"So, you knew them very well."

"Yes. And I miss Joyce every day. They were so happy when they had Charley. It had been a struggle for them to get pregnant. I could always see the sadness in her eyes when I was carrying my boys. But she never let on she wasn't happy for me. Then she got pregnant with Charley, and they were thrilled. They got their little farmer."

Trisha smiled.

"And Charley was the spitting image of his father, too. That boy was out helping his father and grandfather as soon as he could walk. He was riding the horses before he started school. And driving, too. I remember the first time I saw him drive by our house. He was only seven. And he was driving better than me."

Trisha laughed.

"It was hard on the whole family when their dear Nancy was killed. Oh, it was a hard day indeed. For the whole town too. Everyone loved Nancy. And to lose that little baby too; it was such a tragedy. Then Ray got the cancer and passed, and Joyce passed. Oh, I still miss them."

Trisha noticed the tears slipping down Grace's cheeks and grabbed a tissue from the center of the table, handing it to her.

"Thanks, dear." Grace patted her arm with one hand as she dabbed at her eyes with the other. "Would you like some coffee?"

"Let me get it," Trisha said as she stood up.

"The cups are in that cupboard above the stove."

Trisha gathered the cups and filled them with piping hot coffee that had clearly been made shortly before she had arrived. She carried their cups over to the table and sat back down.

"I know Charley had lots of trouble with your father in school, Trisha. George was a year older than my oldest, Christopher. I don't mean to talk badly about your family, Trisha, but George wasn't a nice child back then. He was spoiled. And I have no idea how that happened, because your grandparents were such kind, loving people. But George wasn't as kind. I always thought that boy he hung around, that Robert Townsend child, was to blame for how your father acted back then. Christopher tried to steer clear of your father. And Joyce used to talk about how your father would pick on Charley, too. She was always worried they'd get into a fight on school property and Charley would get in trouble. But then George and Betty Sue got married and had you, and he grew up."

"And that's all you know about my father and Charley?"

Grace nodded before sipping on her coffee. "You can talk to Christopher, if you'd like. But that's all I know."

ꕥ

"How much money are you loaning Charley?" Tess asked Darrell as they walked to the truck to head to town.

"$75,000."

Tess' head spun as she thought about the money she needed to pay her brother. She'd withdrawn $5,000 from their bank account when she was in town getting groceries the day before. She'd planned to wait another week before withdrawing the rest, but wondered if she should do it today. Before she could stop herself, she blurted, "That's a hell of a lot of money."

Darrell's green eyes were intense as he glared at her across the bed of the pickup. "He needs my help. And I plan on helping him. Do you have a problem with that?"

Sensing she was close to upsetting her usually calm husband, Tess shook her head.

They both climbed into his truck and were halfway to town before Tess asked, "What's he need that much money for?"

"To pay off his bank loan. They are threatening to take his land, Tess. I can't stand by and watch that happen. Especially when I have the funds to help him. If the tables were turned, he'd do the same for me."

Unable to let it go, Tess continued, "But that's a lot of money, Darrell. I can't believe he asked you for that much."

She reached for the dash in front of her to stop herself from flying into it as Darrell slammed on his brakes and pulled the truck to the side of the road, quickly shutting it off.

There was a long, uncomfortable silence between them as Darrell stared at the field to their left, then he softly said, "You know, Tess, I went a long time being a bachelor. It wasn't until I got this money that women started showing an interest in me. And I didn't fall for it, because none of them liked me. They liked my money. I married you because I thought you liked me."

"I do like you. It's just that—"

"We both know what I do with my money is my decision," Darrell interrupted. "You signed those papers before we got married."

"I remember."

"If it wasn't for my mother, I wouldn't even have this money. She invested all she inherited and invested it smartly. She would want me to help Charley. I can't understand why you don't want me to help my friend."

"I'm sorry," Tess said, feeling terrible she was giving him any reason to doubt her love for him. She knew it was because of her brother coming to town that she was on edge. "I love you, Darrell. Not your money. I think it's nice you want to help him."

"Good." Darrell glanced back at the road. "Then we're done talking about this, right?"

Tess nodded and felt her heart rate return to normal as Darrell started the truck and they continued on to town.

Charley was parking his tractor in the shed when his cell phone started ringing. He quickly cut the engine and answered.

"Charley, it's B.J. How's it going?"

"Oh, shoot. I was supposed to call you about that job," Charley said, snapping his fingers.

"Oh, don't worry about it. I got better news."

"What's that?"

"Have you heard of McCoy Auctioneering over in Taylor?"

"Sure. I used to go to their auctions all the time when I was a kid."

"Well, Clint McCoy is ready to think about retiring. As you probably know, he's a third generation auctioneer, following in his grandfather's and father's footsteps."

"Yes, I knew that," Charley agreed.

"Like I said, Clint's ready to start thinking about retiring. He has two daughters who both live away from the area, and neither one's interested in the business. He called me to see if I knew of any good beginning auctioneers in the area who might be willing to join him for a few years, then buy him out. And I thought about you."

Although intrigued by the idea, Charley couldn't get his mind past the phrase "buy him out."

"Charley, you still there?"

"Yeah. It sounds like an amazing opportunity."

"Are you interested?"

Thinking about his impending loan from Darrell, Charley said, "Yes. But I don't know if I'll ever be in the financial position to buy him out."

"Well, I don't think that's a deal breaker. He really wants to see the business keep going. Why don't I let him know you're interested, and then he can set up a meeting with you?"

"Yeah, I'd like that. Thanks, B.J."

"You're a great auctioneer, Charley. You have a lot of potential. I know you took my class seriously, and I like to reward hard-working people. I also wanted to thank you, Charley."

"For what?"

"If it wasn't for you knowing that girl, Trisha, I wouldn't have hooked up with Suzy."

"From the convention?"

"Yep. Turns out, she lives close to me, Charley. We've been together ever since. And I heard through the grapevine that Alex and that other woman left the bar together. How about you?"

"Trisha moved here."

"In with you?"

"No. To Hope. Turns out she has family here."

"So, are you two dating?"

"Yes."

"Guess we all had a love connection," B.J. teased. "I'll give ol' Clint a call, Charley. I'm guessing he'll get back to you before the end of the week."

◌

Trisha was almost to town when her cell phone started ringing.

Noticing it was Brad, she quickly said hello.

"Hey, have you seen Scarlette?"

"Um, no. Why?"

"Well, she didn't show up for her photo shoot this morning. They called me to see if I knew where she was, and she hadn't told her manager or anyone she'd broken up with me. I thought about the threat she made to you and started worrying maybe she was in Iowa."

"I haven't seen her, Brad." Trisha shivered a little as she started studying the cars she was passing on the surprisingly busy Main Street. "You really think she'd come here?"

"I didn't figure she would. But I also never figured she'd miss a photo shoot. She loves her job, Trish."

"I think she'd be pretty easy to spot in Hope," Trisha said, finding comfort in that thought as well. "She's not really good at blending in."

"True. I'm sorry to dump this on you, Trisha. Is everything going all right?"

"Yeah, fine. I can't start work for a while longer. First there was the problem with the HR lady. And now Kat had to go to Kansas because her mother-in-law passed away."

"How's Charley?"

"Good. Except his daughter caught us in bed together."

"Oh, shit. Not a good way to make a first impression there, Trish."

"I know. Tyler seems to think it'll be okay. So, I'm hoping he's right."

"Good for you, Trisha. You're talking to your brother."

"I've talked to my parents too, Brad. I went back to the house."

"How'd that go?"

"Okay, I guess. Nothing's really changed in all the years I've been away. I figured Mom had probably redecorated by now."

"Hey, Trish, I'm sorry to cut this short, but I'm needed on set. If you would happen to see Scarlette, don't talk to her. Okay? Just call me."

"I don't think she'd hurt me, Brad."

"Promise me."

"Okay, fine. I promise you that if I see Scarlette I will call you."

"Thanks, Trisha. I'll call you soon."

Trisha shivered again as she hung up her phone and continued through her small town. But now she was carefully examining all the cars she passed to see if there was a skinny blonde in any of them glaring back at her.

When a beep blared out in her car, she almost jumped out of her skin.

"Oh shit," she said, noticing her gas tank was almost empty.

She turned at the next block and drove down the quiet side street, then pulled into the gas station on the edge of Hope.

She was leaning against her car, in the middle of filling up her tank, when a black Cadillac with completely tinted windows flew in the driveway and headed directly for her car, screeching to a stop directly in front of her.

Trisha's heart started racing as she reached for her pocket to grab her phone, quickly realizing she'd left it on the passenger seat of her car.

Thankful several other cars were also in the parking lot and people were watching, she glared toward where the driver was sitting, wondering if Scarlette really had come to town.

Just then, the door flew open and an obviously drunk Robert Townsend stumbled out of the car and marched straight for her.

"You git away from that son of a—"

"Don't come one step closer to me," Trisha ordered, anger coursing through her veins, and she marched straight up to him. She pointed a finger in his face and said, "Leave me alone."

"No." He grabbed her arm and pulled her close. "You gotta get away from him."

"Let go of me," Trisha said, struggling to break free from his grip.

Robert suddenly let go of her and ran back to his car, throwing it into reverse and narrowly missing a pickup that was pulling into the convenience store.

She noticed the crowd of town folks who had been drinking coffee inside were running toward her and quickly realized that was why Robert had fled so quickly.

"Are you okay?" one man asked as he reached Trisha. "Did he hit you?"

"Oh, no," Trisha answered, suddenly very aware of the bruises still on her face. "He was just drunk."

"He's always drunk," another man offered, glancing up as Robert squealed his tires and tore down the highway that led out of town.

Trisha started feeling very self-conscious as people gathered around her, asking questions about what had happened. Before long, a county sheriff's car pulled into the convenience store parking lot.

The officer trotted over to where they were standing, and the crowd started offering their accounts all at the same time.

"Ma'am, do want to press charges?" he asked as he jotted down notes.

"No." Trisha shook her head, dying to get away from the scene.

"I understand he grabbed you."

"My arm. He was drunk and angry. I was in his way. I'm fine."

"Do you know Mr. Townsend?"

"He's a friend of my father's. I think he thought he was doing me a favor by giving me some unwelcome advice."

"Who's your father?"

"George Bailey," Trisha answered, noticing a hush fall over the crowd before several of them started whispering.

"And what's your name?"

"Trisha Jenkins. I'm the eldest child of George and Betty Sue Bailey. I recently moved back," she continued, raising her voice slightly so the crowd could hear what she was saying and she wouldn't have to repeat it. "I appreciate you coming, officer, but I don't wish to press any charges. I just would like to be on my way."

"Of course, ma'am."

Part of the crowd followed the patrolman as he walked toward the front door of the store, and the other part watched her as she got into her car and hurried on her way.

~

Tess carefully tucked the wad of cash into her purse, then walked out of the bank.

"I've got it all, now I just have to wait," she reminded herself.

Guilt started washing through her veins as she thought about Trisha.

She knew she shouldn't have told her brother Trisha was in town. And she definitely shouldn't have offered to help him get to Trisha.

"But I had no choice," Tess reminded herself as she quickened her pace, figuring Darrell was probably already done at the barbershop.

She darted into the drug store and picked up her birth control pills, knowing Darrell had made it very clear he didn't want to have children at his age. He was almost fifty and figured he wouldn't be able to be the kind of father a child would need in his older age.

Tess still felt a little sad about the idea of never being a mother. But she liked the fact that she'd never have to worry another day in her life about having enough money to pay her bills.

She thought of her mother, who had tried to raise her by herself. Tess knew her mother had fallen victim to a life of prostitution when she hadn't been able to make enough money at the fast food joint to provide for her family.

Tess wondered if Carl even knew his father was one of their mother's regular customers.

Her mind was suddenly back to those nights when she'd be alone in the one-room, rat-invested apartment.

Her mother would read her a bedtime story and tuck her in, then would kiss her on the forehead and tell her to stay in bed until she got back.

She went to bed hungry almost every night.

Once school had started, she had been shocked when she'd found out from her best friend in kindergarten that normal mothers didn't leave their children at night.

It had also been while she was in kindergarten that things had gone from bad to worse. Her mother had gone back to working in the fast food places while she was pregnant with Carl. She'd bring home half-eaten sandwiches for their supper.

Even though they seldom had electricity and usually were wearing dirty clothes, Tess had been excited to have more time to spend with her mother. And she had been thrilled when her mother had brought home a baby.

But a few weeks after that, her mom had left her alone at night to take care of the baby, and Tess had quickly grown tired of changing diapers and making bottles.

She sighed, remembering the night the police had shown up and taken Carl and her away. The neighbor had heard Carl crying and had called the police, telling them about their mother leaving them at night.

Luckily, a couple who hadn't been able to have their own children had quickly taken in Tess and Carl and ended up adopting them. Tess and Carl had lived a normal life for several years.

Tess' heart started to race as she continued down the sidewalk toward the barbershop, thinking about the night her life had changed again.

She had turned sixteen a few months earlier, and they had celebrated with a huge party. She had been dropping hints that she wanted a car, and her adopted parents had teased her back, telling her she might get one. Carl had been eleven at the time and had adjusted well to living in the suburbs.

Tess remembered that unseasonably cold night when her parents had lit a fire in the fireplace in the house to warm it up, and they had all gone to bed. The next thing she remembered was waking up, coughing, surrounded by smoke.

Remembering the video in school, Tess had crawled across her room and into the hallway, crawling to her brother's room and waking him. They had opened his window and jumped out, like they had practiced numerous times in their own fire drills.

When their parents hadn't been in their meeting spot, Carl had wanted to go back in. But Tess had insisted they stay in their safe spot.

Unable to stop the tears that threatened, Tess remembered the neighbors getting them and taking them to their house while the fire trucks arrived.

They had kept asking for their parents. But as the night had continued on and the fire had destroyed their entire house, it had started to become clear their parents hadn't made it out.

Tess thought about the next few weeks as she and Carl had waited in limbo to see what would become of them.

Her heart hardened a little more as she thought about her selfish great aunt who had whisked them away to her small house in downtown Los Angeles, and then had left them to fend for themselves as she plowed through the life insurance money their adopted parents had left for her to use to raise them.

The day before she turned seventeen, she and Carl had hurried home from school, packed up some clothes and all the money they could find in the house, and had ventured out on their own.

"Hey, Tess, Darrell's about done."

Tess jumped at the sound of a male's voice. Noticing one of Darrell's friends standing on the sidewalk in front of her, she flashed him a smile. Then she hurried into the barbershop and managed to joke with the guys sitting around.

Once Darrell was done, she followed him out of the shop and to the truck, vowing he'd never find out how she'd survived after that.

Jessica slowly opened her eyes, shivering from the cold air blowing on her. As she tried to sit up, her head started pounding. She peered around, trying to figure out why she was so cold, and jumped when she noticed the stranger staring at her from a chair in the corner of the unfamiliar room.

"Who the hell are you?" she demanded in a voice as loud as her pounding head would allow.

"Your lover."

Confused by what he'd said, Jessica suddenly realized she was naked in a cheap hotel room, and the window air conditioner was to blame for her shivering.

She pulled the dirty sheet up to her chin. "What the hell did you do to me?"

"Nothing you didn't want me to do," he teased, grinning, as he waved a bottle a whiskey at her. "I think you had a little too much of this at the bar, babe."

"I was at the bar," Jessica moaned, trying as hard as she could to remember. She shut her eyes and thought back, suddenly remembering the call from her lawyer's secretary. "He took my daughter. They called and said he took my daughter. I was at Stu's Bar. I was drinking whiskey. And some guy asked me about my sister."

Carl, who was dressed, stood up and walked over to the bed, sitting down beside her. "That was me."

"Get away from me!" Jessica ordered, sliding to the edge of the bed. Noticing her clothes were lying on the floor, she wrapped the sheet around her and slipped out of the bed, then grabbed her clothes and hurried to the bathroom.

"It ain't like I didn't see it."

Jessica shivered as she slammed the door shut and dressed, her vision clouded as she tried to remember how she'd ended up in a hotel with a stranger.

She glanced in the mirror and noticed her limp blond hair was tussled.

"What the hell have I done?" she whispered to her reflection, suddenly thinking about Glen. "He can't find out. He can never find out what I've done. He'd leave me. And he's the only thing I have left."

Jessica took a deep breath, then marched back into the room, tossing the sheet at the stranger. "I'm leaving. Where's my purse?"

"In your car, which is in the parking lot." He grinned at her. "I think the better question is, where are your keys?"

Jessica scanned the room, then demanded, "Give me my damned keys. I want to leave."

"You can leave," he promised as she stood up. "But first, we need to have a little chat."

"Whatever happened here was a mistake," Jessica said, deciding the bossy approach wasn't working with him. "Cleary I was drunk. I'm sorry if I led you on, but…"

Carl's laughing aggravated her even more. She put her hands on her hips and demanded, "What the hell is so funny?"

"You. Sit down, Jessica."

Fear shivered down her spine as she wondered how he knew her name. She steered clear of the bed as she walked to the chair and sat down, biting her nails.

"I'm guessing you'd like to keep our little romp a secret, wouldn't ya?"

"Yes." Glen flashed in her mind.

"Hey, I'm fine with that. I won't say a thing."

Jessica let out a sigh of relief. "Thank you."

"I just need you to do one thing for me."

His grin unnerved her and she crossed her arms. "What?"

"You'll find out when I'm ready for you to find out. Just remember, you owe me. And don't think I don't know where you live or who your family is, Jessica. I had lots of time while you were passed out to go through your purse and your car. I know where you live and where your folks live. I know about your main squeeze, Glen Robbins. I know a lot about you, and when I'm ready, you'll do exactly what I want you to do, and after that, I'll disappear."

"Fine," Jessica said, deflated. "I'll do whatever you want me to do. Now, can I please have my keys?"

Carl laughed and pointed at Jessica's skirt.

She reached in the pocket and felt her anger getting the best of her when she realized she'd had her own keys all along.

She stomped to the door and slammed it shut, declaring right then and there she'd never, ever do anything for him.

Charley was sitting on the front porch when Trisha pulled in.

"Hi," she called out as she hurried to him. "How was your day?"

"Lot of highs and lows." Charley took her in his arms. "How about you?"

"The same."

"I thought we'd have hamburgers on the grill for supper. Is that okay?"

"That's sounds wonderful."

"Great. I have the patties all made up, and the grill is ready to go."

Charley opened the door and held it for her as she walked into the house.

"What can I do to help?" Trisha asked as they continued to the kitchen.

Charley stopped at the white, humming refrigerator and pulled out a heaping plate full of raw patties. He pulled the plastic wrap off the meat and tossed it into the trash, then said, "Can you get the door?"

Trisha opened the metal screen door, waited while he passed through, then shut it. She followed him to the cement patio, then sat down at the rounded table while Charley carried the meat to the already pre-heated grill. She listened to the sizzling of the meat as he strategically placed the patties. Noticing the basketball hoop for the first time, she asked, "Did Pam play basketball?"

"Yes. She was pretty good at it."

"Well, there's something we have in common. Maybe we could get together and shoot hoops sometime."

"She'll come around, Trisha." Charley carried the now-empty plate over and set it down on the table. "She's had a lot of change in her life recently."

"That's what Tyler thought too."

"You've talked to your brother?"

"Yeah. I went by the school. I miss him and want to try to get our relationship back on track. I'm happy to say he wants that too."

"Well, that's good."

"I know he isn't your favorite person right now," Trisha said as Charley hurried back to the grill and started turning the patties. "And I don't blame you for that. But Tyler's a good person. He's not like my father, Charley."

Charley shrugged, keeping his back to her.

"I also talked to my parents today." Trisha got up and walked over to him. "I'm going to get something to drink. Do you want anything?"

"There's pop in the fridge."

Trisha had just walked into the house when her cell phone started ringing. She pulled it out of her pocket and checked the number. She smiled when she realized who it was.

"Hey, Marti. Did you find a new internship?"

"No. I'm still stuck here at Milligan, and it's a nightmare. I was calling to see if you could help me out. Do you have any connections? Maybe I could come to the place where you got your job in Iowa?"

"You want to move to Iowa to do an internship?"

"No, not really. But I'm desperate, Trisha. I have to get out of Milligan. The only reason I enjoyed my job was because I was working with you. Now that you're gone, well, it's unbearable."

"I'm really sorry to hear that, Marti, but I can't ask here. I haven't even been able to start work yet."

"So, you won't do anything to help me?" Marti asked, the anger clear in her voice.

"I'm sorry, but no, I can't. Not right now."

"I thought you were my friend," Marti yelled, scaring Trisha. "Damn you. You'll regret this!"

Trisha's hands were shaking as she quickly hung up, shocked Marti had become so angry. During the weeks they had worked together, Trisha had never seen Marti remotely upset.

Trisha took a deep breath and grabbed two cans of pop, then walked back out.

"What did they say?"

"Who?" Trisha asked, confused.

"Your parents. Are you okay, Trish? You look pale."

"I just got a strange call."

"From that Scarlette person?"

Trisha shook her head, "No, this was from a girl who worked as an intern in my office in California. She wanted me to help her find a new place to intern. She demanded that I try to get her an internship with Just For You, and when I told her I couldn't, she got mad. Really mad. She said I was going to regret not helping her."

"Damn, Trisha, I'm so sorry. Should we call Sheriff McEntire?"

Trisha quickly shook her head. "No, I'm sure she was just upset. A lot of things are changing for her out there with all the restructuring. It's hard enough on you when you're an adult. But to be a college student trying to earn credits through your internship, well, I'm sure she's stressed."

"Still, threatening someone is not the way to get their help."

"No, that's true. Let's just forget about it. Now, what did you ask me?"

"What did your parents say when you went to see them?"

Trisha thought back to her mom's performance. "Maybe we'd better wait until after supper to talk about it."

"What did they say, Trish?" Charley insisted, taking the can from her.

Noticing the fear in his eyes, she said, "Mom implied you did something to her."

"That lying bit…uh, sorry," Charley muttered, stopping himself from cursing his girlfriend's mother.

"I wasn't sure what to make of her comments, but I figured there wasn't much truth to them." Thinking back to her conversation with Grace, she said, "I also talked to Grace Locke about you today."

"Grace? Where'd you see her?"

"She's Kat's neighbor."

"I guess I knew that. Were you at Kat's today? Did Grace stop by?"

"Actually, I stopped by her house. Kat mentioned I should."

"Grace is a sweet lady and a great cook. She was best friends with my mom," Charley said as he continued to tinker with the burgers.

"She mentioned that. She also told me my father was a spoiled brat in school." Noticing the surprise on his face, Trisha nodded.

"Well, I'm not going to argue against that statement."

"She also said your mom told her my father picked on you. Why'd he do that, Charley?"

"I still think you should hear something like this from your parents." Charley started back to the house with Trisha right behind him.

"I tried that; it didn't work," Trisha reminded him as he gathered a clean plate and spatula.

"Why don't you get whatever you want on your burger? I'll go and pull them off the fire. You wanna eat in here or outside?"

"Outside. What do you want on yours?"

"Cookies BBQ. And pickles."

"Cheese?"

Charley nodded and walked outside.

Trisha gathered the condiments and a bag of chips, then juggled everything around until she could open the door.

"Let me help you," Charley said as he hurried over and took the glass pickle jar and bottles of barbeque sauce and ketchup from her.

Trisha nudged the door shut with her arm and followed Charley to the table. After they doctored their burgers, they sat down beside each other and started eating.

"These burgers are delicious."

"Thanks." Charley took a deep breath. "Even though I think your parents should be the ones to tell you, I will."

"Thank you," Trisha replied as she reached for a handful of salty chips.

"Your mother was a year older than Nancy and me. Your father was three years older."

"Okay."

"There's no easy way to tell you all this, so I'm just going to lay it all out there," Charley warned, putting his hamburger down on his plate and pushing it aside.

"Okay," Trisha coaxed. "That's fine."

"Your father wanted Nancy. It didn't matter she was younger than him. He wanted her to be his girl. And he was used to getting everything he wanted. Nancy was very mature looking for her age, I suppose. But Nancy only had eyes for me, and that really ticked off your father. That's why he didn't like me. And that's why he tried to make my life a living hell during his senior year."

"I'm so sorry," Trisha said, losing her appetite too.

"And that bastard never gave up chasing my Nancy, either," Charley growled, unable to stop himself.

"It's beautiful," Pam gushed as Tyler gave her a tour of their new home. "I can't believe how big it is."

"We can have lots of kids," Tyler teased, wrapping an arm around her shoulder. "Come on, honey, I have a surprise for you in the kitchen."

Pam smiled as he led her to the staircase and back down to the first level. They weaved through the living room and started down the short hallway, coming into the kitchen that had an attached dining area.

"Ta-da." Tyler waved his hand toward the table where a prepared supper was waiting for them.

"When did you have time to do this?" Pam asked, her eyes wide, as she noticed her favorite, spaghetti and meatballs.

"Well, I didn't really cook it," Tyler confessed as he pulled out her chair. "Helen offered to make supper for us a few nights a week until we get all settled in. She loves to do that kind of thing, so I couldn't turn her down. I hope that's okay."

"It's great." Pam smiled as he sat down across from her. She took a bite. "This tastes amazing."

"Helen's the best. How were your meetings today?"

"Boring." Pam stifled a yawn. "It didn't help we had to cut our honeymoon short. But I'm looking forward to the kids arriving on Thursday. My room's ready."

"I'm ready too, I think. Hey, guess who came by to see me today."

"Who?"

"Trisha."

Instantly losing her appetite, Pam set her fork down on the table.

"Are you okay?" Tyler asked, noticing she stopped eating.

"What'd she want?"

"Just to talk."

"She was at my daddy's house this morning." Pam leaned her elbows on the table. "They were in his bedroom. I thought something was wrong because his front door wasn't shut, so I went to check on him and…well…I shouldn't have."

"Trisha mentioned it."

"She did?" Pam raised her eyebrows. "So, what are we going to do about this, Tyler?"

"What do you mean?" Tyler helped himself to another piece of garlic bread.

"Well, we obviously need to put a stop to it. We can't have my daddy involved with your sister. It's wrong."

"It's a little different, but it's not really wrong." Tyler shook his head while chewing on his bread.

"I can't believe you," Pam accused, pointing a finger at him. "Your sister shouldn't be with my father. She's a stranger to all of us. And she's gotta be up to something."

"I think she really cares for your father."

Pam rolled her eyes as she crossed her arms.

"My sister's a good person, Pam. She isn't up to anything."

"Until our wedding day, you hadn't even seen your sister since she graduated from high school, Tyler. You don't know she's a good person. You don't know anything about her at all."

Tyler took a moment to collect his thoughts as he pushed his half-eaten plate of spaghetti out of his way. Then he said, "Although I haven't been in touch with Trisha in several years, the caring, kind sister I remember visited me today at school. I love my sister, and I believed her when she told me she cares for your father. I don't think she's up to anything at all."

"How can you be so gullible?" Pam asked, throwing her arms up in the air.

"And how can you be so cynical? Your dad's happy, Pam. My sister makes him happy. Yes, there's an age difference. And yes, it's gonna be a little weird to explain to our friends that your father and my sister are dating. But they both seem happy. And isn't that what's important?"

"No," Pam declared as she quickly stood up, knocking over her chair. "What's important is protecting my father. He hasn't been in any serious relationships since my mother died. Your sister's way too young for him."

Tyler's jaw dropped as Pam stomped out of the room.

Betty Sue slammed the house phone receiver down and jumped up, jogging down the hallway to George's study, fuming mad.

She pushed open his partially closed door and felt her anger rising even higher when she noticed he was sitting on the leather couch with a bottle of whiskey in his hand, watching a pornographic movie on his fifty-five-inch television.

"What the hell is that smut?" Betty Sue hissed as she grabbed the remote from the table and shut off his television.

"I was, um, looking for a ballgame," George stammered.

"I bet you were."

"What'd ya want, Sue?"

"When did you see Robert Townsend?"

George set his bottle down on the coffee table and stood up, stumbling a little as he took a couple of steps toward her.

"George?"

"Well, Sue, I, um, I haven't seen Robert for months. Not since you told me never to talk to him again."

Betty Sue whipped her hand up and swiftly smacked him across the cheek.

George fell backwards, landing with a thump in the leather recliner by the door.

"Don't you dare lie to me," Betty Sue threatened as she walked over and knelt down in his face. "When did you see that man?"

"Last night."

"Damn it, George. I thought you were done with him."

"I was. But he called about Trisha." George rubbed his throbbing check with his hand.

"What about Trisha?"

"He saw her with Walker at The Tasty Cone. He wanted to make sure I knew about it."

"Did he ask for money?"

"Yes, he did. And I told him no."

"Well, at least you did one thing right."

"How did you—"

"Find out?" Betty Sue interrupted. "Because dear ol' Robert caused a scene tonight at Marnie's Convenience Store. He blocked Trisha in and grabbed her by the arm, and they argued. No one heard what they were talking about, so Mary called me to find out if Trisha was okay."

"Is she?"

"How would I know?" Betty Sue flung her arms up in the air. "She doesn't talk to me. Why the hell didn't you tell me she was out in public eating with that…that man?"

George shrugged. "Because I knew it'd tick you off."

"Damn right it did." Betty Sue started pacing around the room. "It's one thing when she's meeting him in private. But for her to meet with him in such a public place. And people are talking about it too, George. Mary said she heard that our Trisha was back in town and dating our daughter-in-law's father. Do you have any idea how embarrassing that is?"

"Yes. A better question is, how are we going to stop this?"

"I'm not sure." Betty Sue suddenly lost steam and plopped down on the couch. She glimpsed over at him and noticed the red splotches on his cheek. "Sorry I hit you."

"Sorry I didn't tell you about Robert."

"I can't believe this. First Tyler marries that man's daughter, and now that man is stalking our daughter. This is a nightmare."

"We have to stop it even if we have to drag her to this house, lock her up and throw away the key. We have to get her away from that bastard."

"Is there more, Charley?" Trisha asked as they sat on his couch wrapped up in each other's arms, covered in only a blanket.

"What do you mean?" Charley muted the movie they'd been watching on his small cabinet television.

Trisha turned to face him. "With my parents? I just got the feeling there was more."

Charley noticed his family portrait on the wall and instantly felt guilty for being intimate with Trisha on their family couch a few moments earlier.

"Charley?" Trisha said, noticing his eyes were glued to the picture.

Charley took a deep breath, then turned away from the photo and focused his attention on Trisha.

"You don't have to tell me if you don't want to. But if you want to, I'd like to know."

"There's more," Charley said as he got up and snatched his jeans off the floor. He pulled them on, then escaped outside onto the front porch.

Not sure what to do, Trisha pulled his shirt on and buttoned it as she followed him out the door.

"Pam doesn't know this." Charley turned his back to her as he stood on the edge of the porch, looking over his cornfield. "She can never know this. Especially now that she's pregnant and married to your brother."

Trisha walked over and wrapped her arms around him. "What is it?"

"You can't tell anyone." Charley turned to face her. "You have to promise me you won't. I can't tell you if you don't promise."

"I promise. No matter what it is, I won't tell a soul."

Charley closed his eyes and took a deep breath.

"You're scaring me, Charley. What is it?"

"This is going to hurt you too," Charley mumbled. "It might even end us."

Panic ripped through Trisha as her heart started to race. Suddenly not sure she really wanted to know, Trisha pulled away. "Maybe I don't want to know."

"You need to know. I have to tell you everything if we're ever going to be able to make it as a couple," Charley replied softly. "I was hoping your dad would come clean. But he's scared. I'm sure he's scared."

"What'd he do?" Trisha demanded, years of pent-up anger toward her father surging through her veins.

"Your father left Nancy alone after you were born," Charley started. "I thought it was over. He was married to Betty Sue and you were born, then Tyler and Jessica came along. Your father seemed like he'd grown up. And Nancy and I were happy. We both were working our dream jobs, and we had enough money to live on. And we had Pam. I thought your parents were happy, too. I lost track of them. Except for my loan at the bank, I never had any contact with them. I'm not sure what changed, but at some point, your father started it up again."

"Started what up again?"

"His obsession with my wife," Charley whispered. "He started following her around. She'd come out of the grocery store, and he'd be sitting in the parking lot. She'd come out of the school late at night, and he'd be there. It scared her, Trisha. It scared her a lot."

Trisha placed her hand against her heart. "My father was stalking your wife?"

Charley nodded.

"There's more, isn't there?"

"Yes. Your father was with a man named Kevin the night Nancy died. Kevin and your dad had been drinking together at one of the bars in town. Your dad wanted to see if Nancy was still at the school and convinced Kevin to drive him there. But your dad wasn't content with just watching her this time. He tried to talk to her. According to Kevin, it scared her. Nancy didn't want to talk to him and took off running to her car. Your dad grabbed her arm and tried to make her listen to him. Nancy pulled away from him and jumped into her car. Your dad made Kevin move over, and he jumped in the driver's seat and took off chasing after her. Nancy was driving faster than she should have been, and they were chasing her out of town. She hit the gravel going too fast and lost control on that first curve on the gravel road. Kevin saw the car leave the road. They watched it as it flipped over and over and over…"

Trisha heard Charley's sobs and quickly realized she was sobbing too.

Once he gained his composure, Charley continued, "Kevin said George got scared and they fled the scene. They never tried to help her. They didn't even call the sheriff's office. If they would have, they might have been able to save her. Either way, she's gone, Trisha, and your father's to blame. His obsession with my wife is what killed her and took her and my baby boy away from me and Pam."

"He should be in jail," Trisha demanded, her face red with anger.

"Neither one of them were ever convicted of anything, Trisha. My wife's death was ruled an accident. No one saw them chasing her, and no one pursued it. Your father's money bought him freedom. I only know it because Kevin confessed it to me on his deathbed before he passed away from cancer a couple of years ago."

"This is so awful." Trisha gathered Charley in her arms and hugged him. "I'm so sorry my father did that. I'm sorry he's caused you so much pain during your lifetime, Charley."

Charley held on to her tightly as his mind drifted back in time to his conversation with Kevin. He'd always wondered if George had had anything to do with Nancy's accident. He'd even mentioned George's obsession to the sheriff. But they had insisted it had been a single car accident, even though there had been another set of tire tracks near where her car had left the road.

"Charley?"

"Yeah?" he asked, glancing into her eyes as she released her grip on him.

"How can you look at me?"

Charley tilted his head to the side and furrowed his brow. "What do you mean?"

"Your suffering was caused by my family. That's the reason you didn't want Pam with Tyler. How can you be with me? Don't I remind you of my family too?"

Charley noticed the panic in her eyes and quickly shook his head. "I fell in love with you the first moment I saw you walk into that conference room in Minneapolis. You can't help being George's daughter any more than Tyler can help being George's son. I figured that out as soon as I figured out you were a Bailey. You and your brother aren't to blame for your father's sins. Don't doubt my love for you, Trisha. It's real. What we have together is real."

Trisha fell into his embrace when he held out his arms.

"I'm exhausted, Trisha. Let's go to bed."

"What's wrong?" Glen finally asked as he sat by Jessica on his couch, both of them surrounded by empty beer cans and whiskey bottles.

"What?"

"Something's up. Talk to me."

Jessica's thoughts quickly returned to the hotel room with Carl. She shivered as she felt the coldness that had surrounded her and silently cursed herself for not being able to remember what had really happened between the two of them.

"Jess, you're a mess. You have been ever since you got home. What's wrong, honey?"

Jessica lost it when she noticed the sincere look on his face.

"Tell me." Glen repeated as he pulled her close.

Not one to rat herself out, she said, "Danni's gone."

"What do you mean, gone?"

"You remember when my dad threatened to quit helping me keep custody of her? He said I had to go home right away, and I was going to, but you stopped me. Well, you got your wish, because I got a call today. Danni's gone, and I'm never going to see her again."

"I'm sorry, honey."

"Well, you should be. It's your fault."

"It is. And we'll figure out a way to get her back. But for now, you can be with me. Stay here with me. I love you, Jess."

"You love me?"

"Yep." Glen laughed. "I wonder when the hell that happened?"

Tears popped into Jessica's eyes as she thought about the fact that just a few hours earlier, she'd woken up in another man's bed.

"Those better be happy tears."

"They are." Jessica climbed over and sat on his lap. "I'm real happy you love me, because I love you too."

They'd just started making out when Glen's cell phone started ringing.

"Ignore it," Jessica begged.

"Can't." Glen pushed her away.

Jessica listened as he answered yes and no a couple of times, then got angry when she heard him say he would be right over.

"Who the hell was that?"

"My mama. She's sick, babe. I gotta go and check on her. I'm sorry. I'll be back soon. Enjoy the booze, honey, and I'll wake ya when I get back."

Jessica forced a smile as he walked to the door and left, then started sobbing again.

"What'd I do? And why can't I remember?"

Tired of reality, Jessica spied a half-empty bottle of whiskey sitting on the kitchen counter. She stood up and slowly made her way to the bottle and took a long swig.

As the room started to tilt, she used her left hand to make her way back to the couch, the bottle still tightly gripped in her right hand.

Tired of missing her daughter and feeling guilty, Jessica took another long swig. Her tears fell freely as she reached for her purse and slid off the couch onto the dirty, worn brown carpet below. Jessica opened her purse and grabbed out her wallet, looking for a photo of her kids.

When she noticed the photo of her sister, taken the day Trisha left for California, Jessica's anger started coursing through her veins.

"This is all your fault," Jessica insisted as she reached for the bottle and accidentally knocked it over. "Oh, shit!"

She picked it up, eyeing the liquid that had gathered on the plastic wrapper on the floor. Then she leaned down and sucked the spilled booze off the wrapper, wanting all of her pain to go away.

The ringing of her cell phone made her head hurt, and she retrieved it off the couch. "What?"

"Hey, Princess. It's time."

"Who the hell is this?"

"It's Carl, baby. Don't tell me you already forgot about our little agreement."

"Now?"

"Why, are you wasted, babe?"

"I don't feel good." Jessica shut her eyes as the room started spinning again.

"Stop drinking and sleep it off, Jessica," Carl ordered, his teasing suddenly gone. "I need you sober tomorrow. We got things to do."

"What things?"

Quickly realizing he'd already hung up, Jessica dropped her phone on the floor and promptly passed out.

Chapter 13

Betty Sue sat alone at the large dining room table, sipping on her coffee. She took a bite of her grapefruit and was quickly lost in thoughts of happier times when she used to sit at that very table surrounded by her children and husband.

"Why did everything have to change?"

"Ma'am, there's a woman asking for Trisha. I wasn't sure what to tell her."

Betty Sue glared at the newest member of their staff. "Did you ask for her name?"

"No, ma'am."

Betty Sue thought about letting the maid handle the visitor. But she was curious, so she stood up. "I guess I'll deal with this. But next time, find out their name before you bother me."

She hurried down the hallway and stopped before she got to the foyer, able to observe the stranger without being seen.

The woman was tall and dangerously thin, with wild, wavy blond hair. Large, dark sunglasses covered her eyes, making it difficult to tell what her face really looked like. And Betty Sue knew she had money when she noticed her almost $500 designer jeans.

"I'm Betty Sue. I hear you're looking for Trisha."

The woman nodded as she pulled off her sunglasses, revealing deep green eyes and to-die-for cheekbones.

"And how do you know Trisha?"

"I'm an old friend. Is she here?"

"No."

"But she's in Hope, isn't she?"

"What did you say your name was?"

"I didn't," the woman said as she abruptly placed her glasses back on her face. "Thank you for your time."

Betty Sue stood speechless as the woman turned and hurried out of the house.

"Well, she was rude," Betty Sue finally said, shaking her head as she turned and walked back to the dining room.

Trisha's mind was swirling with thoughts and emotions as she carried her cup of coffee out to Charley's patio and sat down at the table.

After hearing her father was more or less responsible for everything that had ever hurt Charley, she hadn't been able to sleep.

And it was during those fitful early morning hours when doubt started creeping into Trisha's mind about their relationship. Could Robert Townsend actually be right? Could Charley be using their relationship to finally even the score with her father?

"No, he can't be," Trisha mumbled, shaking her head. "I believe in us. And I'm sure he believes in us too."

But even as she said those words out loud, that little annoying voice in her brain taunted her, playing on her insecurities, tormenting her with the fact that she really didn't know Charley.

Deciding she needed a level head to bounce ideas off, Trisha pulled her cell phone out of her shorts pocket and called Brad.

"Have you seen her?"

"Excuse me?"

"Scarlette. Have you seen her? Is that why you're calling me?"

"No. I don't think she'd come here, Brad."

"Well, no one has seen or heard from her for days. I'm at the airport waiting to catch a flight back home."

"You're really worried about her, aren't you?"

"Yeah. She missed another appointment, and her agent's getting very upset. He said he usually talks with her several times a day, but he hasn't heard from her since the day before she left me. He's been out looking for her and asked that I come home and help."

"I'm so sorry, Brad."

"Thanks. What's going on with you, Trish? You sound upset."

"Well, I hate to add any more to your plate."

"Tell me."

Trisha quickly filled him in on Charley's news and added, "What if he is using me?"

"Before he told you all of this, how did you feel about your relationship? Did you trust him or did you have doubts?"

Trisha thought about it for a second. "I trusted him completely."

"There's your answer."

"How can that be my answer?"

"Because, Trisha, you're a very smart woman. And very observant. If Charley were just using you, then you would've picked up on that. You would've sensed something was wrong. But you didn't. The only reason you're having doubts now is because that Robert person has been harassing you. Trust you gut, Trisha."

"Thanks." Trisha let out a low, long breath of air.

"Better?"

"Yeah. I knew you'd help me with this."

"That's what best friend ex-husbands are for," Brad teased. Then getting more serious, asked, "Have you been to the cemetery?"

"Yes, but only once. It's hard, Brad. I don't think I can do it again without you by my side."

"What about taking Charley?"

Trisha's mind started racing at the thought of taking another man with her to their daughter's grave.

"It'll be all right, Trisha."

"I know I need to go to the cemetery again, Brad. And I wish you were here to go with me, but I can't take Charley. He doesn't know. I'll go today. By myself."

"You're strong, Trisha, and you can do this. I'll be thinking about you."

"I'm sorry about Scarlette. But I'm sure she's fine. Let me know when you land, okay?"

"Okay, bye."

"Good morning."

Trisha's head whipped around at the sound of Charley's voice. She got up and walked over to him. Noticing he bristled a little when she kissed him on the lips, she asked, "Is something wrong?"

"I heard you."

Trisha's heart dropped to her toes. "I'm sorry, Charley. It's just, I didn't sleep very well last night. And my mind was going crazy. I know you'd never use our relationship to get back at my father. I'm sorry that even entered my mind."

Charley's eyes grew wide. "You thought I was using you to get back at your father?"

Trisha nodded. "You said you heard me."

"I heard you talking about the cemetery and wanting Brad to go with you. I didn't know you were also talking about me. About us."

"I'm sorry. That was a lot to take in last night," Trisha said, panicking when she noticed how upset he was getting. "I couldn't sleep and I started thinking too much. Robert's babbling came back to me and I—"

"You believe Robert Townsend over me? Wow," Charley interrupted, his face turning a bright red as he glared at her.

"I'm sorry. I just needed to talk it through with a friend."

"Your ex-husband."

"Yes. He's my best friend. He keeps me grounded, Charley."

"Well, I'm glad someone can." Charley turned his back to her as he started pacing around his yard.

"I know you're not using me. And I know what we have is real." Trisha caught up to him and stepped in front of him, stopping his pacing.

"I can't believe you questioned it in the first place," Charley said, the pain evident in his eyes. "I've been completely open and honest, Trisha. And yet, you still question if my love is real. How could you even think for one second I'd use us to get back at your father?"

"Because he took so much from you."

"I'm not like him," Charley whispered, then added, "and for you to even think I might do something like that makes me think you really don't know me at all."

"But I do know you. I'm insecure, Charley. Please, don't be mad at me."

"I'm not mad. I'm hurt, Trish. And…I'm wondering if this isn't gonna work after all."

"What?" Trisha asked, her heart breaking into a million pieces as panic grabbed ahold of her.

Silence filled the air for a few seconds before Charley whispered, "I need some time to think about all of this."

"No."

"No?"

Trisha shook her head. "I won't let my family ruin our love."

Charley's voice wavered when he declared, "I think they already have."

Jessica sat on the couch in Glen's apartment, her cell phone in her hand. Sober and regretting it.

She thought back to the call she'd gotten from Glen, right after Carl's call. He had wanted her to know he was taking his mother to the hospital because she was sick. And although she'd never met Glen's mother, Jessica wondered how she was doing.

She nervously peeked at her phone and shivered, wondering when Carl was going to call again, and what he wanted from her.

Jessica shivered again and cursed her father, deciding it was his fault she drank too much. And if she hadn't drunk so much, she wouldn't have gone anywhere with someone like Carl.

Deciding she couldn't get through another minute without a drink, Jessica got up and ventured into the kitchen to search for Glen's stash.

"Damn it. I need something stronger than this," she said when all she could find was one can of beer. She popped it open and guzzled half of it down, then continued on to the bathroom.

She took a shower, dressed and finished the rest of her beer, then walked into the living room, sat back down on the couch and stared at her phone.

ꝏ

"Do you have my money?" Carl asked when Tess opened her front door.

Hatred for her brother washed over her as she nodded.

"Well, good," Carl said and pushed his way into her house. "Something smells good."

Crossing her arms, Tess said, "It was breakfast. And it wasn't for you."

"You always were a good cook."

Tess hurried over to the teddy bear cookie jar on the counter and reached inside, pulling out a thick wad of folded-over bills. She carried it back to Carl and thrust it at him. "Here."

"Thanks, Sis." He licked his lips and took the bills from her, then thumbed through the wad. Then he smelled it. "Nothing like chocolate chip-scented dough."

Tess rolled her eyes, then crossed her arms. "You can have the money, Carl, but I'm not gonna help you get Trisha."

Carl laughed, walked over to her kitchen table and sat down.

"I'm serious, Carl."

"I figured you'd back out, Tess. I know you better than anyone else in the world. And that includes that dumb farmer you conned into marrying you. How did you pull that off?"

"Get the hell out of my house, Carl. I don't ever want to see you again!"

"He doesn't know about your past, does he Sis? I didn't figure he did. Most men don't take damaged goods to their bed."

Tess lunged at him, and Carl jumped up, agile as a cat, and grabbed her hand before she could slap him across the face.

He twisted her arm around her back and pulled on it until she fell to her knees.

Carl glared down at her and declared, "I knew you'd back out on me, Sis. You have been letting me down my entire life."

Tess fell to the ground and crawled away from him when he released her. She them mustered up all the strength she could, pointed toward the front door and ordered, "Get the hell out of my house."

"I don't need your help, Tess. I got someone else helping me with this little project."

"Who?" Tess asked, worried for Trisha's safety as she stood up.

Carl laughed, then added, "And don't even think about telling anyone what I'm doing, because you'll go down too. I'll make sure of that."

"I didn't do anything."

Carl held up the cash. "I've been to jail enough times to know that you, my dear sister, are my accessory. If you rat me out, I'm taking you down with me. And I'll make sure I don't end up in the slammer by myself this time."

Tess kept her composure until Carl was out the door and back into his car, then she slid down the wall to the linoleum kitchen floor, sobbing.

"No," Trisha insisted, grabbing his arm as he tried to walk away from her.

Charley's brown eyes welled up as he said, "Trisha, please, I need some time to think."

"I didn't mean to hurt you. I love you."

"You love me?"

"I do. I can't believe how much I love you already. Even though I've only known you for a short time, I know that I love you. Please, don't walk away from me. From us."

"I just need time to think. I'm not walking away from us. Not yet."

"Fine." Trisha brushed her tears off her cheeks. "I'll give you some space."

"Trisha?" Charley called as she started toward the house.

"Yes?" she asked as she turned around to look at him, hopeful that he'd changed his mind.

"Please don't tell anyone else what I told you last night. I know you want to confront your dad, but you promised you wouldn't tell anyone. Pam doesn't know, and it would devastate her to find out what her in-laws took away from us. She's pregnant with a Bailey child and can never find out what happened in the past. Okay?"

"I won't tell anyone. I do want to talk to my parents. But I promise you, Charley, I won't say a word about my father's obsession with your wife."

"Thank you."

Trisha turned to leave, then ran back to Charley and hugged him tightly, kissing him on the lips.

For a moment, Charley returned her kiss as he wrapped his arms around her.

Then he jerked back, the hurt clear in his eyes.

"I'm so sorry I ever doubted us," Trisha said before she turned and ran to the house.

"Has Charley Walker paid his loan yet?" George asked his secretary.

"I'm not sure, Mr. Bailey. I'll check and let you know."

"Great, I'll be in my office."

George walked into his office and was looking through his work email when he heard a commotion in the lobby of the bank.

He stood up and walked to the doorway, not sure what to think when Robert almost ran into him, pursued by his secretary and the man who served as Vice President of the bank.

"I need to talk to you," Robert insisted, glancing at George, then over his shoulder.

"Sit down," George ordered, and then he turned back to the other two and put up his hand. "I'm fine. I'll let you know if I need assistance."

Before they could answer, George shut his door and walked back to his desk, sitting down in his plush, leather chair.

"You've gotta do something, George."

"About what?"

"Your daughter and that SOB." Robert leaned forward in his chair. "He knows what caused his wife's accident, George. He's gonna tell her."

George was temporarily distracted as he thought back to the night that had almost ruined him. He leaned back in his chair and shut his eyes, unable to stop the image of Nancy's car tumbling over and over again.

"Damn it, George. Focus!" Robert yelled.

"Keep your damn voice down," George ordered in a low rumble. "What makes you think he knows?"

"Kevin told him before he died."

George shook his head. "Kevin wouldn't do that."

"You weren't there at the end, George. You didn't go visit him like the rest of us did. I was at the hospital the day before he died, and I saw Charley coming out of his room."

Shocked, George shook his head. "Son of a bitch."

"That's why I've been trying so hard to keep her away from him."

"Why didn't you tell me this before?"

"I thought you already knew. I figured Kevin told you he was gonna do it. He always told you everything."

"I didn't go to see him in the hospital. He called, but I didn't go. Every time I saw him, it reminded me of the accident."

"What do you want me to do?"

"Leave Trisha alone. Let me worry about getting her away from Charley."

"But I need to—"

"Leave my daughter alone, Robert." George leaned forward in his chair. "I'm going to put $50,000 in your bank account, but you need to move away from Hope, Robert. It's time."

"Move? This is my home."

"But you caused a scene the other day, Robert. I'm going to buy a house for you down in Fort Lauderdale. You can be closer to your brother. You need to go home and start packing. Just take what you need. You have to be gone before the end of the day."

"I've never lived anywhere else."

"This is my only offer. Betty Sue insists that I quit helping you. I'm gonna miss you, ol' friend. But it's time. I'm putting your house on the market this week. And I've already hired someone to find you a house down there."

"You're selling my house?"

"We both know my name is on the deed, Robert. The wise thing for you to do right now would be to go home, pack what you need to survive for a few weeks, and take off for Florida today. If you're not gone by six, I won't help you move."

"You really are heartless," Robert snarled as he shook his head. "I've spent my whole life helping you, keeping your secrets, and—"

"And I've spend my whole life cleaning up your messes. And paying your way. Take the offer, Robert. We both know you can't survive without my help."

Robert glared at him, then jumped up and slammed open George's office door, never looking back.

"Mr. Walker hasn't paid his loan."

George glanced at his secretary, who appeared in his doorway, and nodded. "Please shut my door on your way out."

Memories of Nancy Walker surrounded him like a dense fog as he leaned back in his desk chair and sighed.

"Oh my gosh. Trisha?"

Trisha quickly hugged the woman who had been like a second mother to her. "It's so good to see you again, Helen."

"You've become a very beautiful woman, Trisha. I heard you were back in town."

"You haven't changed a bit. I've missed you so much, Helen."

"Me too, honey. You've always been like my own daughter. Are you here to visit your folks?"

Trisha peered up at the house and suddenly questioned why she was there. Charley's words raced through her mind, and she wondered if she really could keep his promise.

"Trisha? Are you okay, honey?"

Trisha offered her a smile. "Sorry. I was just thinking. How come you're out here in the yard? Don't you cook anymore?"

"Yes. I just got back from your brother's house. I stocked up their refrigerator for them. School starts tomorrow, and I figured they could use a little help."

"You always were very thoughtful, Helen. And the best role model I had."

"Trisha!"

Both women glanced at the front door, and Trisha felt her heart sink as her mother marched up to them and waved her long, manicured finger in in Helen's face. "You have lunch to prepare, Helen."

"Yes, ma'am."

Trisha watched as Helen quickly retreated in the direction of the side entrance and disappeared behind a row of bushes.

"That was rude, Mother."

"She has work to do. We don't pay her to gossip."

"She wasn't gossiping," Trisha said, shaking her head.

"I'm so glad you came, honey. Let's go in the house and talk."

Trisha reluctantly followed her mother into the house. They walked silently down the hallway and into the living room.

Trisha stood by the door, watching as her mother walked over and sat down on the antique couch that had been in their home as long as she could remember.

"Aren't you going to have a seat, dear?"

"Why'd you lie to me?" Trisha demanded, thinking about the last time she'd been there.

"Lie about what?"

"You implied Charley had done something awful to you. Why'd you lie about something like that?"

"He didn't confess, did he?"

"He didn't confess because he had nothing to confess. Charley's a good man."

"No, he's not." Betty Sue jumped up and hurried to Trisha. "He's not a good man, and you need to get away from him while you still can."

"I won't." Trisha crossed her arms. "I love him. He's showed me more compassion and love than you ever have."

"Don't talk about that man that way," Betty Sue insisted as she rushed toward Trisha. "And don't you ever talk to me like that again."

Trisha turned to leave and was stopped in her tracks when her mother grabbed her arm. "Let go."

"No." Betty Sue shook her head. "We have things we need to talk about."

"You know, that's the problem, Mom. We can never have a real conversation, because you refuse to be real with me. I need the truth. I want the truth. But you still think I'm a little girl you can control with lies and manipulation. I'm not that little girl anymore. I had to grow up fast out in California when you and Dad turned your back on me. You turned me into the strong woman I am today. And if you don't like that, you have no one to blame but yourself."

"You're going to regret spending time with Charley Walker." Betty Sue tightened her grip on Trisha's arm.

Trisha quickly pulled away. "I love Charley. He's the best thing that ever happened to me."

"Oh, I should drag you upstairs and lock you in your room!"

"That's the only way you know how to deal with things, isn't it? One way or another, you always have to get your way. Well, it's not going to happen. Until you accept my relationship with Charley, I won't be back to see you or Dad again."

Trisha turned and ran out of the house with Betty Sue following her, neither one of them noticing the new maid had been cleaning on the far end of the room the entire time they'd been there.

"Hey, what's wrong?" Darrell asked as he walked up on Charley's porch and sat down beside him.

"Oh, girl problems. It's been awhile since I had to worry about this stuff, and I think maybe I overreacted."

"Being with a woman is an adjustment," Darrell agreed. "What happened?"

"I can't really tell you what we were talking about," Charley started, "but it was about her parents, and now she's wondering if I'm using her and this relationship to get back at them for something they did to me. She was talking to her ex-husband about it apparently. I walked in on the end of their conversation. It really hurts me that she had doubts about my feelings for her. But she says she trusts me. And what I told her last night was pretty serious. Oh, hell, Darrell, I overreacted. Big time. And I told her I needed time to think. But ever since she left, I've just wanted to go and find her and tell her I understand."

"Then do it."

Charley shrugged. "How do I know that's the right thing to do? Everything was so much easier with Nancy. We grew up together. We knew we were in love. There was no baggage or worries about our feelings. We knew each other better than we knew anyone else."

"I don't know much about Trisha. And I gotta admit, I'm a little worried about her being a Bailey. But it sounds like she isn't thrilled with being a Bailey either. And she really spent her growing up years out in California at college, right?"

Charley nodded.

"Don't condemn her for who her parents are, Charley. And don't get mad at her for thinking things to death. It seems to be what women do these days. Don't be too hard on yourself either. I had a little fight with Tess, and I think that was because I over thought something too."

"Is everything okay?"

"Oh, yeah. Fine. I'd better be gettin' on home. Lunch is probably getting cold."

"Thanks for stopping by," Charley said as they both stood up.

"We'll go in and pay off your loan tomorrow. Okay?"

"Okay," Charley agreed.

Darrell had just pulled onto the gravel road when his cell phone started ringing. Noticing it was the bank, he answered.

"Hi, Darrell, this is Samantha down at the bank. I wanted to let you know two large amounts have been taken out of your account by your wife. Our new employee was the one who waited on your wife both times, and she didn't realize she needed to clear that large of a withdrawal through you. I'm so sorry."

"It's okay." Darrell's mind started racing. Not wanting the new girl to get into trouble, Darrell lied when he said, "I knew she was going to make those withdrawals, but for the life of me, I can't remember how much she said she was getting."

"Oh, well, it was for a total of $10,000."

"Oh, yeah. That's right," Darrell said, hoping he didn't sound as shocked as he really was. "Thanks for letting me know. But again, it was no problem. I hope no one gets in trouble."

"Oh, no. We're just going over company policies with her. Thanks for being so understanding."

"Thank you." Darrell hung up his phone and flung it across the cab of his truck.

"Wake up, Princess."

"Glen?" Jessica questioned as she opened her eyes. But her blood turned cold when she realized Carl was lying beside her on Glen's bed.

"What the hell?" Jessica demanded as she slid to the edge of the bed and jumped up. "How'd you get in here?"

"Wasn't hard," Carl admitted as he sat up and smiled at her. "That lock was very easy to pick. It's time."

"For what?" Jessica demanded, tired of waiting to find out her fate.

"Well, I'm a nice guy, so I'm giving you a choice." Carl stood up. "Either we take another romp in between the sheets, or you help me get your sister."

"Get my sister? What do you mean, get her?"

"It's easy. You help me get her into my car, then I'll take her off your hands. For good."

"You want to kidnap her?"

"Kidnap is such a harsh word. I want to take her away for some fun."

Jessica shivered.

"Well, Princess, what's it gonna be? Are you gonna sacrifice yourself for your sister? Or are you going to sacrifice your sister for yourself?"

Happy childhood memories of playing with her big sister started rushing her as she asked, "Are you gonna hurt her?"

"I'm asking the questions," Carl bellowed, scaring her.

"Fine. Her. Take her," Jessica blurted, surprised she felt empathy for her sister when she uttered those words.

"Great. Call her."

"I can't call her. I don't have her number."

"She's your sister, of course you have her number."

Jessica shook her head. "I don't. We don't talk."

Carl shrugged. "Well, then, you're no use to me. And your boyfriend's bed is right there."

"I have her email address," Jessica said, shivering as she looked at the bed.

"Fine, try that."

Jessica hurried to the end table where her phone was charged and picked up it. Then she scrolled until she found the address she had copied from her brother's phone when he didn't know she'd borrowed it. While it loaded, she thought back to that day, remembering how hurt she'd been to find out her brother had been in contact with the sister who had abandoned both of them.

"Give it to me."

Jessica handed her phone over and watched as Carl typed on the small keyboard. She shuddered as he grinned while handing her back the phone.

She felt her heart drop again when he walked over and sat down on Glen's old couch. "Why are you sitting down?"

"We have to wait for her reply," Carl reminded her as he patted the couch cushion beside him. "Come on over and have a seat."

Jessica walked over and sat as far away from him as possible, and then she asked, "How do you know my sister, anyway?"

"I met her out in LA. My sister was a maid for the married guy your sister was doing."

Jessica's mouth dropped open. "My sister had an affair?"

"Yep."

"No, shit?" Jessica's mind started racing as she wondered if she was more like her sister than she ever imagined.

Pointing toward the kitchen table, Carl said, "Now that you've done your work, you can have the gift I brought for you."

Jessica's mouth started watering when she noticed the two new bottles of whiskey.

"Crack one of those babies open, Jessica. We might as well enjoy ourselves while we wait."

❧

"Where the hell is he?" Tess wondered as she dumped the ruined lunch into the trashcan.

She checked the microwave clock and shook her head. "He's always here by one for lunch. Now it's almost four. And he never called me."

She was drying the last dish when she heard his truck pulling into the driveway.

She hurried to the door and met him on the porch. "I was worried sick. You missed lunch."

"Is there anything you want to say to me?" Darrell demanded, his cheeks red as he stared at her.

"I always want to tell you that I love you." Noticing he looked even angrier, she said, "What's wrong, Darrell?"

"The bank called me today."

She felt the blood drain from her cheeks as she sat with a thump on the chair outside the door.

Darrell walked over and sat down beside her.

"I'm sorry."

"Did you do that because I want to loan Charley money? Are you scared we'll run out or something?" Darrell continued, presenting the only possibility he'd been able to come up with while he was driving the county roads and thinking.

"Uh, yes," Tess lied. Sensing a way out, she continued, "I'm sorry, Darrell. You know I'm not used to having enough money to pay my bills every month. I took that out to invest it."

"Why didn't you just tell me?"

"I was scared you'd be mad."

"Look, honey, I'm sorry I got so upset the other day. You have every right to ask me about our finances. I shouldn't have yelled at you. But helping Charley is important to me. Besides, we'll still have plenty of money for bills. I promised on our wedding day I'd take care of you. And I will."

Tess let her tears fall as the guilt from lying to him ate away at her.

Carl studied his watch. "It's almost six. Where the hell is she?"

"She got a job. Maybe she's at work," Jessica said, thinking back to something she'd overheard her mother saying. "You need to leave, Carl. Glen will be back any minute."

Carl stood up and threatened, "You haven't paid your debt back yet, Jessica. And don't even think about telling anyone, or I'll take you down with me. Got it?"

"I won't tell anyone," Jessica said as she corralled him toward the door.

They both jumped when Glen opened it before they could.

"Hey, uh, what's going on Jess?" Glen asked, looking Carl up and down.

"This is one of Trisha's friends. From LA. He's trying to get in touch with her. Thought I could help."

"That's a long shot. You two hate each other. I'm Glen, Jess' boyfriend."

"Carl," he said, glaring at Jessica when Glen turned his back to them.

"Carl was just leaving. Bye," Jessica insisted as she pushed the door shut before Carl could walk back in.

Glen took her in his arms and hugged her tightly. "I don't like you being here alone with a guy like that."

"He's creepy. I can't believe he's a friend of my sister's," Jessica said, holding tightly on to Glen, scared what Carl would do next.

"Trisha, please call me. I'm getting worried," Charley said when he got her voice mail again.

He hung up the phone and glanced at his watch, then walked out and climbed into his truck.

As he headed down the road toward town, he dialed his new son-in-law's number.

"Uh, hello?"

"Tyler, this is Charley Walker."

"Yeah, hi, Charley."

"Have you seen Trisha today?"

"No." Tyler glanced at his closed bedroom door. He got up off the floor where he'd been sitting and trying to coax Pam into opening the door, and walked down the hallway to the living room. "I saw her yesterday. Is everything okay?"

"Well, I think so. We had a little misunderstanding this morning, and I asked her to give me some time to think about something. I figured she'd be back by now, but she's not. And she's not answering my calls. I don't think she's mad at me, but could you give her a call and see if she answers?"

"Sure. I'll call you right back."

Charley's phone started ringing as he passed the city limits sign.

"She didn't answer my call either," Tyler said.

"I hate to ask this, but can you find out if she's at your folk's house? I don't think I should go over there."

"Sure. I'll call you after I find out if she's there."

"Okay, thanks."

Tyler walked back down the hallway and knocked again on their closed bedroom door.

"Pam, that was your dad on the phone. He needs me to do something for him. Please open this door so I can kiss you before I leave."

Not hearing a sound, he slowly turned the knob and walked in.

"Where is she?" He questioned as he stomped around the empty room he'd been talking to for more than 20 minutes.

"Her car's in the driveway. Where'd she go?"

He pulled his cell phone out of his pocket as he started for his car, annoyed when she didn't answer.

"This is your husband. Where are you, Pam? Your dad just called me, and I need to go and do a favor for him. Please call me as soon as you get this. It's important. I love you. Bye."

Now worried about both his sister and his wife, Tyler jumped in his car and took off for his parents' house.

ஐ

Charley coasted toward downtown and almost ran into a parked car when he noticed a moving truck was outside of Robert Townsend's house.

"I hope that old bird is really moving."

As he swung around the downtown square and headed toward The Tasty Cone, he thought back to that morning before Trisha left. His lips burned as he thought about her kiss.

"I've gotta let her know I'm not mad anymore," Charley insisted. The uneasiness that had started earlier that afternoon seemed to intensify as he continued his drive around town, not finding her car anywhere.

"She was there earlier," Tyler said when he called a few minutes later. "Helen, the maid, said she left about noon."

"Well, hell," Charley sighed.

"Have you checked out Kat Roe's house?"

"No. I was getting ready to head that way."

"Let me. Do you have somewhere else you could look?"

"I'm not sure where to look. I figured she'd be back at the farm hours ago."

"Think about what you two were talking about before she left. Maybe she mentioned somewhere she needed to go and you didn't think too much about it at the time. I'll head out to Kat's and see if Chase Locke is around. He might know if she's been there today."

"Okay. I'll call you if I think of anywhere else to look."

While driving by one of the Bailey-owned banks, Charley suddenly remembered Trisha's conversation with Brad. "She said she was going to the cemetery today."

Hoping she meant the Hope Cemetery, he turned around in the bank parking lot and headed to the southern edge of town.

The cemetery was tucked behind rows and rows of beautiful oak trees that had been planted long before he was ever born. He drove through the entrance and weaved around the narrow lanes, keeping his eyes open for any sign of Trisha or her car.

He was about ready to leave when he remembered the section in the far back of the cemetery reserved for children. Feeling a pull in that direction, Charley started up the steep hill and through the narrow opening flanked by beautifully flowering hydrangea trees.

His heart skipped a beat when he noticed Trisha's car blocking the path, and felt the blood drain from his cheeks when he realized both the driver's and passenger's doors were wide open.

"What the hell?" he muttered as he picked up his phone and dialed Tyler.

"I haven't gotten to Kat's house yet."

"I found her car."

"Just her car?"

"I think we need to call the sheriff," Charley whispered, feeling faint. "Something's wrong, Tyler."

"I'll call Sheriff McEntire. Where are you?"

"The children's area of the Hope Cemetery. Get help and get out here. Now!"

Charley's mind was racing in several directions as he sat quietly in the sheriff's lobby.

He peered at the closed office door and wondered if Sheriff McEntire was almost done talking with Tyler.

He leaned back and shut his eyes, his mind instantly back at the cemetery. Tyler had arrived a few minutes after his call, and they had both stood by Charley's truck, staring at Trisha's car.

They had wanted to walk over and look through it, but had known better.

Then several patrol cars had started arriving, and things had gotten crazy as crime scene tape had gone up and strangers had started going through Trisha's car, looking for clues.

He knew her cell phone had been found in the front seat and that the keys to the car were still in the ignition.

He took a deep breath, remembering how scared he'd been when they had opened the trunk to make sure she wasn't inside.

Charley's heart was racing and he took another deep breath, trying to maintain his composure.

He knew officers were still checking in the thick trees around the cemetery, looking for Trisha, and his heart could hardly stand the thought of never talking to her again.

"Charley," Tyler called as he hurried out of the sheriff's office, closely followed by Bill McEntire.

Charley stood and thought how strange it was that just a few days earlier, the three of them had been standing together at the wedding.

"Thank you for coming to the station. I'll be in touch with both of you. If you think of anything else, call me. I know neither one of you is going to rest until we find her, so be careful. And keep me in the loop. I want Trisha back home as much as you do."

Charley nodded as Tyler shook Bill's hand, and then they all hurried out of the station and into the parking lot.

Tyler climbed into the passenger's side of Charley truck, and they both sat in silence as Bill raced out of the lot in his cruiser with his lights flashing.

"We need to compare notes," Charley said.

"You first."

"Okay. I told Bill about Brad Jenkins and his ex-girlfriend, Scarlette, who threatened Trisha."

"Who are they?"

Realizing Tyler didn't know about Trisha's marriage, Charley explained, "Brad is Trisha's ex-husband. They still talk. I guess Scarlette was jealous of their relationship and broke up with Brad and then threatened Trisha."

"If she hurt my sister—"

"Focus," Charley interrupted.

"Yeah, okay. I didn't know Trish'd ever been married. But I guess I'm not surprised. What else did you tell Bill?"

"That a girl Trisha had worked with called her last night. She was upset Trisha hadn't helped her get a new place to intern and told Trisha she was going to pay for not helping her."

"Anything else?"

"Only that my neighbor, Darrell Whiteshell's wife, Tess, knew Trisha in California." Charley thought back to the night Trisha had confessed about her affair with her coach. "I guess Tess worked as the maid for Trisha's basketball coach. Trisha moved in with her coach and his wife after your parents quit financially supporting her. I don't want to go into all the details, Tyler, but Tess and Trisha had some issues, and they aren't friends anymore."

"So, do you think she had anything to do with this?"

Charley shrugged. "I don't know. But she's someone who knew Trisha. What did you tell him?"

"That there was a woman looking for Trisha out at the house this morning. When I talked to Helen, she mentioned a stranger was looking for Trisha. And when Mom wouldn't tell her anything, she left."

"Do you think that could be this Scarlette person?" Charley asked, his heart racing. "Or the intern?"

"Could be," Tyler agreed. "There's something else."

"What?"

"Helen also said that mom and Trisha fought this afternoon and that mom told Trisha she wanted to lock her up until she came to her senses and quit dating…"

"Me," Charley said when Tyler's voice trailed off.

Tyler looked over and nodded.

"Do you think your parents would do that?"

"Hell, I don't know. They do crazy things all the time. That's why Bill wants to keep this quiet for now. He's got several people to question. I guess Trisha had several messages on her cell phone. And she also had emails from Jessica. She wanted Trisha to meet up with her today."

"That's weird."

"It is."

"So, what does Pam think about all of this?"

"Don't know. She's not talking to me. She wasn't home when I left, but her car was there."

"Do you think she's missing too?" Charley asked, terrified.

Tyler shook his head. "No, she answered her phone when Bill called her. She said she'd been out for a walk. She's home now, and she's fine. But she's mad at me, Charley."

"Why?"

"Because I stood up for my sister, and she's mad at Trisha. Walking in on the two of you really set her off yesterday."

Charley hung his head, feeling defeated. "That wasn't a good thing."

"Well, we don't have time to worry about that. We need to start looking for any sign of Trisha we can find."

ဓ

Tyler drove around Hope, taking one city street at a time, checking each driveway to see if he could find any trace of his sister. He knew it was a long shot, but he didn't know what else to do.

He quickly answered his phone when it started ringing.

"Tyler, it's Matt. How's it going? Are you ready for school to start tomorrow?"

"Oh, yeah," Tyler said, shocked he'd forgotten all about something he'd so been looking forward to a few hours earlier.

"Hey, did Susan Bartlett find you? I was supposed to tell you she was looking for you at the school, but forgot all about it."

"Susan Bartlett?"

"Gee, dude, you haven't been off the market that long. Yes, Susan Bartlett. She was a year older than us in school. Great friends with Trisha. Blond hair, green eyes and long, long legs. She liked to tease us."

"Oh, Susan," Tyler said, remembering her. "No, I haven't seen her."

"Well, she was at the school looking for you today. I ran into her in the hallway. She said she'd heard Trisha was back and wanted to see if you knew where to find her. I sent her to your room."

"I headed straight out to the football field after our meetings. Thanks for letting me know. I'll look her up."

"Well, see if you can find out if she's single. You'll see, Tyler, she's even hotter now, and I didn't think that could be possible."

"Thanks," Tyler said as he hung up and turned around in his dentist's driveway. He cut three blocks over and one block down, then pulled into the Bartlett's driveway.

The front door opened on his second knock. "Oh my gosh, Tyler."

"Hey, Susan, I heard you were looking for me."

"And you rushed over to my parents' house? That was nice of you Ty, but I already found Trish. Didn't she tell you?"

"You saw her?"

"Yeah. Right after I was at the school."

"So, when was that?"

"About three thirty. I was headed uptown and saw her walking down the street. We had a good talk. She looks great. I can't believe Jess hit her, though. Sounds like little Jess is still having a hard time of it."

"How long did you two talk?"

"I'm not sure. I guess about thirty minutes. We sat on the bench outside the courthouse. Yeah, the bells were going off when she was backing out. It was four o'clock."

"Where was she heading? Did she say?"

"Yeah, she said she had errands to run. What's going on, Tyler?"

"I can't say. Did you go to my folks' house looking for her too?"

Susan nodded as she crossed her arms. "I hated to. I know Trish got a bum deal from your parents after she decided to move to California. Your mom wouldn't tell me where she was, so I left. I wasn't going to play games with her."

"Is there anything else you remember? Did you see her again?"

"I did, but I didn't talk to her. I went out for my afternoon run, and she passed me on the road to the cemetery."

"What time was that?"

"About five. Is Trisha all right, Tyler?"

"Is there anything else you remember?" Tyler demanded, ignoring her question. "Anything at all, even if you're not sure it matters."

"Well, there was something."

"What?" Tyler asked, leaning closer.

"While we were uptown, this silver car kept driving around the square. It would go real slow when it passed us. The windows were tinted, so I couldn't see who was inside."

"Did you notice the license plate?"

"Yes. It was a vanity plate. From California."

"Do you remember what it said?"

Susan shook her head. "I'm sorry. I don't. But I swear it looked like that same car was following Trisha when she passed me going toward the cemetery."

"Okay, Susan, you need to come with me. We have to find Sheriff McEntire."

"Why? What the hell's going on?"

"Trisha's missing, and it looks like someone ambushed her at the cemetery."

"Oh, no. Let's go, Tyler."

"Hey."

"Charley, what's going on? You look terrible," Darrell said, when he found Charley standing outside his front door at nine thirty, covered from head to toe in dirt.

"Sorry to bother you so late, Darrell, but I wondered if you could give me a hand?"

"Sure."

"Great, grab a flashlight and your shotgun and meet me at my truck."

"Your shotgun?" Tess asked, concerned.

"I'm sure there's just some kind of critter running around. Old Lady White's grandson swore he saw a bobcat in her cattle lot. Maybe Charley saw it too. I'll have my phone if you need me. I'm sure I'll be back shortly."

Tess met him at the door and kissed him. "Don't be gone too long. I love you."

"I love you too, Tessy."

Charley tore out of the driveway the minute Darrell shut his door.

"So, what's going on, Charley?"

"This has to stay between us. You can't even tell Tess."

"Okay. I figured it was somethin' big."

"Someone took Trisha. The cops are working on it, but I can't sit around, Darrell. I have to do something. I have to try and find her. What if she's hurt? Or what if he's…he's…touching her?"

"I'm sure she'll be fine."

"I'm not so sure about that. I thought I'd look through all the abandoned buildings around here. He might be hiding her in one of them. That's why you need the gun. If you don't want to help me with this, I understand."

"Of course I'll help you."

They continued down the road and then turned left. Just as they were pulling up to a cluster of abandoned out buildings, Charley's ringing telephone startled them both.

Not recognizing the number, Charley hesitated before answering.

"Is this Charley? Trisha's boyfriend?"

"Yes. Who's this?"

"Charley, this is Brad Jenkins. I'm Trisha's—"

"I know who you are," Charley interrupted, not wanting to hear the word husband in any form.

"I just got off the phone with Sheriff McEntire. Scarlette doesn't have Trisha."

"How do you know that? There was a model-type blonde at the Bailey house today."

"Sheriff McEntire's talking with that woman right now. She's a classmate of Trisha's," Brad relayed. "The reason I know Scarlette doesn't have her is because…because…we found Scarlette. She had come back to the house sometime after I left for Paris. She killed herself in our bedroom. She's been dead for a few days, Charley."

A knot formed in Charley's throat. "I'm so sorry."

"Thanks," Brad said before breaking into sobs. "I can't…believe…Scarlette would do this to herself. And I…can't believe that Trisha…Trisha…is missing. I thought she'd be safe in Iowa. I want to help. But I can't leave right now."

"It's okay. Trisha would understand. I'm so sorry for your loss. Thanks for calling and letting me know."

"Who was that?" Darrell asked after Charley hung up.

Charley quickly filled him in as they both sat staring at the headlight-illuminated outbuildings in front of them.

"Was Scarlette your only suspect?"

Charley startled Darrell as he punched the dash. "I figured Trisha could handle herself with someone like Scarlette. When they said a blonde was at the Bailey house looking for Trisha, I just figured it was her. I also figured she wouldn't hurt Trisha. But now, damn it, Darrell, anyone could have her."

"What about her sister?"

"Maybe," Charley agreed, latching on to that possibility. "She had been emailing Trisha today."

Charley's phone rang again, and he answered, "Tyler. I know Scarlette is dead and that she wasn't the woman at your parents' house."

"That woman was Susan Bartlett."

"Cliff and Christine's daughter?"

"Yes. She saw Trisha heading toward the cemetery and also saw a car following her. Susan was out running. That was after five. The car had vanity California plates and tinted windows.

"So, it probably is someone she knew from California."

"Looks that way. But Bill doesn't think Brad's a suspect."

"No, I don't either," Charley agreed. He glanced over at Darrell and said, "So that leaves the intern, because the only other person I know that knew Trisha in California was my neighbor Darrell's wife, Tess. But she lives here now."

"The intern, Marti, is in California still at the office. A deputy's on his way out to talk to Tess. They are also going to talk to Jessica. Where are you?"

"I'm checking in old buildings."

"Alone?"

"No, I got Darrell and my gun with me."

"Well, be careful. I'll call you when I know more."

Darrell waited until Charley hung up, then said, "You told them Tess knew Trisha?"

Charley nodded.

"But Tess said they didn't know each other that well."

"She never told you about the stolen jewelry, did she?"

"What stolen jewelry?"

"Trisha told me Tess was her basketball coach's maid. Tess stole jewelry from the coach's wife and pawned it to get enough money to pay her bills. She got fired when they realized she'd stolen the jewelry. I guess Trisha and Tess were pretty good friends, for awhile."

"Shit, Charley. I'm starting to wonder if you were right about Tess all along. She never told me any of that. And I found out today she withdrew $10,000 from our bank account. When I confronted her, she said she took the money to invest it."

"And you believe that?"

Darrell shrugged. "Not really."

"I think I should tell you a deputy is headed out to talk to her right now. Do you want me to take you home?"

"Nope," Darrell answered as he opened the door. "She's on her own. Let's find Trisha."

"Now what?" Jessica mumbled when someone started knocking on Glen's door. She peeked over, noticing he was sleeping through the ruckus, and decided to ignore it, hoping they'd go away.

It was quiet for a few seconds, and then the knocking started again.

"This better not be that lowlife," Jessica said as she jumped up and ran to the door, swinging it open. Her heart skipped a beat when she noticed the sheriff's deputy.

"Jessica Donohue. I need to ask you a few questions. We can talk here or down at the station."

"Do I have to?" Jessica asked, scared, as she peered back at Glen, thankful he was still asleep.

"No ma'am. You don't have to, but we do want to talk to you and will follow the proper channels to make sure that happens if you don't talk with me now."

"Okay, fine. But you do know who my father is, right?"

The officer nodded. "Yes. I'm aware your father is George Bailey."

Jessica hesitated while glancing back at Glen. Not sure what the deputy wanted, and worried it might have something to do with Carl, she said, "Let's go to the station."

Not a word was spoken as they made the quick trip from Glen's apartment to the newly built county sheriff's office on the east end of Hope.

Jessica followed the officer into the building, glancing around, on the lookout for Carl as they walked down a long corridor and turned into a small room.

"Sheriff McEntire will be with you shortly."

"I know Bill. He's my brother's friend," Jessica babbled as she started chewing on her fingernails.

The officer just nodded before shutting the door.

Jessica got up and started pacing around the room while she peered into the corners, quickly noticing the cameras.

She plopped back down in the chair and chewed on her nails again while bouncing her right foot.

"Thanks for coming in, Jessica," Bill said as he walked in carrying two cans of pop. He placed one down in front of Jessica and opened the other as he sat down in the chair across from her.

"What's going on, Bill?"

"Well, I wanted to ask you a few questions."

"About what?"

"Let's start with why you were trying so hard to get ahold of Trisha today?"

Jessica felt the blood running from her cheeks, and she mumbled, "To apologize for hitting her."

"That's why you wanted to meet her?"

"Um, yes."

Bill leaned back in his chair and studied Jessica's face. The moments ticked on as silence fell between them. Finally, Bill said, "We both know that's not true, don't we?"

"I don't know what you want from me. I answered your question."

"This is serious, Jessica," Bill slammed his hand down on the table. "I don't have time to dance this dance with you. I want to help you, but I can't if you're not truthful. Why did you email your sister two times today?"

"I don't want any of this conversation getting back to my boyfriend, Glen. Okay?"

Bill nodded as he leaned forward.

"I met a guy at Stu's Bar yesterday. I had just found out that my daughter was going to live with Clay, and I wasn't happy. I drank too much, and the guy took advantage of me. I woke up in his hotel room. He threatened to tell Glen I slept with him if I didn't help him. This morning he broke into Glen's apartment and told me I either had to help him kidnap Trisha or he was going to…he wanted me to sleep with him again. I did what everyone always expects me to do. I saved myself and offered to help him get Trisha."

"Okay, so you contacted her and she met you?"

Jessica shook her head. "I emailed her, but she never responded. And that son of a bitch sat with me in Glen's apartment all afternoon. I told the guy he had to leave, but he didn't get gone before Glen got home from the hospital. Glen's mom was admitted last night. Anyway, Glen saw him at the apartment. I know the guy won't give up until he has Trisha. And if she doesn't call me back, he's gonna want me again. I won't sleep with him again, Bill. I love Glen. I don't want to hurt him."

"So, you're telling me you haven't seen Trisha all day?"

Jessica shook her head. "She never got back to me. She's probably still mad at me for hitting her. I would be if I were her."

Bill leaned back and studied Jessica's face for a little bit, then asked, "Except for coming here, have you been out of Glen's apartment at all today?"

Jessica shook her head. "Why?"

"What was the guy's name, Jess?"

"If I tell you, he's going to tell Glen what happened in the hotel room."

"It sounds like you were a victim of his, Jessica. If Glen really loves you, he'll understand that and want to protect you from this guy. What's his name?"

"Carl. I don't know a last name."

"What hotel was he in? What's the room number?"

"That old flea bag outside of town. We were in room three."

"I need you to stay put for a little bit, okay?"

"Yeah, sure. Once Glen finds out, I won't have a home to go back to anyway."

Bill patted Jessica on the shoulder, then hurried into the hallway, running into one of his deputies.

"Mrs. Whiteshell refuses to come in."

"We'll deal with her in a bit. I got a lead, but first, we need to get a warrant."

Carl was staring at the picture of Trisha he'd swiped from the many Jessica carried in her purse when someone knocked at his door. He quickly opened it, expecting to find the pizza delivery boy, but froze when he noticed the cops.

"Carl?"

"Yeah. What do you guys want?"

Sheriff McEntire noticed the photo of Trisha in his hand and pulled out his gun while ordering, "Put your hands up, Carl. Slowly."

Carl raised his hands, his mind racing while he thought of all the things he'd done over the last few weeks that could have gotten him into trouble.

Bill quickly handcuffed him and took him out to the patrol car, and then he joined the other officer in searching Carl's hotel room, looking for Trisha.

"She's not here," Deputy Toms announced.

"Damn it," Bill muttered. "But he had her photo in his hand."

"And he has a wad of cash." Deputy Toms pointed to the stack of money on the end table by the bed.

"He wants to talk to you."

Sheriff McEntire looked at the young deputy who had just arrived and asked, "Why?"

"Says he wants to confess."

"I'm gonna take him back to the station. We need to see if we can find any evidence that either Trisha Jenkins or Jessica Donohue were in this room. Okay?"

He hurried outside and got into the patrol car where Carl was waiting, and they started into town.

"I want to confess," Carl said as they started into the building.

"Great. Let's get into one of these rooms where we can talk."

A few minutes later, Bill sat across from Carl, who was guzzling a can of diet pop.

"I didn't rape her," Carl insisted. "She came on to me in the bar. She wanted me. Afterwards, she passed out from the alcohol. It was almost four hours later before she woke up. Then she was mad. I swear, I didn't rape her. She left willingly with me, and you can ask the bartender. He saw it all."

"Fair enough. Why did you have a photo of Trisha Jenkins?"

"Trisha Bailey?"

Bill nodded.

"She's an old friend. I knew her in California."

"Come on, Carl. We know you wanted her sister to help you kidnap her."

"Okay, fine. She knew my sister in California. That's when I met her. She's hot! I just wanted to talk to her. My sister paid me ten grand to take her away from here. Said she was gonna blow her cover with her rich husband. She wanted me and Trisha far away from Hope."

"Were you going to kidnap Trisha Jenkins?"

Carl leaned back and crossed him arms, then shook his head. "Nope. I just wanted the money, and I wanted a chance to talk to Trisha. I'd never kidnap no one."

"Who's your sister?"

"Theresa Hooper. Oh, wait, she goes by Tess now. She's married to a farmer. I think his last name is Whiteshell. Yep, that's it, Tess Whiteshell. And her old man's loaded."

Tess paced around the kitchen, her cell phone glued to the side of her head as she tried Darrell's number again.

"What?" Darrell demanded.

"I need you to come home. Why didn't you answer before?"

"I'm helping Charley. I can't come home right now. I'm sure you can handle whatever mess you got yourself into."

Tess was shocked he hung up and felt her nice, happy life crumbing down around her.

"Damn you, Carl," Tess growled, thinking about her visit from the deputy. When she'd heard the knock, she'd figured Darrell had forgotten his key. She'd been completely caught off guard when she'd noticed the officer standing on her front porch, asking her to go down to the sheriff's office with him.

Then she'd panicked and refused, and he had promised he'd be back.

"I have to be proactive," Tess decided as she ran up the stairs to her bedroom and changed into a pair of black dress pants and a conservative, button-down white blouse. She slipped into black flats and ran a brush through her hair, and then she pulled her purse out of the bedroom closet and ran down the stairs.

After finding her car keys, she ran out to her car and drove as quickly as she could to the sheriff's office.

She took a few deep breaths as she sat in the parking lot, then walked inside.

"I need to speak to Sheriff McEntire. He wanted to ask me some questions," Tess told the receptionist.

"What's your name, ma'am?"

"Tess Whiteshell."

"Have a seat Mrs. Whiteshell, and I'll let him know you're here."

The second hand seemed to barely inch along as she clutched her purse and sat stoically in her chair.

"Mrs. Whiteshell?"

"Sheriff McEntire, I believe you wanted to talk to me. I'm sorry I didn't come with your deputy, but I panicked. I apologize."

"It's okay. Thanks for coming in. Why don't we talk back here?"

Tess followed him down the hallway, wondering who was on the other side of the two closed doors she passed.

"Can I get you anything to drink?"

Tess shook her head. "If you don't mind, I'd just like to help you out so I can be on my way."

"Okay. Have you seen Trisha Jenkins today?"

"Uh, no."

"Do you have a brother named Carl Hooper?"

"Unfortunately, yes. I do. He's a criminal and has done time in a prison in California. He's in Hope and blackmailed me. He told me if I didn't give him $10,000, he was going to tell my husband, Darrell, that I was a prostitute for several years in California. Darrell doesn't know anything about my life in California, and I didn't want him to know, so I took the money from our account without my husband's knowledge, and I gave it to Carl this morning."

"Did you ever ask your brother to kidnap Trisha Jenkins?"

Tess felt her heart dip down to her toes and shut her eyes, then shook her head. She took a deep breath, opened her eyes and said, "But I did tell him I would help him get to her if he promised he'd keep his mouth shut about my past. But I couldn't do that to Trisha. When Carl came to get the money this morning, I told him he could have the money, but that I wouldn't help him get to Trisha. And he just laughed at me. He told me he figured I'd back out and that he had someone else who was going to help him."

"Did you warn Trisha your brother was after her?"

Tess shook her head. "Did something happen to Trisha? Is that why Charley came and got my husband and told him to get his gun?"

Bill's face paled. "When did they leave?"

"About nine thirty."

"Wait here."

෴

"Hello?"

"What are you two doing?" Sheriff McEntire insisted as he paced in the hallway past the three closed interview room doors.

"Looking for Trisha," Charley answered.

"With guns?"

Charley took a deep breath as he slipped his revolver back into its holster and shut off his flashlight. His eyes quickly adjusted to the moonlight. "It's just for protection in case we run into any critters."

"I told you not to tell anyone and not to get into trouble," Bill reminded him. "You told Darrell Whiteshell, didn't you?"

"And you must be questioning Tess Whiteshell."

"Damn it, Charley. Don't mess this up."

"Have you found her?"

"Not yet. But I'm getting close. I know I am."

"Well, when we have her back, I'll quit looking for her."

"Don't get into any trouble. If I have to run out there and help you guys, it'll take me away from this."

"We can take care of ourselves."

Bill hung up and hurried into his office. Then he sat down and started skimming through the notes he'd made on the yellow lined notebook in front of him.

"I've got something for you," Deputy Miller said as he stepped into his office.

"Shut the door and let me have it." Bill motioned him in.

"Glen Robbins called while you were in with Mrs. Whiteshell. Apparently, he has very nosy neighbors who watched Jessica leave with Deputy Smith, and he was calling to make sure she was all right. I went down and interviewed the neighbors to see if they saw anything else. Turns out, the man who lives next door witnessed Carl Hooper breaking into Glen's apartment this morning. He watched to see if he was stealing anything and swears no one left that apartment all day. And Glen verified Jessica was there with Carl when he got home."

"I figured," Bill replied, nodding.

"So, where are we?"

"All three of them had believed, at one time or another, that Trisha Jenkins disappearing would be a good thing. In Mrs. Whiteshell's case, Trisha threatened her future with Mr. Whiteshell because Trisha knew Tess' secrets from California. Jessica has always been jealous of her sister and resents her showing back up in Hope. And Hooper, well, he has a rap sheet a mile long. He's a seasoned criminal who seems to be fixated on Trisha. And even though they all wanted Trisha gone, I don't believe any of them is responsible for her disappearance."

"I got that feeling too. So, where do we go from here?"

Bill shook his head. "I have no idea. All my leads have been exhausted."

"What about George and Betty Sue Bailey?"

"I know they didn't like Trisha with Charley, but I don't think they were desperate enough to act on it yet. Several people saw George Bailey at the bank until after seven. And Betty Sue was at the golf course all afternoon and even ate supper there. I know they could have hired someone, but I don't think they did."

"And Robert Townsend?"

"On a flight to Florida as we speak. He was at the airport at five."

"I hate to ask this, but what about Pam Bailey? Tyler mentioned she was upset with Trisha. And I know she was missing around the time Trisha was kidnapped."

"Pam's a good person," Bill said, feeling protective. "As far as I know, she doesn't have an alibi, but I don't think she'd do anything to Trisha either. Plus, why would she be driving a car with California plates?"

"Was our witness able to remember what was on the vanity plate?"

Bill shook his head. "Only that it was a California plate."

"Sheriff McEntire? Susan Bartlett's in the lobby. She's remembered something about the car."

"That was good timing," Deputy Miller said.

"Have her come on back to my office."

They could smell the flowery scent of her perfume before she walked through his doorway.

"I heard you remembered something."

Susan sat down beside Deputy Miller. "I remembered some of the letters on the plate. And that there was a parking pass on the bumper along with a bumper sticker of a moose."

"Okay, let's start with the plate. What are the letters you remembered?"

"There were two H's and the number fifty-four."

"Were there other letters?"

"I believe so, but I can't remember what they were."

"Were the two H's together?"

"Yes."

"And there was a parking pass. Do you remember what it said?"

"It said SUM and the year. It might have had the word college, but I can't remember for sure."

"And a moose?"

"Yeah. There was a moose on a bumper sticker. That was what I first noticed. It was a cartoon moose wearing a bikini. Does that help?"

"I think it will. Thanks for coming in so late, Susan."

"Trisha was one of my best friends in school. I hate like hell we grew apart. I want to be friends again. I'll do anything I can to help you find her."

Tess paced nervously around the small room when the door opened.

"Sorry that took so long."

"Did you find her?"

Bill shook his head. "No, not yet. But I was hoping you could help me with something."

"Anything."

"We have a witness who saw a car following Trisha today. The car looked similar to this."

Bill handed her a paper with a printout copy of the silver car.

"It had vanity California plates. Our witness can only remember that there were two H's and the number 54 on the plate. There was also some sort of parking pass on the bumper and a sticker with a moose."

Tess' face instantly paled as she leaned forward and asked, "Was the moose in a bikini?"

"Uh, yeah. At least the witness thought it was. Do you recognize that description?"

Tess pointed at the paper. "Coach Halley used to drive a silver car. He worked at the college, so he always had a parking pass on his car. And, he used to have a moose bumper sticker from a lodge he liked to go to when he needed to get away for a few days. It's very secluded and not many people know about it. His family ran the lodge when he was a kid. But the last time I saw Coach Halley and his car was more than nine years ago. I'm sure he's changed cars since then."

"But maybe he kept the same color of car. We think the parking pass was from this summer. Do you know what the rest of the vanity plate said?"

"His said Coach Hal, C-H-H-A-L, in all caps, followed by the number 54."

"Do you have any idea why Mr. Halley would be following Trisha?"

Tess shook her head. "I don't even know why he'd be in Iowa."

"What can you tell me about their relationship? Was he her coach?"

Tess crossed her arms, weighing her thoughts carefully.

"Please, Tess. Tell me anything you know about Coach Halley and Trisha. It could save her life."

Making up her mind, Tess said, "I worked for Coach Halley and his wife. His name is Michael. They didn't have any children, and he loved coaching basketball at the college. They felt sorry for Trisha because no one from her family ever came to her college events and she never went home for breaks or over the summer. When she graduated and her folks cut off her money, she was stranded. The Halleys invited her to live with them. I was working as their maid that summer. Mrs. Halley traveled a lot for her job and left right after Memorial Day that year. She didn't get back home until mid-July. Trisha helped Coach Halley with the summer basketball programs at the college. And…"

"And?" Bill pried.

"I hate to tell you this."

"Please, Tess."

"They had an affair."

"Trisha and Coach Halley?" Bill asked.

"Yes. And it's my fault Mrs. Halley found out. She even punched Trisha. I felt terrible about it, but felt I owed her that much after she…"

"She what?"

Tess took a deep breath. "I stole jewelry from the Halley's to pay my bills. Mrs. Halley didn't call the police. I felt like I needed to repay the favor. I had known about the affair for weeks and decided at that moment she needed to know too. I never thought through what would happen after I told her."

"And Mrs. Halley hit Trisha?"

"Yes. They started yelling at each other, and I left."

"And you haven't had any contact with them since?"

Tess shook her head. "Not the Halley's. And I hadn't talked to Trisha since that day either, until we ran into her at Charley Walker's house."

"Do you think Mrs. Halley could still be angry? Do you think she could be the one driving the car?"

"She never drove his car when I worked for them."

"Anything else you can tell me about them?"

Tess thought for a second, then said, "They were very nice to me when I worked for them. They paid me well and helped me out when most people turned their backs on me. I still feel terrible for stealing from them. I'm sad it ended the way it did."

"Fair enough." Bill stood. "You're free to leave, Tess."

"Am I going to be charged with anything?"

"Not at this time. Thanks for your help."

"I could stick around in case you have more questions," Tess offered as they walked down the hallway together.

"That's fine. You can wait in the lobby."

❧

Pam sat in the chair in their bedroom when Tyler opened the door and walked up to her.

"I'm not ready to talk to you yet." Pam glared at him. "Why in the world would you have Bill check up on me?"

"Look, I know you're mad about what you walked in on," Tyler started as he began pacing. "I'm sorry you had to see that. No one should see a parent doing that. But something much worse than that is going on. And I need your support, Pam."

"What's going on?"

"Someone took Trisha." Tyler walked over and knelt in front of her chair. "We don't know who or why. We can't find her anywhere."

"I can't believe this." Pam leaned forward and hugged him. "I'm so sorry, honey."

"I wanted you to know." Tyler gently pulled back.

"That's why Bill called?"

Tyler nodded. "I didn't know where you were. I was afraid that they…that whoever grabbed Trisha might have…"

"I'm fine," Pam interrupted. "I'm so sorry I worried you."

Tyler shook his head as he stood and started pacing again. "You didn't know. It's okay."

"No, it's not okay. I've been acting like a spoiled little brat, and both you and my daddy needed me. I'm so sorry. What can I do to help?"

Tyler stopped and looked at her, his mind a blank. "I have no idea what to do next."

They were hugging again when his cell phone started ringing.

"It's Bill," Tyler said before answering.

"Can you come down to the station?"

"Did you find her?"

"No. But I did find out something I'd like to talk to you about. Bring Pam and get down here."

❧

"Are you sure you don't want me to drop you off at home?" Charley asked as he and Darrell rushed toward town after getting a call from Bill.

Darrell shook his head.

"Okay."

Fifteen minutes later, Charley ran into the lobby and was directed to Bill's office.

Pam hugged him the minute he walked in. "Oh, Daddy, I'm so sorry."

"Thank you, honey," Charley said, then turned his attention to Bill. "What the hell is going on?"

"Everybody sit down," Bill ordered as he shut his office door. "I wanted you all to know that Trisha is like a sister to me. I probably shouldn't even be working this case, but I am. I have interviewed both Jessica and Tess Whiteshell and I don't believe either one is involved with her disappearance. I have also interviewed a male subject who had ties to both women and don't believe he's involved either. Although he was making plans to approach Trisha."

"Who the hell is he?" Tyler demanded. "Was he working with Jessica?"

"I don't want to take the time to go into all that right now," Bill said. "Thanks to our witness, Susan, and information we got from Tess, we now have a suspect."

"Who?" Charley and Tyler both demanded at the same time.

"His name is Michael Halley. He was Trisha's basketball coach in California."

"That bastard who manipulated her?" Charley asked, thinking back to Trisha's confession.

Ignoring Charley's question, Bill said, "Susan remembered more about the car, including a partial plate and a very unique bumper sticker. Tess worked for the Halleys several years ago and knew Coach's Halley's car, at that time, had that kind of bumper sticker. We checked it out, and he has the same color car now and was stopped for speeding in Des Moines yesterday, so he's in the area."

"Why would he take Trisha?" Pam demanded.

"Trisha and Mr. Halley were involved in the past. We have learned from Brad Jenkins that Trisha had a run in with Mr. Halley last Wednesday.

Brad doesn't believe Trisha told him where she was moving, but he most likely found out from a friend of Trisha's who still works with Mr. Halley at the college."

"So, after all these years, he wants her back?"

Bill shrugged. "I'm not sure. But he's definitely a person of interest. And we have already started looking for him. Since I highly doubt I can talk either one of you into leaving this to us, I wanted to let you know what you're looking for. Just promise me this: If you find them, call me. I want to make sure we get her back unharmed."

Darrell walked into the station, planning on leaving a message for Charley, and noticed Tess sitting in the lobby.

"Darrell?"

Darrell glared at her. "What are you doing here?"

"I'm helping," Tess said. Then she clarified, "I was brought in for questioning in Trisha's disappearance. But I didn't do it. And now I'm helping them. I know whose car it was, Darrell. I know that Coach Halley, my old boss in California, was the person who was following Trisha."

"Did you help him?"

"No." Tess shook her head. "But it's time I told you about my past, Darrell. I'm tired of keeping secrets from you."

"I'm helping Charley."

"He's in talking with Sheriff McEntire. Please, Darrell, at least let me explain."

"Fine, but not in here."

Tess followed him outside, where they sat down on the bench. She took a deep breath, "The $10,000 was for my brother, Carl."

When Darrell didn't say anything, Tess continued. "He came to our house and threatened to tell you about my past if I didn't give him the money and help him get close to Trisha. He also threatened to make things up to ensure you'd never take me back. I was so scared, Darrell. I just wanted him gone. So I got the money."

"And helped him take Trisha?"

"No. When he came and got the money this morning, I told him I wouldn't help him with Trisha. He laughed at me, Darrell, and said he figured I'd back out. He said he'd found someone else that would help him. Then he gave me this."

Darrell noticed the bruises on her arm and couldn't help himself when he blurted, "Did he give you that bruise on your face too?"

Tess nodded as she rubbed her cheek. thinking about the lie that she'd told him about falling and bruising her check. "Yes. I'm sorry I lied to you."

"Why didn't you just tell me the truth? I would've protected you."

"I know. That's one of the reasons I didn't tell you. I was scared what he'd do to our life, Darrell. I want to tell you everything. I can't run from my past anymore. I don't want to lose you, but I see now that lying isn't the way to handle it."

"I'm listening."

"My mother was a prostitute. Carl was born when I was five and I'm pretty sure his father was one of her customers. We were taken away from her before I turned six. Life got better for us when we were adopted by a kind couple, but they were killed in a fire a few months after I turned sixteen. We were sent to live with an aunt who plowed through our inheritance money and treated us poorly. I made the decision to strike out on my own with Carl before I turned seventeen, and I did the best I could. But the streets of LA can be hard on a girl with a limited education and no funds, toting her twelve-year-old brother around.

"We got in with a bad crowd, and Carl turned to the neighborhood gang for support. For the next couple of years, I followed in my mama's footsteps. But I hated that life, and I hated what the gang life was doing to Carl. He didn't want to leave, so I got out and took on two part-time jobs while living in a shelter. As soon as I had enough money saved up, I moved to a better part of town and got my own place. It was amazing having enough money to pay for a place and food. I got my GED and started taking a couple college classes. That's when I met Trisha and she helped me get the job working as a housekeeper for Mr. and Mrs. Halley. Things were good for me until Carl found me. He wanted money and sucked away my life savings, then disappeared again. I got desperate to save my apartment and way of life and stole jewelry from Mrs. Halley. And that got me fired. I tracked down Carl because I needed money to buy back Mrs. Halley's jewelry from the pawnshop so I wouldn't get sent to jail. Carl was working as a drug dealer and gave me money, calling it a loan. I used what I needed to get the jewelry back, and then I split town using the rest of the money."

"Why'd you come here?" Darrell asked, his tone even and his face stoic.

"Because of Trisha. She'd always talked about how beautiful Iowa was and how nice everyone was in Hope. It sounded like such a nice place, so I started making my way across the country to Iowa. I'd go as far as my money let me, and then I'd find a place to stay for a while to earn some money so I could take off again.

"It took me several years, but I finally made it to Iowa. And Hope. I love it here. Then I met you and I…"

"Did you marry me for my money?"

"No." Tess' eyes filled with tears. "I married you because I love you. You took my breath away the first time I laid eyes on you, Darrell. I don't want to lose you, because you're my world. I wouldn't want to live anymore if I didn't have you."

"I'm sorry you've had such a tough life."

"I don't want your pity, Darrell." Tess crossed her arms. "That's another reason I never told you. I want you to be with me because you love me. Not because you feel sorry for me."

"I'm gonna need time to think all this through." Darrell stood up. "But thanks for telling me."

Tess jumped up. "I understand why you need time, Darrell. I'll find somewhere else to stay."

Darrell shook his head. "You stay at the house, Tess. I'll stay at my mom's old house. But first, I'm going to do whatever I can to help Charley find Trisha."

"And I'm going to stay here so I can answer any more questions they might have about Mr. Halley. Trisha and I were very close once, Darrell. I don't want anything to happen to her either."

"Okay, you brought me here to talk. Let's talk," Trisha demanded as she stood on the other side of a crooked wooden table, staring at him through the cobwebs in the almost empty house.

"That's what I've been trying to do," Coach Halley insisted as stepped closer to her. "You aren't taking this seriously."

"The hell I'm not!" Trisha exploded, reaching her breaking point. "You followed me to the cemetery and forced me into your car. Then you brought me here. This house is damp and cold, and there are mice everywhere. How'd you get a key, anyway?"

"It's our house."

"Our house?" Trisha asked, confused. "We don't own a house together. And why the hell would you buy a house in Iowa?"

"You're getting ahead of where we need to be. Quit trying to rush me."

Trisha took a deep breath. "Okay, fine. You lead. What do you want to talk about?"

"Us."

"There is no us."

"There used to be an us. I loved you, Trisha."

"And I loved you too. But it was wrong. You were married."

"We were good together. That summer we had was the best summer of my life. Memories of the times we spent loving each other are what keep me going, Trisha."

"It's over, Michael. It's been over for years."

"It doesn't have to be."

"Yes, it does have to be. We shouldn't have been together in the first place. You were married. It was wrong."

"But I'm not married now." Hope filled his brown eyes. "And you're not either."

"What we had has passed."

"It doesn't have to be that way. We're here together. We can pick up where we left off."

"No, we can't." Trisha shook her head. "We can't ever go back to what we started, because it was wrong. And I've felt guilty about it ever since."

"Guilty?"

Trisha nodded as the feelings she'd suppressed for years came rushing to the surface. "We committed adultery, Michael. There hasn't been a day that's gone by I haven't been haunted by that sin."

"What we had wasn't a sin, and it wasn't wrong. It was beautiful and special. And it's what I want back again."

"We'll never be together again, Michael. Our relationship ended the night your wife found out about us."

"No!" he yelled, scaring her as he slammed his hands down on the old table. "We can get it back."

"No, we can't. Now, either you take me back to town, or I'll walk back," Trisha insisted, fearful for her safety as she started for the door.

Michael ran around and blocked the entrance.

"Get out of my way."

"No." Michael reached over and grabbed her purse off her shoulder, tossing it on the table. "You're not going to leave right now, Trisha."

"The hell I'm not," Trisha demanded as she shoved him out of her way.

Michael grabbed her arm before she could get out the door and tossed her back into the room.

Trisha's hand bumped her purse, knocking it over before she stumbled to the floor.

"I'm sorry. I don't want to hurt you. But you can't leave."

Noticing a small silver tin had been knocked out of her purse, Michael reached over and picked it up. He thumbed through the jewelry, then grinned, "You kept my necklace."

Trisha stood up and peered at the necklace dangling off his finger.

"You do still love me. This is proof."

Trisha shook her head. "No, I don't."

"What's that?" Michael asked, glancing at another item that had fallen out of her purse. His face turned red as he picked it up. "Why the hell do you have birth control pills?"

"I, um…"

"You're sleeping with someone, aren't you?" Michael accused as he threw the container, hitting her in the forehead. "How could you?"

Trisha rubbed her forehead and gathered up all the nerve she could muster. "I'm leaving right now, and you're not going to stop me."

"Yes, I am," Michael vowed, pulling a gun out of his waistband.

Trisha put her hand against her heart. "What are you doing with that?"

"You can't leave me again, Trisha. I won't let you," he demanded, shaking the gun at her.

Trisha threw her hands up. "Okay, I won't leave. Let's talk some more."

"No, I need to think." Coach Halley reached into his other pocket and pulled out a pair of handcuffs. "Put this on one of your wrists."

"You don't have to do that. I promise I'll stay here."

"I'm not stupid, Trisha. You're just lookin' for a chance to leave me again. You want to go back to some other man. I thought this would go so differently. But it's just because you need time to remember what we had. I can give you time. But I can't trust you to stay on your own. Put that on your wrist."

Trisha took the cuff and attached it to her wrist, then winced in pain as he pulled the other cuff and dragged her into the living room.

She shivered when she noticed a new metal bar had been bolted to the wall.

Michael handcuffed her to the bar, then walked into the kitchen and returned with one of the wooden chairs and the necklace.

"Sit down," he ordered.

Trisha sat on the chair and flinched as he moved her hair and latched the necklace behind her neck. She felt his hands resting on her shoulder and tensed, worried what he was going to do next.

"I gotta think this through," he said as he kissed the top of her head, then stepped away from her. "But I'll be back."

Trisha's heart raced as he hurried out of the room. The lights went dark before the door slammed shut.

She waited until she heard his car start up and the gravel crunch under his tires as he started down the driveway, and then she yanked on the necklace, breaking the chain and throwing it into the darkness.

"I've gotta get the hell out of here," she declared as she started pulling on the bar, willing it to give way.

"Okay, we got in contact with Trisha's friend at the college," Bill said. "She did tell Coach Halley that Trisha was moving to Iowa. She said the day after that he told her he was taking some vacation days and left."

"We've gotta get some help with this," Deputy Miller said. "He could have taken her anywhere."

"Brad Jenkins on line one," Deputy Smith announced.

"Thanks."

"I'll keep digging," Deputy Miller promised before leaving.

"Sheriff McEntire?"

"What can I do for you, Brad?"

"Have you found her?"

Bill shook his head. "We think Coach Michael Halley abducted her from the cemetery."

"Damn it. I shouldn't have insisted she go there today."

"Why was she there?"

"We had a daughter who died. And I insisted we bury her there, in Hope. If I would have just listened to Trisha, and let her bury our baby girl in California, none of this would have happened."

"I'm so sorry for your loss, Brad."

"Trisha always blamed herself for Sophie's death. She felt it was her punishment for having an affair with Coach Halley. I can't believe she's having to deal with him again."

"Was he possessive during their relationship?"

"Not that I know of. It always upset Trisha to talk about him. But I never got the feeling he was mean to her. He took advantage of her situation, Sheriff McEntire. He knew her back was against the wall, and he swooped in. Trisha was the victim in their relationship. She's a good person."

"You don't have to sell her to me, Brad. Trisha's like a sister to me. Tyler and I were best friends in school. I knew Trisha very well."

"I just can't believe all of this," Brad admitted as he broke down sobbing. "First my beautiful Scarlette takes her own life and now, now Trisha is kidnapped. In Iowa. I thought she'd be safe there. I always worried about her here. I hated that she lived alone and worked such long hours at that damned job. But she's tough."

"And she's smart," Bill said. "I'm sure we'll get her back home. Do you know of any Iowa ties Coach Halley may have?"

"No. I really don't much know about the guy."

"How are we supposed to find her?" Tyler asked as he and Charley drove around the dark countryside, not sure what to do but too worried to go home.

"I don't know," Charley said as they came to another T in the road. "You wanna go right or left?"

"Right."

They were driving down the road, glancing back and forth at both empty and occupied buildings, when Charley quickly cranked his steering wheel to the right.

"What the hell?" Tyler asked, grabbing on to the door.

"Didn't you see that car? What the hell's he doing driving without his headlights on?"

"Turn around," Tyler ordered as he looked in the side mirror. "Cut your lights and turn around."

"What?"

"Follow that car, Charley. Maybe it's them!"

Charley turned around in the next field driveway, shutting off his lights before pulling back on the gravel. Using the bright moonlight, they both squinted into the distance.

"There it is," Tyler cried, noticing the plume of gravel dust. "It still going north."

"Call Bill," Charley ordered. "We gotta let him handle this. But we can follow them until they get here."

Charley tried to keep the car in sight as he turned left at the next road.

It seemed to be an eternity before they saw flashing lights flying down the road in front of them.

"Block the road!" Tyler ordered when the car suddenly turned around in a field driveway and hightailed it in their direction.

Charley pulled his truck across the road, tugged down on his seatbelt and braced himself for the impact.

But at the last minute, the car aimed for the ditch and crashed into the embankment.

"Shit!" Charley yelled as they both jumped out and ran to the car, looking for Trisha.

"Where is she?" Tyler yelled, only finding a man in the car.

"Tyler, don't!" Sheriff McEntire called as he ran up to the car. "Get back. Both of you."

Charley grabbed on to Tyler and pulled him away from the car, where they both stood watching as the deputies worked to free the man from the mangled mess.

Before long, fire trucks and two ambulances were zooming down the gravel road.

"I didn't see her in there," Tyler mumbled as his vision blurred. "But it's his car. Look at the plates. Where's my sister?"

Fear coursed through Charley's veins as he shrugged, "I don't know, but we'll find her. We have to."

It seemed to take forever for the rescue team to free Coach Halley from the wreckage.

"I didn't get anything out of him. He sustained a head injury," Bill said as he hurried to them.

"Where's my sister, Bill?" Tyler pleaded.

"I'm guessing she's close. He's probably stashing her in a building around here. We need to start going door-to-door, whether houses are occupied or not. We've got to find her. Tonight."

The smell of blood filled the dark room, and Trisha sighed, realizing she was no closer to freeing herself than she'd been when Michael left.

"I have to get out of here. He's gone crazy," Trisha reminded herself, thinking about the gun.

She yanked on her arm repeatedly and tried to ignore the searing pain. She hoped her restraints would give so she could get out of the house.

"Oh, shit," Trisha mumbled when she heard a vehicle coming down the road. She watched the headlights dance across the wall, and fear squeezed her heart when the vehicle turned into the driveway.

"Oh, no. Please, no," she said as she pulled herself to the end of the bar and crouched down.

It seemed like an eternity before she heard someone pounding on the door. Realizing she could hear her name, she stood up and hollered, "I'm in here. Help me!"

Everything played out in slow motion as a flashlight beam danced around the room, blinding her when it hit her eyes.

"Oh, Trisha. Thank God."

"Charley?" Trisha cried, instantly recognizing his voice. "Oh, please, get me out of here. I have to get out of here before he comes back. It's Coach Halley. He took me from the cemetery."

"We know. We got him," Charley said as he took her into his arms and held her tightly against him. "I'm so sorry about this morning. Oh, baby, I'm so sorry."

"Me too. I love you Charley. I love you so much. Please, get me out of here."

"Are you attached to something?" Charley asked, shining his flashlight on the wall.

"I'm handcuffed. I've been trying to pull free, but I can't."

"I have a saw in the truck."

"No! Don't leave me alone," Trisha begged, gripping his arm. "Please, Charley, I don't want to be alone in this house anymore."

"Let me call your brother. He's gotta be close by. He can come and help."

Trisha waited while Charley called Tyler, then held tightly on to him.

"How did you find me?"

Charley quickly filled her in while they stood holding each other.

"Trisha?"

"In here," Trisha hollered.

"You stay with her," Charley said. "I need to get my hacksaw from the truck so I can get that damned thing off her wrist."

"Bill will be here shortly." Tyler hugged his sister. "Are you okay? Did he hurt you?"

Trisha shook her head. "He left when he got mad at me. But I didn't want to be here when he got back. I'm not sure what he would have done then, Tyler. He wanted us to get back together. He said he bought this house for us."

"I'm so sorry, Trisha. I'm sorry it took us so long to find you."

"I've never been so happy to see anybody in my life," she said, managing a small grin. "I'm glad you and Charley are working together."

"Not just me and Charley. Susan Bartlett is the one who remembered the license plate on the car she saw following you to the cemetery. And Tess Whiteshell is the one who remembered Coach Halley's moose bumper sticker. We've been working together to find you, Sis. You've got a lotta people who care about you."

"What about Mom and Dad?"

"We never told them. Helen said Mom threatened to lock you up, so we had to make sure they hadn't done that."

"I brought reinforcements," Charley announced as he walked back in the house followed closely by Sheriff McEntire and several deputies.

"The lights work," Trisha said as flashlights flickered around the room.

Bill turned on the lights and quickly noticed her wrist. "That's bleeding pretty bad. Let's get a medic in here."

"I was gonna saw off the handcuff," Charley said, holding up the small saw in his hand.

"Let me," Bill ordered as he took the saw from Charley and made quick work of the handcuffs.

Charley and Tyler stood back as the medics rushed into the room and started tending to Trisha's wrist. Everyone relaxed when they announced she wouldn't need stitches as they cleaned her wound and bandaged it.

"Can I go home?" Trisha asked Bill, her good arm wrapped around Charley's waist.

"Why don't I go with you to Charley's house? I need to ask you some questions, but we don't have to do it at the station. Okay?"

"Can I ride back with Charley?"

"Sure," Bill agreed. "I'll meet you both back there."

Jessica rolled over and looked at Glen, relieved he was finally asleep. She gently slipped away from his hold and climbed out of bed. Then she walked a few feet and plopped down on the couch.

As she closed her eyes, her mind was back at the sheriff's office when one of the deputies had opened the door and told her she was free to leave.

She'd been surprised to find Glen waiting for her in the lobby and had tried to answer all of his questions without incriminating herself.

Then she had asked if Trisha had been found yet.

Her heart ached as she thought of the answer from the deputy. Her sister was still missing. Someone still had her and was doing whatever he pleased.

Jessica shivered and she tried to focus on her favorite memory of her sister. It had been the summer before Trisha's senior year. Softball season had finally ended, and the two of them had spent the last two weeks of vacation sunning themselves by the pool and talking about boys.

Jessica remembered how fun Trisha had been and how she'd never made her feel like a little sister. She always had treated her the same way she'd treated Tyler. And even though Jessica had only had junior high crushes at that time, Trisha had taken her feelings seriously and had helped her sort out a lot of things that had been bothering her that summer.

"Why'd ya hafta go away?" Jessica muttered, still able to feel the pain and sadness she'd experienced when Trisha had carried her suitcase out the front door and had never come back home.

She jumped when there was a forceful rapping on the door. Scared it might be Carl, Jessica was frozen in fear.

"Jess? It's me, Tyler. Are you up?"

Amazed her brother even knew where she lived, Jessica hurried to the door and threw it open.

"We found her," he said as he grabbed her in a bear hug and spun her around. "She's okay. Trish's gonna be okay."

Jessica started sobbing as she buried her face in her brother's chest, while all the hurt from their past melted away and she suddenly longed to have her brother and sister both in her life.

"It's okay," Tyler promised. "It's all gonna be okay now."

"I'm sorry," Jessica said softly. "For everything. I'm sorry."

"I accept your apology."

"Who had…is she…did Trisha get, um, hurt by the person who had her?"

Tyler shook his head. "She's fine. We found her in time."

"Oh, I'm so glad."

"I gotta get home, Jess. I just wanted to let you know. And, this might not be the right time for this, but if you decide you want some help, sincerely want some help, with the drinking, I'm in."

Jessica nodded, suddenly realizing that for the first time in a long time, she hadn't turned to a bottle when she was upset.

"No pressure, though. I just miss having us all together. I want my baby's aunts in his or her life."

Chapter 14

"Tyler, what a nice surprise. Is Pam with you?"

"No. Where's Dad? There's something we all need to talk about."

"Isn't today your first day of school?"

"Yes. Where's Dad?"

"Probably passed out in the study, Tyler. You know your father."

"Come on, then. Let's wake him up."

"Tyler," Betty Sue called, rushing to keep up as Tyler hurried out of the dining room and hightailed it down the hallway toward the study. "What's this about?"

Ignoring his mother's question, Tyler slammed open the study door, which banged loudly against the wall. Anger and pity washed through his body when he noticed his father was passed out on the couch, an empty whiskey bottle leaning against his side.

"We shouldn't bother him…"

"Wake up," Tyler interrupted, the anger winning as he kicked the couch.

"Whaaattt..uh, hi," George stuttered as he struggled to sit up, knocking the bottle onto the floor in the process.

"I need to talk to both of you. Now. Sit down, Mom."

Worried about his behavior, Betty Sue walked over and sat down by George.

Tyler took a deep breath. "Something happened yesterday."

"Oh my gosh. Is the baby okay?" Betty Sue insisted.

"What? Oh, yes, my baby's fine. This isn't about me."

"What has Jessica done now?" George asked, his mind working again. "You know Danni left for Nebraska."

"Uh, no. I didn't know that. But this isn't about Jessica either."

"What happened to Trisha? Did that bastard hurt her?" George said, his cheeks turning red as he struggled to stand.

"Damn it, listen to me. Please," Tyler begged. "Yes, this has to do with Trisha. And no, my father-in-law didn't hurt her. He saved her."

"Saved her? From what?" Betty Sue asked.

"I want to tell you this before the news gets around town. Trisha was kidnapped yesterday."

"Are you sure that bas—"

"Dad, shut up," Tyler interrupted him. "You can't blame everything that goes wrong on Charley Walker. Trisha was kidnapped by a man she knew in California. Luckily, Charley jumped into action. We got the sheriff involved and were able to find her before the man could hurt her. She's going to be okay."

"Where's my baby?" Betty Sue asked.

"Why the hell are we finding out about this now?" George stood up and started for his desk. "I'm going to call the sheriff's office and demand to know why no one called us. We could have been helping in the search!"

"You weren't included, because you were both suspects."

"What did you say?" George finally asked.

"We all know you don't like Trisha with Charley. And we all know you two are used to getting your way. There was reason to believe you might have hired someone to take her in order to keep her away from Charley. So the decision was made to keep this quiet from the two of you."

"That's bullshit," George insisted.

"Is it?" Tyler asked, his anger starting to get the best of him too. "We all know the two of you were plotting the best way to break up Trisha and Charley. It's what you do when you don't get what you want."

"I can't believe our own son would say such things about us," Betty Sue said, tears filling her eyes.

"I'm not playing this game anymore," Tyler said calmly. "I've followed your orders and tried to be a good son to both of you my entire life. And I'm done now. I'm going to be a father soon, and my priorities are changing. We have an opportunity to be a family again. Trisha's back in our lives. And she's safe. Both of those are because of Charley Walker.

You two need to bury the past and accept their relationship, or I promise you, you won't know your daughter any more than you do now. And without getting into details, I think this experience has also changed Jessica. I think the fear of losing her sister to a crazy man might have been the wake up call my little sister needed to turn her life around. I haven't talked to either one of them about this, but I think it would be nice if we could all be a part of this change. And the only way that's going to happen is if you accept Charley."

"You don't understand, son. He—"

Tyler put up his hand and interrupted, saying, "I don't give a damn what the problem is. I'm telling you right now, if you don't move on from the past, your children and grandchildren won't be part of your future."

"Wait," Betty Sue yelled as Tyler hurried from the room.

"Let him go, Sue," George said, latching onto her arm before she could follow him down the hallway.

"Let go of me. He has to understand that we can't just forget that Charley Walker…"

"What, Sue?"

"That he…he…"

"We both know all of this is my fault. We both know we can't stand Charley because of my feelings for Nancy."

"No, it's Charley's fault," Betty Sue insisted, real tears falling as she turned her back to George.

He hurried over and put his hands on her shoulders. "I'm so sorry I hurt you over and over again, Sue. I don't know why I couldn't stop myself from being attracted to that woman."

"It's because she was special," Betty Sue said, her tears now blinding her. "She was my best friend at one time, George. In elementary school, she was the only person on the entire playground who would talk to me. I always showed up in dirty clothes with stringy hair. The other kids made fun of me, but not Nancy. She'd play with me and give me nice clothes. Her family even let me stay with them for weeks at a time during the summer. I think my grandmother needed the rest."

George nodded, thinking about Betty Sue's parents, who had

abandoned her with her father's mother shortly after Betty Sue was born.

"I'm sorry my feelings for her caused you to lose her as a friend. I shouldn't have used you to get to her. It was stupid of me to think she'd be jealous to see us out together. And I should have never used you that way either."

"Have you ever loved me?" Betty Sue whispered, a dam inside of her heart breaking wide open as the question that had been haunting her for almost thirty-two years escaped her lips.

"Yes," George said quickly as he spun her around and held tightly onto her. "You're a beautiful woman, Sue."

"When did you start loving me, George? I know you didn't love me when we conceived Trisha."

George thought back to the night of their first date when his frustration with Nancy's rejection led him to getting Betty Sue drunk and having sex with her in the backseat of his car.

"George?"

"The moment I saw you holding our sweet Trisha in your arms in the hospital was the moment I fell in love with you. You looked so beautiful that day. I finally realized how lucky I was to have both of you in my life. Even though I struggled with the responsibility, I never stopped loving you. Not for one moment."

Betty Sue managed a small smile.

"Tyler's right. It's time we let this all go. We both know Charley never did anything to either one of us. It was just easier to blame him than accept our role in all of this."

"Do you think he knows you were there the night Nancy died?"

George's head whipped around, and his jaw dropped.

"Yes, I know."

"How did you…I didn't…What?" George stammered.

"Come on, George. I knew you'd been following Nancy around town for months. You might love me, but you lusted after her. And it always would get worse when you drank. I had my suspicions you might be to blame for her accident, but I didn't find out for sure until Kevin was on his deathbed. He asked me to come to the hospital, then told me about that night. Is that why you drink so much now? Are you trying to forget you're the reason Nancy died in that car accident?"

George walked over to the window and looked out over the pool and patio. Memories of witnessing Nancy's car leave the road and flip over and over again assaulted him, and he started sobbing.

"George?"

"It's easier to be angry at Charley," George started, catching his breath between sobs before continuing, "than accept the reality that I killed her."

"You're going to have to do something to make it up to him."

"I don't want to go to jail, Sue," George said, the fear evident in his eyes when he turned to face her. "I can't do that."

"That's not what I'm talking about."

Trisha woke with a start, her heart racing as she sat up and peered around the room.

"I'm at Charley's house," she sighed, relieved, as she lay back down, trying to forget her latest nightmare. Her night had been filled with them.

She reached for Charley and was concerned when her hand hit the cold sheet. She peeked over and noticed the blankets were bunched up beside her, but she was alone.

Trisha slid to the edge of the bed and got up. Wearing only one of his T-shirts, she pulled on a pair of shorts Charley had found in Pam's room and walked into the hallway, glancing in the bathroom first.

Not finding him there, Trisha continued into the living room and through the kitchen, out to the patio.

"Where is he?"

Deciding he must be on the front porch, Trisha turned around and followed her tracks back to the living room. She opened the front door and smiled when she saw Charley sitting on the bench, petting Shooter with one hand and drinking coffee out of his favorite cup with the other.

"Hey," she said.

"Oh, hi. Is everything okay?"

Trisha nodded as she pet the dog and sat down beside Charley.

"You were doing a lot of tossing last night. Did you get any sleep?"

"Some. But I had a lot of dreams. Bad dreams."

"I did too." Charley set his cup down beside him and wrapped his arm around her shoulder, pulling her close. "I'm right here, Trisha. I won't let anything happen to you. I promise."

Trisha leaned against him and smiled.

Shooter nudged her leg and Charley laughed. "You've got a guard mutt too."

Trisha rubbed Shooter around the ears and smiled while looking at the cornfield across the road. "It's so beautiful here, Charley."

"You don't miss the hustle of the big city?"

Trisha shook her head. "Not at all."

"Oh, sorry," Charley said when his cell phone started ringing. He pulled it out of his Western shirt pocket and answered.

Trisha listened as he said yes and no a couple of times, then he agreed to meet someone in thirty minutes before hanging up. "Who was that?"

"I'm sorry. I don't want to leave you."

"I'll be fine."

"It was Clint McCoy from McCoy Auctioneering over in Taylor. B.J., my instructor, called about a job."

"B.J. from the convention?"

"Yes. Mr. McCoy wants to retire and is looking for someone to take over his business."

Trisha smiled. "Oh, wow. That'd be great."

"I love your smile," Charley said, momentarily distracted.

"Are you going to do it?"

"I'm going to meet with him. But B.J. said he wants someone who will buy his business in a few years. I don't know if I'll ever be able to do that. But B.J. didn't think that was a deal breaker. It would be a great chance to learn from an ol' pro."

"And he wants to meet with you this morning?"

"Yes. But I hate to leave you alone."

"I'll be fine. I have my guard mutt," Trisha reminded him, smiling as she rubbed the dog again.

"It could wait until tomorrow."

"Don't put it off. Go now. I'll be fine. It takes a good twenty minutes to get to Taylor."

Charley smiled, helping her to her feet as he stood. "Call my cell phone if you need anything. Okay? And you can take Shooter in the house with you if it'll make you feel safer. We let him in the house during storms, and he's a good boy."

"I promise you, Charley. I'll be fine. I love you."

Charley leaned in and kissed her, then hugged her tightly before hurrying to his pickup and taking off down the road.

Tess cradled her lukewarm cup of coffee while sitting on the front porch, hoping Darrell would be home soon. She had been sitting there for several hours, and as each minute ticked by, that much hope for their future together ticked away.

She thought her ears were playing tricks on her when she heard the familiar crunch of gravel and the gentle rev of the motor as Darrell slowed down and pulled into their driveway.

"Darrell," Tess hollered as she dropped the cup on the wooden planks below, not feeling the splash of the coffee as it hit her bare feet, and took off running for his truck.

"What are you doing out here in your pajamas?" Darrell asked, trying not to notice how terrible his wife looked. He was mad at her, and he intended to stay that way. But her bloodshot eyes, mixed with her bare feet planted firmly on the jagged edges of rock, made it hard to stay focused on his pain and anger.

"I missed you last night," Tess said, reaching for him. "I couldn't sleep without you."

Her eyes welled up as he quickly pushed her hand away.

She was sure she heard him wrong when he whispered, "I'm not here to stay."

"You are here to stay," Tess insisted, chasing him as he hurried toward the house, his driver's door still open. "You stayed in your mom's old house last night, but you're here to stay now."

"No, I'm not," Darrell said as he took the front porch steps two at a time, choosing not to comment on the broken coffee cup by her chair.

"You can't leave. Please, don't leave. I'm sorry. I should have told you everything. Please, Darrell, give me a chance. Please!"

"I still need time to think," Darrell said as he hurried up the stairs to their bedroom.

"Think here," Tess begged, following him. "Please, don't leave me again. Please. I can't survive without you here."

"I can't stay, because I don't know if I can trust you. I might never be able to trust you again."

"I'm sorry." Tess felt her legs start to shake as Darrell fetched a suitcase out of the closet. As he started throwing his clothes into it, she blurted, "Are you moving out?"

"For now."

"I'll leave. This is your house," Tess said softly, her fight suddenly gone.

"No. You stay here. The sheriff needs to be able to find you."

Tess nodded as her tears started to fall.

Always the gentleman, Darrell walked over and brushed them off.

Tess felt a glimmer of hope as she noticed the look of love that briefly showed in his eyes.

Then he stepped back and zipped his suitcase.

"Are you going back to your mother's house?" Tess asked softly, realizing his mind was made up.

"Yes. I'm glad we don't have renters in there right now. It gives me a place to stay."

"What can I do to make this up to you? Please, tell me Darrell. I'll do it. I'll do anything."

"I have to get away and think some more."

"I love you. I will spend the rest of my life making this up to you."

"Reach out to Trisha if she'll let you." Darrell picked up his suitcase. "Make this right with her. After you do that, call me."

Tess watched as he hurried out of the house.

She jumped as her phone started ringing. Hoping it was Darrell, she quickly answered.

"Hi, Sis."

"You bastard. I don't ever want to have anything else to do with you. Do you hear me? You've ruined my life!"

"Well, I guess we're even then. You shouldn't have ratted me out, Sis."

"We both know I wasn't the only one answering questions at the police station. Whomever you got to help you with Trisha must have given you up to save himself. I'm just glad you were too late to get to Trisha."

"This time."

"Leave her alone, Carl," Tess warned, his comment causing a shiver down her spine.

"I will. For now. And I'm leaving you alone too."

"I'm sure. You're probably halfway back to LA by now. Don't want to wait around to see what charges they'll slap you with, do ya?"

"They ain't got anything on me. I do have some business to see about. But I'll be back, Tess. That's a promise."

Trisha checked the back door to make sure it was locked, and then she walked back through the house and checked the front door again.

"Just making sure," she said, feeling more nervous than she thought she would.

She walked over and sat down on the couch, wincing in pain when she hit her sore wrist on the armrest.

"Oh, damn," Trisha mumbled, holding her arm gingerly as her thoughts quickly returned to the moment Coach Halley had attached her to the wall. She could see the gun in his hand and felt herself tensing up.

Her ringing cell phone made her jump. She checked the number, worried who might be on the other end. Realizing it was Sheriff McEntire's personal cell number, she answered.

"Hey, Trisha, I have some information for you. Is now a good time to talk?"

"Yeah, it's a great time."

"Are you still at Charley's? I could come on out."

"That'd be great," Trisha said, relieved someone would be joining her.

She had just set her cell back on the couch cushion when it started ringing again. Noticing Kat's number, she quickly answered.

"Are you okay?"

"I'm fine. How'd you find out?"

"Chase," Kat continued. "Is it true? Were you kidnapped?"

Trisha filled her in, finding it helped her feel a little bit better to talk about it with her friend.

"I'm so sorry that happened to you. Are you safe now? Is he in jail?"

"Last I knew, he was in the hospital for injuries he sustained when he tried to get away. Sheriff McEntire's on his way out now, so I should know more shortly. How are things going for you in Kansas?"

"Okay, I guess. Things are strained between Vic and me. I think he's been cheating on me with someone, Trisha. I had a feeling in my gut that might be going on, but the way he's been acting makes me think I'm right. As soon as some of his relatives go home, we're going to talk about us. I'm not sure what's going to happen."

"I'm so sorry, Kat. I wish I were closer so I could help you with all of this."

"I wish I had been home to help you. I'm so glad you're safe now."

Noticing Bill's car, Trisha said, "Sheriff McEntire's here."

"Okay, call me if you need to talk."

"You too."

She stood up and hurried to the door, unlocking it before Bill started up the front porch stairs.

"Hi, Trisha. Here's your purse back. Sorry I forget to send it out with Deputy Miller last night when he brought your phone."

"That's okay. How's it going today?"

"Pretty good. Your car is at the county building, and you should be able to retrieve it as early as this afternoon. We've been able to find out a little more about Michael Halley's life for the last few years. I thought you'd like to know."

"Come on out to the kitchen. Would you like something to drink?"

"Pop's fine," Bill said when Trisha opened the fridge.

She grabbed two cans and sat down across from him.

Bill opened his can and took a swig, flipped open the manila folder he'd brought with him, and started skimming through his notes.

"We got ahold of his mother. She said Michael and his first wife divorced several years ago. She said they were never able to conceive and grew apart. She also said they both admitted to affairs before they divorced. A few months after that divorce was final, Michael married a woman who worked at the college. They weren't able to have children either, and his mother said that caused unhappiness in their marriage. They also divorced, and it was finalized two weeks ago. His mother said Michael had been living with her and he'd been moody. Then the day he met up with you at the college, he came home happy. She said he told her he ran into a woman he used to date and that he thought it was a sign you were meant to be together again. She said she tried to talk him out of pursuing any relationship, because she felt he wasn't emotionally ready for that kind of commitment yet. The next day, he found out the college was firing him. He'd been there for many years and was very upset. She said all he talked about was you, but he never mentioned your name. Just that he had a relationship with a former player after she'd graduated and he wanted her back. They had words, and he left. She hadn't seen him since."

"I can't believe they'd fire him."

"Apparently they're offering the job to your friend Shawna, but she only found out this morning. She called to let us know he'd been fired. She's really worried about you and feels terrible she told him you were in Iowa."

"Oh, I don't blame her. If he was hell-bent on finding me, he would have. It's not like I was hiding or something."

"Michael has recovered from the injuries he received in the accident, and his mental state is being evaluated. Several charges have been filed against him, but his mother hired a very expensive lawyer."

Trisha leaned back and crossed her arms." Well, I do have to take some responsibilities for my actions back then, but I know this isn't my fault. Sounds like he's been dealing with a lot."

Bill nodded. "I think someone just pulled in."

Suddenly nervous, Trisha asked, "Could you see who it is?"

Bill patted her on the shoulder as he stood up and walked through the house, opening the door as a young man was getting ready to knock.

"I have a package for Charley Walker. Is that you, um, Officer?"

"No, his girlfriend's here. Can she sign for it?"

"Yeah, sure. That's fine," the man said.

Trisha moved from where she'd been listening and stepped outside, signing for the package. Then Bill watched as the young man walked back to his car and drove away.

Trisha checked the return address. "It's from my dad's bank. Who was that man?"

"I'm guessing he's from that courier service out of Taylor. Why would your dad send Charley a package?"

Suddenly remembering her father was threatening to take away Charley's land, Trisha's cheeks turned a bright red. "Because, he wants to make sure Charley never gets a moment of peace."

"Trish? Are you okay? You look like you're ready to blow up."

"Oh, yeah. I'm okay. I'll be fine. I just can't believe my parents sometimes. They were the whole reason I stayed away so long, Bill. I'm glad I have Charley and Tyler to help me out."

"Well, I, for one, am glad you're here."

Trisha waited as Bill answered his ringing phone, then turned his attention back to her.

"There are some other things I need to talk to you about, Trisha, but we have an emergency back at the office. I'll give you a call when I get a chance. If you need anything, anytime, you call me. Okay?"

Trisha nodded and accepted the hug he offered.

ꟷ

Jessica sat on the couch waiting for Glen to wake up. She'd been tossing and turning all night, thinking about everything that had happened in the last 24 hours and debating what her next steps should be.

"Jess? Are you okay?" Glen asked as he sat up. "What's goin' on?"

"We need to talk." Jessica patted the couch cushion beside her. "Can you come over here?"

"This sounds serious, Jess," Glen said as he stood up, pulled his jeans over his boxers and walked over, sitting beside her.

"I need help."

"I'm here for you, honey. I love you, no matter what."

"I want to quit drinking, but I don't know how to do it. I've already lost my kids because of it. I don't want to lose my life."

Glen reached over and pulled her tightly against him. "We need to get you into rehab, baby. I have a friend who went through that, and it helped him a lot."

"Well, my dad's tried it several times, and it didn't do him any good. I'm like my father, Glen, so it probably won't do me any good either."

"What if I go too?"

"You'd do that?"

"Yes. But I don't have money to pay for it. Do you think your parents would?"

"They're done with me."

"Your dad loves you, Jess. He's always tried to help you. Call him and tell him you want to go to rehab. Or better yet, talk to him in person."

"I don't know." Jessica eyed her shaking hands. "I want a drink so bad, Glen. I need it."

"Let's get you in rehab today." Glen pulled her to her feet.

"Today?" Jessica asked, suddenly rethinking the entire idea.

"Yes. Today. Right now. Let's get you checked in, then I'll talk to your dad. We'll figure out a way to pay for it if they won't, babe. I promise you, I'm gonna help you beat this."

"What about you? I thought you were going to do it with me?"

"I will, I promise. After I talk to your dad. Let's get you help today. Okay?"

Jessica thought about what he was saying. She was tempted to put it off another day. Or have another drink. But then her little boys and Danni's face popped before her eyes. She thought about waking up in Carl's bed and the feelings of panic and shame when she'd realized she couldn't remember any of what had happened between them. Making up her mind, she said, "I'm ready, Glen. Let's go."

ꟿ

Trisha was sitting on the couch, staring at the envelope from her father, when she heard the crunch of tires in the driveway. Panic tore through her. She knew no one was supposed to be coming yet, and she feared who was outside.

She jumped to her feet and ran to the door, making sure it was locked. Then she peeked out from behind the curtain, not sure how to feel when she noticed Tess was getting out of a fancy car.

"What does she want?" Trisha said, wondering whether to open the door when Tess started rapping on it.

Deciding she had to find out, Trisha unlocked the door and pulled it open.

"Oh, good. You're here."

"What do you want?"

"I just want to talk to you. Please, Trisha. There's something I need to tell you."

Trisha thought it over, then slowly stepped back and waved Tess in the door. She shut it behind her and locked it, then followed Tess to the couch and sat down.

"I'm so sorry for what you've been through." Tess glanced at the bandages on Trisha's wrist.

"Why are you here, Tess?"

Tess took a deep breath. "My brother, Carl, is infatuated with you, Trisha."

"Carl?" Trisha asked, confused. "I barely even remember him. What makes you think that he—"

"He's out of jail, Trisha," Tess interrupted. "He was here, in Hope. He blackmailed me. He wanted me to give him $10,000 in exchange for him to not tell Darrell about my past. I was desperate to get him out of my life, and I told him you were here. I knew he's always wanted you."

"Me? Why? I only met him once."

Tess shrugged. "That was enough for him to become infatuated with you. I gave him the money, Trisha. And I offered to help him get close to you."

Trisha felt a shiver down her spine and slid to the side of the couch, "Stay away from me, Tess."

Tess threw up her arms. "I didn't do it, though. When he came to get the money, I told him I wasn't going to help him get to you. He laughed at me, Trish. He said he already had found someone else to help him. I don't know who that person was."

"Coach Halley?"

Tess shook her head. "I don't think so. I think Coach Halley was working alone."

"So I had two crazy men after me?" Trisha asked as she stood up and started pacing around Charley's living room.

"I guess. Carl called me this morning, and I think he was headed back to California. I'm guessing he's afraid he's going to be arrested for something here and got out of town before they could cart his sorry ass off to jail. But I wanted you to know he threatened he'd come back someday."

"So, what? Am I supposed to live in fear?"

"I don't know, Trisha. I'm so sorry for all of this. I really am."

Trisha noticed Tess seemed sincere and thought back to her conversation the night before with Sheriff McEntire. He'd told her Tess had been very helpful in their search to find her. She sighed and sat back down on the couch.

"I'm sorry."

"Thank you for helping the sheriff, Tess."

The two sat in silence, both obviously lost in their own thoughts. Then Trisha asked, "Why did you come and tell me all of this?"

"Because I feel terrible about what I've done," Tess said, then added, "And because Darrell left me."

"I'm sorry about that."

"You were right. I should've been completely honest with him from the beginning. I never told him about the jewelry, Trisha. I was so afraid

I'd lose him. But he knows about it now. He knows all about my past. Now when he looks at me, I see the anger, but I also see the pity. I don't want his pity, Trisha. I want his love."

"I don't really know Darrell, but from what I've seen, he seems like a nice man."

"He's the best man I've ever met. And now, because of all of this, I might lose him for good. Do you think he'll ever come back to me?"

Trisha looked over and was flooded with memories from their friendship. She reached over and took ahold of Tess' hand, squeezing it. "He will, Tess."

Tess squeezed back as she blurted, "I've missed having you for a friend so much. You were the first real friend I ever had, Trisha. You never expected or wanted anything back from me for being friends. I'd never had that before. You and Darrell have been the only two people in my life who weren't nice to me because they wanted something from me. And I've done terrible things to both of you. Maybe I don't deserve Darrell after all."

"Give him some time to think things through. Then go to him, Tess. Make sure he knows how you feel."

"You think I should? He told me he'd come to me."

"Be patient, Tess. I think he really does love you. I think he'll want to come home."

Tess offered Trisha a small smile. "Thank you, Trisha."

~

Tyler panicked when he noticed Pam was standing outside his classroom. He gave the kids a problem to work on, then hurried to the hallway.

"Is something wrong with the baby? Or you? Or Trisha?"

"No, oh, no. Sorry. Everything's fine. I was just wondering how the talk with your parents went."

"Oh," Tyler said, relief washing over him. "Thank goodness. I saw you standing out here and totally panicked. Obviously. What about your kids, Pam?"

"They're in an assembly for another twenty minutes. I wanted to see you and thought this might be a good time."

Tyler glanced back through the window at his class, thankful they were all still scribbling their math problem in their notebooks. "I don't know if I got anywhere with Mom and Dad. But I laid it all out on the line."

"I know that wasn't easy for you, honey. I'm proud of you."

"I'd love to kiss you right now. But I'd better not. Don't want to break any rules."

Pam winked.

Tyler laughed, then gave her a quick peck on the cheek.

"I'll see you at home," Pam said, waving as he went back into his classroom.

She watched as he casually joked with the kids and smiled, thinking what a good teacher he was. Then she hurried back to her own room and started getting things ready for their next subject.

"Pam?"

"Daddy?" Pam said, noticing him standing at her doorway.

"The secretary said it would be all right if I came on down."

"I'm so sorry about Trisha." Pam hurried to her father and hugged him tightly. "And I'm sorry about the other day. I've missed you so much."

"I've missed you too, baby. And I'm sorry too."

Pam shook her head as their hug ended. "It was my fault. I shouldn't have assumed you'd be, that I could…"

"You can always come home."

"I know I can. And I want you to know I will respect your privacy more now that you have a girlfriend."

Charley smiled as he thought about Trisha.

"How's she doing Daddy? Is she really going to be okay?"

"She will be. She's a strong woman. I'm so thankful we found her when we did."

"Sounds to me like you're a hero."

Charley quickly shook his head. "It took a lot of people working together to bring Trisha home. I'm so relieved he didn't…that he…"

Surprised to see her father so shaken up, Pam hugged him. "He didn't hurt her that way. And he never can get close to her again. Thanks to you."

"I probably need to get going," Charley said as they both heard the commotion of little footsteps hurrying down the hallway. "I just wanted to stop by and talk to my little girl."

Pam grinned and nodded, then Charley stepped out of the room as her twenty seven students rushed in, several of them excitedly telling her about their assembly program.

Pam felt the rush of adrenaline as she gently herded her group to their chairs and smiled, thinking how proud her mother would be to see her teaching in the very classroom she had taught children in so many years earlier.

Jessica sat in the waiting room. Her hands were shaking, and her stomach was in knots. She glanced in the direction Glen had gone and fought the panic that was running through her.

Thankful for the distraction when her cell phone rang, she answered it without looking to see who it was.

"Hey, Jessica."

"Carl." Jessica said, recognizing his voice.

"I wanted to let you know I'm leaving town for awhile baby. But I'll be thinking about both you and your sister. And I'll be back someday to collect what you owe me. Got it?"

Jessica quickly ended the call and got up, heading for the closest exit.

"Jess," Glen called, quickly catching up to her. "Honey, please, don't leave."

"Glen?" Jessica questioned, thinking back to her phone call with Carl and feeling shame wash over her as she thought about the fact that she'd cheated on him.

"Honey, it's almost time for your appointment. I called your father. He's agreed to pay. There's nothing to worry about now, honey. He wanted me to tell you he's proud of you."

"Proud of me?"

Glen hugged her tightly. "He's proud of his daughter."

"Jessica Donohue?" A nurse called.

"It's time, Jess. Are you ready?"

Jessica started toward the nurse, then turned around. "What about you? Aren't you coming?"

"I will, I promise. But I need to check with my mom and make sure she's still feeling okay. It might take a bit, but I'll join you as soon as I can. Okay?"

Jessica shut her eyes and took a deep breath, then opened them and nodded, "I'm ready."

Charley hurried into his house. "Sorry I was gone so long."

Noticing Trisha was sitting on the couch staring at a manila envelope, he hurried over. "Trish? Are you okay?"

"Oh, hi," Trisha said, glancing at him. "I'm sorry. I didn't hear you come in."

"What's that?"

"It came for you." Trisha handed it to him. "It's from the bank."

Charley felt his heart skip a beat as he took the envelope.

"That bastard. I'm so sorry my father has done so many terrible things to you, Charley."

"Did you open it?"

Trisha shook her head. "But I can only imagine what's in it. He's taking your land away, isn't he?"

"He can't." Charley started looking for his letter opener. "I'll go down tomorrow and pay that bastard off. I can't wait to see the look on his face."

Finally finding the opener, Charley carefully slid the metal tool under the flap on the envelope and popped it open. Then he took a deep breath and pulled out a pile of papers.

While skimming them, he muttered, "Oh my God."

"What?" Trisha asked as she hurried to his side.

"It says paid in full." Charley held the papers out to her. "Doesn't it?"

Trisha scanned them. "It does. Did Darrell go down and pay it already?"

"Maybe he did." Charley pulled out his cell phone and dialed his friend.

Trisha listened as they talked, then shook her head as he hung up. "Darrell didn't do it."

"We need to go down to the bank and find out what the hell's going on. I don't know what kind of trick they're trying now, but I won't let them get away with it."

Charley took her hand in his as they hurried out of the house and jumped into his pickup.

His heart raced as they hurried into town and into the bank, watching in awe as Trisha demanded answers from George's secretary.

Before long, they were waiting in George's private office.

"We'll get to the bottom of this, Charley. I promise we will."

Just then, the door opened and a petite, older woman with short, gray hair walked into the room and shut the door.

"Hello. I'm Mrs. Wilson," she said as she stopped to shake both of their hands. They waited while she walked around the desk and sat down. "I am Vice President of Home Town Bank. As you may know, we have banks in four other towns besides Hope."

"Yes, I knew that," Charley agreed, puzzled as to why she was giving him a history of the bank instead of answering their questions.

"I was asked to speak to you on behalf of Mr. Bailey," Mrs. Wilson continued as she pulled a folder out of the black briefcase she'd been carrying. She moved the briefcase to the side of the clean desk and opened the folder. "Our business today is in regard to your farm loan."

"Yes. I received this notice. It says my loan is paid in full. But I never paid my loan."

"We demand to know what's going on with this matter." Trisha sat forward in her chair, angered her father had sent someone else to do his dirty work.

"Yes, of course. I'll answer all the questions I can," Mrs. Wilson said. "Your entire bank loan has been paid off."

"How?" Charley demanded.

Mrs. Wilson thumbed through her papers. "An anonymous person has paid off your loan. Here are your papers. I need you to sign by the X's and date them, and I will be able to give you the deed to your land."

Suspicious, Charley shook his head. "This can't be right."

"It is, Mr. Walker. I was there when the person paid off your loan. It's a done deal. We just need you to sign the paperwork. Here's the copy of your loan papers. See at the top? It says paid in full."

"And my ground is still mine?"

"Oh, yes," Mrs. Wilson said. "Everything remains yours. Home Town Bank has been paid the money owed to us. If you could sign here."

Charley took the pen she handed him and started to sign when Trisha demanded, "Was this anonymous person my father, George Bailey?"

The expression on Mrs. Wilson's face gave nothing away. "The person who paid this loan wished to remain anonymous."

"We both know this was a significant amount, Mrs. Wilson. Charley has a right to know who did this."

"I agree. But I can't offer that information. If you have questions, I suggest you contact our customer service representative. I'm here to finalize this and give you the deed to your land."

Charley looked over at Trisha, then signed his name and dated the papers.

"Okay, we're all set," Mrs. Wilson declared as she placed the signed papers into her folder, then handed him an envelope. "This contains the original deed to your property, plus the loan papers marked paid in full. If you have any questions, please give me a call. My card's also in the envelope."

Charley stood as she did and shook her hand when she offered it.

"You two have a wonderful evening."

Still confused, they followed her down the hallway and into the bank lobby, then headed straight out the door.

"We've got to get to the bottom of this."

"I need to go and talk to your father," Charley said as they reached his truck.

"Okay, I'll go with you."

"I need to talk to him alone."

Trisha looked at him, her blue eyes wide.

"Let me take you out to Kat's house so you can get some clothes. I'll go talk to your dad and come back and pick you up. Okay?"

"Well, I suppose. But I'll go with you if you want me to."

Charley shook his head. "I need to do this alone."

Fifteen minutes later, Charley was headed back to town from Kat Roe's house, alone.

He peered at the packet and pulled off into a field driveway. Then he pulled the papers out of the envelope and sat staring at the deed he and Nancy had signed a few months after their wedding.

He noticed her handwriting, and tears filled his eyes as his mind started replaying that day. He could still see the smiles on his mom's and dad's faces as he and Nancy signed the deed to the farm that would become the only place they ever lived together.

Memories of their wedding and their first Christmas started replaying in his mind as feelings of guilt washed over him.

"I'm sorry I'm moving on without you, Nancy," Charley murmured, unable to stop himself from thinking about the conversations they had had regarding how excited they would be when they paid off their loan.

"But I didn't pay it off," he reminded himself as he shoved the papers back into the envelope and took off for the Bailey mansion.

Carl sat in the bar down the road from the dirty hotel in a small, eastern Nebraska town.

He sipped on his mixed drink while thinking about the women he needed to get even with in Hope.

"I'm gonna start with you, little sister," he promised in between sips. "You ratted me out for the last time. Then I'm gonna move on to Jessica. I'm sure her sweet lips were loose as could be while she was saving her own cute little ass. I'm gonna have to teach her a lesson in keepin' her word."

He took another long sip, then sighed, "And after I get done with both of them, I'm moving on to the prize. Trisha Bailey. I'm gonna get her out of that one-horse town before anyone even realizes she's a'missin'."

ↂ

"Mr. Bailey, you have a visitor," Helen said as she stepped into his study.

"Oh, okay. Who?"

Charley stepped in from the hallway. "Me."

George waved Helen out of the room, and she shut the door.

"I thought you might show up."

"You did that so I'd quit seeing her, didn't you?" Charley accused, glaring at him as he sat down on the leather couch in the corner of George's study.

George leaned back in his chair. "Did what?"

"Cut the bullshit. I know you paid off my loan. You're the only person I know who has that kind of money."

"Your friend Darrell does. How do you know it wasn't him?"

"Because I asked him."

"Fine," George sighed. "I did."

"I'm not gonna stop seeing Trisha," Charley declared as his anger rose.

"That's not why I did it."

"Then why the hell did you do it?"

"Look, I know we're never going to like each other. We've spent too many years hating each other."

"I can agree with that."

"For whatever reason, my daughter loves you. And I want my daughter to be happy."

"And?"

"And I figured after all the hell I've put you through, I owed you something. This is my peace offering."

"It was $75,000."

"We both know I can easily afford it. By paying off your loan I've taken a step toward repaying my debt to you for all the hell I caused both you and Nancy. And I've ensured that my daughter won't spend the rest of her life struggling with you."

"Rest of her life—"

"Look, I know. Okay?" George interrupted. "I don't understand it, but I know. You and my daughter are going to be together just like my son and your daughter are together. I can't say any more, but it's important to me to know Trisha will be financially secure."

"You make it sound like you're not going to be around long." Charley leaned forward and peered at him. "Are you sick?"

"I think our business here is done. You got the answer you came for. Now, please leave."

"I'll accept your peace offering, George. Thank you. But you need to know my wife didn't deserve what you put her though," Charley said, finding a confidence deep down inside. "You also need to know my relationship with Trisha has nothing to do with you or anything from our past. I wouldn't do that to Trisha or you. I fell in love with her before I even knew she was a Bailey."

"Fair enough." George remained seated, but gripped onto the arms of his leather desk chair.

Charley got up and started for the door, then turned around. "If you are sick, you need to make things right with your daughter. Even though she's angry with you, she still loves you. She's still your little girl."

Trisha was unlocking Kat's door when her cell phone started ringing. Noticing it was Brad, she said, "I'm so sorry about Scarlette."

"Oh, Trisha, I'm so glad to hear your voice. Are you really okay?"

"Yes." Trisha hurried into Kat's house and locked the door behind her. Then she sat down on the bench. "I'm fine. I heard you helped the sheriff find me."

"I did what I could from here. I really wanted to be there helping in the search, but…"

"You need to be there for Scarlette's family. I understand that."

"I was going to come today if they hadn't found you yet. Are you really fine? That bastard didn't hurt you, did he?"

Trisha picked at the bandage on her wrist and shook her head. "No, he didn't have a chance."

"Thank God. I'm going to come and see you. Just as soon as I can, I'm jumping on a plane and flying to Iowa."

"Is there anything I can do for you?" Trisha asked. "I know you loved Scarlette."

"I did at one time, Trish. I think it was the drugs. I don't know why she started taking them, but they destroyed her. The Scarlette I fell in love with never would have taken her own life. She never would have killed herself in our house."

"I can't even imagine what you're going through."

"It's hard. I'm selling the house, though. Between the memories of us and now this, I can't live there anymore. I'm staying in a hotel right now. I'll find a new place to live."

"I wish I were closer so I could help you through all of this. I might be able to fly —"

"No, Trisha, don't come back here. Not for this. You've been through enough. Why don't you just enjoy your time with Charley? Then your job will start up."

"That's true. But you're welcome anytime, Brad."

"This might not be the time, but I need to tell you something, Trish."

"What?"

"The reason I wanted our daughter buried in Hope was because I always felt like that was her real home. That someday, we'd find our way back to the small town where your roots run so deep. I'm sorry that I didn't communicate with you before I set all of that into motion back when we lost her. But I'm so thankful that you're home now and can be with our baby girl."

Tears streamed down Trisha's cheeks and the lump in her throat made it hard for her to talk.

Sensing it, Brad continued. "I'd better go, Trish. I have to get down to the funeral home. But I had to hear your voice for myself. I miss you, Trisha. And I love you. You're the best friend a guy could ever have."

Trisha cleared her throat as she brushed away the tears. "Okay. Take care of yourself, and I'll take care of our baby girl."

௸

Tess thought she was dreaming when she turned around from the stove and noticed Darrell was standing in the doorway with his suitcase in his hand.

"Oh my gosh, Darrell? Is that really you? I must be dreamin' again."

"It's me, Tess. I'm back."

"For good?" Tess asked, hopeful that everything was going to work out for them.

Darrell set the suitcase down. "I've been thinking about us all day. I wasn't sure what I was gonna do. But then after I got your voicemail saying you'd talked to Trisha, I got a phone call from Trisha too."

"You did?"

"She's the reason I'm here, Tess."

"Why?"

"Well, I know you made things right by her. I also know you warned her about a call you got from your brother. And I don't pity you, baby. I think you're pretty damn strong and brave. I know if it weren't for you, Trisha might still be out there with that crazy man. You haven't done everything right, Tess. But we all make mistakes. And I hated like hell sleepin' away from you last night. I couldn't stand the thought of doing it again. And I'm hungry."

Tess grinned. "I fixed your favorite."

"It smells great."

"Let's eat then," Tess said as she started gathering plates out of the cupboard.

Darrell took the plates out of her hands, then took her into his arms and kissed her. "Now, we can eat."

௸

Finding her dad standing in her classroom doorway again, Pam asked, "Daddy? What's going on?"

"I need to talk to you about something," Charley said, still confused by his meeting with George.

"Okay. I'm ready to leave. Why don't you come to my new house? I'd like to show you around."

"Oh, well, okay."

"It's at Fifth and Watson. Number 1399. It's a two-story, white house. Just follow me, if you can keep up."

Charley noticed her grin and chuckled as he thought about all the times he'd begged her to slow down when he was teaching her how to drive. "I'll try. Did you have a good day?"

Pam locked her classroom door and they started down the hallway. "It was so much fun. I have great kids. They are excited to learn."

"Your mother would be so proud," Charley said, trying not to think about all the times he'd walked down that very hallway when he had met his wife in her room.

"Sometimes it's hard to be in her classroom, but most of the time, it's wonderful. It might sound crazy, but I feel like she's with me. Helping me."

Charley smiled as they walked out into the warm afternoon sunlight, "I don't think that's crazy at all."

Pam smiled back, and they were both lost in their own thoughts of Nancy as they walked through the parking lot to Pam's car.

"My truck's parked over there." Charley pointed to the other side of the parking lot. "I'll meet you at your house."

He trotted over to his truck and waved as Pam drove by him, then pulled out onto the quiet city street and followed his daughter seven blocks to her new home.

He cut the engine and sat in the truck, looking up at the small mansion his daughter was living in, and tried not to curse George Bailey.

"She's living in a safe house," Charley reminded himself. "Be happy for her. At least she's not living in that damned mansion."

"What do you think?" Pam asked, grinning as he got out of the truck and walked up to her.

"Looks like a mini version of the Bailey mansion."

"It's big," Pam agreed. "But it's really nice. Come on in, and I'll give you a tour."

Charley smiled, encouraged by his daughter's enthusiasm as she showed him all the rooms.

Then they settled at the kitchen island, each with a glass of water.

Pam started chewing on her fingernails. "What do you want to talk to me about?"

"I want to tell you where I went back in June. It's time."

"I'm ready to find out. I've been worried about this."

Charley took a deep breath. "You know that my crop share agreement is ending this fall. Right?"

"Yes. You got notice in May that Mrs. Montgomery's family is selling the ground, so you won't be able to farm it anymore."

"Right. And I can't make enough money farming my own ground to pay my bills. So, I decided I needed to find a job to supplement my income."

"What kind of job?"

"Your mom and I used to talk about what we'd do when we got to this point. We figured someday the custom farming work would come to an end. And the one thing I've always been interested in, other than farming, was being an auctioneer."

Pam smiled as she leaned back in her chair. "I remember all those auctions we went to when I was little, but I never knew you wanted to do that for a living."

"Farming is my dream, Pam. But auctioneering has always been my second interest. Last June, I attended an auctioneering class in western Iowa. They have one of the best programs in the nation out there, and I learned a lot."

"Why didn't you tell me this before?"

Charley held up his hand. "We'll get to that. A couple of weekends ago, I went to an auctioneering convention in Minneapolis. That's where I met Trisha. She was at the same hotel for a marketing convention."

Pam nodded, silently encouraging her father to continue.

"The reason I didn't tell you any of this was because I thought I might have to sell the farm." Charley noticed the fear in Pam's eyes and quickly said, "I don't, though. It's all going to work out."

"I don't understand. Why would you have to sell the farm?"

"I'm having major money issues, Pam. Living paycheck to paycheck is getting harder. I had to use my savings to afford auctioneer schooling. I wiped it out with that trip to Minneapolis. And then I got those damned bank papers—"

"That Tyler's father harasses you with," Pam finished.

"Yes. I've always felt that George was waiting for me to be in this position so the bank could take my land from me or I would have to sell it to pay them off. And it was close, honey. But Darrell was going to help us out so we could keep the farm."

"Was?" Pam asked, her brow creased with worry.

"He was. But, he doesn't have to now."

"How come? What changed?"

"George Bailey paid off my loan. I got the paperwork and my land deed from the bank today. My lawyer's looking it over, but said he thought it was legitimate."

"Wow, that's so nice."

Charley held up his hand. "I still don't trust George Bailey. I think he's up to something. But he says he did it because he wants peace between our families. I'm hoping he's sincere about it, because I want that too."

"Well, I'm just glad you don't have to sell our family farm. I want my little boy or girl to grow up exploring that land like I did."

"I want that too," Charley agreed. "There's something else I need to tell you."

"Okay."

"I was offered an auctioneering job today. Clint McCoy with McCoy Auctioneering over in Taylor is ready to think about retiring. He wants to hire me as an assistant auctioneer. It would give me a chance to make some money but still give me the flexibility I need to keep farming. And when he does retire, I'll be first in line if I want to buy his business. Plus, it gets my name out there."

"I think that's amazing, Daddy."

Trisha was busy packing up her clothes when she heard the crunch of tires on gravel. Figuring it was Chase, she hurried through the house and out the back door, stopping dead in her tracks when she noticed her mother getting out of her car.

"What are you doing here?"

"Looking for you." Betty Sue shooed away Kat's dog and kittens while walking up to Trisha. "Thank God you're okay."

"No thanks to you," Trisha said, her sharp voice accidentally scaring away the animals.

"We didn't know about it until this morning when your brother stopped by."

"I know. We both know why no one told you, don't we? You were suspects. My own parents were suspects in my disappearance."

"We should have never been treated in that manner." Betty Sue put her hand to her heart. "I think we should sue that sheriff's office."

"We both know the thought had crossed your mind. And your lips. You're so desperate to keep me away from Charley Walker, you'll do anything. Even pay off his bank loan."

"What are you—"

"Save it," Trisha interrupted, surprising her mother. "We both know Dad wouldn't have come up with that idea on his own."

"Your dad didn't pay off that loan as a bribe to keep Charley away from you."

"Oh, so now you know about Dad paying off the loan."

Exasperated, Betty Sue huffed. "It was my idea."

"Why? What kind of hell are you plotting for Charley now? I can't believe my own parents would be so cruel. Well, now wait. I guess I should know how cruel you can be. After all, you tried to punish me over and over again for going to college in California."

"And we were right. That man who took you was your basketball coach, Trisha. If you hadn't gone out there, you wouldn't have met him."

"That might be true," Trisha agreed, anger seething through her. "But if you and Dad hadn't stopped supporting me, trying to force me to come home, I wouldn't have ended up having an affair with him either! I could have rented my own apartment instead of ending up under his roof, alone with him. Completely vulnerable, upset that my entire family had turned their back on me, with no money. And no chance to save up any money either. Who does that, Mother?"

"You had an affair with him?"

Trisha laughed, "You mean your gossip squad hadn't found that out yet? They're slipping."

"Was he married?"

"Yes, mother. He was married to a woman who'd invited me to her house for every holiday and break. A woman who took pity on me because I had no one who cared about me. A woman who didn't deserve to be cheated on by two people she trusted."

"Then why did you—"

"Because he was kind to me," Trisha interrupted. "He was the first person I'd met who made me feel special. Feel loved. He knew I had nowhere else to turn. And I can see now how wrong it was of him to get involved with me. He was my coach. My authority figure. But I was an adult, I knew right from wrong, and I still did it. And I paid dearly for it too."

"I'm so sorry, Trisha. I didn't want to cut you off financially. That was your dad's idea. He wanted you home."

"And so did you. I'm sure it was Dad's idea. But I'm also sure it was your idea to refuse to come to my games. And to refuse to come out to see me at all."

"You should have come home on the breaks, Trisha. That's what college kids do."

"I was busy on all of those breaks, either playing basketball or working to better myself for the next season. It was like a job, Mom. And I loved it. And I wanted to share my passion with my family. But no one ever came."

"I'm sorry. We were wrong. All the times we tried to control you were wrong."

Surprised, Trisha wasn't sure what to say next.

"I'm glad you're okay, Trisha. I miss you. I miss our family. And I'm here, begging for a second chance. I don't want to fight with you anymore. And neither does your father. We want our family back together. We will accept your relationship with Charley just as we have accepted Tyler's marriage to Pam. You also need to know Jessica checked herself into an alcohol rehabilitation program in Des Moines today."

"Jess did?"

Betty Sue nodded as tears filled her eyes. "I love all of my children, Trisha. I've made many mistakes as a mother. Please, just think about it. I want you back in my life. I want to be a part of your life and your brother's and sister's lives. And I want to be a grandmother to all my grandchildren."

Trisha felt her own eyes welling up when she saw that real tears seemed to be streaming down her mother's cheeks.

Betty Sue brushed them away with her hand. "I'll spend the rest of my life making it all up to you, Trisha. I promise I will. I'm so glad you're okay."

Betty Sue took a step toward Trisha to hug her, but Trisha stepped back, hating she still wasn't sure if her mother was telling the truth.

Betty Sue appeared resigned as she turned away, walking back to her car.

Trisha watched as her mother drove down the driveway, then let her tears fall.

Charley almost plowed into Kat's garage when he noticed Trisha was kneeling in the yard, her hands to her face.

He threw his gearshift into park and pushed the door open, not stopping until he was kneeling with her.

"What's wrong?"

"My mother," Trisha said, surprise clear in her eyes. "Where'd you come from?"

"Didn't you hear me pull in?"

Trisha shook her head as he helped her to her feet.

"What'd your mother do?"

"She apologized. Said she was sorry. She also said she wants us all together as a family again."

"How'd she know you were back here?"

Trisha shrugged. "I'm used to my mother. She's always had ways of finding out what she wanted to know."

"Did you get your things packed?"

"Yes. I have enough packed for a week."

"Let's get it and head home."

Trisha followed Charley into the house and handed him the suitcase, then locked the back door while Charley put the case into the truck.

As they arrived at the edge of Hope, Trisha said, "Charley. I need for you to head out to the cemetery."

Charley shook his head, "I don't think that's a good idea, Trisha. There are bad memories for you there."

"I need for you to do this for me. Okay?"

Charley nodded and turned on the next street he came to. He looked anxiously over at Trisha as they pulled through the gate and started past the rows of stones and flowers.

"Please head back to the children's section."

"I know he took you from there."

Trisha glanced over at him. "Do you know why I was there?"

Charley shook his head. "I assumed he chased you there."

"I want to show you something," Trisha said as they drove through the one-lane gate and over the hill.

Charley's eyes froze at the spot where he located her car. He felt the hair on the back of his neck stand up as the emotions he had been feeling that night rushed back to him.

"Park here, Charley."

"Trisha, this is the very spot where your car was found."

"I was here for a reason, Charley. I need you to come with me."

Charley shut off the engine and climbed out of the cab. Then he hurried around the truck and took Trisha's hand when she offered it to him.

They started walking hand and hand down a row of markers, and Charley felt sadness sweep over him as he started noticing the names and dates chiseled in the different shades of stones with teddy bears and other toy etchings.

His heart ached as he thought about the baby boy he'd lost when Nancy had died.

"I was here because of this."

Charley peered down at the small, gray stone with the lamb and felt a lump in his throat when he read, "Sophie Sue Jenkins."

"My daughter," Trisha said softly as she held his hand tightly.

"Oh, Trisha. I'm so sorry," Charley said as he put his arm around her and pulled her close. "What happened?"

"She was stillborn in my third trimester. Everything was going so well. I followed all the doctor's orders. She was kicking, and I was over the moon. Then one day, she wasn't kicking at all. I was worried, so I went to the doctor. And she was gone, Charley. Just like that. One day I had a beautiful baby girl growing inside me and I was making plans for our life together, and the next day, she was just gone. We found out later that a genetic birth defect caused it. I felt like it was all my fault."

"It wasn't your fault."

"I thought it was. I thought I was being punished."

"For what?"

"The affair. With Coach Halley."

"What happened to Sophie wasn't because of that. Her death was a sad tragedy, not a sign."

"How can you be so sure?"

"Because I don't believe it works that way. For whatever reason, God needed Sophie to go back to Heaven. It wasn't anything you did, honey."

"But I never got to hold her or play with her. Losing her contributed to our marriage falling apart. My whole world was happy for a few years, then crashed down again."

"My world crashed down around me, too," Charley reminded her. "And even though I blame your father for Nancy's accident, I can't just put aside my beliefs. I don't think anyone goes to Heaven before it's their time."

"What about your baby boy?"

Charley looked down at the stone. "I admit I don't understand it all, Trisha. But I trust God. It's that trust that keeps me going."

"I wanted you to be the first one here in Hope to know about Sophie."

Charley took Trisha into his arms and hugged her tightly. "I know this was hard on you, honey. Thank you for sharing it with me. And thank you for telling me about Sophie."

"How'd it go?" George asked as Betty Sue walked into the study and sat down on the leather couch.

"Okay. I think I got through to her. Looks like you survived talking with that snake."

"Yeah. It took all my strength not to knock him into next week. But it's done. Please, tell me again the real reason I bailed him out? I've been setting all this into motion for years, and just when I have his land in my hands, you made me pay his loan off myself."

"Trisha. Your love for your daughter is greater than your hatred for that man."

"But we aren't really okay with them dating, right?"

Betty Sue laughed as she shook her head. "Hell, no, George. We were backed into a corner today by our son. I believed him when he said this was our only chance to put our family back together again. And I want them all to think we are going to welcome Charley and Pam into our family with open arms."

George leaned back in his office chair and asked, "And just how long do you expect me to keep up this charade?"

"A few months. Let everyone get comfortable believing we are accepting these relationships."

George thought about his illness and couldn't help but wonder if he even had a few months left.

"Something wrong?"

George shook his head, deciding right then and there he would never tell anyone in his family he was dying from cirrhosis of the liver. He knew he could only blame himself and his drinking for his illness. But he wasn't ready yet to believe any of it was true.

"Today was a tough day. I'm ready to go to bed. Are you coming?"

"I'll be right up, dear."

Although she knew what he was planning on doing, Betty Sue nodded and walked out of the room, reaching into her pocket the minute she was in the hallway. She pulled out three small pills from her silver tin and tossed them into her mouth, swallowing them down dry, then continued up the stairs.

George pulled the half-empty whiskey bottle out of the bottom desk drawer and took a long, slow swig, downing half of it.

It burned going down, but George enjoyed the burn.

Then he put his bottle back into its hiding spot, turned off the light and headed to his wife.

"It's so peaceful out here," Trisha said as she sat curled up with Charley on his front porch bench, Shooter lying at their feet.

"You make it perfect."

"What a day. Hey, what did you find out at your meeting with that auctioneer?"

"Oh, we had a great meeting. He wants me to start out as his assistant. I would be able to learn the ropes from him while still having time to farm and get my name out there. He would like to work for about five more years, then I would have the option of buying his business."

"We might be able to afford it by then. I'm going to make good money when I start working at Just For You."

A grin spread across Charley's lips.

"What?"

"It feels right making plans for our future, Trisha. Isn't it amazing how we found each other? If either one of us would have decided not to go to Minneapolis, we might not have ever met."

"It seemed like such a waste of time when they told me they wanted me to go. But I'm so glad I did."

"Me too. I love you, Trisha. Almost losing you yesterday made me realize how much I do."

Trisha smiled and kissed him as he leaned in.

"Me too. Deep down, Hope is where I've wanted to be for so long. And because of you, it's where I can be now. It's where I belong."

"Let's go to bed." Charley stood up and pulled her to her feet. "I want to make love to you all night long."

Trisha smiled, feeling happier than she had in years as she took his hand and walked to his bedroom, excited for the next chapter of her life.

Acknowledgements

Thank you - Leigh and Stephanie for your editing expertise and insight; Roxanne and Kathy for your proofreading talents and Michael for designing this wonderful cover.

To Angela – thank you for supporting and encouraging me throughout this entire journey. Your suggestions and advice from the first draft and on have helped bring Hope to life.

To Brenda and Jan – thank you for reading the early drafts and for offering support, suggestions and proofreading advice.

To my brother and his family – thank you for allowing me the freedom to be creative and for all of your help and encouragement. Also, a special thank you to my nephews for inspiring me to reach for my dreams every day.

Thank you to my mother who offered every kind of support I needed from the start of this journey. This book became a reality because you have been on board with this dream since the very first sentence of my very first story was written with a pencil on paper.

To Mae and Barb – you both always wanted to see my work in print. Thank you for your encouragement in the early days of my writing career. Your belief in me helped me to start to believe in myself.

To everyone who has supported my dreams of becoming a writer and to everyone reading this book – thank you!

About the Author

Debbie Tindle Parker lives in rural Montezuma, Iowa with her husband, J.O. They have two cats, two dogs and three adorable miniature horses. This is Debbie's first fiction novel. The Parkers have released two nonfiction books – *Iowa's Tradition: An ABC Photo Album of the Iowa State Fair* and *Family Reunion: Midwest Old Threshers.*

Please visit www.ourfrontporchbooks.com to find out more about the books available from Our Front Porch Books and to find information about the annual Montezuma All-Iowa Writers' Conference.

Watch for Book Two in the Hope Series

About the Author

CPSIA information can be obtained
at www.ICGtesting.com
Printed in the USA
LVHW04s2319290618
582304LV00001B/129/P

9 781983 871566